John Evans lives in ... an American corpo... nology and finance. ... next book.

www.john-evans.com

Also by John Evans

GOD'S GIFT

GORDIUS

John Evans

ARROW

Published in the United Kingdom in 1998 by
Arrow Books

1 3 5 7 9 10 8 6 4 2

First published in the United Kingdom in 1998 by Arrow

Arrow Books Limited
Random House UK Ltd
20 Vauxhall Bridge Road, London SW1V 2SA

Random House Australia (Pty) Limited
20 Alfred Street, Milsons Point, Sydney,
New South Wales 2061, Australia

Random House New Zealand Limited
18 Poland Road, Glenfield,
Auckland 10, New Zealand

Random House South Africa (Pty) Limited
Endulini, 5A Jubilee Road, Parktown 2193, South Africa

Random House UK Limited Reg. No. 954009

A CIP catalogue record for this book is available from the British Library

Papers used by Random House UK Limited are natural, recyclable
products made from wood grown in sustainable forests. The
manufacturing processes conform to the environmental regulations of
the country of origin

Typeset by SX Composing DTP, Rayleigh, Essex
Printed and bound in the United Kingdom by
Mackays of Chatham, Chatham, Kent

ISBN 0 09 922572 7

**For Geoff and Stewart
My Brothers**

Con-Text

The Book Reads On . . .

Where does it end?

Behind the words of people, in the words themselves and in the spaces between those words is The Book.

From outside of time, through time and, perhaps, beyond time is The Book.

It will end precisely where it began, and will begin again.

The Book.

The First Knot

In the beginning was the Word,
and the Word was with God,
and the Word was God.
John 1:1

Chapter 1

It was the best sex Jenna Miller had had in months. Okay, so it was the only sex, and now it was being interrupted by the phone and she didn't like it at all.

'Ignore it,' she said, gripping him with her hands and her vagina.

'It might be important. It is late,' he said, shrinking away inside her.

Jenna wanted to remind him whose fucking flat he was in, but realized he might be right. Reluctantly, she lifted herself off him, watched his cock fall limply to one side, picked up the phone, said hello.

Silence. A breath possibly, but she was not certain. Jenna thought she had heard something. The whisper, more breath than voice. She drew a breath of her own and said hello again, more of a question now. The whisper again, this time with its familiar wordless rhythm, a pattern that held meaning locked away within itself. How many times now? she asked herself.

The line went dead.

Jenna put the phone down, stood and pulled the sheet away with her.

'Who was it?' he asked.

'No one. Wrong number,' she said.

How many times now? On the phone, on television, at the cinema.

Something occurred to Jenna. This was the first time it had happened in front of someone else, not just in her head. Now it had spilled out and found its way into someone else's mind. It was no longer imagination.

'A wrong number?' he asked, and his banal repetition of her own words would have been annoying had she been paying any real attention to the man on her bed.

7

The bulb in the lamp had blown and sex had taken place under the unforgiving glow of the ceiling light. He had fallen out of his clothes lazily, pushing bits of his body around indifferently. His hair was dyed black to the point of frizziness, as if he'd crimped it in a sandwich toaster. His body was yellow like sour milk. Sick lapped at her tonsils. Stop, she thought, but could not.

His scrawny body was hairier than she'd anticipated. Jenna had come across him in the York pub and he had droned on about cider before pushing himself upright and standing there as though she should run herself up him. An hour later, they were up against a wall in the Slimelight, he kissing her badly while shaking his head in time to the out of time music and trying hard to look dangerous. Most of the leather he wore smelled of sweat, not all of it his. Cigarette smoke, beer and urine were the other main ingredients, but she guessed he was used to waking up in puddles of his own making. Just before joining him on her bed, Jenna had tripped on his leather jeans and found herself wishing he would leave, instead of lying there and squeezing his skinny cock between his fingers. He was disgusting, but she fucked him anyway.

In the pub, while they could still hear each other, he had made an inept job of trying to appear dark and interesting instead of just shabby. The moment he opened his mouth and reeled off the names of half a dozen bands that Jenna found depressing, she felt her face rearrange itself into the mask of apparent interest, the muscles so used to it they were practically over-developed. She could hold the expression for hours, able to nod at the appropriate place simply by divining the rise and fall of his voice tone and the changes in his body language. After twenty minutes, he was confident that he would get sex from her. When she realized this, Jenna tuned in for a few seconds, like channel-surfing, and stayed long enough to hear some snippet about his fascination with death and blood and industrial music, and then she was gone again, there but not there.

'Are you okay?' he asked her.

She needed to get to the bathroom, the urge to pass water making her feel as if she were about to flow over.

'Who was it on the phone? Did they upset you?' he asked.

Please don't start caring about me, she thought, not now.

'There was no one there, I told you. Wrong number. I don't know who it was.'

Jenna knew who it was, the murmuring voice beneath the surface. Jenna knew because she had placed it there herself.

It was Jenna's own voice.

The Jenna everyone remembered from four years ago was trying to escape from beneath the calm layer she had smoothed over all of that trouble. The voice had been so potent that silencing it had been a long and testing process. First, she deprived it of the things it needed most – no alcohol or cigarettes for six months had starved it into weakness. No drugs either. Apart from the pills, which had been a feature of her life since it was barely into double figures. For Jenna, drugs were simply a question of legality. Sometimes they were and sometimes they weren't. They helped her stay in check, diluted her feelings until they were bearable. Narcotics were a way of taming the voice, enchanting it. Apart from that one bad time, Jenna had shaken off all the bad times and the old ways by making them part of some person who now seemed alien to her.

That was only one part of the process. The clean sheet left behind, all its ink washed away by chemicals and the concentration of her pure will, needed something new written on it. There needed to be something to put in place of the old Jenna, and that had been the most difficult part. The work still not fully completed, leaving a certain emptiness to the new Jenna, in some respects.

How had the voice made its way from her mind and out into the world? What had allowed it to do that? How had Jenna dropped her guard, after feeling as though she had been clenched for the last two years?

Panic shifted gravity in her stomach and Jenna hoped it was not going to start again. Whatever the gaps in her personality, she had built too much of an other self, one that would not co-exist easily with the old one. She didn't want to fight a battle, still less lose it. Not now.

For almost the whole of the last year, she had been calling to herself; whispers under the surface, sometimes lying beneath noise and other times folded into silence. A long sentence uttered like a prayer but not enough force behind it to form an intelligible sound wave.

Jenna headed for the toilet.

'I'll be waiting right here for you,' he said, twirling his cock as though it were a cowlick of hair.

Jenna pushed the door shut and fell back against it, holding the room behind her at bay.

This is not going to happen to me again. I am a grown-up now.

Look at yourself, Jenna. They told her to do that when she felt like this. As though it were a fat picture of her on a refrigerator, there to remind her how bad it could get. Look at yourself, Jenna. In the mirror door of her bathroom cabinet, she studied herself and the reflection studied her.

Jenna knew she was too thin, limbs seeming long and parallel as if she had been drawn in haste by a child. Weight would not increase, even without the cigarettes and in periods where she forced four or five Big Macs a day into herself. She was careful with her body, arranging herself so that what might have appeared gangling came over instead as poise. Jenna retained a girlishness which, through her teens, had alienated boys her own age and attracted attention, sometimes welcome, from men older and more certain of their objectives with her. Under the treacle-black dye and the mauve lightning streak she painted in every Friday night, her real hair colour was warm and blonde and set off the tawny colour of her eyes and the angularity of her cheekbones.

A chill seemed to fall in any space Jenna occupied, so she

always had a cold, frosted look to her. Her beauty had a hollowness to it, her face really a china mould for something else. Even at rest, her features became what appeared to be a pout through which she measured the distance required from others. When she became agitated, her bottom lip would jut and a long sigh build from a swelling in her chest. The majority of people assumed she was sulking all the time.

Twenty-eight. When did that number get so big? I am in control. No you are not. You never have been. When was the last time that numb smile felt real, when it communicated anything to your soul? That bad time, she thought. That was the last moment I truly knew who I was, and now I carry it as no more than a memory. That was when I was in control.

Who *is* in control then?

Not you, she said. A voice said.

Jenna was from money. She was also heading towards money, but right now she was somewhere in between. I don't believe in money, she liked to say to her parents. In truth, she wanted to remain agnostic about it, living off its physical proofs and then, when her father died, she would repent and accept money into her life. Jenna felt as though she were on a leash, a short one that could be reined in suddenly. And any piece of slack offered, Jenna snapped it tight the first chance she was given.

You kicked so much, before you were born and then as a baby, her mother was fond of saying. She never seemed fond of the memory, only of repeating the story until the harshness seemed to go from its meaning. You were trouble from the start, that was the insinuation whispering through the words. Trouble punctuated with high drama.

Six intensive-learning weeks after her seventeenth birthday, Jenna had a car which was written off in an accident whose details were still blurred by the amount of cider she had consumed before getting behind the wheel. Still, it had led to the nose job of her mother's dreams, with partial sight in her left eye and recurrent sickening headaches.

In her first term at Bristol, Jenna almost died of alcohol poisoning, coming round in a private room with a sore chest and the sight of her mother, scolding and apparently disappointed at the random and unfocused manner of her daughter's near demise.

The wrist-cutting, eight weeks later, was far too focused for anyone's liking. For Jenna, it was nothing more than a well-managed and frightening ride, a roller coaster she knew could not come off the rails but which petrified her nonetheless. Taking pills would have felt like imploding, conceding to an eternal sleep. The slashes were more direct, visible marks of her anger at others being vented on herself. She cut across the veins, knowing it would clot and buy her a little more time, giving the lecturer she had been sleeping with the previous two weeks more of a chance to get there. Again, she passed out. Always absent from the key dramas of her life. Again, she opened her eyes to be faced with her mother wearing an expression that said decisions had already been taken.

For nearly seven months after the slashing episode, they hid her away, and Jenna was ready for it. She felt the need to catch her breath. Ensconced in the country house with her mother who kept as discreet a distance as the three staff. Her father did not visit, although his presence was felt in the shape of the two individuals despatched at different intervals to talk with her about her feelings. Muted and apologetic, they had been bought off, she could sense, paid by her father to stay away from the bad places in her head.

After the break in the country, university never to be discussed again, they left Jenna to herself once more. A long chain of credit cards with ever-decreasing but still full spending limits led her father to agree a monthly allowance on a secondary card, but he had really been forced to do so after Jenna had been stopped outside Harvey Nichols with a small, unpaid for and not inconsiderable Donna Karan accessory in her bag.

After her father's pronouncement that Jenna was to

learn the value of money by putting some effort into obtaining it, several phone calls were made and a slot opened up for her in the shape of a job answering telephones and having others trust and rely on her. When that did not work, other calls were made and the same-shaped slot opened up in a different place. Another call. Another slot. A drift through a period where she did her best to get in the way at home led to her parents' offer of a flat linked to a promise of commitment from Jenna – commitment to herself as much as to the next job her father found for her. When the slot opened up, Jenna realized she needed to make herself the right shape for it, however hard it proved, because she loved the idea of her own flat too much not to. It became what she liked to think of as her tied cottage.

And where had all that finished up? Here? In bed with someone who would linger for as long as it would take to wash the crusts of him off her, things once wet that would dry on some part of her; chest, stomach, legs – wherever.

Is this all I am? she wondered, and the thought opened her up like the pages of a book about to be read.

'That isn't all you are, Jenna.'

The whisper became speech.

It was back. The voice she had been expecting for so long.

But it was not her own voice. Not the voice she had been expecting.

The man was standing behind the clear plastic shower curtain pulled across the width of the bath. There was yellow scale on it, but the man was visible.

He was naked. Jenna looked hard, trying to make out his face through the mistiness of the plastic.

He had no eyes.

She tried to move but her body was weighed down, as though gravity in the room had changed. Fear did not paralyse her; it was trying to mobilize her, but a greater force held her down.

'Who are you?' she asked, and it felt as though an unseen

hand was working her jaws and making the words come out.

'I am who you will become. It is your time, your turn.'

The man rubbed the tip of his finger over the podgy surface of his belly, the scrape of skin against hair clearly audible. A purple indentation immediately appeared where his finger had traced and a pattern began to develop on the man's stomach.

The energy inside Jenna, her life force, felt as though it were synchronized with the movement of the man's finger over his stomach. The line he traced around on his skin was familiar, as if it had been inside her, waiting for someone to awaken it.

'It goes on forever, but you can see it.'

'Sorry?' Jenna asked, though she had heard him the first time.

It was the whisper made into speech, its pulse and pattern as familiar as her own name.

'The knotwork goes on forever but you can see it. Infinite patterns visible to the eye. It's seeing forever.'

Vomit bubbled in her throat, hot and lumpy.

'You could follow it around and around all day and never stop. Unless you got tired,' the man said. 'I could do this all day and my finger would never stop moving. Only when I got tired.'

'You'd have to stop somewhere. Back where you started,' Jenna said, looking at the man's stomach.

Her words did not belong to her, she knew. And yet they had been spoken somewhere before; it was as if she were reading a script.

'Besides,' Jenna continued, 'you can start anywhere you want. It's arbitrary. And it doesn't really go on forever, it's only a line joined up.'

'I agree. If you think of it as a line that only goes in one direction. When did we start doing that? Thinking of things as a line? Don't you find the pattern of infinity comforting?'

The knotwork gave way and the skin on the man's

stomach split like wet tissue paper. Long red tendrils spilled from him, nothing that looked as though it should ever have been there in the first place. The mass of raw flesh looked heavy as it fell out of the man. Wormy guts slithered and oozed down the curtain as if with a life of their own. Jenna jolted and used all her strength against the force that tried to hold her in check.

The curtain made its usual scratching sound as the plastic eyes skidded along the metal bar. More had come out of the man than could possibly have been inside him and it flowed around his feet and up his legs like rope.

Jenna pressed her back harder against the door but as soon as she did, a force gripped the sheet that was wrapped around her and used it as a sling to pull her the short distance towards the edge of the bath. As she neared, the sheet unfurled so she was naked in front of him.

The man had put his fingers into the empty hollows where his eyes should have been and was fingering them as long strings of red gut-like matter continued to expel itself from him with a squelching sound. He stood in a sea of his own viscera, his legs not visible below the knee.

'I have something to give you. I am going to give you the power to be free, to find out what you are,' the man said.

Jenna felt his hand work itself up the join of her legs. She gasped as he reached the top and rough fingers tried to ready the dryness between.

'What are you going to do?'

'Something very special and very nice.'

'What is it?'

'Do you trust me?'

'I don't know. Will it hurt?'

'Am I hurting you now?'

'No.'

His hand reached further under her, lifting her slightly.

'Or now?'

'Ah! No, I like that.'

'So you trust me then?'

'Yes.'

15

His hand had gone. Jenna looked down at herself and saw his fist poised between her legs, gripping a long string of the crimson entrails, the blood-shiny sinews knotted over each other and pulsing together. She looked up and felt the last moment of true fear she ever would, crying out as his fist shoved at her and she felt the strands enter her, able to discern each as it probed and insinuated itself, becoming part of her being.

He leaned forwards and she looked into the craters of his eyes, the flesh and tissue in them old and dried by the air.

His hand smoothed down between her legs and wandered over the scratchy path of skin that led to her behind, the bilious blood of each long worm lubricating the trail.

'No,' she said, and whimpered as her rear was breached, not by his hand but by something long and thin shooting upwards and touching her insides.

Jenna's head fell back in agony and she opened her mouth to cry out. As she did, it was filled, stuffed to the back of her throat. She began to gag, her throat constricting around several wriggling strands. Jenna tried to vomit but the invading strands forced harder, already well down her gullet.

Jenna's whole body was invaded by the fleshy cords and she shook in time with them. It was difficult to tell how time was passing. She was dazed and in pain but also nauseated that she could be so conscious of what was happening to her, as though she had woken in the middle of an operation only to look down and see her insides on the operating table.

The bath was almost empty, the tangled mess no longer there. It sickened her to know where it was. A feeling came over her that she was about to faint. Her knees became weak and she realized she was holding the man's forearm to steady herself. With a sound somewhere between a slurp and slap, the last of the fibres disappeared into her mouth, tickling her lips as they did, and she gasped for air.

A long shudder took hold of her back and tingled through it. Jenna waited to pass out and then realized she was not going to. That was not what the feeling signalled.

She was having an orgasm.

'No,' she pleaded, her hands tightening into the skin of the man's arm, nails breaking it.

There was nothing she could do, it was as though she were being stimulated manually by the swirling threads, each end charged with electricity and sparking off her own nerves.

Pleasure did not come with the release. It was the most painful experience of her life as the walls of her vagina went into spasm and her body broke down into syncopated and irregular jerks over which she had no power. Each wave of the climax was like the lash of a whip and she cried out, shrill and high, tears running down her face.

Silence. Briefly.

Then, as usual, absence.

Jenna was face down on the floor of the bathroom when she came round. She lay still for a few moments, knowing that the first move of her body would be the thing that confirmed the truth or falsity of what lingered in her mind. Summoning resolve, she flexed her body and felt a sharp pain in her lower back, her groin and her behind. She swallowed and her throat felt like a mess.

It had been no dream.

She listened.

The whispers had become her only true voice, the voice in her head she could trust. It was the others she would no longer stand.

Jenna swivelled slowly and came face to face with her reflection in the mirror. She gasped. Her hair was back to its natural blonde, lighter though, as if she had been on a sunny holiday. Her eyes burned at her and the pallor was gone from her cheeks. Under the surface of the skin on her neck, Jenna thought she saw a tendon pulse and then realized it was one of the tendrils slithering through her. It was as though she had been transfused with them and they pumped new life and energy through her. It did not feel like her own reflection as it looked back at her. I look like life itself, she thought.

'I'll be waiting right here for you,' he had said, twirling that stringy thing between his fingers. All of his words streamed through her, the things he had said when he was coming on to her, stored away inside without her even realizing it. It was a drone and it was painful.

Silence the voice.

This is not life itself, she thought, staring into the watery glass. This is death itself, and not his naïve and inane dressed-in-black, vampire idea of death.

Unrolling the last four metres of the dental floss, picking her nail scissors up off the shelf and retrieving a tin of scouring powder, Jenna managed a smile as she re-entered the bedroom, ready to silence the first voice.

'I'm back,' Jenna said.

When she spoke, it was with the voice of The Book.

Chapter 2

And the knot moved.

It happened in a way that made everything around it seem clumsy or still. The knot, which had been pushing on silently like the roots of a tree, suddenly burst out and made itself present once again.

It stopped Mike Kavanagh dead. He stood and listened, as though someone had called out his name. The silence was too empty and the air too still. Real, but too real. Fabricated. Kavanagh realized what had happened. For just a brief moment, he had slipped across a small fissure, stepping on a crack in the text as though it were a pavement.

It had begun again.

The feeling was familiar. He had not felt this way since . . .

Los Angeles. The beach. The earthquake.

The two separate knots of dull metal which hung from a chain around his neck hummed and became warmer against his flesh. He began to hyperventilate and his body convulsed gently, as though warming up to something bigger.

Kavanagh shuffled on the spot, alternately trying to go with the involuntary direction of his body and fight against it. Either way did him no good. It was useless to fight it and he would have to ride it out.

'Ve,' was the half word that escaped his lips. 'Ve. Ve.'

His head was bobbing up and down and his breath became a pant that had a note of its own, interspersed with the forming word he sputtered.

'Very.'

It came out and it was like taking a cork from a bottle, freeing the rest of the words queuing up behind the first.

'Very special and very nice.'

'No!' he shouted, finding his own voice once again.

He shuddered and managed to mumble, 'Oh shit.'

Instinctively, he reached for the two pendants round his neck.

They were gone.

The feeling came over him that he was going to vomit. His stomach rolled and it felt like there was something in there that should not be. He heaved, the front of his chest and ribcage moving unnaturally, stomach contracting. Nothing happened but he immediately felt the tight sensation at the back of his neck and the strain in his shoulders, pains which would linger for several days. Come on, he thought, puke if you're going to. It was the way he felt when he drank too much, not quite sure if he wanted to be sick.

Kavanagh put his hands up to his eyes and felt tears as hot as boiled water forcing their way out of his tightly shut lids. He coughed and gagged, grateful at least that it stopped the words. He wretched and his tongue furled up in his mouth, his throat feeling like there was broken glass in it. For several moments he choked on nothing, his head close to the carpet. I am in control of this, he told himself.

When he next looked up, his vision was watery.

Through the blur, on the floor in front of him, was The Book.

It had been four years since he last saw it and yet it was so familiar to him it might only have been a moment ago. For The Book and its geological timescale, it *was* only a moment ago.

He blinked hard and rubbed the water from his eyes.

The book was almost a foot long and eight inches wide. Between its covers, the pages were compacted tightly and were perfectly white, the way The Book always seemed at first glance. Nearing it cautiously, he smelled the newness of the paper, and it was comforting, as was the finely woven and pleasant green of its cover.

Kavanagh could understand, respect even, the power it

had, the compelling nature of it. There wasn't a person on Earth who could resist opening it up to see what was inside, not realizing they were opening themselves. But Kavanagh had seen The Book in its true colour, had lived with it in him for almost four years. He recalled all he had learned while waiting for it to begin again.

And the things it had made him do.

He watched as The Book changed under his gaze, silently reading him and writing him.

Veins joined up three craters on the cover. In two of the dents, shining with a soft glow like a night-light, were the two knots which had only moments earlier been around his neck. The delicate weave of the cover was no more, and left in its place was mouldering wood, mossy-smelling and damp. Now, The Book looked fragile, something to be handled with care for fear of tearing a page.

Looking at the space on the cover where the third knot should have been, Kavanagh began to weep quietly. The space was like the one he felt within himself, the one he made for Nancy Lloyd, still lost somewhere in the infinite swirling pattern of the knot which went on forever and yet was visible to the eye. He cried because Nancy was gone and also because he knew this was the start, the chance to get her back.

For several minutes, Kavanagh and The Book read each other. Reader and writer, read and written, all possible activities interchanging between the two of them.

Kneeling on the floor and reaching over, not daring to touch the knots on the cover, he opened The Book and was enveloped by the page. For the missing third knot to come back, for it to bring what it had taken, all Kavanagh knew for sure was that he would come face to face for the last time with the thing that called itself Nathan Lucas. A man older than all time who was gradually running out of it as he became progressively younger, getting to zero. The product of The Book, the only real secret it contained, Nathan Lucas had touched all their lives in some way, not least that of Kavanagh's daughter.

He would have to face Nathan Lucas one more time. Only one of them would walk away from it. He still felt far from ready, but knew The Book chose when it began again.

The page folded around Kavanagh like the wings of an angel, and in a single burst of white light, The Book was gone. He was left standing in the middle of his living-room. Around the chain on his neck, the two metal knots jangled against each other as though calling to their lost sibling.

Through a small crack in the text, where once it had begun and ended, so it had begun again.

Lucy stroked Nathan's short blond hair closer to his head and pulled his warm, naked body into hers. Every curve and crevice of it was more familiar to Lucy than her own. With careful hands, she examined him, feeling the slumber of his body and longing for it to be in motion with her own.

The phone rang.

Lucy Kavanagh jolted to attention, the hazy soap-bubble of memory quickly burst. Later, she would wonder if she hadn't really been waiting by the phone as though expecting the call, thinking about Nathan all the time.

'Hello?' she said.

'Luce, it's Dad. Please don't put the phone down,' he quickly appended to the sentence.

There was a silence at both ends of the line and she heard him take a long, deep breath before speaking.

'I want to see you. I need you to come back here, to England,' her father said.

Lucy was about to answer, to offer an instant response, but instead she paused for a few seconds. The tone of his voice, more than its sound, stopped her from speaking. Instead, memory filled the space where words ought to have been.

'It's started again.' He paused. 'It's time.'

Lucy sighed.

'Will you come?' he asked.

She did not like the urgency, the same fervent pleading

that had pushed her so far away in the first instance. Lucy had hoped he was going to cope on his own, to move on.

'What choice do I have?' she asked.

'When can you get a flight?'

'I'll have to check with Wadlow, he knows all about them,' Lucy said, realizing she already knew the flight times. How long had she been waiting for her father to make this call?

'Luce, I want to explain . . .'

'I don't want to hear. Not now. I'll see you the day after tomorrow.'

'Which airport? I'll come and collect you,' he said.

'I can make my own way. I have the new address,' she clipped back, replacing the receiver and knowing he would not call back. The next time they spoke, it would be face to face, and the first time they had done that in eighteen months.

Lucy Kavanagh, only just twenty, sat and cried for fifteen full minutes after putting down the phone on her father. When she was done with it, she went to find Wadlow Grace.

Chapter 3

Luke Smith stood in front of the full-length mirror in the spare room and held his own gaze for as long as he could. Through windows set high into the slope of the roof so they formed fanlights, sunlight filled the room at the top of the house and Luke stood under it as though a spotlight were trained on him. The mirror bounced his image back at him, but gave nothing away, no hint of any life in the glass, just the reflection of a fifteen-year-old boy, a little too tired around the eyes, perhaps, but no hint of the four things on his mind.

Monday. School. PE. Steve.

Luke held one of his delicate hands out in front of him. There was no dirt under what remained of the nails, no calluses or scuffs, just a few sore fingertips, nothing he couldn't handle. His body was lean, a thin waist, not much of a chest and hardly any hair on him. Luke looked smooth even fully clothed, only a couple of pimples on his forehead and the left side of his mouth, blemishing him in a way that was not unpleasant. He covered his face with his hand and squinted at himself through open fingers. He did not trust what he saw.

Monday. School. PE. Steve.

Luke's mind was overrun by the dread so familiar at the start of every week since they had moved to London.

From the outside, with its long, thin windows and privet hedges, the new house could have been a distant cousin of the one they used to inhabit in Southend. Rather than being a comforting reminder, the family resemblance between the two buildings made Luke pine sadly. The new house did not contain them, its four detached outer walls not forming the kind of shell in which to feel safe. The garden backed on to a stray, unwanted piece of Epping

Forest, left over from an intersection of several fences. A blank space between borders, it was a grey area, the kind of straggling woodland in which bodies turned up. No amount of heat could give the warmth and succour Luke felt in the old house. This place did not want them, still less need them. All their furniture, which was not much, was the wrong size, shape or colour, the empty rooms of the house an unwilling canvas.

The mirror had travelled with them, his mother nervously supervising its passage from the old house to the van to the new house. Wide and tall, it was the sort normally attached to the back of changing rooms in clothing shops and sometimes his mother would stand and admire herself in it. Standing before it this Monday morning, wearing only green boxer shorts with white polka dots, Luke studied himself. He always looked serious without being sullen, and even when he grinned it was held in obvious check. His brow did not help, especially when he scowled from under it, making it seem heavier than it really was, denying the prettiness of eyes cut sharply into his face and the lashes that curled out in gentle turns. He hated people who noticed the snub of his nose and called it cute. His mother always did that as her hand swept through his long, light brown hair, lifting the gold streaks that shot through it and telling him he was beautiful.

The reflection blinked.

Luke had not blinked himself.

He remained as still as he could, conscious of all the low-level functions of his body, the organs keeping him going. The reflection mocked him, imitating him perfectly, never doing anything contrary to Luke's will until he was off his guard. The day before yesterday, or perhaps the day before that, as he had stood side on to the mirror with his attention directed to programming tracks into the portable CD player, he saw his reflection wave to him from the corner of his eye. By the time he had turned around, everything was back to what had come to pass for normal.

What if I don't really look like this at all? he wondered.

Every time I stand in front of the mirror, have a photograph taken, see myself reflected in a shop window, it might not be me. What I see in the mirror could be completely different from the image everyone else sees. I may not be brownish-blond, my eyes might not be green, my skin could be black, not gold. How would I know? Really know?

For a small part of a second, as his concentration on the image lapsed, there was a sudden twitch in the glass.

How close would I have to get to lose my reflection? he wondered. He tried to think about something else.

Monday. School. PE. Steve.

Steve.

Old enough to know better but too stupid to care, Steve Faulkes had been retaking the same exams for three years in a row, the oldest non-staff member of the school. Also the most pernicious person Luke had ever come across, and so pointlessly so. Steve took delight in his own lack of goodwill, pleased to make something, anything, more difficult and unpleasant than it needed to be. It was as though something ten years earlier had made him angry and he was still seething. Steve's life was based on this putative outrage and the retribution meted out to anyone unfortunate enough to be in the way.

One morning, not long after he started the Alder School, Luke was the one in the way. Steve had used his one critical faculty to recognize Luke for the easy prey he was.

It was break time and the only redeeming feature of the Alder when compared to Luke's old school was the sale of tea and toast each day at ten forty-five. It was a comfort, the smell of the warmed bread at the same time every day, almost like being at home in the old house, the one in Southend, not London. Luke queued up with a cup of tea, no sugar, and two slices of toast with low-fat spread. Luke thought he might be able to settle in this school after all as he stood in the queue and immersed himself in the swell of excited break time chatter. There was a chance he could be just himself and get away with it. Perhaps, the same way as when he stood before the mirror, he had let his guard down for a moment. The flash gun Steve carried with him everywhere went off in Luke's eyes and Steve laughed at Luke's flinch. Taller and heavier than Luke, with the arrogant physical confidence of the truly graceless, Steve pushed in front of him. Luke did not intend to say anything, but it was not good enough for Steve to win, Luke also had to lose, and be aware of it.

'I'm just going to stand in front of you here,' Steve said. Facing Luke as other people in the queue looked away, Steve touched the lip of his glass to the lapel of Luke's blazer and tilted it until strawberry milkshake just touched the fabric. 'Of course, if you don't like it, we can go outside. Or, I can kick the shit out of you in here. Doesn't bother me which.'

Luke's silence brought a satisfied and knowing smile to Steve's face. Steve was investing in Luke's timidity, like a nest egg to be called on in the future. Two days later, the same thing happened again in the queue, except this time Luke paid for Steve's milkshake, a doughnut and four slices of toast.

That was how it had started.

In the days that followed, Luke and Steve became familiar with each other, bully and bullied establishing the ground rules. Words spoken from Steve as he walked past, the threatened growl of an impending encounter more important than what was said. A hard thump in the back. A trip-up in the quiet corridor that led to the technical drawing annexe. Each physical interaction with Steve made Luke feel smaller, hunched uncomfortably into himself as Steve seemed to grow larger. More toast bought for Steve and then no longer gifts, just money. Then, it started to happen out of school, Steve waiting for Luke one Saturday afternoon. 'I own you now,' Steve had said. 'You belong to me,' he continued, recycling the lines from a film or TV show.

Maybe he was right. As Luke looked into the glass, he wondered if he owned even that, his own image. It seemed to smirk at him and that sent a shiver through Luke, enough to mobilize him towards his room, knowing she would be downstairs waiting for him.

'Morning,' she said when he entered the kitchen.

She was at the table set to one side, where they perched for hurried meals. It was near the window and she had it open to blow cigarette smoke out. With a guilty look she took one more quick puff of the cigarette, stubbed it and tossed it through the opening.

'There's some cereal and a slice of toast. It's got cold,' she said, standing and rubbing her hands on her sides.

'I have to go,' he said, slowly shaking his head as though giving it a lot of consideration. He stood awkwardly, playing with his fingers. He turned.

'Luke, darling.'

It stopped him and he faced her again. 'I'll be late,' he sighed.

'Make sure you eat something on the way. Take it with you.'

He looked at her.

How much money did she get for the three houses in Southend? What value had she placed on their future? he asked himself. She tried to exclude him from the detail, batting questions away with an adult hand and the implication he would not understand. From what he could understand, a development company had wanted the two properties she owned which were semi-detached and were keen enough to offer on her other house, their home, as well, enabling her to make a clean break. How much did she reckon was enough to see him to independence and herself to the grave?

'Why did we come here?' he asked.

His mother was not flustered by the question, was used to him asking it almost out of the blue, as though she knew it was on his mind continuously.

'Because we could afford it. Because this is where I came from originally. We have to make the best of it, darling. How else can we do it?' she asked.

He fidgeted, hating it when she turned the question round on him.

'I don't know,' he mused, sounding almost shy. He wanted the continual asking of the 'Why did we come here?' question to bring her to her senses like a slap round the face, to make her realize there was no good reason.

'Did you take some medicine?' she asked.

He nodded. 'There's PE today.'

'Take something with you to eat,' she said.

'Can I go?' He tried to sound gentle.

'There are duties that will need doing later this week,' she said, cutting across him. 'You could stay at home today, if you wanted to. Get them done sooner that way.'

Monday. School. PE. Steve.

'I have to go. There's a test today. Important.' He lied weakly.

Her arms opened a fraction wider and Luke took a step forward to walk into her embrace. He could smell the smoke as she hugged him too tightly and as she kissed his cheek, he felt the heat of a tear as it passed from her skin to his.

'Stay home,' she said to his back as he left the kitchen.

Monday. School. PE. Steve.

He kept on walking.

The whistle blew, sending a shrill and piercing ricochet across the cold gymnasium of the Alder School, rattling around its high corners and through the ancient wooden equipment. The boys fell silent almost all at once, only the two most leery risking continuing their conversation a second beyond the others.

Chewing quietly on a thumbnail, Luke felt goose bumps on his legs, partly from the fridge-like air in the gym and partly because he was nervous, wishing he'd eaten and annoyed at himself that he had let nerves kill his appetite. He was wearing navy blue nylon shorts which crackled when he walked and a red top of rough hessian material. Reduced to a simpler, starker uniform, the differences in the boys around him were more pronounced. Some appeared abnormally tall and thin, half-finished men whose puberty tugged them ahead of the others in the race to adulthood. Fat boys looked alarmingly bloated, their hips pushing out sideways against the red sackcloth and the navy shorts straining to contain them.

An oblong annexe grafted on to the back of the Alder School, the gymnasium was almost like a chapel. Nothing else happened in there other than worship at the altar of physical sport. The floor was sacrosanct, and to tread on it with an ordinary shoe, or even to put a toe on it, was to commit a hideous crime.

Robins, their PE teacher, had been a decent athlete in the past, nearly making it to the Commonwealth Games in the discus, prevented from competition by an injury. He still had the tracksuit the whole team had been given that year, a year when most of the boys in front of him were still wetting themselves. He wore it from time to time – sports days, important football matches and parents' evening. He was heavier and older, but the puffed-up glory of an almost-ran still showed.

'Okay,' Robins said, 'circuit training. You're the first group in today, so you get to set up the equipment for everyone else. You two bring the vaulting horse out. You and you bring five basketballs and the three medicine balls.' Robins took his authority to be above the need to use a name when giving orders. 'You three pull the bars out from the wall – and make sure they're locked down properly. The rest of you, grab two mats each out from the store and line them across that end of the gym and everyone sit on them.'

Robins blew the whistle again to indicate that a military-style scramble of forces was to ensue. The boys all ambled slowly and quietly towards their allotted tasks. He blew the whistle again.

'Come on! I know it's Monday morning but get lively, you look half asleep.'

Robins resorted to drill sergeant clichés the moment he

had a whistle in his hand. He moved about the gym super-vising and pointing to where he wanted equipment put. Most of the boys wanted to play football or, if they had to be in the gym, to use the trampettes and the big thick crash mat. He shouted at them to go more quickly, telling them they only had a forty-minute period.

'Okay. We'll go off at thirty-second intervals. You start by running along that low beam, ten squat thrusts at the other side – proper ones – then run to the vaulting horse. At the other side, go to where the basket is, pick up a ball, run back and do a lay-up shot – make sure you take the right number of steps. Then, over the first set of bars and run along the high bar between the two, holding on to that girder on the ceiling. When you're down off the other side – and climb down, no jumping – I want ten sit-ups with the medicine ball. Then back here when you're finished – and sit on the mats.'

Robins was virtually unable to speak a sentence without appending another accusatory command to the end, already filled with admonishment for failure to comply.

Sitting towards the back of the tight group on the mats, the grassy cotton fabric icy on his legs, Luke looked up at the bars and the thin one connecting them at their tops. They called them monkey bars, the sort that wheeled back flush with the wall and were brought out and locked down to the floor when in use. At infant school, Luke remem-bered there being a similar set and he had loved them, their low, safe friendliness. When he had first seen the bars at the Alder School, his stomach had turned over.

It was one of Robins's favourites, to wheel them out and connect them with a metal pole he made the boys run across. To do so, it was necessary to reach up and hold on to the girder that was a roof-supporting joist. The whole process involved being seven or eight feet off the ground with only a slim mat to land on. They had done this three times since Luke arrived at the Alder School and each time he had skirted past it behind Robins's back. He swallowed and chewed on his top lip, which felt chaffed.

'Cousins, over here and time the gaps on the watch.'

Cousins, who had a note excusing him, walked over in his white towelling socked feet, shoes left in the changing room, and took the blue plastic stopwatch. Luke looked on enviously.

There were moments in Luke's life, like when the phone rang or someone turned up at the door, that he thought he might be psychic. When Steve had picked on him the first time, even with his guard down, Luke had sensed something was wrong, almost like he had a radar. He's going to pick me first, Luke thought to himself as he turned his gaze away from Robins. It was no good, Luke felt as though he were magnetic, drawing the teacher's energy towards him.

'Right, you first,' Robins said.

'Sir?'

Luke's hands were shaking slightly. He blinked a few times and tried screwing his eyes up to clear his head, but it made him feel worse. He frowned.

'You heard, lad. You first. Cheer up about it.'

Robins smiled at Luke in a way that was neither friendly nor fearsome and he felt weak, like the flu had come over him in the last five seconds.

Luke hated being watched by the others in the group. Even now, he was still the new boy. He was an outsider, and as he walked slowly to the first mat, his stomach churning like a toilet cistern filling up, he heard whispers and giggles.

The whistle blew and he tried to block everything out as he ran across the first low beam which was barely six inches from the ground. It was the same as the other beam, he told himself, just not as high off the ground. He did his ten squat thrusts and as he was halfway through, he heard the next person being signalled off. At least I'm not the only one on the circuit now, he thought. Luke felt so tired. He ran and made it on to the vaulting horse, the harsh suede rubbing his cold legs as he shimmied over to the other side and ran towards the basketballs positioned under the post supporting the net. He began to breathe more heavily and felt his body warm against the coldness of his kit and the gym around him.

Luke glanced at the monkey bars and then at Robins, trying to judge where the teacher would be when he got to them. Would he be able to skirt past them? Would someone grass him up? Noise had begun to pick up as more boys started on the circuit and there was the sound of Robins shouting at people, but not at him. He had gone unnoticed as he ran to the basket and stepped into a passable miss on his lay-up shot. He quickly did it again, successfully this time, ignoring someone's derisory shout from behind him.

The noise and activity level was at its height now and he hoped it would provide the cover he needed. Luke ran towards the monkey bars, pretending he didn't know where he was going, gradually arcing outwards as he prepared to go straight past them, energy draining from him.

Robins appeared next to him, blocking out his escape route and running almost in time with him.

Luke stopped dead in his tracks as though he had run into a brick wall. He looked up at the ceiling, the girder with its long and many times painted-over rivets, no decent hand holds on it. The metal bar joining the two sets of monkey bars was ridiculously thin, like a piece of scaffold. The alloy crossbars that formed the ladder seemed to get further apart.

He could not move. Luke stood and stared up at the ceiling, thinking about climbing and height, wondering what was so familiar and so frightening about it.

'What's the matter?' he heard Robins ask, annoyance stirring in the tone.

Luke didn't know what the matter was. All he could feel was the shifting of memory, like something waking inside him that had been asleep, or dead even, and was only now coming to life. There was a humming sound, like the approach of a plane far in the distance, and Luke felt queasy. The hum became louder and then oscillated, a rhythmic warble.

33

'Smith. Smith.' Robins again, but farther away this time, the pulsing nearer, awakened and now full of life.

The noise was not drawing closer, Luke realized – he was moving farther away, going somewhere else.

'What are you doing?' Robins asked.

'Something very special and very nice.'

'What is it?'

'Do you trust me?'

'I don't know. Will it hurt?'

'Am I hurting you now?'

'No.'

'Or now?'

'Ah! No, I like that.'

'Go on, lad! Up the bars, quick now!' It was Robins. Through the haze of voices he heard Robins and tried to focus on it as a way of pulling himself back. He looked at Robins then looked back up at the girder.

'Fuck, not again,' Luke heard a boy say.

'So you trust me then?'

'Yes.'

'Take off the rest of your clothes then.'

'Up the bars. Come on!'

The roof was getting farther and farther away each second, the girder now fifty or sixty feet up.

The whistle blew long and loud and Robins shouted for quiet. The other voices in his head faded. Silence came quickly and Luke felt eyes on him. He looked at Robins, who was looking back at him, anger on his face.

'What's wrong?' Robins said, sharply and impatiently.

'I'm not climbing up there. You can't make me.'

As the words left his mouth, Luke was aware immediately of two mistakes he had made. He should have used a word like 'couldn't' which would have implied inability rather than obstinacy, and he should have appended 'sir' to the end of such a sentence.

'Get up those bars – now. You're holding up the rest.'

'No.'

'Pardon?'

34

'No.'

Robins looked flustered, as if he could not decide what was making him more angry. Luke refusing to climb the bars or Luke not calling him 'sir'.

'Get up those bloody bars now,' Robins said, looking as if he were about to explode.

'Fuck off!' Luke shouted. 'Fuck off, okay?'

Luke's heart-rate had come down from the exertion but was now back on its way up from adrenaline.

'Alright, son,' Robins said, leaning into him as though squaring up for a fight.

'Leave me alone. Fuck off,' Luke said, a half-sob.

'That's enough! Go. And. Get. Changed,' the teacher ordered, each word spoken with the same heavy force and intensity.

Luke was aware of the acute stares from the rest of the group as he turned and walked past Robins and made his way to the changing rooms, no further words exchanged between him and the teacher. Luke couldn't tell precisely, but some of the boys seemed impressed by his display of defiance, even if it was not enough to spark a mutiny. He heard the whistle blow and the action resumed quickly. Luke headed for the changing rooms, needing the Lion bar that was in his bag. He should have eaten, the way Mum had told him to.

The flash gun went off in his face as he entered the changing rooms.

'What are you doing in here?' Luke said, blinking and trying to see Steve through the white-hot square over his vision.

Luke wondered if Steve would have been more passive if he hadn't been so physically large. He had short red hair and a pigeon chest. It was as if this was the best thing to do with a lumbering body like his, put it in the way of other people.

Steve was on him instantly, pushing him back against the wall, his breath in his face, smelling of crisps. 'What are *you* doing here, you mean. You're supposed to be doing PE.'

'You better not touch me, Steve,' Luke said, the words sounding as weak as he felt at that moment, pinned to the wall by the bigger boy.

Steve reached out and the movement brought a flinch from Luke, a cower that made Steve laugh.

'What's this then?' Steve asked.

His hand was cold against Luke's neck and Luke felt two fingers gripping the metal chain.

Luke put his hand on his chest, trying to protect what was on the chain. 'Nothing,' he said, beginning to squirm.

Steve seemed to detect value on the end of the chain and was not going to listen to Luke. He pulled harder and Luke felt the links burn against his neck.

'Don't,' Luke cried out.

The pendant slipped up over the high V-neck of his top and Steve caught it with certainty, moving his head closer to peer at it, struggling to see what was on it.

When his head came back up, there was a smile of pure satisfaction on his face, as though he had unearthed a treasure whose value his mind could not even begin to calculate.

'I am a diabetic?' Steve read theatrically. He tested the words again, painting them onto Luke, who stood and felt shameful. 'I am a diabetic.'

Held on the end of the chain like a dog on a leash, all Luke could do was nod slightly. 'I have to take insulin, or else I could go into a coma,' he said, wondering if there was any compassion in this ugly lump of a human. Most people, when he chose to tell them, were sympathetic and intrigued.

Steve lifted the chain over Luke's head in a way that had something delicate, almost intimate about it.

'What are you doing?' Luke asked. Every time he was confronted with Steve, he found himself asking the same question, never able to understand the older boy's motives.

'Taking this off you.'

I know that, Luke might have said had he been braver. 'Why? I have to wear it in case I'm in an accident, so they know what drugs and stuff to give me.'

Steve either hadn't heard or didn't care as he stood and caressed the pendant and chain as though it were alive.

'Can I have it back, please?' Luke asked.

Steve just looked at Luke, as though the question had been asked in a foreign language, unintelligible to him.

Inside Luke, in what could have been a noise or physical vibration, like an earthquake, something rumbled. It was the same energy he had felt flow in the gym as he had stood and remembered whatever it was. Before he had time to interpret it, his hand had shot out and roughly grabbed the pendant back from Steve; he heard him cry out as the chain snagged on his finger. Steve looked as shocked as Luke felt.

Staring down into his palm, Luke studied the disc. It felt warm, as though it had been left near a fire.

Something moved. *It* moved. The metal disc.

Luke jolted. The pendant erupted like a geyser. A fountain of metal spurted a thousand strands that landed in his palm, swarming and writhing over his open hand. The metal was alive and could have been emanating from the centre of his hand, like some part of him hidden beneath the skin. There was force in the movements of the loose strands and it reminded Luke of pictures he had seen of steelworks, where molten metal flew into the air and danced.

Steve was not seeing it. Luke looked at him and he seemed frozen, perhaps still shocked by the boldness of Luke's actions. Steve seemed to have slowed down and was moving on a different path of time. That was how it felt, even though Luke could not fully comprehend the sensation. It was as if Luke had been cut free by the overflowing sinews of metal and he was able to inhabit the spaces in between time.

Luke looked over Steve's shoulder and saw himself

37

standing there. The reflection smiled in the way it always did. The whole of the world has just become a mirror, Luke thought dreamily.

Steve must have read Luke's confused expression because he turned and looked. When he quickly turned back, Luke realized Steve could not see what he saw. The reflection stood and mouthed silent words at them. It was like seeing a ghost of himself. Luke looked at the mouth of the image and was trying to make out the words when he realized that his own mouth was moving also. The reflection held its hand up and involuntarily Luke's own arm rose, the fountain of metal almost white and hissing slightly.

Sound came out of Luke's mouth but it was nothing he recognized. His throat rasped and his tongue made involuntary movements in directions it had never taken before. Luke felt sick, as though something obscene were spewing from him. It scared Steve, Luke knew, because he could sense it in the way the boy stood, frozen.

The noises continued and it reminded Luke of vomiting, forcing something from himself in a violent and uncontrolled manner.

I'm talking backwards, he thought. These are real words turned around on themselves. I'm saying the opposite of what my reflection is saying. I am *its* reflection.

'What's wrong?'

It was Steve. Luke swivelled his head slowly and knew his expression was saying, Can't you tell what's wrong?

'Are you having a fit?' Steve asked, and his words were carried through the gap between the two boys.

Luke carried on looking at Steve and mouthing reversed words at him, their sound like a high-pitched scream of pain.

The reflection was about to take on another form, its true one, Luke knew, and he struggled to stay focused on it, but it was too late and his vision faltered as his mind seemed to close down all at once, like being given an anaesthetic. He crumpled into darkness.

Steve had fled when Luke came round. His throat was sore and in his hand was the disc, restored to its normal shape but still warm against his palm, throbbing like a tiny heart.

Chapter 4

What would it feel like to go off the deep end right from the first? There was to be no build-up, nothing gradual, she realized. Jenna was going to experience it all, the first time round. Or so she hoped.

She stood in the middle of the shop as around her they ran, few even reaching her waist. The centrepiece of the shop was a piled-up collection of cuddly toys, all familiar from their original appearances as cartoons. The colours matched the films of her memory perfectly and to see them all in the same place was touching, as though they had come together for a convention. The big bear, the yellow lion, the black and white spotted dogs. Or, they looked like something from the killing fields of Cambodia, a massacre of cartoon cuddlies all piled on top of each other in a mass grave waiting for the earth to be piled on. Did they have skeletons under the fur and cloth? Would she be able to recognize the skull of a mermaid or the boy from the jungle? There must have been a hundred toys, possibly even more than a thousand, and she had been watching a uniformed shop assistant with a big behind carefully arranging them, speaking the occasional unselfconscious word into a fur ear. Jenna could picture the row of Barbie dolls that had kept this girl company through her over-weight teenage years. The suede-like seat of the uniform trousers created a second skin, the outline of her panties visible beneath. Jenna heard the two layers of fabric rub together and then the sound of skin on skin, blood trickling through veins.

What would it feel like? All the way off the top and into the deep end?

Would they be warm, all those toys lying on top of her? What kind of cover would she need to go missing in there?

She could buy a collection of toys and skin them, fixing their pelts on to combat trousers and T-shirt, a new Technicolor camouflage. A bank of television screens worked relaying advertisements for new films or cartoons, and parading the back catalogue of movies, some of which she had been dragged to herself, the first bar of a song able to send a disturbing sense of memory through her. One or two of those songs could even bring on a tear. Under the music and the chirping dialogue was a static hiss, noise boiling up to the steamy vapour of words.

There must be security, more than the visible presence. Silent eyes surely whirred away, filming her even then as she stood fixed to the spot, just another parent happy to let her child run round unattended – that must have been what people thought of her. Could she hide herself under the mass grave of soft toys without being seen? Perhaps she would have to wait in there all night, the only indication of her presence the slow rise and fall of the wooden boy without strings. Only the guns for company. The assault rifle, lying across her chest, heavy and warm. The revolver in a shoulder holster, the butt pressing into the soft lymphatic flesh under her arms. Against the bone of each hip, bruising it gradually, automatic pistols. Strapped to her inner thigh, pointing towards the join of her legs, the eight-inch hunting knife with the serrated tip, its sheath stiff and giving off the animal smell of leather. In the breast pocket, beating away as her heart pumped, the hand grenade. The pin called to her, the way presents had under the tree, begging to be unwrapped.

There would be little time for reloading. It was a one-shot deal, literally. What would it feel like, for real?

Part of her wanted to be discovered in hiding, a small hand pulling at a piece of fur attached to her. A parent and shop assistant called over and then she would rear up, screaming and firing. What would the panic be like? Would their noise drown out the music, the sound of the bullets? There was a lot of glassware and crockery and that would make an impressive shatter. Having to shift the weapons up and down to adjust for the height of each target would be difficult, but she could practise that too. There would be an order, an apparent downward cascade into inertia. The assault rifle first, then the two automatic pistols. The revolver would put an end to the bullets. Once out of ammunition, she would start with the knife. Each of these, she realized, became more discriminate. The automatic weapons would spray without favour or conscience. The revolver would require aiming. The knife even more precise. Jenna shivered. Would anyone else see this sense in the carnage – that she was winding down? She hoped so, because then, when she pulled the pin from the grenade, put the bulb in her pocket and ran headlong into the largest group left standing at that point, they would realize that she was far from done.

What would it feel like? Would I feel like me? she wondered.

'These ones are great,' the dyed blond shop assistant said, bounding up like a sniffer dog.

Not him, please, she tried to plead in her head, making room in there for her own voice and hardly recognizing it. The end for this boy was already there and she could read it on him, as though he had gone backwards and it had already happened.

How old was he? Not old enough to drive yet, cycling in enthusiastically, eager for another day and wanting more of the world to pass through him. How could she take that freshness, the belief, his faith, and twist it, knot it up until it was no longer what it had been? Already she could sense him, reading him and what he was thinking about her, the brazen pornography of his imagination almost exciting in its naive and pared-down manner.

'I bet you'd love me to do that, wouldn't you?' she asked him.

'Sorry?' he asked.

Jenna jogged him over the thought and watched his confusion as he lost the thread.

'I love your hair,' she said, looking slightly down on him.

'They don't like it here,' he said, almost whispering. 'It doesn't look as good as yours.'

'Isn't it an officially approved colour?' she smiled.

'No,' he said, smiling also. His teeth were independent, slightly askew rectangles of well-brushed enamel. Jenna imagined the feel of them on her tongue and then tried not to, hoping to hold back the hunger she felt.

'Well, if you were in a box I'd take you home,' she said.

He laughed, those teeth making the grin goofier than it should have been. His eyebrows hinted at his real hair colour. He was still a boyish and compacted pod, the sudden and potentially ugly spurt to early manhood not yet there.

After he had left her to browse on, she watched him playing with two small children, hiding and seeking between the pillars, poking his head round and widening his eyes at them, squealing almost as much as the toddlers. Where did the energy come from? It floated in the air, was stored up as potential force. So was pain, his pain. He looked up and caught her eye, the smile more downcast, a frown of acknowledgement, as though he were now reading her and he too knew where it would end and the suffering along the way.

'This is a nice place,' he said.

No it isn't. It's a terrible place, she thought.

'Thanks,' she said.

A safe distance apart on the sofa, she looked at him and let the silence hold for too long, making him fidget. Jenna touched her hair and then spoke.

'How long have you worked in the shop?'

'Nine months. I only do Thursday and Saturday. Half a day Thursday.' He nodded, as though checking it with himself.

'What do you do the rest of the time?'

'I'm at college. Just started A levels.'

When he came a second time, breath hissed through the

notches in his teeth, his eyelashes fluttered and the small cups of his chest heaved violently. Jenna had not seen his face the first time, just felt his hands tighten on her head, fingers pushing into her hair, and tasted his semen, hot in her throat and clogging her nasal passages. This time, Jenna had put him on one of the dining-room chairs she had moved into the middle of the room and made him sit on his hands so she could manipulate him with her own.

From the initiating moment, when Jenna had reached and put her hand on the flies of his trousers, a quiet amazement seemed to take hold of him. His cheeks blushed in a prickly wave that continued onto the border of his shirt collar. When Jenna asked him to strip for her, she thought he was going to protest, but he complied. Several times after that she expected resistance as she instructed him to turn this way and that, arching his body in different and increasingly revealing postures. His discomfort was pleasing. Jenna could interpret his consternation, the short-circuiting of his expectation to be in charge because he was the man, or whatever he was. And the confusion because he liked it. He was enjoying the fear of not being in control.

Jenna found his pleasure upsetting, and the feeling gnawed at her; the sensations he was having at her administration were troubling to her. She could feel a boundary approaching, a moment where he would be suspended in pure pleasure before realizing he was about to tumble into something far different.

She laughed inwardly at the mock-porno way she leaned over and whispered into his ear, as though wanting him to hear what she wanted but afraid to listen to herself. His look of surprise was pierced by a bolt of fear that dissolved and left only willingness behind. He wanted to please her.

Jenna eased him on to his hands and knees.

'What are you going to do?' he asked.

'Something very special and very nice.'

Jenna took a moment and then began to explore him, his spine rigid with anxiety as she stroked and then let the gently cupping hand sharpen into just a finger, a dull point she rested against expectant and unyielding muscle which she tried to coax into submission. When she realized it would not respond to teasing, she slicked her hand and became more aggressive with it, putting some weight into the motion, using her shoulder. One finger became two, then three, until she was working him with her whole hand, her knuckles a barrier.

And then there was no longer a barrier.

Their shock was mutually vocal when Jenna made a sudden ingress from which there seemed no turning back. For a time, a long time, they were locked in their own private orbits of awe, the silence almost reverential and broken only by his gasps and the movements of his straining body. He was so tight around her wrist.

There was look of satisfaction when he stood upright, disengaged, his movements slightly tired from the exertion of submitting. His whole face was now a blush oiled with perspiration. He looked different somehow, as though now a part of her. His heart was loud in his chest and she could feel the blood wash around it, the noise of his life. It was deafening.

He held out his hands to her, offering her an embrace, a kiss lying at the end of it.

Jenna punched him hard in the mouth, coming up against the bony gums and sharp teeth, feeling them slice into a knuckle. She had hit him hard enough to knock him off balance, as though she had pushed him away but left his life-force in place. This was not part of the game, not a part he was expecting. As he tried to recover, she followed with another blow in exactly the same place, but harder.

'What are you doing?' he asked, and the words sounded wet, his mouth sluicing with fresh blood.

Jenna slapped him across the cheek, the crack stinging her palm.

Naked and bleeding from the mouth, he was flustered. Things were moving too quickly for him. There was not enough time to gather up clothes, find his way out of the flat and run. Decisions paralysed him. And Jenna knew he

could sense her seriousness, that this was no simple exten-
sion of the sex. He made as though about to bolt nude from
the room and Jenna knew she could not let that happen.

From the fireplace, Jenna gripped the long, heavy poker,
swung it from far behind her head like a golf club, and let it
make contact with his left leg, on the side of the knee.
Jenna heard the joint give way, the crunch and crack as he
fell. He yelped but she knew his life-force was strong and
that the blow would only slow him down. She stood on his
ankle and hit him with the poker until she was certain his
leg was broken. He gripped the edge of the rug and
screamed. It reminded Jenna of his orgasm.

'Oh fuck,' he wept.

His mouth was filled and taped far too tightly for him to
make a noise. She wanted to trap the pain inside his body
and let it run round like electricity. Some of the daze was
clearing and he seemed to be able to focus on her, she
noticed, as she crouched over him to glue his eyelids
shut. He fought against it and she suspected it must be
stinging.

'If you don't keep still, I'll cut slits in your eyelids and,
trust me, you don't want to see what's coming next.'

His body arced suddenly and he hissed.

'Sorry,' she said. 'This is called an indwelling foley
catheter. I know a lot about these, believe me.'

Jenna had bent him backwards over the table, like an
animal strapped to the bonnet of a car. His back was ricked
unnaturally and she had pulled his bound wrists and ankles
towards each other using a short length of nylon rope.

The noise he made through his nose might have been an
attempt to form the word please.

'We'll be done soon. I promise.'

There was a click. The light on the steam iron had
turned from red to green. The air smelled of its white-hot
metal fuelled by electricity. Using both hands and all her
body-weight, Jenna applied the iron to the fleshy part of
his belly just below the ribcage.

Switching to one hand once there was less need for pressure, she leaned over and pinched his cute nose shut, gently soothing his forehead with kisses until there was no more sound to trap inside him and he no longer moved.

Chapter 5

The light had started to fade as Kavanagh stood at the bottom of one of Greenwich's long grassy slopes, waiting for a man he had seen only once before. That time he had emerged noiselessly through a wall of light that was almost blinding. Now, light seeped from the sky and the air was already more chill than it had been at the start of his twenty-minute wait.

Checking his watch, he realized Lucy must be making ready to leave New England. Such a gentle move in the knot and already they were being pushed together, the way they had been previously. Kavanagh fingered the chain around his neck, knowing the pieces of metal it held were the ultimate source of fracture between himself and his daughter, and also the way to mend the break. When he saw her again, he would change things, make them better.

The Los Angeles earthquake of 1997 was the moment when it had all become real for Kavanagh, as though the words of a story he had been reading suddenly breached the borders and made their way into the world, uncaged from the confines of the page. It had been real, seemed real at least, and then it had turned into a memory formed only by doubts; questions ranging from the minutely detailed to the all-encompassing, *Did it even happen?*

Kavanagh shivered and checked his watch again, wondering if he were waiting for nothing.

Under his feet, a tremor, he was sure. He swallowed hard and listened into the silence, waiting for a sign of some kind.

Kavanagh looked up to the top of the incline, its horizon lined by the twilight sky. The peak was high enough to make him feel the stretch of muscles at the back of his neck. Like searchlights that could touch the clouds, two parallel beams pointed from somewhere over the crest of the incline, close by. His eyes were fixed on them, the dense yellow shafts glowing in the mauve of the clouded sky.

Abruptly, the beams reached the top of the hill and pointed down at him, the first indication they were moving. The bank of light became one, too bright to distinguish the separate beacons.

Car headlights.

Kavanagh was not familiar with Greenwich, but he was certain nothing over the other side of the hill was accessible by car, just a similarly sheer and grassy bank.

The car drew closer to him, silent and floating as it eased down the incline. His eyes adjusted to the brightness and as the vehicle came nearer he was able to see behind the shield of brilliance. It was an American car, old and over-sized, wings and fins making it look aquatic. The amphibious look was not so inappropriate as the great vehicle floated across the grass. The colour-scheme was cream and green, like a kitchen from the Fifties; and Kavanagh wondered if that was the period. He did not know enough about American cars to hazard a guess at what it might be; the fact that it had loped over the hill with such silent grace had rendered his thoughts incoherent.

The car pulled up and the door opened. Alexander Cameron stepped out from the passenger side, on the right, and quickly pulled at his scruffy clothing in a gesture seeming more for Kavanagh's benefit than his own.

'Mr Kavanagh. Michael. It's been so long.'

The car made no sound. Kavanagh tried to see who was driving, but could not, as though the driver's seat were in a blind spot.

'The last time was after Nancy,' Kavanagh said.

'Yes. I'm sorry about the way that had to happen, Michael. I can call you Michael?'

'Yes.'

'Let's walk together,' Cameron said.

'What about the car?' he asked, glancing at it, the size and sheer presence of it troubling to him.

'It will be there for me when I need it. To take me where I have to go,' Cameron said.

'Where's that?'

'To where the story ends for me.' The old man looked up into the sky and then down at the ground. 'I had to cross the meridian to get here. He's running out of time, you know that,' Cameron said.

'Nathan Lucas? Yes.'

'He must have been in his seventies when I first knew the truth about him. Then he was in his late forties when he took my family from me. And then your wife.' Cameron paused.

'He told Lucy he was eighteen.'

'No one can know for certain. I expect now he will be fourteen or fifteen years old. Gradually whittling away to nothing. Getting to zero. You know what has happened, don't you?' Cameron asked him.

'The knot moved,' Kavanagh said, instinctively touching his chest as he spoke.

'Yes. He will want what he considers to be his.'

'Lucy is arriving tomorrow,' Kavanagh said.

'Yes. Mr Grace and I have spoken. Is she ready for the truth, Michael?'

'I don't know. I don't even know what I think is true.'

'You must deal with what she believes to be true, Mr Kavanagh. What goes on in her head is of crucial importance. She still believes your wife's death was connected to the Trust?' Cameron asked.

'Yes, but not in the way we know it to have been. After Helen was killed and Lucy went into counselling, she began to wonder about her own sanity. I realize that more now than I did at the time. Lucy thought she was going mad. As far as she's concerned, I was trying to bring off a deal with Trellis and in the process I met Nancy Lloyd, a new woman, and she found herself a boyfriend in Nathan. For her, Garth Richards is the one responsible, killing people here, following me to the States and kidnapping me. He, Nancy Lloyd and probably Nathan Lucas all died in the earthquake in Los Angeles.'

'She has no memory of meeting me in America,' Cameron said, not really a question.

'Lucy remembers nothing about you, about reliving the afternoon she found her mother or the time we spent on that fabricated beach.'

'But you remember it all, or at least it is all in you, stored up and waiting,' Cameron said, almost speaking for Kavanagh.

Cameron was right. The details were inside him. In 1997, for a short time, other people had been allowed to dwell in his dreams. Kavanagh had built a place in his own imagination and that place had taken on a physical form. With the desperate power of his mind, he had created a version of a beach in Los Angeles, a way for him to save his daughter from Nathan Lucas. And then he had torn his dreams apart, an earthquake splitting the fabric, but not without consequences.

The real Los Angeles felt it too, shivered as though afraid, teetering on a precipice, the sea ready to catch it should the city tumble. The earthquake took hold and pockets of the city fell into themselves. Kavanagh looked around him and saw the real consequences of what had happened in an unreal world. In his ears, the sound of panic, voices shouting across each other as they called for help or for loved ones.

The scene reminded Kavanagh of the news footage he had seen of the riots in the city, a visible tension. Behind him, Wadlow Grace had his arm over Lucy's shoulder, dwarfing her with his fat body. Lucy was staring at the paving, her body shaking. Kavanagh did not know what to do, had not known what to expect. Perhaps he was unprepared because he had not really expected any of them to emerge alive from the fabricated world he brought into being.

'Wadlow has concerns for your daughter,' Cameron said,

bringing Kavanagh out of his thoughts. 'Nathan Lucas invaded her in the same manner he did Nancy Lloyd. Lucy is now carrying something he wants.'

'I know. The last two years, two and a half, have been difficult for us.'

They came to a bench and Cameron gestured to it. They sat.

'The last time I saw you, Nancy said something that stayed with me,' Kavanagh said. Cameron looked ahead and Kavanagh studied the side of his face as though it were the outline of a map. 'She said that you wouldn't have been there with us if you didn't know something. She was right then and I'm sure she'd be right now,' Kavanagh continued.

'You miss her as badly as Wadlow Grace.' Cameron sighed. 'You understand, as I do, Mr Kavanagh, that the pattern of this story is incredibly intricate, the most complex of all stories. Others will become involved, are involved already through their past, not even realizing it. Somewhere, lost in that criss-cross, running underneath it like a major artery, is a kind of roadway that will lead to Nathan Lucas.'

'I've been waiting for that,' Kavanagh said. 'I thought, deep down, something would have shifted when the century ended. It was so obvious, that was why I thought it might happen.'

'It was not without significance.'

'What part do you play in all of this, Alexander?' Kavanagh asked.

'Not the one written for me. Remember, Nathan Lucas is like my father, but I was also meant to be like his, the one who would take care of him as he became too young to fend for himself. If that had written out in the way intended, I would be looking after him now and running the Trust, Gordius, call it what you will. You might have been in the picture too. But it did not turn out that way, as we know. Now, my role is to point you in the new direction.'

'What do you have for me?' Kavanagh asked.

'Something that will help you, make things clearer about what your daughter needs to do. Where she needs to go.'

Cameron reached into the breast pocket of his jacket and produced a postcard. He handed it to Kavanagh, who studied the fading picture on its front.

'You've seen this place before. Haven't you?' Cameron asked gently.

Kavanagh nodded.

'For me,' Cameron said, 'that place was where it began and most likely where it will end. Lucy will find what she is looking for there.'

Kavanagh pocketed the card.

'What do I have to do?' Kavanagh asked.

'Stop Gordius. Stop the Gordian Movement.'

Cameron's words were measured and precise, as though the task would be simple.

'How do you stop something like that?' Kavanagh asked. 'One is organized so tightly it is impenetrable and the other is so ragged there is nothing to find.'

'There is an old air base bought by the Cameron Trust in 1961. It is in Cambridgeshire, secluded, and already the first are arriving, discreetly and quietly.'

The latest gatherings of the Gordian Movement had been in the hundreds of thousands. Wadlow Grace had attended one of the biggest ever, in America on the eve of the millennium. Those who followed the knot, who believed they heard its call, were looking for the patterns, trying to make sense of things even as order rapidly slipped away from them. By contrast, the Gordius Corporation did its utmost to distance itself from the Gordian Movement, carefully denying any link, either financially or ideologically. Kavanagh had spent time looking for such a connection, but he could not find it. There was an apparent spontaneity to the Gordian Movement that gave it a peculiar strength. There was something anarchistic about it.

'I understand your consternation. There are things that will provide the bridge between Gordius and the movement that takes its name. I know they both seem too large, amorphous,' Cameron said. 'But, imagine for a moment that it is organic. You can kill or at least paralyse something organic by going to its heart and its brain. The Gordius Corporation is, by certain measures, one of the largest on the planet. The Gordian Movement is not without significance either. Consider how many religions take shape as no more than cults, but it is the Corporation that is by far the more important of the two. It feeds the Movement, gives it resources, provides it with direction.'

'I haven't been able to see any of that, Alexander. Look at the controversy around the book the academics wrote – earthquakes and literary theory.'

'But enough people wanted to believe it, with or without evidence, Michael. How many people subscribed to that theory? More than a million.' Cameron paused and gave Kavanagh a long look. 'I, more than anyone, should know how to keep things hidden, make sure there is no evidence. We had enough experience of it with the Trust. The world relies so much on what is written, enshrined in books, law, records and contracts. Witness the legions of lawyers ensuring everything is recorded in some way. All of your previous career was built on similar foundations. None of it mattered. What did matter were the promises made, the things that were said and never recorded. When my father first encountered Nathan Lucas, they did not write anything down. He saw the hunger in my father, read it in him, his desire for children, for the Trust to become powerful. Nathan Lucas made him promises. Gordius is the same. People are making promises, Michael. Some of them may even be blind to what they are doing, the possible effects. There are things said between the Corporation and the Movement that we will never be privy to, but they are there, beating away at its centre, like a heart, giving it direction, like a brain.'

'Where is the heart and brain of Gordius?' Kavanagh asked.

Light distracted Kavanagh and he looked to his left. The

car was pulling up on the footpath in front of them. It had moved through the air without disturbing a molecule.

Cameron stood.

'Where do *I* have to go?' Kavanagh asked, feeling a sudden urgency, aware that his time with this man was at an end.

The old man touched Kavanagh's breast pocket, reminding him of the card he had been given.

'That place has been on your mind for too long, but it's not down to you to go there. Send your daughter there, Michael, and it will put her on a path that leads back to you.'

Kavanagh swallowed. 'What about me?'

Cameron opened the door of the car.

'Wait,' Kavanagh said.

Cameron turned to him and took his hand as though to shake it. Instead, he cradled it carefully in his own and looked directly into Kavanagh's eyes as he spoke.

'Once your daughter is on her way, you must go and see Wadlow Grace. That will lead you to where you need to go, to the heart and brain of it.'

'And then what?' Kavanagh asked.

'A new beginning?'

Kavanagh was angry. The old man had asked it like a question. He had wanted more from this than an old post-card and some obscure words.

'Goodbye, Mr Kavanagh.'

The door closed.

Kavanagh watched the car fade into the distance, certain he would not see Cameron again.

Chapter 6

She was not there when Luke got back home and the heating in the house was off, the boiler still not functioning as it should. On his way home, nervous about getting there, he had eaten more chocolate than he knew was best. Now, Luke made straight for his room, needing a short shot to even him back out.

But it was gone. She had taken it. It was that time again, he thought. Luke could either wait for her or raid his stash. He supposed he should have done something to get his heart going. Instead, feeling cold, Luke undressed and climbed into bed, snuggling into the quilt, enjoying it as the feathers, warmed from his body, soothed the heat back at him. There had been the first icy moment when his skin touched the material of the duvet, but that soon gave way to the secure feeling of heat. It did not last. Luke felt bad from the PE lesson, physically and mentally. He had managed to get himself changed and out of the way before the lesson ended. Afterwards, he had gone to Robins and apologized. 'Sometimes it's good for me to be told to fuck off,' the teacher had said, smiling.

Luke shivered. Would anything soothe him? he wondered.

In movements so routine and unconscious they could have been automatic, Luke flipped himself on to his back and quickly removed his boxers, raising his knees and tugging the shorts off his ankles. When his hand reached his groin and took a firm grip, he was ready and for a few short moments he tormented himself with images that seemed profane before the intense and sudden pain of the release eased his mind for a few thrashing seconds, his groaning loud and unearthly even to his own ears. His breathing returned to normal, its only rhythm anxiety, and he

56

mopped his chest and stomach with the shorts. Maybe that will bring my sugar down, he thought.

There was a creak – a floorboard, he thought – and it stopped him completely. Had he imagined it? he wondered. He cocked his head to one side and tried to hear, certain he could make out the sound of feet creeping along the landing and down the stairs. Had she heard him? Luke jumped from the bed and dressed himself. Once more he thought about his secret supply, but knew it would be better to go and see her.

Bella Smith had been 42 when Luke was born. Having an older mother did not bother him as much as it seemed to bother her. Now she was three years from 60, it scared him to imagine what that increment would do to her. The attention he had been expected to lavish on her when she turned 50 was still fresh in his memory and he had been only 8 on that occasion.

Fine lines had begun to appear near her eyes and mouth in recent years, as though she were cracking at weak spots, life finding the points of strain on her face. Even though the grooves were always carefully filled with powder and blusher was applied as an attempted diversion, she continually drew Luke's attention to them, as though he were in some way responsible. Bella Smith's faint brown eyes reflected back only the bad they had seen, ready to well up as heightened emotion would lubricate them. Luke had rarely seen the real colour of his mother's hair except when roots hinted at it, only to be smothered quickly by a new shade. At the moment, it was the colour of copper pipes, falling away from her head in loose, home-permed ringlets.

His earliest memory of her face was a segmented painting, areas of colour in contradiction to each other. Mouth framed behind shining lipstick, eyes filled in with green and outlined in a heavy black. The blusher. The powder. She may have been trying to hide beneath it, but Luke thought it was more like a cry for help, painted bold and bright; as though she were trapped in there.

Luke tiptoed into the front room, wanting a second to

compose himself. On the wall was a large painting of two cottages facing what his mother had told him was a village green and a pond. To Luke, the pond had always looked primordial and slimy, as though it would bubble and something unformed would crawl from it and heave itself towards one of the cottages. Two identically sized pictures of galleons were at angles to each other on the wall facing the bay window, each of them sailing away from the viewer and off towards something better. In front of the television set, a rug the size and shape of a single bed was laid out, and here used to be Luke's favourite position for watching television after school, in the old house of course. Against each of the side walls was the same old three-piece suite, the upholstery almost lime green and clashing with the blue in the wallpaper. Chairs and sofa were separated by the boundary of the coffee table, also good for resting a foot up on while reading.

She was in the kitchen moving things from surface to surface, ambling in the way she always did when she was waiting for him. He wondered if she had been listening to him in his bedroom and it made him feel awkward.

'I didn't know you were here,' she said, not turning to look at him.

'It's cold,' he said.

'I phoned them about it today. Someone's coming at the end of the week. Are you hungry?'

'Not really. I don't feel very well.'

She turned and looked at him. 'Don't I get a cuddle?'

Luke walked to her and gave her a quick hug.

'You should eat something,' she said.

'I had a Fuse on the way back. And a Lion bar.'

'Luke,' she sighed, disappointed.

'I can't help it,' he said. 'I hate it there.'

'Let me get the medicine. Wait here, babe,' she said.

Luke leaned on the counter and looked out of the window at the damp garden and the patch of forest beyond. He could hear his mother rustling about and he knew what she was doing, going to the supplies he was not

58

meant to know about.

'Here we go,' she said, coming back into the kitchen with a fresh hypodermic and the familiar glass bottle. She laid them on the table and went to wash her hands at the kitchen sink.

'Shouldn't we check my level first?' he asked weakly.

'You don't trust your mum?' she clucked. 'I know how to sort out a bit of chocolate.'

She sat on one of the chairs at the table and rolled the bottle between her palms as though it were a small creature requiring great care and attention. Luke tried to see what kind of insulin it was but, as usual, she had taken the label from the bottle. It would be one of her cocktails. He knew better than to ask. She cleansed the flat target area on top of the bottle with a small wipe she had removed from a sealed pack. Luke licked his lips and watched as she unwrapped the hypodermic, waiting to see how far she would draw it back, how much she was going to allow him. He had asked her if he could use a pen device to inject, but the independence that had smacked of meant the idea had never made it beyond the few mumbled suggestions.

It was not going to be enough, he thought, as she pushed the tip through the top and injected it with air. She turned the bottle and pulled the plunger to draw the liquid, the motion slow and measured. Holding it up to the light, she tapped the syringe and tutted, annoyed at herself.

'Air bubble,' she muttered.

She tried it again and Luke saw the barrel of the syringe fill with the insulin. There was no air this time and she looked pleased with herself.

'Can't do it through your shirt, babe,' she said, and he realized he had been daydreaming as he watched the chamber of the hypodermic filling.

Luke stood in front of her and hitched his shirt up. She stroked his belly and gave it a pinch, making him jump back.

'You used to love that when you were little,' she laughed. 'This belly could do with a wash,' she said, scratching at something crusty just below his ribs. Luke looked away and felt his cheeks redden. He was about to speak when she grabbed a bigger pinch of skin and he felt the tiny puncture of the needle. Luke gave a slight gasp, feeling the pierce followed by the unnatural cold of the alcohol on the wipe she held over the needle. He heard her sigh as she depressed the plunger and then withdrew it, wiping him with the moist tissue.

'Sorry, babe. There, let's make it better.'

He felt her lips kiss his stomach where the needle had been, one hand resting on his hip.

'Thanks,' he said, moving away quickly and tucking his shirt messily back into his trousers.

'Did you have a nice day at school?'

Monday. School. PE. Steve.

'Not really. I don't like it there, Mum.'

'I hated my school. It's nearly Christmas. Our first Christmas here. We'll have to decorate and get a tree. Then you won't have to think about school.' She looked around. 'This place needs some things doing to it,' she said and he saw her disappear into a line of thought that was entirely her own as she pondered. 'There are duties that need doing,' she said when she came back to the present.

'I don't feel well,' he said.

'That's the cold. When are you going to bring some friends back from your new school?'

Luke closed his eyes and tried to stay calm. 'Can I have something to drink?'

'Bring them back for tea.'

'I don't have any friends. There's no one to bring back, alright? Do you want me to cook something?' he asked, still standing in front of her as she sat and held the syringe. 'Mum?'

She was biting her lip, tasting a word before she said it. When she looked at him, her eyes were narrow.

'You're a hateful boy, Lucas,' she said.

'What do you mean?' he asked, coughing a little.

'I used to catch your father doing that. What you were just doing.'

'Mum . . .'

She ignored him. 'The first time, I made him carry on, made him show me what was so special, better than anything I could give him.'

'I wasn't,' he said, his plea almost a sob.

'Do you want me to do that to you? Make you show me what you were up to in your room? Do you?'

'I didn't, I promise . . .'

'Do you?' she asked again.

His face felt as though his skin were about to fall from it.

'No,' he whispered.

'Go away,' she said, looking at him with tear-filled eyes. They began to run down her cheeks. 'Leave me alone, Lucas.'

Upstairs, he went into the spare room and stood in front of the mirror. His reflection gave him a welcoming smile, pleased to see him again.

Chapter 7

The Gordius Building was nine floors high but seemed taller to those who stood at its door and peered upwards. Erected on the charred ground of the original Pendulum Building, it was a memorial to the lives lost – not only in the fire, but before it, when Garth Richards, one of Pendulum's employees, had killed four of his co-workers and a string of others, the extent of which might never be fully known. Those who had witnessed the fire spoke of its contained intensity, as if the building were a kiln. Other buildings around it were untouched, as though the building had spontaneously combusted. A year after the fire, the Cameron Trust, the corporation which owned Pendulum, changed its name to Gordius. The change of name followed a period of heavy expansion and acquisition and a certain amount of coming-forward from the shadows of the hitherto publicity-shy Cameron Trust. If observers had expected the already mysterious Trust to retreat further into the shroud, they had been wrong. The monolith with narrow windows and artificially weathered stone was a monument to the former Cameron Trust and a celebration of Gordius. Where once there had been Pendulum, the headquarters of Gordius had risen from its ashes.

But Jenna didn't really give a fuck about any of that. At one time it might have been interesting in a trivial manner, but this morning the Gordius building had called to her in a way it never had before, as though demanding her presence before it. For a moment longer than normal, Jenna gazed at the copper knot clinging like a spider to the brown marble. Take the step, she said to herself. This is where you can finally part company with yourself.

Jenna entered.

There were enough people employed at the Gordius

head office to make the collection of faces a familiar tapestry, too many for the sort of conspiracies she had been the victim of in smaller companies. At such places, everyone had known the job had been created for her by the ugly power of her father.

Marketing occupied a quarter of the eighth floor and Jenna was an assistant, which meant unskilled secretary she soon realized. Jenna became a sort of hand maiden to the creatives, people whose flow could not be interrupted by anything as mundane as buying their own coffee, clearing up after themselves, answering their own phones, getting their own sandwiches.

Today, Jenna would have to go through those motions to get what she really wanted. On her desk she had placed a Styrofoam cup whose plastic lid seeped froth through the pinhole on its raised centre, while next to it a Danish pastry was darkening its brown paper bag as if it might be bleeding into it.

The group of companies owned or controlled by Gordius was as incestuous and complex as a royal dynasty, its branches heading in sudden and unexpected directions only to fold back on themselves.

In terms of companies with their own individual names, the children of the family, there were 176 separate entities. These fed upwards and sometimes crossways until they reached a country. Then, there were layers of Gordius that straddled countries and continents. The criss-cross seemed to have no start or end. The closest there was to a final level were three large companies, turning over more money than small nations, into which many of the arteries flowed. After that, Gordius was reached, and yet Gordius was everywhere, its energy flowing in all directions and seemingly through dimensions as its tendrils insinuated themselves into the body of the family.

And what had they chosen to represent this, the family crest?

Mounted on the far wall of their office was the Gordius logo, an exact replica of the copper knot by the front door.

For the previous nine months, Gordius had been involved in one of the most aggressive re-branding campaigns ever witnessed. The knot logo had developed from a mere watermark hidden under the skin of the company letterhead and out into the forefront. Most of the companies owned by Gordius had previously sported the symbol in some discreet fashion. On several, the knot had been there since before the Cameron Trust even changed its name, the pattern no more than a slightly raised area on the bottom left corner of a page, veins barely visible.

The marketing department was to be the nexus, a hub for the knot. The simplistic and brazen manner in which Gordius went about the matter was one of the things that made the greatest impression on Jenna. There was no discussion, no consultation about what all the various strands wanted. The logo would be branded, like a hot iron on to an unwilling animal, across the whole of the Corporation. One pattern, one philosophy.

None of it should have been alarming. Jenna thought about the brands that were imprinted on her consciousness already – golden arches, Coke, Disney, Mercedes, the list went on. But, they had always been there, as though they pre-existed not only for her, but for everyone on the planet. Gordius was different because she was witnessing the birth of something that was far more intelligent than that which bore it, as though a fully developed adult had sprung forth from the womb.

They were responsible for the 31 companies in the United Kingdom, any resistance or inertia of people in the actual companies bulldozed to one side. Everything was to change and change quickly. Any piece of paper that might once have borne the moniker of independence was replaced by the knot of Gordius. Companies which had identifiable brand histories stretching back over 50 years disappeared overnight. Signs had been pulled off buildings and the silent, squatting copper spiders had taken their place.

On billboards, including those rated the most seen of any in the country, simple knot patterns were placed, sometimes easily visible and at other times requiring more involvement to determine what was occurring in the frame. Wherever people made a connection with something external to themselves, the knot was waiting for them. Newspapers, magazines, television, radio, cinema, the Internet. It was not so much a campaign as a design for living. They were not advertising what Gordius was or what it did, just the fact that it existed. The knot was staking a claim on minds.

Something trembled in Jenna's head, as though one of the tendrils had wormed its way into a frontal lobe. She swallowed and found a heavy pack of phlegm sitting in the back of her throat, its shape almost distinguishable as she eased it down her gullet. Memories shimmered in her mind, but they were not hers. In the air around her, an energy hung that was not part of the building as such; it just floated in the atmosphere, enclosed only by whatever building happened to be around it at a given time. Like the old building that used to be here, she thought.

The first voice was muffled, as if someone were in the room with her but not speaking clearly, a sound effect on a piece of music. The next was a distant shout struggling to break through an echo, reverberating on itself until the sound was lost in a chopping noise.

Something very special and very nice.
LKG two hundred million.
May I ask who's calling?
Infinite patterns visible to the eye.
Have you seen the rooms on the ninth floor?
So you trust me then?

Jenna let her shoulders sag and pressed more of her weight into the chair, trying to increase her gravity. It felt as though her face, or the inside of her head, was attempting to push itself out. Her tongue quivered and this time the words whispered from her own mouth, no longer imprisoned in her mind.

I need to get ready.
Don't worry, I won't be making any noise.

Kill me. Kill me. Kill me.
Have you seen the rooms on the ninth floor?
Something very special and very nice.
Have you seen the rooms on the ninth floor?

'There aren't any,' Jenna said, clearly and loudly in a voice that was not hers. It was a man's voice. She put her hand to her mouth, the bass of the voice leaving a tingling sensation on her lips.

Any what? she asked herself. Rooms on the ninth floor. Like the old building that used to be here.

Something had happened in this space. A phone had . . .

The phone on Jenna's desk warbled and the normally pacifying trill jarred her brain.

'Garth –' Jenna stopped herself and flexed her jaw, as though trying to chew the unfamiliar word into something digestible. 'Jenna Miller,' she said into the receiver.

'Popsie, it's Gordon. Can you run round here?' a thin-toned male voice asked.

She stood.

A tall piece of work in Alan Mikli glasses, his short hair glazed to the sheen of dried fruit, Gordon Irvine would sweep around the office of Gordius as though his Red or Dead shoes were mounted on castors, either that or he was still wearing the rollerblades he sometimes commuted to work on. Carried along on a waft of Issey Miyake after-shave, he generally wore a ribbed top, something that would stay close to his gym-honed body.

The clutter of Gordon's desk was organized with all the artfulness of a *GQ* photo shoot. A book on yoga, one about feng shui, a copy of *Loaded* magazine, two empty tins of Fosters lager. A picture of Ursula Andress emerging from the sea in *Dr No*. A book by someone called Dennis Cooper and one by Kathy Lette. His Mac, the headset he used instead of a handset when on the phone, his Psion Series 6, the sleeve from his blood pressure monitoring kit, a CD Walkman, a Nokia mobile phone.

Stuck to the side of the terminal, so it jutted out like an

ear, was a picture of Edward Furlong, the boy from *Terminator 2*. Dressed in a leopard fur coat and clutching a cuddly bear almost the size of him, he was more waif than stray, more girl than boy. Jenna knew that Gordon's references to this picture and to the one of Ursula Andress were meant to keep people guessing, intrigued about him.

Jenna read him in a single glance and knew this was why she had come to work today. He did not acknowledge her presence and she realized he had not made the call to her. Gordon had not wanted her to be there, and would have wanted it even less had he been able to see what Jenna had just glimpsed of him.

'Gordon, you used to work here, in the old building, didn't you?'

'Yes,' he said, glancing up only for a second, frowning back at the page in front of him as though he did not want to have a conversation. 'What did you do to your hair?' he asked, not sounding interested.

'How many floors did it have?'

He looked up and laid the page down on his desk.

'That would be a pretty weird thing to remember,' he said.

'I know,' she replied.

'Of course, I do remember.' He smiled and paused.

Jenna wanted to know, so she was prepared to let him have what he wanted – her interest.

'How come you know?' she asked.

'When they rebuilt, they wanted to put a huge fuck-off skyscraper up, one that would have dwarfed Canary Wharf, but they weren't allowed to. They squeezed one more floor on and that was all. I think this building is basically the same height as the old one, but there's nine floors instead of eight.' He looked up. 'The ceilings might be a bit lower, actually. Why the question, popsie?'

'How much do you know about what happened here, in the other building?'

'You're morbid this morning. You really want to know?'

'Yes,' she said.

'Get it from Library. They should have all the press coverage archived on CD, even some of the TV footage. We saw the fire brigade video once as well. Why the sudden interest? You know they don't like it talked about.'

'They?' she asked.

'Gordius. It's the past.' Gordon stopped and stared at the surface of his desk. He picked up a copper knot, one of several that were at various points on the desk top. He held it up and moved it round in his fingers. 'Is it calling to you, Jenna?' he asked.

'Sorry?' she said, confused by the way he had changed his tone, slipping into something more solemn.

'This morning. I was watching you outside the building, staring at the knot. You've never seemed interested in it before. Are you hearing its call, feeling the pull it has?'

'Don't be silly,' she said.

'There's nothing silly about it, or any reason to be embarrassed.' He held the metal up and twirled it through his fingers with the skill of practice. 'It's easy to fall into this. It's so seductive and it's so simple. It makes me feel good.'

Jenna stood and watched his hand, not certain how it made her feel.

'What do you know about the Gordian Movement?' he asked.

'What we all know. The company line. They're nothing to do with us. We have no connection and no interest in any connection. Gordius Corporation and the Gordian Movement are separate entities.'

'You do have the company line,' Gordon said. 'I'm impressed. Do you think we could do what we do here all day and not become involved?' he asked, working the knot through his fingers faster. 'It just seems to go on forever, even as you look at it. How can you not be involved?'

'Involved?' Jenna asked. She stared at him. 'How could I become involved, Gordon?'

He looked momentarily uncertain.

'Are you free on Tuesday night next week?'

Jenna nodded.

'Good,' Gordon said, as if something had been decided for him. 'Then I'll involve you.'

Jenna smiled and brought her fingers to her nose, smelling them.

Chapter 8

Kavanagh had resisted every urge he felt to go and meet
Lucy at the airport, instead spending the time nervously
moving from chair to chair, looking out of the window and
along the road before Lucy's plane could even have landed,
just in case she turned up early.

Greeting her at the door, he had kept his features in the
neutrality he had been practising the whole morning,
despite thinking she looked well and had gained some
needed weight.

'This place needs tidying,' Lucy said, walking around
the living room as though afraid to sit anywhere.

'It has been tidied,' Kavanagh said. 'Are you going to sit
down, Luce? You are staying?'

'Of course I am. Where else would I have to go?'

Lucy sat down. Kavanagh had not touched her, kissed
her or hugged her. It had been almost two years since they
had been in the same room together. She was unknown to
him, someone new. He glanced around and wondered how
the room would seem to her. Perhaps it did look a mess.
Kavanagh tried to imagine how *he* might seem to her.

'It will be nice if we can spend time together, Lucy. We
need to catch up. I might have to go away soon,' Kavanagh
began carefully.

Lucy laughed.

'What?' he asked.

'The last time you said that, well . . .' Her voice trailed
away and seemed to say, Look what happened that time.

Kavanagh nodded. She was right.

'Are you working?' she asked.

'No,' was all he said, hoping that conversation could be
left to later. 'How's Wadlow?'

'Good. You'd hardly recognize him these days. When

did you move here? Last year, wasn't it?' she asked, still regarding the surroundings with something like disdain.

'Yes.'

After they had managed to get out of Los Angeles, neither of them could face the old house. They camped out in a hotel for three months and then moved into a short-term rental on an extravagant house in St John's Wood, Kavanagh hating being surrounded by taste that was not his own. The house they moved to after that, not far from Dover, had been the one they were in when Lucy decided to leave for America. Kavanagh felt lonely without her and found himself back in London, in the current house, a three-bedroom in Farringdon, barely touching the edge of the West End, and still in isolation. The loneliness was an empty space inside and it followed him wherever he moved.

'How have you been? I've missed you, Luce.'

'No one calls me Luce any more, Dad.'

'You can still call me Dad,' he said, trying a smile.

Lucy did not smile. She rubbed her temple and he thought he saw her wince.

'We have to talk about some things,' Kavanagh said.

'All I've ever done is talk about it. With Kim and now with Alanah.'

'Alanah?' Kavanagh asked, immediately recoiling at the cynical way he had used the name. No one in the serious psychiatric business could be called Alanah.

'She's helped. A lot. She's taught me not to make life easier for everyone else. That's not part of my duty.'

He could hear an edge in her voice.

'Maybe, but *we* have to talk, Lucy, you and me. It's no good talking to others. They won't understand,' he said.

'Understand what?' she asked.

'Understand what happened when I was in Los Angeles, when you and Nathan came looking for me.'

'I don't understand that and neither do you, Dad. Nothing happened. Even the things I think happened don't seem real. Some of it was in my mind and maybe it was in yours too.'

71

'You can't just pretend that none of it was real. Nathan Lucas was going to hurt you.'

'Nathan wouldn't have hurt me.'

'Lucy, you don't remember what happened, do you?'

'You know I don't. Nathan and I were at Nancy's apartment and when I came out of the shower, she'd gone to see Wadlow and then Nathan went out, to the shops I think. There was a knock on the door.' She paused. 'Then the earthquake started.'

'Sorry. This is wrong of me, to make it difficult for you. You shouldn't have to speak about it like this . . .'

'Talking about it is not the thing that makes it hard, Dad. Nathan and Nancy died in the earthquake. We lost them and we should be trying to move on. This doesn't help us.'

Kavanagh lifted the chain over his head and laid the two knots on the top of the oak coffee table. They jangled into each other as they came to rest.

'Your life has a couple of blank spaces in it, Lucy, doesn't it?'

'Sort of. Alanah and I are talking about that a lot.'

'And do you talk to her about the dreams you use to fill in those spaces?' Kavanagh asked.

'What do you mean?' she asked, shifting about.

Kavanagh was uncertain of whether or not to continue. How fragile was she? She looked older and stronger, but under the surface he could sense the same tenuous Lucy. Had she come far enough back from the edge that this was safe, that he would not tip her over and be unable to save her?

'You dream that you're at Nancy's in America and after the knock, you open the door and an old man is there who tells you his name is Alexander Cameron, the man old Tom Richards used to tell you stories about. You slam the door, afraid, because you think he is the one that killed your mum. He tells you about the power of the knot you used to wear around your neck, how it was not really made by Mum. In fact, it's the reason she died, because it was part of something else and someone else wanted it enough to kill her for it.'

'No,' Lucy said, staring at the knots on the table.

'In the dream, the old man tells you to go into the light and find out what happened to your mother. He offers to give you back that blank space in your mind, the piece you've blocked out since Helen was killed. You find yourself back in the house, going in the way you did the afternoon you found her body up in the attic, except it's different this time. You're earlier, and now you're confused, because the past, present and future suddenly make no sense when you're travelling on the knot. You see Mum and you see someone with her, not me. It's Nathan Lucas and he is the one who kills her.'

'It's only a dream, Dad. Did you speak to Alanah? Did you find this out from her?' Lucy asked, sounding upset.

Kavanagh hated himself, but continued. 'He takes that screwdriver and opens her up in the middle, as though he might have been looking for something. You head for the kitchen, where you feel safe, where you always see the ghost, the Lady. She gives you the knot, time spinning round and round on itself now. You still don't know who you've seen, but then you turn and it's Nathan, covered in your mother's blood.'

'You shouldn't know all this,' she said, shaking her head.

'He would have done the same thing to you as well. You even felt the tip of the screwdriver on your stomach as he kissed you. I had to get to you, Lucy, to save you. I turn up in this dream, don't I?' She did not answer so he continued. 'You know what I did next, to Nathan, with the screwdriver, and I know you hate me for it, even though you think it's only a dream. You were in danger. After that . . .'

'We were on the beach,' she cut in. 'Except it was a dream beach, all black and faded. The man who worked for you, Garth Richards, was there and so was Wadlow. A gun goes off and then the ground moved.'

'How often do you dream the dream, Luce?'

73

'I never stop dreaming it, it's just sometimes my eyes are open and other times they're closed.'

'This is why we need to talk. *I* understand. Others can't.'

'Nathan wanted me to help him. He asked me to.'

'You think that's what he wanted you for? To help him?'

'Sometimes, when I dream or daydream, it can be so precise and it makes sense. Other times, it's, I don't know, it's . . .'

'Just like a story,' Kavanagh said. 'An unfinished one.'

'Why did you ask me to come here?' she asked.

'For the same reason you came. It feels right, doesn't it?'

'Yes. Unless this is part of another dream,' Lucy said.

'Neither of us could dream up a house this horrible,' Kavanagh said, surprised at his own levity.

'That's true,' she replied and grinned. 'It is pretty nasty.'

'You're not wearing as much jewellery or as much black as you used to,' Kavanagh said. 'You grew out of it like I always said you would.'

'I still have my dark moments,' she said, a small smile.

'I want you to wear one of these, just for a while. See if it talks to you, helps you.'

'Alanah and I picked out a crystal for round my neck. Is it alright to wear it on the same chain?' she asked.

He nodded and watched her deft fingers thread the knot. The room felt airier than it had for a while and he realized the difference her presence had made. 'I missed you, Lucy.'

'I missed you too, Dad.'

'I feel like I drove you off.'

'Whatever. It doesn't matter now.'

'Are you seeing,' he faltered, 'do you have anyone at the moment?'

'No!' she said, her shoulders rising but the smile still there. 'Are you?'

'No,' he said, with less energy than her.

'When are you going away?' she asked.

'In a week or so. I want us to spend some time first. Luce, don't you have a hug for me?'

'I want to, but it feels awkward,' she said.

'Why don't you put the therapy on hold for a second, Lucy, forget what you think about the feeling and just go with it. You may be a woman, but you're still . . .' his voice trailed off. 'Oh God I can't believe I was about to say that.'

'When did you become cliché king?' she asked playfully.

Kavanagh raised his arm and held it out level with his shoulder, looking into the space he wanted her to occupy and then looking at her. She was uncomfortable.

'Luce,' he said.

She moved suddenly, as though not wanting to spend too long analysing it, and then she was next to him, pressing into him the way she always had, still smelling like Lucy, still breathing like her. Kavanagh kissed the top of her head and stroked her hair. However strong she was trying to appear for him, in his arms she still felt as fragile as she ever had. In the last few years, it had been easy to fall into himself, to forget why he was acting like a man possessed, following roads that led nowhere.

The warmth of her made the lonely space feel a little less empty.

Chapter 9

Luke stared through the window of the shop he had just stopped outside, wanting to go in. Heroes. Stupid name for a shop, but he thought comics were stupid anyway, something you read when you were a kid and then gave up on once you were older. The window was clean and sharp and he could see himself in the middle ground. The shop did not have the clutter he would have associated with the sort of people he imagined frequented it. His one trip to a comic shop in London, on a day jaunt with a Southend friend, had been enough for him. The heat of the basement and the big air conditioning unit freezing stale air and putrefying it through its insides was something he could still bring to mind. That whole shop had seemed as if it had bad breath.

He drew a breath as he entered and was prepared to hold it for the duration of his stay, but inside Heroes the odour of polythene warming under electric light and the expensive whiff of merchandising all combined into an atmosphere he found welcoming.

The two men behind the till were talking about a film they had seen the night before and their conversation was unbroken by his appearance. Both were unshaven and managing to look ragged and overweight in black; one in a T-shirt from a festival which revealed as much about his age as his taste in music.

Luke browsed and picked up snatches of their conversation, which moved on to *Logan's Run* and then *Planet of the Apes*. It came back to comics.

'When Galactus turns him into the Silver Surfer –'

'Norrin Radd, you mean,' the other interrupted.

'Yeah. It looks like he went into the wash cycle in a machine, the way he turned into an atom. It's drawn a bit like the logo for Ariel Automatic.'

The other one laughed. 'Yeah, but when Galactus goes round sucking the life out of all those planets, do you notice how he appears in space beside them, ten times the size of the planet he's next to?'

'Yeah?'

'What do you reckon he's standing on?'

'What do you mean?'

'Well, he just floats there, but it looks like he's standing on something.'

'Maybe he has his foot on a moon or some asteroids.'

'I can't see why Galactus would want to eat a tiny planet like that if he's so big. It wouldn't fill him up.'

'Maybe it's like a Malteser to him?'

'Yeah. He doesn't wanna ruin his appetite.'

'Earth, the planet you can eat between meals without ruining your appetite.'

'He should have a king-size Mars.'

'Yeah. Or a Milky Way.'

They both sniggered.

Luke sighed and went to the second-hand section where they were out of earshot. Expensive and rare editions were pinned on the wall, high enough to require a ladder.

Something very special and very nice.

Luke looked round, thinking one of the men had spoken, the voice was so close. He peered round the corner and saw they were still engrossed in their conversation.

A pile of comics, upright and leaning back in a box, gracefully tumbled forwards, like playing cards in the hands of a magician, making the firm sound of paper on paper and the faintest puff of air as they made contact. Luke looked at where the pile had parted. There was a comic with harshly drawn and long-limbed figures on its cover, their bodies shaped from shadow rather than colour. The writing appeared to be Chinese, more likely Japanese, he reckoned, like those brightly coloured cartoons with young, big-eyed boys and chesty women, lots of motor bikes and machinery. Something about the images was sexy but comforting at the same time.

77

Another pile tumbled, but with more force this time, as though it had a mind of its own and knew precisely where it desired to fall open. Luke inspected the cover that had been revealed. It was familiar and yet it made no sense to him. Superman, two Supermans, were wrestling. They were dressed identically, but one had white skin as opposed to the fleshy tones of the other. Their hold was almost like an embrace as they fell through an opening in the ground and on to muddy rubble beneath them. At the head of the page, like a crest, the familiar Superman logo streamed away in the opposite direction to its normal streak, the text reversed like mirror writing. The comic was called *Bizarro's World* with a backwards number three inside the letter 'O' of *World*.

Luke picked it up and held it close to his face.

Steal me.

This time, the voice was in his head. Luke had never stolen a thing in his life, had enough money in his pocket for it anyway, but that wasn't the point, he knew. No way, he thought. Carefully and quietly, he pulled the clear bag open.

Steal me.

The voice was more commanding and it annoyed him. No, I'm not going to steal it. He replaced the comic in the bag. It had been his intention to refile it studiously. He would have done so, put it back where it belonged, he was sure, if only he'd moved faster towards the box. Instead, he lifted his shirt and quickly shoved the comic into the front of his trousers. Luke's heart speeded up and he was instantly sweating against the squeaky polythene. Surely they would hear it as he walked? Put it back, he thought.

Instead, he grabbed several more, ones not in plastic, not even bothering to look at the covers, and shoved them next to the first one. Even as he panicked, his hands shaking, there was a peace and certainty at his core that could have belonged to someone else, as though he were watching himself on a film. Or in a mirror, he thought. The extra thickness in his waistband made the trousers feel tighter and he knew he had to leave the shop.

Casually, Luke lingered near the till, fingering a *Far Side* mug and pretending to look at a *South Park* T-shirt before walking casually to the door, stopping to look at the small notice board and then leaving Heroes.

Once outside, what he had just done suddenly seemed clearer to him and it felt as if the whole world had watched him commit the act and was now talking about it. He walked faster, feeling an urgent need to put distance between himself and the shop, convinced one of the shop assistants had already lumbered from his chair and would be waddling after him. Turning the corner, out of sight of Heroes, he broke into a run towards the closed-down swimming pool. Its car park led from the back to the front of the building, cutting short a long corner, and resentful holes had quickly appeared in the builders' wire fences as locals sought to restore their old shortcut while the site lay empty. Luke ducked through one of the gaps.

Soon the tall, windowless building would be demolished to make way for a superstore. Luke headed down an alley alongside it. People at school talked about how they used to swim here, but already it had been replaced by one nearby with a slide made from a transparent pipe which came out of the side of the building and disappeared back into it again.

Luke stood in front of a chipped orange skip, its side almost as tall as he was. He pulled out the comics and looked at them, wondering what had made him take them.

Daredevil. Captain America. 2000AD. Superman.

'What are you doing?' a forceful male voice asked as he was about to pitch the comics into the skip.

The voice startled Luke enough to raise a small yelp and make him drop one of the comics. He turned and was faced with a compact man, obviously confident and exuding an air of menace to the situation. He must have been in his fifties, possibly sixties. This was a man who had been in a lot of fights but never got hurt. His small eyes seemed to peer round his big nose and his cheeks droop a fraction, making him jowly and grim-looking, his sense of humour his own business. His hair was streaks of pure silver and jet black, harshly cut, in Luke's imagination at least, by a very traditional barber. There was something official about his appearance, the simple white shirt with a tie knotted tidily into its neat collar.

'Nothing,' Luke replied, cringing at how lame his response was.

The man had positioned himself in front of Luke in such a way that he closed off all angles of escape, although as Luke studied the man he realized trying to run off would be feckless. You can't make me do anything I don't want to and you will not make me move, the man's stance seemed to say. I am a man and you are a boy.

'Not going to read them then?' the man asked, glancing down at the sheaf Luke held.

Luke felt his cheeks redden and his hands bled sweat on to the stolen comics.

The man bent down and picked up the comic that had fallen.

'Didn't they give you a bag for these, son?' he asked, moving his head from side to side like a dog as he looked at Luke, as if he would have been able to smell a carrier bag.

Luke said nothing, afraid he was going to cry.

The man stared at Luke and then scratched his cheek, smiling at the same time. He looked down and then up at Luke from under his eyebrows and narrowed his mouth in a grin as he seemed to take the measure of him. Something violent entered the moment and butterflies fluttered in Luke's stomach.

'Please,' Luke said, not certain what he was imploring the man to do or not do.

The man seemed to change gear, as though he had been somewhere else and only just realized where he really was. Luke could feel him turning down his aggression as though using a dial.

'You've never nicked anything before, have you?' the man said.

Luke withered on the spot, unable to speak.

'Tony Wood,' the man said, putting his hand out and transforming the lean grin into a smile.

Luke tried to mirror the smile and stuck his arm out awkwardly, surprised at the firmness of the grip that held his hand.

'You got a name then?' Tony Wood asked.

'Luke Smith,' he replied.

'I look after this place, part of the security firm.'

'People still cut through here all the time,' Luke said.

'I know. It doesn't bother me that much as long as they stay out of the building. They're dead scared some tosser will break in, fall in the empty pool and kill himself. The whole place'll be bulldozed soon and then no one will be able to break in anywhere and there'll be one more fucking supermarket in the world. You like reading comics then?'

Luke faltered as the conversation came back to its original unwelcome track. 'Not really,' he said.

Tony Wood laughed and it made Luke feel silly.

'I've pinched so many things I didn't like. You could always sell them to someone at school that likes them. You shouldn't really be stealing things, Luke Smith,' he said.

'I have to get back,' Luke said, making it sound the way it did in films, an implication that someone was expecting him and would be worried about him.

Tony Wood nodded and moved to one side.

'You look after yourself, Luke. Be careful. It's not worth getting into trouble over stupid things, believe me.' He moved forward once more, blocking Luke's way again, and laid a heavy hand on his shoulder.'Come back and see me if you want. I'm here most weekdays. There's a bell on the door round the side, where the fire exit used to be.'

'Thanks,' Luke said, rolling the comic in his hands in a way he hoped would bring the moment to a close and wondering why he would ever want to come and see this small and unsettling man. 'I really need to be getting back.'

'Alright. Take care, son.'

'Thanks.'

Luke walked briskly, not certain what had scared him more, stealing the comics or meeting Tony Wood.

Chapter 10

Numbers flashed past Lucy's eyes and she made lightning calculations, quickly reconciling birth to death, taking one from the other and letting the result be a measure. What number felt good? Where was the threshold? Seventy or eighty? The numbers with impossibly small margins made no kind of sense to her. Babies and young children. Lucy expected she could move from stone to stone and eventually find every number from one to a hundred encoded on a tablet. Melodramatic verses gave no clue as to who lay interred, or what they had amounted to prior to the final calculation. A name and a number. When it was becoming just algebra, Lucy still felt the occasional pang on seeing the same surnames and same dates of death but a difference in birth dates wide enough to suggest whole families had been lost. All of it turned over in her head and was soothed by the crunch of gravel, the smell of grass and the sheer openness of the space.

On a trip to Los Angeles, Wadlow Grace had taken her to Forest Lawn Cemetery and shown her the preacher's grave and also the place where he had last seen Nancy Lloyd. The left side of Lucy's head gave a throb, the pain like a metal rod pulsing from the outside of her eyebrow, through her ear and down into her throat. The pain had been growing more severe in the past few months, but she had kept it secret from Wadlow and she was certainly not going to get Dad worrying about it. How had Dad been so accurate about her dreams, filling in details she had missed out on herself? Perhaps she had become too dependent on Alanah, reassuring and always able to rationalize Lucy's feelings and fears into manageable sentences.

Her mother's grave was in a private plot, well-tended and laid out with geometrical precision. The headstone was white marble with black lettering. Some reasonably authentic-looking artificial flowers were stuck into pots at the base and it was clean from the frequent washing of a morbid cousin on Mum's side. The stone was set into grass and surrounded by a small area of lawn, no large flat slab to indicate the size of a coffin or the presence of a body underground. The first couple of visits, she'd been wary about standing on the grass too near to the headstone, knowing she was standing directly above the coffin.

'Hello, Mum,' she said unselfconsciously. 'Every time I come, I do this,' she added, wiping her eyes. 'Sorry. I don't want to upset you. I just wanted to come and see you while I was here. It's been a long time and a lot has happened. I think I should have stayed here and looked after Dad. He's in a bit of a state, but he can't see that, of course.'

For 20 more minutes she stood and talked to her mother, bringing her up to date, telling her more than she had told Dad and more than she would probably have told her mother had she been alive. Lucy had been thinking a lot about her mum as a woman now she felt more like one herself. She wished they could have been adults together. Lucy told her mother about Nancy, knowing she would have approved of Dad trying to find someone new. The talking relaxed Lucy, a way of laying her life out in front of her like a map and then surveying it. The process was very . . . therapeutic. She balked at the word.

Lucy looked around to see if the cemetery was empty. It was and she knelt on the lawn in front of Mum's grave, putting her face close to the grass. She willed something to happen, a hand to reach and pull her in, smothering her with cold earth and finally blocking it all out. She concentrated on sounds, waiting to hear one that was different, unearthly.

Nothing.

There were still things to be done that day. Lucy said goodbye.

The old house in Hampstead, where memories had begun

and ended. Lucy stood across the road from it, hiding herself behind a tree. Parked cars obscured her view. Lucy could remember every room, the colour and smell of them. She could remember feelings of happiness, if not the specific events causing them.

Something very special and very nice.

Lucy remembered entering the house.

Am I hurting you now?

She remembered.

Take off the rest of your clothes then.

But the house was impotent now, its power over her gone. The energy had flown from its walls and into her. There was a point somewhere in her head where it was playing over and over again, its effects spreading through all her behaviour and manifesting itself only in dreams. Now, the house was closed up, windows and doors sealed by sturdy metal shutters. A board with the name of a property company and the discreet logo of Gordius in the bottom corner was planted in the fleshy earth near the gate.

Lucy gripped the knot so tight it dug into her palm. She looked down at it, as though about to scold the knot for hurting her. Loosening her grip, Lucy fingered it on the chain. She would have to surrender it back to Dad, she knew that, but before she did, Lucy was going to make certain it would also stay with her.

Lucy stood at the door of the average-looking house in Camden. It had a glass porch with two small doors pressing together. A pair of muddy wellingtons and two umbrellas, one a business-like black fold-away, rested in one corner. In bright orange letters made from insulation tape, the word TATTOO was unevenly spelled out vertically on one of the side windows. A small brass plaque read, 'Captain Steve' and numerous initials followed the name, too many to inspire confidence. Lucy felt a gurgle in her stomach. She pushed the bell and waited.

A man with grey hair greased back over his head in a

Fifties style opened the door. He wore dark blue Levi's and a white vest, showing off his old but sinewy body. There was a shiftiness that made the man appear as though he were about to run off. Lucy thought he looked like an old sailor, so perhaps he had been the captain of a boat. She also thought she could see nicotine stains in his hair. The man looked at her through the glass and seemed as if he was about to close the door in her face, but he opened one of the side doors instead.

'Yeah?' he said.

'I want a tattoo,' Lucy said.

'How old are you?' the man asked.

'Twenty,' hoping her tone said, Is that a problem?

The man looked at her for a moment before reaching his inky blue arm out to open the other glass door.

The man led her straight upstairs to the parlour, giving Lucy only the briefest chance to peer into the living room when she was halfway up the stairs. A young woman sat in front of the television set, back flat to the sofa, legs stretched out and a can of 7-Up resting on the bare skin above her navel where her short top ended. Lucy eyed the skin for a second, the soundtrack from an afternoon television show just audible.

It was like a barber's shop. The walls of the parlour were decorated with eastern designs as refracted through a western eye. Garish dragons and other monsters frolicked in the splendour of their bright red and gold. There was a photograph of the man standing outside a big house and Lucy bent her head to look at it.

'That's me at Graceland,' Captain Steve said. 'Elvis's house in Memphis,' he added, as though Lucy might not know what he meant. 'Fucking brilliant. Bit small, but brilliant.'

'Is this in America too?' Lucy asked as she squinted at another picture, hoping to break the ice by showing an interest.

'No, that was at a rally down by the sea, in Brighton. One of the first '55s to roll off the Plymouth line. Worth a bomb now, wish I hadn't sold it.'

Lucy nodded, wondering where she was meant to sit.

'What do you want doing?' Captain Steve asked, his tone wry like a barman serving a boy his first drink.

Lucy lifted the pendant off her neck and handed it to the man, feeling naked without it.

'It's a complicated pattern and it'll take a while. Is this your first one?' he asked.

'Yes,' Lucy said. 'Of course.'

Captain Steve smiled.

'Why don't you have something simpler? I've got books of stuff you can look through.'

'I want this one,' Lucy said.

'Where do you want it?'

'Just on my arm,' Lucy replied, tapping her outer left arm below the shoulder.

'Are you left- or right-handed?' Captain Steve asked.

'I'm right-handed.'

'Have it done on your right arm then. The muscles'll be better on that arm.'

The statement, with its hints of strength and pain, sent the first tremor of doubt through Lucy. Captain Steve harboured no such qualms.

'What I'll do,' he said, slipping the chain from the pendant, 'is make a copy of this and then we'll transfer the outline to your arm. What colour do you want it doing? This doesn't have a lot of colour to it.'

'I'm not sure, what do you think?'

'Do the outline in blue and then if you want I can fill it in with a colour.'

'Can you fill it in with white?' Lucy asked.

'Yeah, it'll look a bit different to your skin, but it's not that noticeable. Like this,' the man said, holding out his left forearm.

On it was a portrait of Elvis, smiling in slim profile, the areas around his jaw filled in white like a cross between blusher and clown make-up.

'Yes, sort of like that,' Lucy said.

'I'll go and get a copy of this, then. Get your coat off and sit yourself there.'

Captain Steve went through a narrow door hung with coloured plastic streamers. Lucy took off her coat, assuming she could just push up the sleeve of her T-shirt. She sat on the small leather stool Captain Steve had pointed at and rested her right elbow on the table. This is the silliest thing I've ever done, she thought. Dad would go mad. The equipment around her was old-fashioned, like something made by a mad inventor. She assumed the small gun on the end of an extending arm like a dentist's drill was the thing that would ink her. Like a postmark, she thought.

'Bugger me,' Captain Steve said, appearing through the streamers. 'This thing doesn't want to be copied. I've set the copier light and dark and it won't come out, like it's invisible. I'll do the transfer freehand.'

Captain Steve switched on a tape player and as 'You're the Devil in Disguise' began, he asked Lucy, 'Do you mind?'

She replied no, eager to get on with it.

When the equipment was switched on, it hummed. She watched as ink was dropped into glass jars, swirling through and dissolving, the white one looking like a glass of soluble aspirin. Captain Steve wet her arm and shaved the fine blonde hairs from Lucy's arm with a disposable razor fresh from the pack. Lucy could hear a lecture from Dad orating itself in her head, concentrating on lack of hygiene and the risk of infection. As Captain Steve moistened the piece of paper with his copy of the knot on it and stuck it to her arm, Lucy knew she couldn't back out now.

'Love Me Tender' was almost loud enough to cover the ominous drone of the machinery. While they waited for the copy to transfer its outline, Lucy carefully reworked the chain through the pendant and hung it round her neck once more.

'We could have heated it up and branded you with it,' Captain Steve laughed. 'Mate of mine tried it with a swastika and ended up in hospital. Branding wasn't even that popular at the time. Where'd you get it?'

'It's been in the family for years,' Lucy said.

Captain Steve removed the paper, peeling it away carefully. The interlocked lines were faintly imprinted on Lucy's arm. Captain Steve put the needle into the machine and switched on a white table lamp, pointing it at the pattern.

It didn't hurt as much as Lucy had expected. The gun was like a sewing machine as it fired back and forth into her arm, Captain Steve explaining how shallow the depth was. It tingled and stung, but there was no single, definable hurt like with an injection. Captain Steve rambled on and nodded his head in time to Elvis. He was like a hard-boiled egg at Easter, the felt tips having well and truly taken to him. There was hardly an area, apart from his face, neck and hands, that wasn't drawn or written on.

Once, Lucy imagined, Captain Steve's body would have been as blank as a fresh sheet of paper and now it had been written all over. He was like a walking diary, his skin a journal of his life in words and pictures. Words and pictures that were indelible and yet as temporary as Captain Steve, going when he himself was gone.

'Why don't you have any on your hands or neck?' Lucy asked, drawn into the curious intimacy of this moment with a stranger.

'What, like a diving swallow on my throat? I do a few of those round here. And on the hands. Me, I can put on a suit and tie if I have to and you'd never know. I won't do faces. Necks if I'm sure they really want it. Names too, I don't always like doing. And I never do it if they're pissed. You have to get a feeling about the person first. Hold still, I'm going to fill in with the bigger needle.'

Captain Steve frowned with concentration, his eyes making circuits over the pattern on Lucy's arm. 'You could get hypnotized doing this one. I'm starting to feel sleepy already. Only joking, don't worry.'

It took almost two hours and cost most of the money

she'd brought with her. Captain Steve put a square white plaster over his work.

'In a few hours, take this off and wash it gently with lukewarm water and then let the air get to it,' Captain Steve said as Lucy pulled her shirt sleeve back down.

'Will I be able to go swimming?' she asked.

'No, I wouldn't. You never know what's in there. All those dirty pricks, fannies and arseholes. You might get AIDS,' Captain Steve said, lighting a roll-up cigarette. 'Stay away from hot water as well. Be careful when you're in the bath or shower for the next couple of weeks.'

Lucy walked to the station as the sun finally gave up for the day. The pattern was tingling into her arm, the dull pain there seeming to find cadence with the one in the side of her head.

Chapter 11

Luke jerked awake into the darkness of his room, startled by the movement of something that was now still. All he could hear was the sound of his breathing and the agitated scratch his feet made into the sheets as he left sleep. Usually, the workings of his own mind roused him but tonight his body was reacting to something outside of itself. He felt hot but had no desire to remove the covers, unwilling to be exposed to the darkness, wanting neither his body to touch it nor his eyes to see it. Instead, he closed his eyes and remained lying on his back, trying to let brain and body synchronize so he could think more clearly.

The sweats and feverish images had been with him all night. Balled up at his side were the shorts and T-shirt he had removed while still under the bedclothes. There had been similar nights in the old house. It was dark and hot, wherever he was. He waited.

'Luke.'

His name spoken on the half-breath of a whisper, carried along on the dark and sending a tingle through his collar-bone and down one side of his body. He did not move, as though stillness might offer some form of protection. Were he to take the sheet off his face where it lay like a shroud and open his eyes, Luke knew there would be a shape, a mass that might have formed from all the dark edges of the room, ready to swallow him.

As though carried by a light breeze through an open window, the sheet became lighter as it lifted slightly and Luke cringed, trying to cower but with nowhere to hide.

Beneath the sheet, a hand stroked the top of his foot, lighting on the hairs that had so recently started to flourish there. Following the trail of new growth, fingers slid over his shins and then on to the calf muscles, over the sprouting on the front of his legs and on to the hairless join of his inner thighs. It was only when the hand cupped the hairy sac that Luke realized he had been holding his breath, because it expelled through gritted teeth as a harsh whisper that might have been the word 'no'.

Tears filled his eyes but his body denied him the sob he felt in his chest. If only he could cry, he was certain it would stop. Instead, the tickling between his legs had made him painfully hard and he gasped with a passion that nauseated him as he was squeezed and caressed.

The sheet was lifted from his face and his eyes had already adjusted enough for him to make out the shape of his mother's head.

'Don't cry,' she said, rubbing under one of his eyes with a thumb. 'Time for some duties.'

Luke felt the distance open up, the way it had the very first time. How long ago had that been? He had put as much space between himself and the experience as possible, but parts of him had to stay and they were contaminated. That first time, he had only one question, because he literally did not understand what was happening.

'What are you doing?'
'Something very special and very nice.'
'What is it?'
'Do you trust me?'
'I don't know. Will it hurt?'
'Am I hurting you now?'
'No.'
'Or now?'
'Ah! No, I like that.'
Luke had been eight. For a week.
'So you trust me then?'
'Yes.'
'Take off the rest of your clothes then.'

She flicked the bedclothes off him in a single deft movement and leaned over to kiss him, planting her hot mouth on his and letting her tongue work through his lips. Luke knew to be tight-mouthed would only prolong things, so he relaxed and allowed her to manipulate his lips with her own.

When she pulled away, he managed the only word he ever did, as though it might be a reminder to her, to snap her out of it and make her realize who he was – and who she was.

'Mum.'

'Be a good boy, Lucas. Time for duties.'

Chapter 12

'Do people ever frighten you?' Jenna asked.

'Everyone gets afraid, of others.'

'Not like that. Do people ever come in here and tell you things that scare you? If someone tells you that Jesus is living in their house, his face is looking out at them through the open door of a cupboard, his eyes lighting up, switching on and off, and he's smiling, and crying blood, and then snarling at them, but they're the only one that can see him, doesn't that scare you? Don't you wonder if it might just be real, that there could be this whole army of demons and ghosts that are laughing at people like you, the way you keep them out of trouble by explaining them away?'

'If you put it like that, yes. I feel a little scared now, just because of you saying that in such a vivid way.'

'I have some family news,' Jenna said with mock cheer.

Kim did not speak. She sat and waited for Jenna to continue.

'Mother and Father have decided to go travelling before they die,' Jenna said.

'When are they going?'

'Well, from what she said, it sounded like Christmas Day or quite soon after it.'

'How long are they travelling for?'

'Most of the year, all of their lives, they didn't seem clear on the subject.'

'You seem annoyed with them?'

'Do I?'

'Are you?'

'They want me to tell Martin for them.'

'They asked you that?'

'Perhaps they know I am a better sister to him than they were a mother or father,' Jenna said.

'Were?' Kim asked, questioning Jenna's use of the past tense.

'Well, he is dead as far as they are concerned. And they might as well be dead from his point of view. Maybe you're right, Kim. They use me as their lifeline to him.'

'Would you rather they told him themselves or would you prefer to do it?'

'I would rather they weren't going anywhere. That caught me by surprise, when I found myself thinking about them like that.'

'How do you think you will feel when they do go?'

'I don't know. All I can think now is that it will seem different, like having a memory about it already, or remembering something that never really happened to you.'

'Will you feel sad without them? Happy? Angry?'

'All of them?' Jenna asked.

The largest part of the hour with Kim had passed. After the apologists her father had reluctantly agreed to, Kim was a ray of light and one that Jenna had found all by herself. 'What will we do?' Jenna had asked Kim at their first meeting. 'Have a very long conversation over a very long period of time and learn enough about each other so that we can help you.' 'How will we know when we're done?' Jenna asked. 'We'll know,' Kim replied. Bits of it were so obvious that Jenna wanted to laugh, basic reflection techniques and questions about how things made her feel, but Kim was also guileful, able to see links that Jenna did not, make connections where Jenna could see no fit until the ends were touching and buzzing with currency.

'Are you going to tell Martin that your parents are off travelling?' Kim asked.

'I know they won't tell him, so someone has to. Do you always believe what people tell you in here?' Jenna asked.

Kim smiled. 'I try to understand why someone might want to lie.'

Jenna liked the calm and almost immediate manner with which Kim would respond, never flustered by questions about what Jenna considered to be her art.

'But it's a bit easy for you, no offence. This reminds me in some ways of astrology, which I think is a lot of shit. I met this sad guy at a party who was covered in pendants for every sign you could think of, beard, dark mauve clothes, the whole bit. I told him I thought astrology was a lot of bollocks and he said, "You must be a Pisces." They've always got a get-out, even though I'm Taurus. If I said to you analysis was a lot of bollocks, you'd probably say that was interesting and we should discuss it.'

'I think I would ask why you've been coming for almost two years,' Kim said, a warm grin on her face.

Jenna smiled back. Kim paused and continued to stare at her through the hazy light in the room.

'Well,' Jenna said, her standard pause with Kim.

'We haven't talked about work,' Kim said. 'How are things there?'

'I think Gordon has asked me out on a date.'

'You weren't expecting him to do that?' Kim asked, her voice neutral.

They had spoken a lot about Gordon and how negative Jenna felt towards him. Their jury of two was still out as to whether he represented Jenna's father, brother, college lecturer or several other previous boyfriends, or if he was just Gordon in his own right.

'I don't know. He's such a stupid cunt, I'd like to cut him open and arrange all his organs in a feng shui pattern around his desk, ask him if that helps his energy flow, his ch'i.' Jenna snorted, making a swooping gesture with her arms and then leaning back in the chair, pushing her legs open.

'There's a Jenna we haven't heard for a while,' Kim said.

'Do you think of it like that?' she asked interested. 'As though there really was this whole other Jenna that just went away on holiday?'

'It's a convenient device that lets us put boundaries around certain parts of your past. We've talked about that,' Kim said.

'It feels like I'm on this never-ending reality quest, like I will come to the conclusion of this great long journey and the real Jenna will be waiting for me at the end of it.'

'Well, I don't like to use these sorts of analogies as a rule, but what you have to ensure is that when you get to the end of the journey, assuming that journey is life, the Jenna you meet there is the one you are expecting, the one you made. That sounded more like a cliché than an analogy, actually,' Kim said.

'I think it would be disappointing to get there and just find yourself, like looking in a mirror. It would be far more exciting for it to be something else, something so wild it just rips the guts right out of you.'

'You have more of the adventurous spirit than most people, Jenna.'

'Just here for the ride,' Jenna said, a small cackle accompanying the comment.

They fell into silence for a moment or two, Kim looking at Jenna in a way that was calming rather than annoying. There were times when Jenna would gladly have sat there and said nothing for an hour, paying just to bask in the comfort of Kim's gaze.

'I started to hear the voice again, the old Jenna,' she said.

Sadness seemed to tinge Kim's features.

'It woke up,' Jenna continued, 'as though it had been there inside me the whole time, listening to me.'

'Have you started to have destructive feelings?'

'Yes, but I'm scared, Kim, because it feels different this time. The voice is stronger than I am. For a little while it was whispering, muttering away, but now I'm the one who has to shout to be heard. I'm not the one in control any more.'

'You came here today,' Kim said.

'I saw a film once where the killer was able to impersonate different people. That was how he got away with it.'

'You feel as though you are impersonating someone else?' Kim asked.

'No.' Jenna looked into Kim's eyes. 'The voice is impersonating me.'

Kim frowned.

'That,' Jenna went on, 'or it really is me and all the shit I've been pretending to do for the last couple of years was just the impression I wanted to give everyone, that everything was alright and there would be no more trouble.'

'Has there been more trouble?'

'It depends who you ask,' Jenna replied almost before Kim had finished asking the question.

'Is that why you changed your look?'

Jenna ran her hand through the short strands of blonde hair, noticing there was a slight sweat in the follicles. *I* didn't change my look, she thought, feeling a swirl inside her stomach, something like a corkscrew going through her intestines. 'I think so,' she said.

'What should we do?' Kim asked, sympathetically.

'There's nothing we can do. I'm going all the way down this time. Off the high board and into the deep end. It's going to end badly.'

'We took you off that path once before. There's nothing to stop us doing that again.'

Jenna felt like she was going to cry. 'I wasn't going to come today, but I wanted to speak to you, to let you know that you've been helpful and that I've enjoyed the feelings over the last months. However it turns out, it's not your fault, Kim.'

'I can't tell if you are someone who wants to walk away from this or if you want me to drag you back into it,' Kim said.

'This isn't like that,' Jenna said. 'I'm here because I want to say thank you for being a help to me, for giving me the chance to hear myself, to hear all the things I could be. But, I'm the one who makes the choice, you know that, and even if it doesn't turn out well from your perspective, you were still a great help.'

Jenna knew Kim was familiar with her tactics, the walking away just to be chased. *I will follow you a certain way because I really do care*, Kim had told her once, *but there's only so far I or anyone can go. So?* Jenna had retorted. *So don't push your luck*, Kim had replied.

'If you're in this frame of mind, the date with Gordon might not be a good idea,' Kim said.

'You could be right, you probably are right, but it's arranged now. And it's part of everything. It's all linked up.'

'Do you remember how we talked about the way you thought Gordon was persecuting you?'

'Oh, I'm sure he still thinks he is. To tell you honestly, Kim, when he asked me out, I knew I was the one who had made it happen, that there was a bigger reason to it. Maybe I'm the one who's persecuting him.'

'It doesn't sound to me like you're going to have the best time of it, Jenna.'

'Oh no, I'm sure I will. I do mean it, you know, about not being able to come back. I have some things to take care of here and then I'm going to get to the truth of everything. I sound mad, don't I?'

'You sound excited, agitated and a little confused,' Kim intoned.

'I know. Isn't it fucking great?' Jenna laughed.

'Talk to me about the things to take care of,' Kim said.

'Have you ever heard the phrase, I can tell you, but I'll have to kill you?' Jenna asked.

Kim nodded.

'And you still want me to tell you?'

Kim nodded and smiled.

Jenna licked her lips.

Chapter 13

Luke set his school bag down by the radiator in the hall and listened. Music, not much more than a drone, was coming from upstairs. From where he stood, Luke could see down the passage and into the kitchen. No sign of her there. The smell of the oven wafted to him and he knew she had been baking. The music paused and then continued. He hesitated, throat dry, and looked at himself in the hall mirror, staring his reflection down and daring it to do something. Luke hung his blazer on the round bollard of the stair post and quietly climbed towards the source of the noise, the different parts of it separating out as he got closer, allowing him to hear the pattern of a tune. Old music. A steamy hiss pervaded the melody, trumpets tinny and pianos plinking. Climbing stairs to the sound of this music was familiar and nerves tingled in him. His mother was humming, a warble that was either side of the note she intended to hold. The sound of heels tapping the bare floorboards, keeping time through movement. Luke stood in front of the slightly open door to the spare room, his eyes stinging slightly from the seeds of tears. He rubbed his palms against the fabric of his shirt, transferring nervy moisture. Luke sighed and pushed the door open.

Bella Smith was dancing alone, making a tight circle by shifting from foot to foot and gyrating her hips ever so slightly. Her hands were held across her chest as though smothering someone with an embrace. As she sidled round and he could see her face, Luke saw her eyes were closed and her lips and eyebrows knotted as if speaking to someone, rather than mouthing hollow words and humming at the same time.

Her eyes popped open. 'Baby,' she said.

'Are you alright, Mum?'

'Fine, baby. You look smart. Very handsome.'

Luke fiddled with his tie.

By the side of his portable stereo, on the ledge of the unused fireplace, was a bottle of vodka, its top upturned at its side, a smeared tumbler close by. The bottle was a third full, fuller than the one he had checked the day before, meaning she had finished that one off and most of the one now on the mantel.

Luke knew the music. It was the only tape she ever listened to when she was like this. Benny Goodman. Sad and depressing to him.

'Pour a drink for your mother,' she said.

'Mum,' he said, trying to keep the word even, not too loaded with reproach, already beginning to feel dizzy.

'It's a special day, you know that.'

Luke poured some vodka into the glass, over halfway. No ice to water it down with. He handed it to her.

She sniffed at the liquid and then held the glass out to his face, pouting at him with her bottom lip. Like a baby, he let her feed him some of the noxious wash and it burned his throat, making the underside of his tongue feel as though it were withering in his mouth. He stared at her as she licked the print of his mouth from the edge of the tumbler and then emptied it in a dramatic movement followed by a single swallow. He continued to look at her, waiting for her to proceed.

'Do you like my outfit? They called it the New Look. Mr Dior himself had a hand in this one.' She giggled at her own double entendre.

'It's nice,' he said, licking at lips dried out by the alcohol.

The dress fitted close at her shoulders and sprayed out at the waist to just above her knee. It reminded Luke of the skin of a fish, silvery blue and scaly, the surface cracked like wax. It was too tight for her and her stomach showed. The dress revealed too much of her body, showing age that could not be plastered over with make-up, the gristly bumps on her neck, the hanging flesh in front of it.

He hated the music so much, each song encouraging her body to sway slightly. She went off back into the melody, her own tuneless reverie forced over it.

'I should take some medicine soon. I didn't have very much this morning,' he said, making it sound as practical as possible.

'You can have some soon, as a reward. But there are some duties that have to be done before that.'

She held her hands out to him, looking at him as though she were offering everything she had. Luke took her hands, stepped towards her and put an arm round her waist, lifting her right hand with his left, and they began to dance. The heavy shoes he wore for school were clumsy and he kept scuffing the left into the right as he tried to move fluidly. At first, his body was rigid, back very straight and legs stiff. He caught sight of himself in the mirror and was surprised at how relaxed he looked. She rested her free hand on his shoulder and occasionally her hair brushed the side of his face.

With her speaking soft words into his ear, inaudible but sensible through the sadness of the vibration, they danced to two songs in the chilling room as the light dimmed outside, their cold hands joined.

'I need to take some medicine soon, Mum,' he said, afraid to make his voice more than a whisper. 'I had to eat something on the way home because I was hungry. I'm feeling a bit high.'

'Not yet. We're not finished yet,' she said into his ear. 'The special day. Your special day.'

'Mum.' He closed his eyes and tried to find a place he could go.

'Wait here,' she said, breaking away from him suddenly. 'Such a special day,' she mumbled as she left.

'It's not my birthday,' he said to her back.

Luke listened to her descending the stairs and turned to survey the reflection. Sometimes, he was in control of it, the piece of glass like the pivot of a see-saw, weight shifting back and forth. When, like now, he felt despondent, his energy rushed into the glass and nourished the other self in there. He stood and let himself empty into the mirror, wishing he could cross the line into safety before she got back. His reflection understood perfectly and smiled. At first, the expression was warm but it quickly became mocking. Luke put his hand out, reaching for the image, whose arms remained at its sides. Luke was not certain what he wanted; the reflection to hold out its hand and lead him through into a world where everything would be reversed? Perhaps the reflection would grab him savagely, tugging him through against his will. Luke felt light-headed, needing insulin. The eyes of the reflection became encouraging and imploring.

'Here we are,' his mother said, entering the room.

She walked unsteadily, with a tray almost too wide to be comfortable for the span of her arms. Two fat bottles of Coke, the two-litre size, and a shocking pink iced cake the size of a dinner plate provided the weight on the tray. His mother bent to put it down in a manner so ungainly Luke could hardly watch. When she let herself drop to the floor, with a thump, the dress pulled at her, the midriff separated into rolls. Coke fizzed and ran down the side of the bottle when she removed the top, even the sound of it sugary and sticky. Cupping the bottle so tightly she made indentations in it, his mother filled a large American-diner-style glass all the way to its wide brim.

'No candles, baby,' she said. 'Pour me one and sit with me.'

The picnic happened three, perhaps four, times each year. Occasionally it was on his actual birthday, but it did not seem to matter when. He watched her as she took to the cake with a bread knife, sawing at it as though it were made of wood. Home made, specially. He had seen what went into them. Sugar, mostly.

'Can I have some medicine, please?' he asked.

'Soon.'

The slab of cake fell off the knife and hit the tray, crumbling into shiny granules. She picked the pieces up with her hands and dropped them on to a plate. A tiny square of sponge was framed by a mass of icing that looked like partly dried cement.

'You're not drinking,' she said.

The Coke was warm from where it was kept under the stairs, near the boiler for the central heating. It bubbled in his mouth and made his teeth feel dusty and porous. Could he get out of the room long enough to lift his bed and push his fingers through the hole in the sack material underneath, getting to the secret store? The only way to leave the room would be to say he needed the toilet, but he knew she would not allow him to; that would defeat the object for her. Even if he could get out of the room, there wouldn't be enough time, and he'd still have to come back, whatever happened.

'Drink it all down. In one go, Lucas,' she said, sipping from her glass. 'Eat some cake. It's specially made.'

In the frosty air of the room, Luke felt sweat forming on his brow and his back. The first mouthful of the cake made him shudder, so sweet it was almost sharp. He pushed two big handfuls in, wondering if sheer mass would block out the taste. It insinuated itself everywhere, at the back of his throat and under his tongue, dribble coming from the corner of his mouth. He sluiced the next glass of Coke round, and it felt hot as it slipped down.

Already, the sugar was accelerating through his system as though the steady flow of blood had suddenly transformed itself into a gushing torrent. In his field of vision, patches of colour began to appear.

Queasiness set in after the second piece of cake, his mother regarding him over the rim of the vodka glass as she held it to her mouth. Luke felt as though the sugar had absorbed all his weight and now he could lift off the ground. His whole body, not just his head, felt weightless. He drained the third glass as the tape clicked into auto-reverse, a painful moment of silence before the music started once more. Most of the cake was gone and the plastic bottle, with the wrinkled sheath of red plastic for a label, was already over half empty. Luke felt the first small pressure on his bladder.

His mother clambered to her feet and held her hand down for him to take and follow her up. Luke stared at it, worrying he would faint should he stand up too suddenly.

'Come along,' she said. 'It's your birthday.'

Benny Goodman's clarinet whistled sadly in the background, building to a scream.

Luke stood, concentrating as hard as he could. With a lingering movement, his mother pulled his tie open, sliding the long thin end through the knot and removing it from his neck.

'What happened to the top button of your shirt?' she asked.

'I don't know. I must have lost it,' he whispered.

Her nails dug into his Adam's apple and scratched the crest of his collarbone as she opened the next button down.

This time, she squeezed him more tightly when they danced, the tray pushed into the hearth. The last of the first Coke bottle was in a glass, next to a nearly full one of vodka, on the edge of the fire surround. He felt over-tired, awake and asleep. Luke gradually let more of his weight lean against her as both his strength and his will faded.

'Poor baby. You're not well. Finish up your drink.'

Luke had lost track of time. The tape might have been through a whole other reverse sequence. It felt like night-time and the windows were blackening with dusk, certainly. She pulled him along to the mantelpiece, picked the glass up and shoved it at his face, as she had done earlier with her own glass, but more forcefully this time. Half the second bottle had gone now. Luke opened his mouth, the edge of the glass knocking a numbed tooth, and swallowed as much as he could, until it ran out of his mouth and down his neck, wetting the collar of his school shirt.

'There,' she said, hugging him so tightly he could feel the rise of his chest with each increasingly laboured breath.

In the mirror, two figures he did not recognize, wearing the same clothes as Luke and his mother, twirled precisely and effortlessly, the background seeming like a ballroom, a dark cavernous space pushing into the distance of the mirror.

'Need to go the toilet,' he slurred, as if he had just started out of a dream. The feeling in his lower groin and stomach had gone from pressure to cramp.

His mother bore some of his weight as she led him towards the bathroom.

'I can manage,' he said, his tongue feeling swollen.

'Don't be silly,' she said.

Luke stood in front of the toilet and felt himself slump, putting his hands out to steady himself against the wall.

'See, you can hardly stand. How can you manage?' she asked, tutting.

She was behind him, and he felt her hand on his flies.

'I'm alright,' he said, sweating.

Her cold fingers delved into his boxer shorts, through the gap in the front.

The urge to pass water faded just as his need to do so increased. He focused only on the need, the outcome, not the mechanics of the moment. He closed his eyes, but it did no good. The cramp twisted painfully and her cold fingers continued to hold him. Releasing four very even breaths through his mouth, feeling as drunk as the time he had tried two tins of strong lager, Luke felt his insides release and the flow began.

'That's a good boy,' she said.

The long stream made a heavy noise as it fell directly into the bowl, its source apparently endless now it had begun, and he felt the tension across his back and stomach ease off. He shuddered and his head felt hot and tingling. The urine smelled heady and it made him feel nauseous.

'So hot and so, so sweet, too,' she said, the sound of the flow interrupted.

She fell to her knees.

'Please,' he said.

This time, he was able to go somewhere else, lost in the darkness behind his eyes as he switched his body off.

An hour later, as Luke lay on his bed naked and glistening, he was never more grateful to the feel the sharp puncture of the needle in his stomach.

After she had administered the medicine, he felt her adjust his body, shifting it into an unfamiliar and uncomfortable position.

'What are you going to do?' he asked.

'Something very special and very nice.'

Chapter 14

'Some say he's not even blind,' Gordon said.

Jenna looked across the roof of the recently parked car, trying to make out Gordon's features in the poor light. A plume of breath vaporized from his lips, the evening cooler than Jenna had expected, and she felt under-dressed in black jeans and a close-fitting top that firmed her chest with Lycra.

'You mean he can see?' she asked.

'Yes, but not in the way we do. He has insight from blindness.'

'So he is blind?'

'He went blind because of his diabetes. Before that, he was a professor at a university, teaching English. When he was diagnosed and later found he might go blind, he learnt Braille. That's how he sees what we can't. He found the patterns in the text with his fingers, felt them running under the surface in a way we couldn't because we just looked at them on the page.'

The drive had been along ever more covered roads, streetlights diminishing until they were reliant only on the headlights of the car, following the brake lights of cars in front. Eventually they had slowed until they were in a queue, its end unknown. Further along, smartly dressed stewards in cheerful tabards with only a small knot on the breast stood and pointed. They were waved through a gate wide enough for a single car and the threshold was crossed, out of the public domain and into the private one of the Gordian Movement. Every step of the journey was signalled by a hand, directing them through the mass of parked cars until they reached a space and Gordon carefully positioned his Renault in it.

From cars around them, people were leaving in well-ordered and unacknowledging silence, heading towards something she could not see.

'Where in Cambridgeshire are we?' Jenna asked, wondering if the flatness of the terrain accounted for the cold, despite the low clouds that mashed down from the sky.

'Near Huntingdon.'

'Have you been here before?' she asked.

'A couple of times. Twice.'

'And you've seen the blind man?'

'Once, but I didn't meet him. This used to be an airbase.'

'You told me,' she said.

'Not an American one from the Eighties, with nuclear missiles and stuff. This was before that. It was used in one of the wars, I think, but now it's owned by the Movement.'

'There aren't as many cars as I was expecting,' Jenna said, peering round.

'There's another car park on the other side, twice the size of this, and not everyone gets here that way. Some come by buses, some walk, others are here all the time.'

'No wonder we call this lot freaks,' Jenna said.

Gordon did not smile back. 'Let's get moving,' he said.

'I didn't think think this sort of thing still went on, and we're both too old in any case,' Jenna said. 'I haven't been to a big concert for ages.'

Gordon took her hand as she was speaking and Jenna thought about shaking it away or crushing each bone in it, using them to break each other, like pencils in a case. Instead, she said nothing and they stood in the queue, Jenna cold and a bit depressed, not sure what she had been expecting from this.

The building had loomed large from the outside and now it was genuinely cavernous, a large space hollowed out and filled with light and sound. It resembled a warehouse or a covered football pitch more than an aircraft hangar.

It was a TV studio. Jenna looked at the gantries and the lighting rigs, the clean plastic appearance of the false floor.

'Is this where they broadcast from?' she asked Gordon.

'What do you mean?'

'The TV channel, is this where it comes from?'

'I don't know,' he said, pulling at her hand to lead her further in. 'It's one of the largest indoor venues in Europe.'

'How many people are here?' she asked.

'It's hard to say – at least ten thousand.'

The individual queues, the lines of traffic, of people on foot, all fed into this space and became the same. Music played, as did many giant screens, nourishing the hungry with the diet of the knot. The range of ages was wider than she had anticipated, having expected mostly teenagers in baggy clothing allied to something extreme on the fringes of sport and involving wheels and potential injury. Instead, there were groups that looked like families, young, old, black, white, as though the cross-section had been selected in some way.

'Come and look at this,' Gordon said.

Towards the middle of what was a dance floor without dancing, a copper knot the size of a table was set into the opaque white plastic. The same knot they had spent the last year imprinting on to anything that would take it. No one walked over it, a few circling reverentially.

Jenna stared down at the knot, feeling a touch of vertigo as though she could tumble into it and never land, endless free fall. 'Impressive,' she said, unable to look at Gordon as she spoke. While she gazed at the limbs of the knot, absorbing their intimacy with each other, she felt Gordon's thumb run down her spine, gently leaping each bump of her vertebrae until it reached the waistband of her jeans, pausing before cautiously outlining the crease that ran down the rear of them.

'Is that okay?' he breathed into her ear, cupping her behind in his hand, squeezing in a heartbeat rhythm.

She reached behind herself and took his hand, moving it down further until it was between her legs. Then she reached down from the front and met his hand, clasping it and kneading it into herself, feeling hot against her underwear.

'Soon, I promise,' Jenna said, turning and taking a small bite at his lips before kissing him and popping her tongue half an inch into his mouth.

As Jenna pulled away, Gordon exhaled as though he were about to lose his breath.

'When?' he asked, hoarsely.

She moved closer to him once again, not making contact with his mouth this time, but moving to his cheek so she could speak softly, touching the crotch of his trousers as she did. 'You could do me like you would that boy in the picture on your desk. Or we could find a boy, together. You can do anything you want. To me. To him. Think of the things you could watch me doing with a boy like that. There could even be one here. There are so many things . . .' She let her voice trail off.

Gordon's cheeks were flushed and the front of his jeans was stiff in her grip.

'How about him, over there?' Jenna said, releasing him and motioning into the crowd at no one in particular.

He kept his attention on her for a few moments, but then he was looking where she had pointed. The things going on in his mind were impressive, and Jenna almost wanted to stay with him and try some of them out, but she had other plans. While he was distracted, Jenna carefully began backing away, watching him become smaller and then engulfed by the bodies. By the time he was flicking his head from side to side, confused and flustered, Jenna had become part of the crowd.

The thud of the bass drum caught her somewhere between her stomach and groin, but it was the bodies around her which were deafening, thousands of heartbeats, voices, blood flooding through veins, fluids leaving bodies, twisted moans of pleasure, even thoughts and desires, all coursed through her. Their source was the knot, as if it were a receiver picking it all up and relaying it to her. Jenna felt elated and depressed, sick and happy. She needed to latch on to one of these bodies, grab a small piece of the noise and assimilate it, make it quiet.

'Sorry. Hi!' a woman said, bumping into Jenna.

She was in her fifties, very broad face and quite heavy. Jenna wondered where she was from, what she did, what she was doing there.

Don't lie to yourself, Jenna, she reprimanded herself. You can't make her anonymous. You can know everything about her, you already do.

Jenna opened the woman.

Louise Carroll. Fifty-three. Divorced. Two children. Boy twenty and girl seventeen. Runs administration at a software company and likes her job. Has a dog and goes to dog shows, walks dogs for friends and neighbours.

Enough.

Louise was looking at Jenna quizzically, as though sensing she was being read.

'I'm sorry,' Jenna said, 'that was very rude of me. You know nothing about me. Let me introduce myself.'

She held out her hands and the woman took them. They both jerked forwards and Louise's grip tightened even though she wanted to get away. Jenna fed her just a taste, knowing the full contents of her brain would kill the woman dead on the spot. She gave her a glimpse of The Book, letting it flow into the woman so that it bypassed her conscious mind and became a part of her being, hard-coded into her. Jenna watched the woman's expression change as the knowledge swamped her.

'That's okay. You can be afraid if you want to. It's a lot to take in. You're seeing forever. Look at all those sad bastards who sit with their legs crossed for years, waiting for this sort of knowledge to come along, and here I am, giving it to you for free. Imagine what it would do to them if they really knew what was waiting for them on the other side of all that meditation and reflection. It would kill them, don't you think?'

Louise said nothing.

'Isn't this what you came here looking for? Isn't it what you wanted? I can't take it back now. What were you expecting?' Jenna gripped Louise's hands tightly as she spoke, the woman's own strength returning and fortified by fear. 'What did you think nirvana was going to be? Flowers and bells and music and perfume? It's all in me.'

'Leave me alone,' Louise said.

'You will be alone soon enough. I can tell this is all a bit too abstract for you, a lot to take on board. Let me give you something specific to focus on, to sharpen your mind a bit. This is what we're going to do together,' Jenna said, leaning closer and squeezing.

Jenna narrowed her vision until she could see only Louise's eyes, wanting to see the small flinches and the roll of the lids. Then, tears.

'I know. I know. It's okay to cry. It's going to hurt, a lot, but you'll be helping me. Look at it that way. Are you ready?' Jenna asked.

'No.'

'Good. Come with me,' Jenna said, letting one hand go and leading her away.

When she emerged from the toilet, Jenna stood and ran her eyes along several of the TV projection screens, watching the flow of bodies and the patterns the light made on them. Something was not right about what she saw. As one of the cameras swept over the heads of the crowd on screen, it pushed into a throng and gave a good close-up. Different people in a different place. She looked around and reckoned there must have been at least a hundred TV screens. Were they each showing a different crowd? In different parts of the country, different countries even?

Where were the cameras?

She looked up into the high ceiling of the hangar, trying to see where they would be. The lights burned down and she squinted to see what was behind them. Shapes, moving. Her feeling of depression became light and floated free of her. A destination, a reason for her presence, had presented itself.

Jenna surveyed the edges of the auditorium, looking for a way in, somewhere she could breach the crowd and see what was going on behind its collective back. Walking in a straight line, bumping shoulders with beatific revellers, she made for the far left corner of the arena. It wasn't like trying to find a backstage entrance, because there was no stage. Under cover of shadows and feeling so unassailable she knew she could never be seen in any case, Jenna put her foot on a piece of rigging, taking a handhold, and then, almost without realizing it, she was climbing towards the ceiling, unnoticed by the throng she had left behind her. The heat grew as she approached the roof, the noise dying below her. When Jenna was above the lights, she stared down at the bodies, not made much smaller by the distance. Like it was a tightrope, Jenna ran across a thin black bar that supported a row of lights, leapt a foot or two from the end and was on a walkway. At no point did she feel fear, or elation at her lack of fear. She did what was necessary simply because she needed to.

He was standing on a gantry, looking into nothing and fiddling with his clothing while several people moved around him as though he were an object. Jenna could not make out what they were doing.

'We're cross-checked and ready,' said a voice.

'Pump it louder for another half a minute, blind them and then kill the lights. Drop me through the dark as you bring the spots up. Get the line off quickly this time.'

It was the blind man.

'Thirty and counting,' another voice said, the crackle of walkie-talkie static.

A heavy groan of bass came through the busy treble and the harsh mid-range of sound, as though it had risen from the depths. It was nauseating, oscillating in time with her guts and making Jenna's head feel heavy. Below her, there was consternation as the noise became louder and the lights grew brighter. The rhythm and noise were disgusting, that was the only word she could find. The sound felt as though it had gone beyond just her hearing and permeated into every sense.

Darkness.

Silence.

It seemed as if the whole crowd had drawn a collective breath, their suffering under the glare of the light and the blare of the music unexpectedly cut short.

The screens flashed different images in the dark, radiating from beneath a large knot that dominated each frame like bars imprisoning what went on behind it. There were the sounds of excitement, panic and confusion. Then there were screams as the ground moved, only for a moment, but strong enough for Jenna to feel the movement of the suspended walkway as it swung. A tremor. Jenna wondered if there was an earthquake simulator installed.

The blind man was standing on the edge of the gantry, a gate pushed to one side.

Spotlights fired like strobes into the dark, landing on no particular area as they did, but picking out points of confusion, allowing a stricken face to be viewed for a fraction of a second.

With no apparent fear, the blind man stepped off the edge and floated in air. In between beams of light, just touched by their edges, he glided down. Later, Jenna presumed, there would be reports that the blind man had appeared from nowhere, serenity in the midst of panic, some people claiming to have seen him drift down from the heavens, as though he could fly. She was impressed at the quality of the wire flying, almost disappointed that very few people would get to appreciate it. Jenna kept her eyes on him, watching as he descended into a small space on the ground. The wire flew up as quickly as a whip.

The music picked up slowly, as though it too had been confused by events, the lights following suit.

Jenna moved to the edge of the walkway, leaning against the wire that formed a handrail, and peered down into the crowd. The blind man had landed near the knot, the opening perfect for him. It did not take long for some nearby man to realize who he was. Not long enough, and Jenna suspected he was planted there for that purpose.

The blind man was talking, chatting with a young

woman near him, as though nothing out of the ordinary had just occurred. In a way that seemed casual, a spotlight found him, Jenna followed it back up and saw one of the men on the gantry operating it.

'They're here watching a fucking magic show,' she said to herself, shaking her head with sadness.

A light whistle of feedback and then the blind man was speaking, a throat microphone broadcasting his voice into the hushed arena. For the first time, Jenna felt what the crowd would be feeling, a sense that this figure had appeared as if from nowhere. It should have been laughably bad, and in some ways it was, but there was also a facet to the moment that was curiously touching, fragile almost. It was not the belief of the masses that spoke to Jenna, it was their desire and need to believe.

'Just before the last century went to sleep, there was a movement, a reverberation of something larger that had gone before it.'

Jenna scanned the faces, all with a similar rapt expression, caught up in words that had found cadence with some need they each shared and expressed collectively through their presence.

'In 1997, I was in Los Angeles when the earth shuddered into life and opened its mouth to swallow sixteen thousand, four hundred and eighty-nine people. This was the movement of the third knot, the shock wave of trying to bury The Gift. He was on the earth at that time, walking in the opposite direction to us, and He had enemies. We are His friends.'

The blind man held his hands above his head, his image filling every screen and his voice reverberating from each speaker. Applause broke out.

'Two years later, in New Mexico, hundreds of thousands of us waited, watching the sun fade on the day of last things, many expecting The Gift to return through the earth, where He had been placed. Why did so many people, more than they could dare report, converge in that place, on that day and at that time? Because they saw the patterns. They could each sense the order that was forcing through the chaos, struggling to make itself heard.'

He stopped again, but this time there was no clapping, just an expectant silence. On one of the screens, Jenna watched the blind man's face, saw the sweat that ran in a long rivulet down one side of it. He looked as if he were listening to a voice inside himself, nodding his head and frowning, deciding whether or not to share what he was hearing.

'Where does it end?' He asked the question into perfect silence. 'Behind the words of people, in the words themselves and in the spaces between those words is The Book. From outside of time, through time and, perhaps, beyond time is The Book. It will end precisely where it began, and will begin again. The Book. A new beginning.'

Some whispering, people placing mouths against the ears of others.

'The Gift will be back, soon. He comes from water, walking backwards. He brings time, ready for the long journey.'

There was a flash like lightning as the lights died and came back to life again within the space of a few seconds. The blind man stood over the knot and light radiated up from the floor, the arms of the knot binding him in a web. The upward direction of light made him seem ethereal, a spirit floating. The radiance washed over him and then seemed to go through him, penetrating the pores of his skin and coming out again. Jenna stared down and it began to seem as though the light were now coming from the man. Lines began to form as though he had turned into nothing more than thin strips of matter. The lines grew wavier.

A mechanical noise behind her caused Jenna to startle and turn.

The blind man was standing there. Jenna took a couple of steps towards him.

'It's just a simple projection device,' he said to her, as though he had known her all his life, could see her. 'I'm already on my way back up as soon as the lights are killed. What is your name, young lady?'

'How do you know I'm a she?' Jenna asked.

'I can sense a female presence, part of the wave *you* give off. And the way you walk, the sound your feet make, a waft of perfume.'

'You really are blind then?'

'Of course. It would be foolish of me to fabricate something like that. It was darkness that led me to the patterns, to the truth.'

'These people come all this way, just to hear you say a few words?' she asked.

'I'm not a preacher. I'm not a guide. I'm just one who sees the pattern hidden in the text. I know things.'

'Do you know me?' Jenna asked.

He smiled. 'I don't know. Perhaps. May I read your face?' he asked.

Jenna began walking towards him.

'I can find you,' he said, and she stopped.

The blind man put his hands on her cheeks and Jenna closed her eyes, enjoying the feel of his soft hands on her skin.

'All the Braille makes my hands especially smooth,' he said, obviously feeling Jenna's smile. 'You've come here because there are things calling to you. Voices that are speaking to you.'

'Oh, they don't just speak. They scream and scream until they feel like they'll never stop,' Jenna said.

'I can hear them,' he said, nodding.

'There's something else you should hear,' Jenna said.

Abruptly, she reached up and grabbed his hands, squeezing each of them with her own. She and the blind man were galvanized, pulled together and pushed away at the same time, perfectly held by a force that was part of neither of them.

'Can you read that?' she asked, the words an effort as her body strained to make itself a conduit.

'Let me go,' the blind man sputtered.

Jenna closed her hand around one of his wrists and squeezed it hard enough for him to cry out. With her other hand, she pulled his glasses off and they fell to the metal walkway with a clank.

'I'm here to make people see,' she said.

His eyes were dead, gazing into an endless black distance. He was more handsome without them – even in his state of panic there was a kind of curiosity twitching the edges of his features. All of his skin, not just that of his hands, was well-kept, smooth and almost without lines, as though he would leave no marks on anything.

Jenna pulled hard on his wrist and kicked his legs away from him as she did so, following him down and landing hard on top of him on the creaking gantry. She sat on his chest and pinned his shoulders with her knees, restricting the movement of his arms. Her first instinct, the origin of which she could not be certain, was to sink a thumb into each eye socket and bear down with all her weight.

Instead, she fitted the heels of each of her hands into his eyes, feeling air escape as she pressed, her flesh held to his by a vacuum. His eyelashes scratched at the delicate skin of her palm and she realized he was blinking. As she held him, his head trembled as if he were clenching his teeth too hard.

'I'm here to make people see.'

When she took her hands away, it was like removing bandages. He continued blinking, more rapidly now, but his eyes seemed different, the previous dark infinity now bright and bounded by physical objects.

'I'm here to make others see,' Jenna said.

From the back pocket of her jeans, she removed the nail scissors she had taken from the woman earlier. They fitted her palm so perfectly that the sharp point protruded from the side of her hand as though part of her body. He was still blinking and adjusting to the novelty of restored sight as the metal tip made contact with his right eyeball and she quickly gouged into the tough membrane, tearing it and feeling the bones of his eye socket as she pressed further in.

He screamed and kicked his legs, banging them nosily up and down.

By the time she started on the left eye, he had closed it in a reflex reaction to the pain, so it took a little longer and a bit more force to remove the eyelid, but she did so by kneeling on his throat, pulling the lid up by its lashes and trimming it off with the scissors. His stare was bloody and unnerving as the lidless skin twitched, the eye alive once more, looking for what it had lost. Jenna peered down into the single eye.

'I'm here to make people see,' she said. 'Other people see.'

A minute later, there was nothing to stare at her any longer.

'This is a better place for the wire than that harness,' Jenna said as she looped it round his neck several times and made a good effort at a knot.

Picking him up with a fireman's lift, she hefted him along on her shoulder until she was at the edge of the gantry and then she let him fall, watching his body tumble with dead weight, almost graceful until he ran out of wire and the motion was halted with an ugly jerk.

Above the heads of the crowd, he hung like a puppet.

By the time Jenna had found her way onto the roof, the communal scream was loud enough to be heard across the clear space of the night.

Chapter 15

For Wadlow Grace, the future was measured out in ink. The size and shape of what lay ahead was marked out on paper, measurable but unintelligible.

On the pages of his dead brother Randall's notebook, it was inscribed in a naggingly short and indecipherable string of ink, lines knotting into each other but forming no words. It was as if Wadlow and the notebook were one and the same; that the notebook was living and breathing or that Wadlow himself was no more that the artful arrangement of ink on paper. Each time he opened Randall's journal, more became clear.

Everything he had done since last reading it was there before his eyes, in the fastidious hand of his dead brother, right up to the moment where Wadlow had opened the notebook and started to read.

Everything that was to come remained a mystery.

If he put the book down and the picked it up immediately, opening it once again, this action would be recorded in the notebook. The only thing he could glean or guess at was how much longer he had left before the swarm on the page would become clear, the story of his life written and concluded.

There was not much ink left.

If the future lay in an impenetrable block of ink, then what of his past? All that had gone before, his life with his family in Tennessee, then with the preacher in New England? None of it provided co-ordinates, pointed out a direction to travel. In his existence so far, there was no pattern he could discern, as though he had been made up solely for the purpose of a larger story, a story of which he formed only a small part.

Wadlow had seen changes in himself in the last few

years. He was no longer the heavy and sad-looking man he had been. After Los Angeles, his appetite had dried up dangerously for several weeks, and his body had been shocked by the sudden deprivation. It responded by making him dizzy, a fainting spell or two. He let it continue for almost five weeks, picking at small scraps of food where once he would have eaten three large servings. In this period he did not lose weight, he just felt sick the whole time, dizzy, hungry but with no appetite, feverish and irritable, always fidgeting.

In the middle of a panic attack one afternoon, his body drunk on its own fluids, he stopped in front of a mirror and looked at himself, shouting at the image. He sobbed and it hurt his empty stomach, made his chest tender. Something passed out of him that afternoon, a sort of grieving. Looking back up at himself in the glass, he felt sober and in control once again. A huge fat man with red eyes and a mouth that was no more than a cut in some dough. It made him feel pathetic.

When the preacher had found Wadlow in Memphis, he was a teenager, lean and handsome. Once he fused himself with the preacher, it was as though Wadlow had lost touch with himself. From the first time they made love, Wadlow felt himself slip away, and he liked the feeling. It was easy to let yourself dissolve into someone like the preacher, who seemed to have room enough in there for Wadlow, able to incorporate him the way he took so many things in his stride. From the age of seventeen, he did not have to be himself. By the time the preacher died, Wadlow had become a man without even noticing. With the preacher dead, it was not a case of being alone, a stranded half of something once whole; Wadlow just did not know who he was.

To repay his body for all the abuse he had given it for nearly two decades, Wadlow started being kind to it. His body became his project, his obsession. With the correct amount and type of food and some fledgling exercise, body mass fell away from him so fast he could almost feel the weight lifting. His heart took a grateful rest, beating slower and more contentedly. Even though the distance his weight had to travel was far, the journey was quick and several sets of interim clothes filled the gaps as his body rode a downward roller coaster all its own, even the occasional large pepperoni pizza or tub of Chunky Monkey unable to place a brake on it. As the descent evened off and Wadlow's body came to rest, nearly nine months later, he was out picking clothes, choosing who he would be, when he noticed someone looking at him; his body, his project, his interest, had attracted the interest of another. Wadlow could not recall a time in his life when that had happened; it must have, he reasoned, but he had never been conscious of it. How closed his life had been. Ma, Pa and Randall all he knew and then, after them, the preacher.

When Lucy Kavanagh arrived at his door, he had been thin for the better part of four months, just long enough for him to believe this was how he would always be. Lucy did not recognize him at first, but he watched it dawn on her in the form of a smile that stretched her face and made him smile back. After that, once she was sitting in his dayroom, there was less smiling. As he listened to her recount the situation with her father, the difficulty she felt around him, Wadlow found himself imagining her sharing the house with him, filling some of the empty spaces. It made him feel selfish, knowing he ought really to persuade Lucy to go back and work things through with her father. It was not his place to come between them, he told her. She would have to work it out for herself, he continued. What actually happened was that Wadlow called Mike Kavanagh and said Lucy wanted to stay with him for a while. The normally even tone Wadlow was used to in Kavanagh's voice changed, although to what, Wadlow was not absolutely certain. He did not tell Lucy, but he thought he detected relief in Kavanagh's voice.

A while became nearly two years. Long enough for her to make a mark on the place that was highlighted by her absence, the leaving as sudden as the arrival. Wadlow didn't know if he would even see Lucy again. Whatever comfort they had taken in the stillness of the recent years, things were now moving under the surface once more.

As he reached for the notebook that was never more than two or three feet from him, Wadlow thought he had done so instinctively until the feeling became recognizable. It was no impulse. It was written and he was being guided by the unseen hand of The Book.

For the first time since that afternoon in his old book shop in the New England town of Raynsford, there was something new on the page, words that had evolved from the primordial slime of ink.

He comes from water, walking backwards. He brings time, ready for the long journey.

Before his eyes, lines and shapes changed into words.

As he looked at the unintelligible mass beyond, three more sentences sharpened through the mess, allowing him to glimpse what was about to happen. He looked down at them.

The phone rang. Wadlow answered with his name. It was Alexander Cameron.

The phone rang. Wadlow answered with his name. It was Alexander Cameron.

The Second Knot

Every good gift and every perfect gift is from above,
and cometh down from the Father of lights,
with whom is no variableness,
neither shadow of turning.
James 1:17

Chapter 16

Home.

The place Luke went when there was trouble. Up before it was light, on one of the first Central Line trains and off at Stratford. Was he running away from home? His new home? No, he thought, I'm running away *to* home. For how long he was not sure, but he brought all the insulin from his stash. A few shirts, a pair of jeans in addition to the ones he wore, some tracksuit bottoms and all the clean pants and socks he had. Along with the insulin, he had been putting aside some money, as though unconsciously preparing for this moment. There was also money in his savings account. Not much, but enough to keep him going for a while in Southend. Home. And then?

In the sudden manner of British Rail, the train went into motion and it seemed almost as if the ground beneath him had begun to move. It was only just after seven and Luke felt sick, not ready to take on the day at such an early hour. He had never been on a journey like the one he was planning without his mother and he was excited and scared. Luke was confident he could manage his diet and his medicine without her. His bag had several leaflets and instruction manuals. While reading one, he realized it was not insulin he was dependent on. It was her.

Would she be able to cope without him? Guilt took a small nibble at him but he resisted its sting. There was no life left for him in Southend, he knew that, but it was a chance to pretend, to get away from London, from Steve Faulkes, from his mother. Luke looked out of the window and his view was blocked by his reflection, the one thing that would go with him everywhere. It smiled at him, seemingly pleased with his actions, as though he were walking into a well-laid trap. Luke shivered and closed his eyes.

In little more than an hour, he was home. There was more salt in the air, a chill in the wind and misty rain came down in fine droplets that rested on his black vinyl Nike jacket. The town flowed through safe and familiar grooves of memory. The dirty vanilla of the ice-cream factory loomed over him as he crossed the large, almost empty, pay-and-display car park and on to the road that ran behind the seafront, the open back doors of arcades and pubs. Mop buckets and brooms leaned against walls and a man with a moustache smoked in a doorway. Past one of the clubs, steps leading down to it, there was a smell of stale beer not even the rain could damp.

It would be nice to go along the rainswept seafront, pretending everything was alright. Had everything felt alright, even when he was here? Would things have been peaceful for him if they had stayed? He doubted it.

Luke looked at the early sea rolling in. People at school in London found the idea of living at the seaside exciting – big, bright and cheerful. How many people had seen the place in the depths of winter when hardly anything was open? This was a place people *used* to come to.

The seafront was a mix of arcades, pubs, hotels and restaurants. There were a lot of FOR SALE and TO LET boards on closed-up premises. There was a betting shop and a burger bar, plus a few chip shops. In season, the air was full of the sounds of machines and people and the smell of various foods deeply submerged in hot fat – chips, donuts, fish.

Along the sea wall and the railings of the promenade were deck chairs, huts, a few kiosks and a sign advertising sea cruises to World War Two wrecks. The sea wall sloped down to the dirty and uninviting beach. Traffic sped along the front on its way to somewhere else, slowed only by the long speed bumps.

Standing on the promenade, he looked over at the fair, set off to one side of the entrance to the pier. It was closed, not that he missed it. It had been a long time since he'd been on a merry-go-round. In the old shoe box at home, there was a Polaroid picture of him sitting on a wooden horse, the chemical colours rendered far brighter on paper than they ever had been in reality. Now long strings of coloured bulbs crept like ivy around the outer fringes of the fair, the opaque and unwashed globes seeming to choke the place. Dirty, oil-stained green tarpaulins covered the few rides half-heartedly, faded limbs of red and yellow paint poking through gaps. The dodgems each had their own brown canvas zip-up body bags, long antennae poking through defiantly.

He took in just enough of it to remind himself, but not so much that it would make him feel sorry for himself. That wouldn't do, not for Nanna.

Luke was ready to press the bell again, either that or walk away, when he sensed movement behind the bubbles of glass in the front door. It was not the slow, comforting motion of Nanna, though. He swallowed as the door opened, unconsciously shifting his bag out of sight by sliding it to one side with a foot.

'What do you want?'

'Is Nanna there?' he asked.

'She's our nanna, not yours. *We* don't call her Nanna,' the girl replied, her sentence coming back at him with a confrontational rhythm.

'Is she here or not?' Luke asked, trying to show some fight of his own.

'No.' She seemed to soften. 'She went out to the shop.'

'Can I come in and wait for her?' he asked.

'She's *our* nanna, not yours,' she said and Luke wondered if this were the loop of the conversation.

He picked up his bag and took a step forwards and she moved to one side.

She was right, of course. Marlene Dixon was not Luke's nanna, but his mum had treated her as something like a mother and Luke felt that privilege had passed on to him, albeit second-hand. Marlene was a grandmother to two, but neither of them were Luke. She was the mother of one of their ex-tenants, a couple with two daughters, one older than Luke and the other two years younger, who was sitting on the chair opposite him, staring and moving her feet about exaggeratedly.

Luke had not seen this house before, the place the Dixons had ended up in after his mother had sold the houses, including their home. The room was more comfortable than anything in Luke's new London house.

'She won't be back for ages,' Jane said, regarding him with only her left eye, which was widened in suspicion as though Luke were about to steal something.

The living-room was filled with ornaments, intricately worked china and solid pieces of brass, no dust evident in even the most hard-to-get-at crevice. The Dixon house was always the tidiest, Mum had said, referring to the old houses. There had always been a welcome there for Luke on his infrequent visits, always with Mum, and one of the few situations where Luke saw her with other people, a gentle social occasion always tinged by the fact that Mum was the owner of the house. Whatever souring in relations had followed the sale of the houses, Luke had not been privy to it. On their last day in Southend, which had seemed like too much of a rush, Luke's time was so devoured by his mother's needs that there had been no time for goodbyes with the Dixons. Luke and his mother had upped and left, the more difficult negotiation of getting the Dixons out of their home left to the anonymous property company that now owned it. It had made Luke understand the phrase 'Take the money and run'. He looked around at the familiar furniture in a new location. His mother had managed to uproot more than just the two of them.

'Where's your mum?' Jane asked.

'In London,' Luke replied, nodding for no real reason he could identify. 'Where's yours?'

'At work. She said you wouldn't have the front to come round here, not after what your mum did, but Nan said you would. They argued about it,' she finished mischievously.

'Shouldn't you be at school?' he asked.

'Shouldn't you?' she responded instantly.

'Fair enough,' Luke said.

'I've got my period. Nan said I can stay at home. It's bleeding a lot.'

Luke scratched his left eyebrow and quickly found an ornament to focus on. He sort of knew what she was talking about, in theory, but to know she was sitting there and might actually have been bleeding made him feel odd, as though she needed looking after. She was too skinny and her jeans were wearing shiny and white at the knees and, he had noticed on the way in, on the behind as well. A small face and very round eyes made her seem intense at times, although she seemed quite able to turn that into indifference more or less at will. She could have been pretty, but Luke could not get far enough past her attitude to decide.

'Which shop did she go to?' Luke asked.

'I don't know. She didn't say.'

Luke hated her, mostly because he knew that was what she wanted him to do.

'Maybe I'll come back later,' he said, sitting up in the chair.

'You can't stay here,' she said, looking at his bag.

'Will you tell her I called?' he said, knowing she would not. She just looked at him. 'Will you?' he asked, realizing he was feeling upset and that his eyes might even have been watering.

She said nothing. Luke sniffed and sighed, stood, picked up his bag and walked out of the room, not bothering to look at her or say goodbye. Where would he go now?

'She's not really at the shops.'

Luke stopped and looked over his shoulder at her.

'She's not well. That's why I'm off school, to look after her.'

'Where is she then?'

'Upstairs asleep.'

'What's wrong with her?' Luke asked.

'Don't know.'

'You're really fucking stupid, do you know that?' he said, dropping his bag.

She shrugged and scrunched up her nose.

At the top of the stairs, Luke cautiously pushed back doors that led off a strange landing. The third one he tried opened onto a room with closed curtains. Warmth and a recognizable, almost satisfying, smell drifted from the room. Nanna's breathing was laboured and Luke could not tell if she were sleeping or wheezing. He went in, pushed the door closed and approached the large bump in the bed-clothes.

Nanna opened her eyes and smiled, not appearing surprised, just pleased to see him. He bent and placed a kiss on her cheek and it made him feel tearful, reminding him that he had, technically, run away.

'Have you taken insulin?' she asked, levering herself to a more upright position.

Luke nodded and snuffled, threatened tears subsiding. He knew what she would say next.

'I used to inject my mum. Not as easy as it is now, the old glass syringes. You have to look after yourself, Luke, with the sugar. She never did.'

'I know, Nanna. I do. I'm being careful.'

'You look more grown up,' she said, patting the bed where she wanted him to sit.

'What's wrong with you? Do you want anything?'

The old woman raised her eyebrows. 'You could die up here and never be found. I had a fall last month, just sprained my wrist, but it's knocked the wind out of me. Some days I have no strength.'

'Is Jane looking after you alright?'

'That one can't look after herself. If I said I was getting up now to make a sandwich, she'd let me, and she'd let me make her one too. She'll learn,' Nanna said, stroking Luke's hand.

Luke could not remember a time he had seen Nanna ill. Sickness was not something he associated with her. She was always the one worrying about him, was he eating properly, being careful. True, she was not full of energy, making her home in the well-worn high-backed arm chair which had been in the living-room of the old house but was now here in the bedroom. When he pictured her, it was in that chair, roll of toilet paper on the side table for tissues, the backs trodden down on her greasy slippers and the mint smell of Polos in the air like a pot pourri. She was always pleased to see him because he brought a small piece of the world to her.

'So there's nothing you want?' he asked.

'I'm alright. Did you come all this way just to see me? How's your mum?'

'She's okay. I wanted to come and see you, probably go and see if the old house is still standing.'

Loud music started up from downstairs. Nanna made a face.

'Nothing's been done to it yet. Or our old place. Both standing empty.'

Luke hesitated. 'Nanna. Could, well, could I stay here for a little while? Only for a couple of days.'

'What's the matter, Luke?'

Suddenly, without so much as a quiver of his lip to warn him, tears came. Several long streams and then he was sobbing properly. He let himself slump on to Nanna and she stroked the back of his head as he cried into the bed cover, glad of the music and hating the idea of Jane being able to hear him.

'It's alright,' she said, and as he lay there letting her soothe him, it seemed as though it might be alright and he allowed himself to pretend for a while that it was.

'It's school,' he said, sitting up, sniffing and wiping at snot with his cuff. 'And London. I hate it, Nanna. Why did she have to sell the houses?'

A second wave of tears came from somewhere deeper than the first and his eyes began to sting. All his emotions seemed to mix in the confusion of tears. Luke had cried enough times before to know how temporary the relief was.

'What's wrong with school?' she asked.

'I hate it. I'm not going back.' The words were bloated by the air he heaved out with his sobs.

'Is someone picking on you?' she asked, staring at him and narrowing her eyes.

It was the most obvious question for her to ask, the same one Mum asked whenever he was moping about on a Sunday night. Are you being bullied at school?

'No. I just don't like it. I'm not going. I'm not going back.' He shook his head emphatically from side to side.

'We all hate school, Luke, but we have to go. There must be more to it than that. Is there a teacher you don't like? You used to love school when you lived here. Bella used to say you were happier there than you were at home with her. You have to tell me if there's something wrong.'

'Can I stay here, Nanna? Please. Not for long.'

'You have to tell me what's wrong. If not, I'll have to phone your mum and tell her I can't get no sense out of you. She won't like that, Luke.'

Luke weighed the options. Nanna could be strict. He needed her to phone Mum and smooth things over, at least for a couple of days until he'd worked out what he was going to do. If Nanna got Mum excited, there would be trouble. Luke wiped his eyes, played with his fingers and stared at them as he did.

'There's this boy. A trouble-maker.'

For the next ten minutes he gave her the full catalogue of Steve's crimes against him, surprising himself at just how much had gone on. It was the first time he had told it as a cohesive story. There was a good feeling about passing it on, especially to someone like Nanna, but it also made him see how much thought had gone into Steve's campaign against him. At several points in the tale, he cried again.

'Mum's back.'

It was Jane.

Luke turned his red eyes to her, no longer caring what she thought.

'Tell her I want a word with her,' Nanna said.

'I told her he was here,' Jane said, as though the words

had an unpleasant taste.

'Get her for me, Jane,' Nanna said.

'He can't stay,' Jane said. 'I already told Mum that's what he wants to do. She said he can't.'

Luke sat in the middle of the exchange, almost glad they were speaking about him as if he were not there.

Nanna sat up abruptly, threw back the covers and swung her legs over the edge of the bed. The movement, its suddenness, seemed to bring Jane up short.

'What are you doing, Nan?' she asked.

'If you won't get her for me, I'll do it myself.' Nanna winced at a pain that seemed to be in her side. 'And I'll tell her how you've been looking after me.'

'Alright, I'll get her,' Jane said. 'But he can't . . .'

'Jane,' Nanna cut in sharply and the girl stomped off.

'Nanna,' Luke said.

'Don't you worry. You can stay here. I'll phone your mum for you.'

'Mum?'

Luke was not sure if he had shouted the word to eject himself from whatever dream now bubbled potently under the surface or if it had been a fearful reaction to a movement outside of sleep, something moving in the room.

He was fitted awkwardly on to the sofa in the Dixons' living-room, the only visibility afforded by streetlights shining through thin curtains. There had been words between Nanna and her daughter, harsh words that left sharp points on the silence that followed – around the dinner table too small for all of them, Nanna struggling stubbornly down the stairs to provide moral support for Luke. He felt as though he had not spoken in hours. Nanna had made Jane bring her chair down, despite Luke's offer to do it, and in front of the television they stared in silence, any remark a dig. When Nanna announced she would be going back upstairs, Luke had practically jumped from his seat to accompany her.

Luke breathed heavily in the darkness.

Nanna was sitting in her chair, looking at him.

Luke jumped and a small cry escaped his mouth.

'You were shouting and talking gibberish in your sleep. Couldn't understand a word of it.'

A glow backlit one side of her head and she looked like an apparition pasted on to the dark. The back of Luke's T-shirt was sweaty, his feet cold where they poked from the small, grudging blanket Jane had virtually thrown at him. He sat up and spun round, bringing his feet on to the carpet.

'How long have you been sitting there?' he asked, wondering what time it was.

'I don't sleep as much as I used to. No need to. Got a good long sleep not far round the corner in any case,' she said with no trace of humour.

'Nanna, don't say that.' Their voices were almost whispers, hushed beneath the ambient noise of the room and the clicking of the clock on top of the television. 'You should be careful of those stairs. You wouldn't have fallen in the old house,' he said, his tone regretful.

'Luke, you can't think like that. It's not your fault your mum decided to sell up. Bella will have had her reasons. I might have done the same myself. That's what I keep telling Dianne,' she said, referring to her daughter.

'The money, that was what she did it for.'

'A lot of people do things for money, Luke. You will too one day.'

He didn't want her to be so reasonable. 'We were doing alright. She spoiled everything. Just for the money.'

'I know you're upset with her, Luke, but you can't stay here forever.'

'I'm making trouble here. Sorry.'

Nanna tutted. 'I don't mean because of Dianne. Sooner or later you have to go back to your mum and face her, tell her about what's happening at school.' She moved slightly and the chair creaked.

'I can leave next year anyway.'

'And that's still a long time away. You can't go on like

this. Talk to your mum.'

'I tried to stop her selling the houses, Nanna. I did.'

'I know you did, darling.'

'She shouldn't have sold them. They were left to her by my dad.'

Nanna nodded. 'And by rights they should have been yours. We can live anywhere,' she said, motioning around the room with a hand, 'but those houses should have been yours. That was what upset me most.'

'Mum never talks about Dad now. I wish I could remember him. Sometimes I imagine I can, but I know I was too young.'

Through the dimness, Luke could see Nanna was studying him and her eyes looked damp.

'You are such a beautiful boy, Luke. My mum died giving birth to me, you know that already. They say you are what your mum and dad make you and I used to feel like I was only half a person because of it. But it can make you stronger as well, Luke, and we should both know that. Is your mum good to you, Luke? Treating you right?'

The old woman seemed to be wandering a bit, so Luke nodded and made an affirmative noise, but he felt uncomfortable with the drift of the conversation.

'Do you remember me telling you where I lived on my own, before we all came to Southend?'

'Portsmouth?' he said.

'Plymouth,' she corrected. 'Dianne was still living in Cambridge and I was there in Plymouth on my own. I liked it there.' She stopped and looked away.

'Are you alright, Nanna?' he asked.

She was twirling her index fingers over each other as she clasped her hands across her slightly paunchy belly. 'I knew Bella then,' she said. 'Your mum.'

'Mum lived in Southend from when she was eighteen. She met Dad here when she was twenty-five. That's when she moved into the old house,' he said, explaining it carefully to her, as though they were detailed instructions on how to get somewhere.

'The first time your mum ever set foot in Southend, she was carrying with you, nearly four months gone.'

Luke hesitated, no longer sure she was just rambling. There was a certainty and clarity to her tone.

'She was living here since she was eighteen,' he repeated. 'She moved away from her family because she had trouble with them and she came here and got a job.'

Nanna moved her head up and down. 'That's what she told you and that's what she told me to tell you as well. I knew her when I was in Plymouth and she was already carrying you when she turned up in Southend.'

'What about my dad?' he asked.

'I never knew him. Bella was pregnant when she left Plymouth and the houses were here waiting for her when she arrived. A little while after you were born, we all moved here.'

'But, my dad,' he said weakly. 'Mum met him when she was twenty-five. They lived together in the old house from when they married and I was born when she was forty-three. Dad died just before I was a year old. You've told me all this as well, Nanna.' He hoped the mathematical logic of ages and dates would be enough to convince her.

Nanna was crying. She wiped one of her cheeks with her tapered fingers. 'Luke, you would tell me, wouldn't you, if there was anything, you know, not right between you and your mum.'

'Of course I would, Nanna.'

'You never needed to know, not before now.' She paused. 'Things are alright with you and your mum?' she asked again.

'Yes,' he said, with more emphasis and irritation. 'Nanna, you can't be right about this. My dad owned all three houses and he had a heart attack when I was eleven months old.'

'Me and her knew each other. Beforehand. I remember when she got caught with you and she said time had come for her to move on. I don't know to this day who the father might have been and Bella wasn't saying, but I could tell it was the reason she had to leave.'

There was no meandering, no misty recollection or hard-to-recall details. Nanna was stating facts, calmly and methodically.

'I don't know what to say,' Luke said, exhaling.

'She was old when you were born, Luke, and she'd had a whole life by then. Some mothers have children leaving home by the time she had you. There's bound to be things about her you don't know.'

'Why lie to me about who my dad was, then? Both of you, lying to me.'

'That's for you and her to sort out, Luke. I thought she would tell you, when you were still a little boy but old enough to understand. I was surprised when she didn't and then when she let on to me what she had told you, about the heart attack, I was annoyed with her. I didn't even want to know, for myself, but she should have told you, because those are your rights. It might have seemed easier for her to do what she did, but she owes you the truth.'

'Do you know what the truth is Nanna, really?'

'No. Everything I know, I've told you. There are things that might go on between a mother and son that are no one else's business, even if it's things that don't seem right. That's not for me to poke my nose into.'

Luke shifted uncomfortably, thrown by what she had said.

'Do you know who my dad was?' he persisted.

'Bella never told me, I swear it, Luke.'

Nanna put her hand down the side of the chair and it came out holding an envelope. She reached a short, jumper-clad arm out to him, her fingers trembling slightly. Luke leaned forwards and took the envelope from her from her.

'I don't want to keep secrets from you any more, Luke. There're keys in there. Two of them. And an address. You're practically a man now, Luke. Go and look, see what's there and see if it makes sense, if it helps you.'

'What's there, Nanna?'

'I haven't been there for nearly fifteen years. It's safe, don't worry about that. Go tomorrow and see. I've got some money you can have. Have you got enough insulin?'

'Yes. Where is this?' he asked, looking at the address on the envelope.

'It's your mum's house in Plymouth, where she lived before she came to Southend.'

Chapter 17

Since her arrival at Dad's new house, she had been avoiding the rooms used for storage. Dad had alluded to them several times, at first sounding practical about it, in case there was anything of hers she needed, or of Mum's.

Lucy stood in the larger of the two spare rooms, surveying the boxes that held Mum's jewellery – making equipment, beads, some of her clothes. These were the same boxes that had been in the old house, the one where she died. Lucy and Dad had packed them up together, about a month after the murder, a kind of silent pact struck between them that their cooperation in such a painful task meant they would never dispose of them without mutual consent. The way Dad had mentioned the spare room again the previous night suggested to Lucy he thought the time might have come to have a clear-out.

Looking at Mum's boxes and then the ones that contained some belongings of her own, she realized she had moved away from these things a long time ago, not just after the physical move to America. She might as well have been as dead as her mother for what use any of these items would be. The thought made her feel guilty.

Her old comics, never quite a collection as she had found the idea of a commitment to that a little too worrying, were piled neatly in one of the boxes, reaching the top of the tea-chest-sized cardboard carton. There was nothing else in the room except for boxes and the harsh rose-pink of the flowered wallpaper, a remnant of a previous tenant, Dad had told her with apologies. Lucy leafed from back to front through some of the Japanese comics, the stories familiar and the structure of the stories even more obvious now she had been away from them for a while.

Junk she recognized from her dressing table cluttered a

smaller box, wires from her personal stereo twisting irritatingly around a hairbrush. There was a crushed-velvet hairband in dark mauve, the colour of old aubergines, and a brighter clip in a see-through orange that could have been a crystal. Bits of her mother had found their way into the box, through a stray earring and two pendants she had fashioned for some birthday or other.

The previous night she had dreamed more vividly than ever before, certain it was because of her proximity to her father, the knots and the tattoo on her arm. In the stillness of the spare room, she kept a watch out of the corner of her eye, feeling she would catch a glimpse of the Lady, the way she used to, as though the ghost travelled with the artefacts rather than being fixed to a particular location.

Lucy was unsettled because she could feel herself slipping back into the person that was packed away in the boxes in front of her. She wanted to call Alanah and hear her voice, get a prescription consisting of a few well-constructed sentences that placed a fixed line of sanity through all that was happening in her mind. Under the sleeve of her cardigan, the tattoo on her arm stung.

In the silence of the room, through the still air, Lucy heard breath exhaled gently and then she felt a tingle as though a friendly finger travelled the length of her spine, from the small of her back up to her neck.

She stood, frozen, hoping this was in her mind.

Chapter 18

Luke stood outside the house in Plymouth, staring and trying to think what the building reminded him of, apart from the generality of the other houses. It nestled two from the end of a cul-de-sac which faced directly on to railway tracks, the last five houses all empty. It looked similar to the old house in Southend and a bit like the one in London, the family resemblance more that of cousins than siblings. Unwelcoming signs fended off would-be entrants, forbidding access by order, although quite whose order, the notices gave no hint of. The one that interested Luke had metal shutters in a concertina fashion across the door and the windows, whereas tight steel security was not in evidence on any of the others; these were closed by feeble window boards of differing ages, graffiti seemingly thrown on and barely sticking.

Approaching the house and standing where the gate should have been, he regarded the uneven earth of the front garden, which was blanketed by a straggle of weeds with the threat of unseen prickles woven through it. Two glass bottles stood on the window ledge, one broken with algae clinging to the shards. A chocolate wrapper had been trodden flat into the ground and a pile of seemingly identical free local newspapers was hidden half-heartedly beneath the hedge, the bold blue banner faded by the damp that had seeped through the whole bundle.

Pumice-like brickwork was gnarled enough to make the wall scalable, plenty of hand- and footholds. Behind the latticework of one of the shutters, a windowpane was broken, but the hole was too small to allow a view of what lay inside the house. Gingerly and without looking at its underside, Luke tossed aside the cushion that leaned against the metal gate stretched across the front door. The gate reminded Luke of one he had seen in a lift. On the door behind it, paintwork peeled as though planed off.

The keys which Nanna had given him were warm from his pocket. The lock for the gate was a neat-looking slit integral to its construction, while the front door was secured by a heavy padlock and hasp. The differing sizes of the keys reflected this and Luke slid the smaller of the keys into the gate lock, surprised at how easily it turned, as though recently used. There was no rusty squeak of metal separating as he pulled the gate aside and made for the padlock, feeling some kind of momentum building within him. It was the same, well-oiled story with the padlock on the street door, and in only a few moments the door was open and he stood in its mouth, feeling as if the house could swallow him.

Like the locks, the house was old but well-maintained. No one lived here. No one had lived here for a long time. Lit only by daylight through gated windows, the place seemed hazy, as though a thin cloud of talcum powder were hanging in the air. It smelled fairly neutral, a whiff of damp but nothing worse than that, or so he thought. When he was a few paces further in, he took a deeper draught of air and there was a familiar, burnt smell to it, topped off by something sweet. It was more like a memory than a smell and he shrugged it off.

The hallway and the steep flight of stairs to his right were still carpeted. Nowhere in his first impression was there the thought of danger concealed within the house. Rather, Luke felt like an intruder, more afraid of being caught.

The living-room was empty apart from its carpet. Indents in the weave laid out a blueprint of where furniture had once stood. Along one side wall were the eight foot-prints of two armchairs, their sister sofa presumably the four indents near the opposite wall. Marking out a no man's land between them would have been a coffee table. The light patch near the windows was probably where a rug had once been. There were similarly bright patches on two of the walls, perfect squares which would have been occupied by pictures, one very large on a wall of its own and two arranged at diagonals to each other on the wall facing the bay window.

Just an ordinary living-room, the only unusual thing its preservation and the security afforded to the house in general. All of the rooms downstairs were the same, empty with only the ghostly imprints of previous inhabitants to show they had been lived in. Feeling bold by the time he had reached the kitchen, Luke began opening cupboards, finding nothing but empty shelves that smelled only of time.

At the top of the stairs he took a right turn and walked into his mother's room. Luke stopped short, catching himself making the assumption. But he was right. This would have been his mother's room. The smell was there again, no longer so plain. The colour of the wallpaper and the carpet all hinted at her. This room was the sort of place he could picture her in. It was harder to imagine her on her own, rattling about a house too large for one person. For Luke, his mother had existed only as long as him.

Realization palpitated in his throat and he felt a hot flush. He left the room and went to the one next door.

Luke drew in a breath in time with opening the door. This room was not empty. The single bed under the window was made up, its pillow askew. A pair of grey trousers lay thrown on top of it, one leg hanging off as though they were about to climb down and walk away. The curtains were closed and he had to peer hard to make out the posters on the walls. Two were for films. *Gremlins*, which he had heard of, and another called *The Dark Crystal*, which he had not.

Luke walked to the window and opened the curtains.

A football team was lined up in a photograph on the wall facing the film posters. Plymouth Argyle, the 1983 team photograph. A homemade pennant hung from a fitting on the wall with the words 'The Pilgrims' drawn on it in a careful but amateurish hand. Luke walked over to two pictures of players on their own, again hand-mounted, cut from magazines. Tommy Tynan. Andy Rogers. The names meant nothing to him. The room was in the kind of state that, had it been his own, his mum would have been on at him to tidy it.

She had not been alone here.

A square hi-fi system, scratched black and red plastic, had a blue electric guitar leaning against it. On the floor next to it, a pair of football boots and two pairs of trainers scuffed to the point of cracking.

It was a boy's room, Luke could see that. But from when? The date on the yellowing poster?

The chest of drawers was a mess. A coffee cup with some headphones embracing it. A hand towel and a pair of pants hanging from a corner and, on top, a black plastic watch, some loose change including a few coins he did not recognize. Cassette tapes, a pair of sunglasses and a digital clock radio, unplugged. On the small patch of wall above the dresser, almost like a shrine, was a collage of pictures of women, scissors and glue in evidence once again. Long hair and top-heavy breasts dominated the mostly swimsuit-clad figures. One or two were fully naked and Luke stared. He slid back the top drawer of the dresser and it was stuffed with badly folded socks and pants. The next drawer down had shirts and the one on the bottom, sweaters and the detachable hood from a coat.

On the floor, just poking out from under the dresser, was a white plastic card. *Video Star*, it read. And a membership number. 972. And a name written under the laminate in black ink.

Luke Smith.

He almost fell to the bed, sitting and feeling as though all his energy had been sucked away by this discovery.

It clicked into place. Everything he had seen since entering the house, all the impressions, had suddenly ordered themselves in his mind, throwing him off balance.

The living-room was exactly the same as the one in the old house in Southend and the new one in London. The furniture had been set out in precisely the same order, from the three-piece suite to the pictures on the wall. Every room was the same, apart from the one he stood in currently. This room was out of keeping with the rest of the house.

The spare room.

Luke bounded out of the bedroom and into what he already knew would be the spare room. His feet made a loud noise on the bare floorboards. The room was completely naked, as though there had never been any furniture in it.

There was only one indication there had ever been something in the room. On the wall was a patch of paint brighter than the rest, the size of a door.

Where the mirror would have been.

Chapter 19

Jenna's brother simply stared at her, no emotion visible.

'Aren't you pleased to see me? I only came because mother made a fuss,' Jenna said, wondering if the small twitch at the side of his mouth were a smile.

Jenna reached across the bed and picked up what looked like a pair of sunglasses and held them out to him.

'Are you going to talk to me or not?' she asked.

He blinked at her twice.

'With this?'

One blink this time.

'We are communicative today. The old way then?' she asked.

Two blinks.

Jenna went round the side of the bed and fished out the clear plastic sheet with symbols. 'This drives Father mad,' she said, smiling for both of them.

She positioned the board so she could see his face through it and study him as his eyes moved around.

The injury to Martin's spine had been described by his doctor as complete between the fourth and fifth cervical vertebrae, complete meaning that nothing below the site of the injury would function – ever. More functionality might have resulted from more immediate treatment, but that hindsight helped no one. In the first three comatose and ventilated weeks, it had not been certain Martin would even be able to breathe unaided. The doctors made it sound very procedural, the next step in what was already bad beyond belief. Calmly they spoke of diaphragmatic pacemakers.

Jenna had been sitting with him when he began to emerge from the coma. At the time, his traction position was face down and Jenna was sitting cross-legged on the floor, studying her brother's face. The feeling swept over her that he was about to come round and she watched consciousness literally dawn on his face. It made her panic. She knew his first question would be, Why can't I move? and Jenna had no idea how she was going to answer.

But there had been no words.

Jenna sometimes wondered what bits of Martin were really left. Below his severed spinal cord was a barren country and above it, a traumatic brain injury, the left lobe damaged. His thoughts were trapped in there, refracted through his shattered mind like a reflection in a broken mirror. The wiring, the ground circuitry of his head, was damaged, and so too was the current that flowed through it. There had been speculation and disagreement among his various doctors as to how much of Martin's abnormal brain function was due to biology and how much to psychology. It seemed perfectly fair to Jenna and did not puzzle her – if she had been in Martin's situation, she would have gone mad too. Jenna stared at him, wondering if there were a ghost in the machine, a spirit floating freely around the practically dead body.

The gallery of images mounted on see-through plastic was their own secret Ouija board, isolating family, friends and doctors with its intuitive and private language.

Martin's eyes rested on the smile and then tracked to the other side on to a pair of eyes, held there and then went to the transfer of the sun, which also had a smile.

He was pleased to see her.

'How are you?' she asked.

The rain cloud. The red cross. A trumpet.

The doctors had been annoying him.

'Tell them to leave you alone then,' she said.

The girl. The question mark. The angel.

'I'm trying.'

The man.

'As if,' she said simply.

The pointing finger – he did not believe her.

'There's no one. Who'd have me Martin?'

Martin made a circuit with his eyes, alternating between the picture of the man, the picture of a heart and the picture of a woman. The rhythm of his gaze had a levity to it, Jenna could feel it. He kept it up for a full thirty seconds before making an exaggerated sweep to the picture of a baby and then a house, coming to rest once more on the sun.

'No happy-ever-afters here,' she said.

The rain cloud.

In its attempt not to look like a hospital, Martin's room resembled a film set, a pretend homeliness with a hidden barrage of instruments and drugs. However hard they tried, there was nothing they could do about the smells. Before moving him here, to what her parents liked to call 'the home', Martin spent 119 days in hospital. Even when Jenna had accepted that he would never get better, something she had reconciled herself to within the first week, she still expected Martin to stabilize somehow, as though his body would simply go into a kind of waiting state until his brain ran out of energy.

That was almost four years earlier and now she knew that was not the case. Martin was given valium to alleviate the occasional spasms and his low blood pressure was monitored constantly by the team of carers her father paid for to be with him at all times. In the last year, he had begun to show the first signs of osteoporosis. The team maintained his body as though it were a building temporarily unoccupied, keeping it ready in case its owner should return. They manipulated him, moved bits of him he no longer could himself, managed his bowel and bladder regime.

Melanie would never have coped. Martin had met her on his Master's course and she had, Jenna thought, stayed on in London when the course had ended only to be with him. She was a round girl with a face as bright as the picture of the sun on the plastic, and Jenna had never managed to be anything more than impolite to her. The acute drama at the hospital, the high-pitched frenzy Jenna and Martin were at the centre of, had its own kind of distracting energy, a supercharged 'now' where there was no long term. In those moments, Melanie had seemed strong because there was nothing else to be. Once that died down and they started to grapple with what was wrong with Martin, a still and silent future suddenly opened like a crack in the ground and it was too wide and deep for Melanie. She had not had that much love to give in such a concentrated form.

Martin looked at the brain, the woman and the face which neither smiled nor frowned. Don't think about Melanie, he was telling her. She's gone and it doesn't matter.

Jenna wondered if she loved Martin herself. The feeling was reconfigured by his new mental and physical state, and she found herself doing things she thought he would want her to, as though she had to read his mind or do the thinking for him. If there had been love, it was now channelled through duty, actions based on vague ideas of what Jenna would want for herself if the situation were reversed. Except that was not true. If she were the one on the bed, she would be begging Martin to kill her.

Staring at the homemade board, it was easy to pretend, of course. Martin retained an ability to use symbols, but that was really as far as it went. The roots of all the words, dug deep into the pia mater of his brain, had been cut loose and drifted as nothing more than weeds. He still comprehended, was able to be the recipient of words, but what came back in reciprocity did not make conventional sense. It was not clear if Martin could still actually read words or if it was only speech that made any kind of sense to him. What went on in there? she asked herself. Sometimes she found herself guiltily hoping that his brain was so damaged he did not really know what was happening. Words went into him and it was possible to see their effect, but nothing was reflected back. Was his head full of so much sense, unable to escape, that it left him mad?

There were times when Jenna looked hard at the figure

on the bed and wondered if it were really Martin at all, the one she kept safe and undamaged in the confines of her memory.

Martin had been at the start of his second year studying for a PhD in Japanese military history. It had not been the path her father desired but Jenna served as a timely comparison and she guessed her father secretly hoped that once Martin had flushed the academic germ from his system, his hand would be ready to take hold of the family business tiller. The neutrality Martin had always shown to Father still showed, never spilled into anything as active as love but, again, Jenna was the benchmark against which such things were measured.

Now Father had equipped Martin with technology that would have been the envy of many governments and armies. The eye-glasses were similar to the ones fighter pilots apparently used to control weapons systems, reading the movements of the wearer's eyes and translating them. Jenna had worn them a few times, amazed at the menu of options it presented, from simple switching that controlled Martin's immediate environment through to the facility to construct language. There was a synthesized voice capability and it made Jenna giggle whenever it was switched on, sounding like a speak-and-spell machine. There were no swear words in the machine, a neutral language of paralysed happiness Jenna was sure her father had insisted on. He would have done the same to her if only he could. Her father wished it were Jenna there on the bed, she knew that. He thought it was her fault.

Jenna rested the board down on the bedspread, signalling that it was time for Martin to listen. It would be easier for her if she did not have to read his reactions.

'The old fuckers sent me to do some dirty work for them.'

Martin stared at her, intent and grave.

Jenna let out a long and short-tempered breath, angry at them all over again. 'They want to travel. See the world,' she said in an exaggerated voice, mock happy. 'They've decided to spend Christmas at some fucking hotel and then they're off the day after, going to Portugal or Prague or somewhere beginning with a P.'

There seemed to be no reaction.

'Do you understand me?' she asked.

He blinked twice. He did.

'And it doesn't piss you off? That they've decided to dump you?'

One blink, almost a shrug with his eyelids.

'Well it fucking irritates me, especially that old cunt. I was going to tell my therapist about him, but she was very dismissive of the whole area, convinced that everyone had false-memory syndrome. She was a nice therapist, helped me see what was going on inside me. I did the same for her. We had a very good look at what was happening inside her and I think she was really very happy. It's a bit like when you look at chicken guts and see if the crops are going to flourish. I really felt I could see the happiness gushing through her, all those cheerful bits of fresh meat jumping about together. I suppose I can tell you all this. No one understands me like you do,' she said, laughing at the irony of the statement. 'And it's not like you can really tell anyone.'

He was rolling his eyes towards the plastic sheet on the bed. He wanted to communicate with her.

Jenna watched as Martin's eyes focused and he became serious. Slowly and with obvious care, he picked out six pictures from the board, resting on each for the same amount of time.

Martin looked at her, questioning. Jenna stared at the question mark. She did not understand. Her breath made a mist on the glass. He made the same path again and it made Jenna frown.

A boy. The sea. The arrow that pointed to the left. The clock. The aeroplane. The arrow that pointed to the right.

Martin's pupils dilated and his irises seemed to darken, the way a dog's might if it were about to pounce. With obvious irritation he repeated the combination.

'A boy going somewhere? In the past? Did he swim?'
Jenna hated it when she had to ask questions.

One long blink. The eyes were off the board. He was
annoyed.

Jenna made the same journey his eyes had, going from
boy to sea to back arrow to clock to aeroplane to forward
arrow, trying to make sense of it. She too became frustrated. The thin layer of sense between them could not
contain whatever it was Martin wanted to express.

'I'm sorry. I can't get that one. You've beaten me. You
win for now.' She gave him a grin. 'Think about it some
more, Martin, and tell me when I see you again. The next
time I see you, the fuckers will be gone. And then I'm
going to show you how much I really do care for you. I'm
going to make it all stop.'

Chapter 20

Luke was still angry when he arrived back at the house in London. He went straight in and started looking for her.

'Why didn't you tell me?' he asked, as soon as he found her, sitting in the spare room on a chair pulled in from her bedroom.

She was looking at the mirror and smoking, a full ashtray beside her and the room almost cloudy with the haze of smoke. His mother looked at him and seemed to know exactly what he was talking about, as though it were the only secret she might have kept from him. She looked at him sadly and pulled on the cigarette again. He cast a quick glance at the mirror before looking back at her. She stubbed at the cigarette and removed another from the pack, holding it unlit.

'Why didn't you tell me?' he asked, his voice rising.

'You sound irritable, babe. Do you need some medicine?'

It made him angry and it welled up in him until he was almost standing on the balls of his feet, trying to make himself taller.

'Do I need some medicine?' he shouted.

'Don't get angry, Lucas. It's not good for you.'

'I went down to Plymouth after I left Southend,' he said.

'I know,' she replied, sliding open a matchbox. 'Marlene phoned and told me you had, that she'd given you the keys.'

Luke was flustered. He had expected her to be more angry when she found out where he had been and that Nanna had helped him. She struck a match. He wanted her to rise to the moment, to get angry as well so he could trade off some of his energy with hers.

'I went to your old house. The one you lived in before

you went to Southend. The one where you lived with my dad and the other Luke Smith.'

Luke was nodding almost sarcastically as he spoke, enjoying the bullying feeling of his words even though they seemed to be having little effect on her.

'I never lived there with your dad. I left there to get away from him.'

'Why did you give me the same name?' he asked, feeling tears. 'What happened to him? Did you leave him there?'

'No I didn't leave him there,' she said, looking at him properly for the first time since he entered the room.

'What then?' Luke asked.

'He died,' she said quietly.

Luke said nothing, trying to weigh up the loss of something he had never really had, that was not really related to him.

'So he was my brother?' Luke asked.

'Half-brother.'

Luke sat on the floor a few feet away from her and looked up, the way he used to when she told him stories. The muscles of his face ached from the frowning.

'Tell me how he died.'

'It was a punishment, on me. Me and his father hadn't been, you know, together in that way for more than four years. I fell pregnant with you, by someone else, and I didn't know what I was going to do. His father was a sea-going man, back for a time and then gone again. I knew he got up to things when he wasn't with me and he didn't really care for me or Luke that much.' She smiled for a moment and Luke saw it was covering sadness. 'He used to say we were like an anchor, the things that were solid and in the same place.'

'Why was it a punishment, him dying?'

'I was excited when I found out about you, pleased even though I knew it would cause trouble. Luke's dad was away, not due back for three months when I knew for sure I was pregnant.'

'What happened to him? To Luke?'

'The sea had him. To this day, I don't know if he threw himself in or if it reached out and took him. He was seen down on the front and they said one minute he was there and the next he was gone. I asked if they thought he chucked himself in and they couldn't answer, like they never knew.'

'Did he know you were pregnant?' Luke asked.

A tear formed on the outside corner of her eye and rolled down the make-up on her cheek. 'I never got to tell him.'

'Where was his dad?' Luke asked.

'Away at sea,' she said, drawing on the cigarette and holding the smoke in as though trying to block the words.

'Did they call him back?'

She shook her head. 'No. I didn't want that, him being involved. There was hardly anyone knew. I waited a week, which I thought would be long enough for the sea to spit him back out if it was going to. It never did. It kept him.'

'You never told anyone?' Luke asked, straightening his back.

'What could they have done? He was mine and mine alone.'

'That's not right,' Luke said, shaking his head. 'You said someone saw him. What about them?'

'That was Marlene. She saw him down there. I had been friends with Marlene since before I met Luke's father and she knew me well enough by then to know I needed to get away.'

'Nanna,' Luke said, as though the word had taken on a new meaning. 'She knew? That's like, I don't know, a bit like you killed him.'

'All we did wrong was to stay silent. Luke, I was unhappy. He was all I had. When I lost him, I knew it was a punishment for the joy I felt about you. Can you understand that?'

'No,' he said, sullenly.

'It was my chance to start again. You were my clean sheet. My boys. The most important things in the world to me.'

Luke fidgeted nervously on the floor.

'But someone must have missed him,' he said.

'There was his school, a few of his friends, but I was the only one who really missed him, because I was the only one who really cared about him. And Marlene. It was time to move on. She helped me.'

'What about *my* dad?' Luke asked. 'Nanna wouldn't tell me who he was.'

'That's because she still doesn't know. She was already lying and covering up for me. I knew Luke's father would be back and I needed to get away before then, but the next place he might look would have been Marlene.'

Luke rubbed the sides of his head with the heels of his hands. 'Oh God,' he said, feeling irritated and frustrated, annoyed by the messiness of the whole situation. There were so many straggling ends, questions he wanted to ask. 'How did you get the houses in Southend?'

'Your father arranged for them. It was a good solution, Luke. It helped me stand on my own feet, it got me away from there and it got Marlene away as well.'

'Why did you have to stand on your own feet? Why wouldn't my dad help us more?'

'He was married already and he had other children. We would have made things too complicated for him and it would have made it hard for me as well.'

'What about me?' Luke asked. 'What about how it made things for me?' He felt tears in his throat and swallowed on them.

'I did what I thought was the right thing. The other alternative would have been to stay in Plymouth, had you taken away before you were born and carried on living alone. Your father didn't want me and he didn't want you, is that what you want to hear me say? Because it's true, Luke. What he did for me was out of a sense of duty.'

'The house I went to in Plymouth was closed up and empty except for his room.'

'That was the way I left it. I couldn't find it in myself to bring anything. It was a new beginning, the clean sheet.'

'Didn't his dad come back looking?'

'Your father contacted me three months after I went to Southend and said it had been taken care of.'

'What did that mean?'

'I never asked and he never told me. I was finished with that place.'

'The stuff here that was in Southend, was it down in Plymouth too, the furniture and all that?'

'Most of it I took. I wanted to keep things the same as they were.'

'So you could pretend I was him?' he asked, anger leavening his voice.

'I suppose so. I was upset, Luke. I took everything I had and wanted to start all over again, leaving all of his things there but still having the memory. One day I thought I might want to go back and that's why your dad closed the house off for me. Kept it all the way it was.'

'How come he had three houses in Southend?'

'He had more than that, Luke. Your father was well off. I got some money from him to get started and the houses so I could pay my way. It was made clear to me after that that we would be finished and it suited me as well.'

'So tell me who he was. Who was my dad? Is he still alive?'

She shook her head. 'He was older than me. His children are adults now.'

'Why didn't he leave us any money?'

Again, his mother was staring into the mirror as though it were an endless pool.

'Because I didn't want it that way and neither did he.'

'Well the two of you seemed to have worked it all out nicely. What about me?'

She said nothing, casting her eyes down.

'What?' he asked. 'Is this what you're looking at? Have you missed it while I've been away?' Luke stood abruptly and took a handful of his crotch and hefted it upwards. 'Did you use to do that to him too? Did you tell his dad that? Would you tell mine if he was alive?'

Luke grabbed her hand and forced it on to the flies of his trousers, rubbing it over the bump and making sure she could feel him.

'Is that what you want to do to me?' he asked.

'Stop it,' she said.

'If you want me to stop, why don't you just take your hand away?' he said.

'Because I know you don't really want me to,' she said.

Normally he could make his brain go away, off somewhere else, and Luke knew she could sense that and it displeased her. If he was able to please her, make her rested in her mind, it would be to his benefit. That was the thought he was going to use to block out everything else, a way of being there but not being there.

As she gently unbuttoned his trousers, he reached behind her and found the clasp of her dress, letting himself be pulled into an embrace as he did so. She worked down his trousers and then his underwear. Luke stepped from them. When she lifted the front of his shirt and moved her head closer, he closed his eyes and clenched his teeth.

Luke lay next to her on her bed, waiting for the rhythm of sleep to desensitize her to his movements. As she drifted into sleep, Luke had been stroking her flesh, gently nuzzling at the chain around her neck with his teeth, ignoring her contented sighs as he tried to work the clasp to where he wanted it.

It must have been almost an hour before he felt safe enough to ease himself up to a sitting position, making sure there were no sudden changes of weight distribution on the bed. When he was upright, he carefully picked the chain from the sagging skin of her neck as though it were a delicate fibre of hair. With a fingernail he unhooked the clasp and separated the two ends of the chain, carefully setting the end nearer the bed on the mattress. Like a game at a fair, he reached over her, petrified his arm would touch her and wake her, and lifted the key from where it lay, threading it along and then off the end of the chain.

In too much of a rush and afraid the noise might rouse

her, Luke did not bother dressing. Naked, he padded along the hall and down the stairs.

Luke knew she thought the hiding place under the stairs was unknown to him. He smiled to himself as he set the green box on the table and inserted the key, his breath short with the anticipation of what he might find.

All the papers in the box were neatly bundled despite the varying sizes of the documents and envelopes. There were several batches, some held together with elastic bands and one with a morbid black ribbon. He pulled a band from one and laid its contents out on the table. Some legal documents with lots of small pre-printed writing and addresses typed at skewed angles on to dotted lines. The Southend address. Some documents with the crest of a building on the headed paper, something about insurance. In the next pile, the documents were much the same, the Plymouth house featuring more. Some bills for gas and electricity, all with his mother's name on.

Luke untied the careful bow in the black ribbon and looked at the final set of papers. The things it contained were not so formal. They were mementoes, a postcard and two photographs.

The postcard was from a seaside town called Dray, and the picture on the front was of a hotel called the Palace, the name written in script on a white section at the bottom of the card, surrounded by a swirling trellis of lines. There was no message on the card.

One photograph was of his mother, on the seafront, much younger and seemingly happier, her hand resting on the door of a big American car in a way that suggested she had seen it parked in the road and wanted to pose next to it.

The other picture stopped him short and brought a shiver on. Luke peered at his dead half-brother as he sat on a sea wall and looked sullenly back at him from the photograph. In the background, the sea that would take him chopped around. The resemblance was enough to make it eerie and Luke looked around the kitchen, investigating all the dark shadows that now seemed more threatening than they had moments earlier. This boy would have been 30 now, Luke thought, wondering what a big brother, a much bigger brother, would have been like. What was it like between him and Mum? Had it been better? Was he able to do something, avoid something that Luke himself had not, able to distract her attentions from him?

At the bottom of the box was a brass key, about the same size as the one for the mortise lock on the front door. The oval key tag was almost the length of the key. Luke rubbed the ridged pattern on the end of the fob and read the number printed evenly across it. Nine Twenty-Eight. On the other side, Palace Hotel, Dray.

Luke picked up the postcard again and studied the hotel, a pier growing from it like a tail, out into the restless water behind. In the photograph of his mother and the car, far in the background and shrouded in a light mist, the building was visible once again. He paused for a moment and took a breath before looking at the picture of the other Luke. There too, just in a corner of it, but now practically unmistakable to Luke, was the Palace Hotel.

Chapter 21

Lucy felt a tinge of fever and in a psychosomatic way was concerned she might have caught something horrible from the tattoo or that it had gone septic and the pus had spread, making ready to kill her. Lucy had washed it like Captain Steve said, but instead of letting air get to it, she'd put another plaster on, afraid to look at it. If she ignored it, it might go away.

Lucy looked at the plaster, trying to see if the edges gave any hint of mould or gangrene. Around its border beyond, her arm was smooth where the razor had been drawn over it. The hairs on her arm were light in any case. It was time to look.

Do you trust me?

The plaster came away easily, less sticky than it had been four days ago. There was little pain for her hairless skin and she pulled the dressing towards her rather than away, so she could delay seeing the tattoo until the last possible moment.

Am I hurting you now?

There was no blood, no septic arm, no scab. Instead, the shape of the knot was there, clean and distinct, as though it had been on her arm all her life. It was drawn more finely and with greater precision than Lucy imagined Captain Steve had with his capability. The plaster too was clean, no trace of blood or anything else. Gently, she rubbed the tattoo and her skin was soft. The drawing was no more than an inch and a half square and the dark outlines and white blocking melded nicely with her skin tone. No one could take it off her now.

So you trust me then?

Lucy took the real knot from the chain and held it over the tattoo. It matched perfectly, no lines showing from under it, every intricate twist incorporated into her, the central bow swirling endlessly and the other lines pointing off sharply like hair sticking up.

Take off the rest of your clothes then.

The knot was the only thing that had emerged from the dark wordless gap of that day. Entering the house. The knot in her hand. Something moved deep down in her memory, but nothing came to the surface. It was happening somewhere else, in a place where things like time and words didn't seem to matter. It was always now.

A panic came over Lucy and she tried to contain it with some breathing exercises. Alanah, with her long robes and wind chimes, could always soothe her, reassuring her that everything was in her mind and therefore perfectly able to be controlled. Lucy knew the real reason she ran to people like Alanah, because she wanted convincing that it was all just something her damaged mind had manufactured as a way of dealing with the hurt.

My mum was killed. I thought the house was haunted. I met a boy. Tom Richards' son went mad, killed some people and kidnapped Dad. There was an earthquake while we were in Los Angeles looking for Dad. Nancy died in the earthquake. That was all that happened. These phrases were her mantra, the rational onslaught against the other things that might really have happened.

What about the dreams then?

She flicked at her arm as though a fly had landed on it. She batted at it several more times before she became fully alert and looked at her arm.

Under the surface of her skin, like a freshly dug worm, the tattoo was moving.

Lucy recoiled, hitting it and trying to get away from it, as though she could flick it off her arm and leave it writhing around on the bed. It seethed and moved the way internal organs did in operations on the television. The knot wriggled and throbbed, alive on her and with a life all its own. Her arm stung as badly as when the tattoo had been done. The tendrils shifted with the nauseating fluidity of seaweed in the tide.

Lucy closed her eyes, waiting for the movements to stop. She concentrated on nothing, letting all thoughts slip away from her like leaves falling from a tree. It was like waiting for a cacophony of music to finish, every instrument and voice thrashing on in mordant discord. It wasn't like a pop song which would just fade away. It would end with all the flourish of a piece of classical music, getting more and more frantic as it pounded towards its climax. Lucy waited for the silence as all the images in her head got brighter, the voices louder. There was a final crash and a respite of perhaps two or three seconds when there were no voices, no thoughts and no dreams. She was absent from herself for a long and refreshing moment.

Lucy opened her eyes into the silence and felt her heart pound in her breast. She held the pendant over the top of her tattoo.

They were completely different. Still knots, but each taking a different path.

Lucy grabbed up a cardigan and pulled it on, hiding her arm from herself. She stood and left the room, wanting to get away, to be moving.

'Are you okay?' Dad asked when she entered the living-room.

'Fine. Why?'

'You look pale.'

'It's cold up there. Don't you ever put the heating on?'

'It doesn't get used, that room.'

Lucy handed him back the knot. 'Here,' she said.

She watched him place the knot back on the chain with the other one and saw the change in him, a sort of relief that oozed from him. How could he be so convinced about those old pieces of metal, she wondered, and then remembered how attached she had been to one of them. The power was seductive.

'Where do you think they came from?' she asked.

'I don't think they came from anywhere. They just always *were*. Are you sure you feel okay?'

'I didn't sleep well. In the dream, last night, I remember the part with Cameron very clearly. Usually, that's the haziest part and I can't understand what he's saying, like he's not tuned in properly. Some of it was still jumbled, but I remember asking him what was in The Book.'

'And what did he reply?'

'That there was nothing. He said it would have been easy to imagine a great book containing all the stories of the world, but that was not how it was. Every story was not in The Book, The Book was in every story. Then he changed what he was saying, kind of. Nothing except for the secret of God's Gift. Then, and this scared me, he started to say something I knew he hadn't before, as though he were really there in my dream and had woken up and taken on a life of his own.'

Her father was studying her face. 'Go on,' he said.

'He said the secret of God's Gift was how the story ended. He comes into the world complete, goes from end to beginning and leaves it as nothing. The story comes to an end because its most central character is travelling in the opposite direction. When he gets to the end, the stories end. He starts out in infinity as the largest number possible and he reaches zero.'

'Those were things he told me, Lucy.'

'I know. He said that to me in the dream.'

'And did he tell you that this central character, moving backwards through the story, was Nathan?'

She nodded. 'I'm scared, because I can feel something ready to burst into my head, something that's been brewing since as long as I can remember.'

He played with his hands. 'Why do you think that?'

'When Mum was killed, that was the point where it started. That was how I used to think about it. The ghost in the house, the bad dreams, the therapy. But that isn't true. The ghost of the old lady that I started to see when Mum died, I knew that was connected with Mum being murdered. But I saw her long before that, when I was little.'

'Why didn't you say anything about it?'

'It was our secret, mine and Mum's. We didn't think you needed to know,' Lucy said, feeling a sense of her mother's presence through memory. 'All of these things, your old company, Tom Richards and his son, Nancy, Nathan, all of it is linked up. It didn't start when Mum was killed, I know that. But I can't get any of this to make sense. What happened to Nancy, Dad? How did she die?'

He touched the knots around his neck. 'Nancy had one of these, like you did. Not quite like you did,' he said, reaching over and touching the left side of her face. 'Nancy never kept it on a chain round her neck. How long have you been getting the headaches?' he asked.

'What do you mean?'

'The ones you had after Los Angeles. They went away, but they've come back again, haven't they?'

Lucy did not answer him.

'Nancy had one of these,' he continued, 'but as I said, she didn't carry it round her neck. It was inside her, Lucy. In her head, because that was where Nathan put it. She had been with him in the same way you had, years before. Nancy thought she was dying with a brain tumour and that that was the cause of her headaches. It wasn't. She had one of the knots in her head.'

Lucy felt her lips move against her will, mumbling breath into half-formed phrases. 'No.' She shook her head decisively. 'That can't happen.' She touched the side of her aching head, wondering if it were really in there, concealed behind the bone of her skull and enmeshed with the matter of her brain, sucking her thoughts out and sending them round its own arc. 'But what happened to her?' she repeated.

'She disappeared. I spent a long time trying to think of a word that described what I saw. Disseminated. Nancy didn't disappear. She disseminated. Sometimes I'm certain she died and other times I'm certain she is still alive, somewhere. Lost in between the lines of the story.'

'She died in the earthquake, Dad. Lots of people did. Maybe Nathan did too.'

'You were there on the beach, Lucy, you saw him fall into the ground. Wadlow was there.'

'But that was only in the dream.'

'Let me show you something,' he said, standing and retrieving the draughtsman's folio case from the side of the armchair near the bookshelves. Lucy had noticed it her first day back but had made no comment on it.

Her father opened it and pulled out a bundle of papers of varying sizes.

'These are in chronological order, starting from when we got back from Los Angeles after the earthquake. I've left in the main ones, with the biggest jumps.'

'A square?' she asked, looking at the hand-drawn but still precise shape on the scrappy piece of paper on the floor in front of her.

'I spent about six months just drawing that shape. It's a process of reverse memory. Building it up from where it started.'

She sighed at the circularity of his words. Her father turned over a few more sheets and the precise edges of the squares softened from something geometric into something more natural.

'Ten months had gone by before my memory offered a clue. I started drawing smaller squares onto this sort of rectangular shape,' he said, turning over a few more pages. 'It took me a few weeks to realize the squares were windows. I was drawing a building. The long ears that had started to grow on the rectangle were turrets.'

Lucy looked on in silence.

'At first,' he continued, 'I thought I had spent nearly a year doodling a bad version of the Tower of London. It was the only thing it reminded me of. Does it remind you of anywhere?'

'No. It's just a building,' Lucy said.

'The walls are granite and I don't think it's as tall as I'm drawing it. See how detailed these ones are?'

He flipped more rapidly.

'You know where this is then?' she asked.

'I saw it once. When I was with Nathan.'

Lucy sat up straighter just at the mention of his name. 'When?'

'Somewhere between the swimming pool where Garth kept me and when I saw you on that beach. I walked right past it.'

'In the dream? It's not a real building?' she asked.

'It's very real.' He laid a postcard on the table and it looked like the little brother of the drawing. The name of a town and of the building, a hotel, were on the card. 'It's where part of the story began and ended.'

'Dad, don't keep talking like that. Be precise.'

'I want you to go there. Is that precise enough?' he asked.

Chapter 22

Jenna supposed by ordinary standards she should have been extremely drunk by the time she let him take her back to his house in a taxi, using the motion of it to make faux casual brushes against her, but Jenna had been able to hold her drink even in normal circumstances and now food and drink no longer affected her. He had refilled her glass each time it had neared the half-empty level and then there had been a brandy, and another. Most of the time, he had talked about the blind man and how badly he personally had been affected by what happened. Jenna suspected this was a ploy for sympathy and comfort and went with it. It was their excuse for getting drunk and seeking solace. Before dinner, some vodkas – three, she thought. Slowly, Jenna watched him become intoxicated and it just made her see more clearly and feel more precise in her actions. By the time the cab delivered them to the kerb, he was bold enough to take her hand and lead her out of the back of the car. Jenna stepped forward clumsily and bumped into him, giggling, he doing likewise.

'I really wanted you to see the place,' Gordon said, opening the door and holding out his hand as though offering her the whole space in his palm. 'I spent a lot of time getting it the way I wanted. It harnesses the energy. People still laugh at you when you talk about ch'i, but if you don't feel comfortable and in balance, there's not much else.'

'I thought you had a place in the Docklands,' Jenna said.

'I moved. Too many poison arrows and overwhelming buildings.'

'Right,' Jenna nodded. 'So you designed all this specially?'

'It started long before I walked through the door. The location had to be right. I had to feel good about it, the right flows of wind and water, the correct set of buildings nearby. I turned down nine places without even going through a door,' he said, evidently proud.

Two identical sofas in dark blue fabric with high, rounded backs and two armchairs were grouped in a square around a low wooden coffee table. A tall cabinet in one corner of the room was topped with healthy-looking sunflowers in a fat metal vase. Jenna made impressed nods of the head, thinking it looked like a waiting room or a museum gallery.

She stood in the middle of the living area while he disappeared behind a screen and she heard the clinking of icecubes on glass. He reappeared with a drink in each hand and an expectant smile on his face.

'I hope you're not trying to get me drunk,' she said.

'I think we're both well past that stage,' he replied, swirling the glasses in his hand. 'Shall we?'

'Shall we what?'

'Sit down,' he said.

'I'm so surprised you don't have a girlfriend,' Jenna said, sipping from the glass.

'You don't have a boyfriend hidden away somewhere then?'

'No. My only long-term relationships are with my therapists.'

His interest seemed to perk up. 'Really,' he said, a faint slur in his word. 'I'm quite interested in alternative counselling. I was thinking of taking a course on it. Does it help?' he asked.

'Well, you get to have a steady relationship with someone that isn't messed up by fucking,' she said.

He laughed and she followed suit.

'What's so wrong with the fucking? Why does that mess it up?' he asked, and Jenna watched his knee slide perhaps half an inch closer to her on the sofa.

'There's nothing wrong with fucking, I just don't believe it's healthy in the context of a relationship.'

'Does that mean I'm going to have to forsake a relationship with you?' he asked, sniffing a laugh.

'Oh yes,' she said, stretching herself out, 'it's one or the other, Gordon. You can be my friend or you can fuck my brains out,' she laughed.

'I might need a minute to think about that,' he said.

'Sometimes, it would be nice to have this sort of friend that you do things with, go out, get pissed, have a laugh, and then you happen to go home together and fuck like minks,' she said, letting her tone become more wishful.

'Well, we seem to get along, don't we?' he asked, clinking his glass against hers.

'Yes,' she said.

He moved nearer to her and brought his face to hers, until she could feel the heat from it. Gently, he planted a kiss. 'Why don't we see if we can get the other part right?' he asked.

'I don't know,' she said.

'I'm feeling very horny,' he added.

'I can tell.'

'What did you say to me, the other night? About the picture on my desk. I thought we were going to, soon?'

'Maybe I'm getting to like you too much,' she said.

He ignored her attempt to lighten the moment and his hand wandered on to her thigh.

Jenna made no move. She froze herself in position, wanting him to cross the boundary willingly, giving him a chance.

Gordon's lips made contact with her mouth and almost immediately she felt his needy and insistent body pressing on hers, his hands groping. He had manoeuvred himself to be a fraction in the ascendant to her posture and the muscles in her neck were stretched from the way he had pushed her head back, exposing her throat.

'Can I use the toilet?' she asked, breaking away from him.

'Now?' he asked, irritably.

'I want to, you know, put something in,' she said.

'I've got condoms,' he said.

'I'd rather. It would make me feel more comfortable.'

'Okay then,' he said. 'But hurry.'

In the bathroom, she opened her bag, pulled her knickers off her ankles and squatted down in front of the washbasin, holding it with one hand to steady herself as she used the other to insert. Her muscles gripped and she stood, wondering if she should put her knickers back on or not. How hard did she want to make it?

When she re-entered the living area, he was still ticking over in a high gear, his face flushed and his movements betraying restlessness.

Jenna fitted herself into the corner of the sofa furthest from him and he instantly closed the gap between them, leaning across her and throwing an arm over her in a way that was more restrictive than protective.

'Gordon, can I have some coffee?' she said, turning her head away from him.

'Later,' he said, pleading in his voice.

'Please. I feel woozy,' she replied.

'I thought you wanted to?' he asked.

Jenna did not reply immediately. He kissed her on the mouth, less fervently than before.

'Could you make me some coffee?' she asked again.

'No,' he said, pecking at her and sounding jovial.

She cowered back from him, pressing her body into the corner of the settee.

'Uh,' was all she managed to sigh through the heavy kiss.

Gordon's hand was on the outside of her bare thigh, gripping the muscle firmly and cupping under her leg, gently but insistently levering it open.

Jenna slipped deftly to one side and stood, letting him fall into the arm of the sofa. She moved round the coffee table, so it stood between the two of them.

'What's the matter?' he asked, wiping his mouth with the back of a hand.

'I don't feel like it.'

'You did a minute ago,' he said.

'I changed my mind,' she replied.

Gordon grinned at her and rubbed his palms together. 'I'll have to chase you then,' he said, laughing.

He made as though he was going to chase her round the small square track that was the outside of the coffee table. Jenna hesitated and then followed suit. They made a few laps of the table until it felt absurd.

'Gordon. Please.'

He took a step up on the table, cutting across and shoving her – hard. Jenna fell forward on to the sofa, landing heavily on her left arm. He had stopped laughing. Before she had turned fully to see what was happening, he was on her, pinning her shoulders and kissing her, using a handful of her hair to position her head. Further down, she could feel his knee trying to make its way between her legs. She twisted and shut her legs, the bones of her knees pressing tightly against each other.

'No,' she said. 'Don't.'

'Why did you put your fucking cap in then?' he asked, sweating.

'I wanted to and now I don't. Please don't do this, Gordon.'

When he had done kissing her, he pushed his hand over her face, smothering it and pushing her nose painfully to one side. He used more of his weight to force the point of his knee into the soft join of her thighs. Jenna held out for as long as she could, but his weight was too great and she separated. She flailed her legs about, trying to flip one or the other up and round the intrusion of his body, but he had anticipated it and pressed himself too far into her, forcing her up into the back of the sofa.

'Please. No. Stop,' she said.

Even in the grip of anger, violence and arousal, it took Gordon three serious attempts to tear her knickers off, but he managed to get one side of them free, so she was exposed even as the remainder clung to the top of her left thigh, something she found unaccountably irritating in the middle of everything else that was going on.

With her cramped into position and bared, he pulled the

buttons open on his DKNY jeans and slipped himself over the top of grey jersey Paul Smith boxer briefs. Without looking at her, he took himself firmly, guided himself at her and gave a shove and then lunged down using the full mass of his body.

Gordon's mouth stretched as though it were trying to swallow his whole face and his scream volleyed off the carefully arranged surfaces of the room.

'That doesn't feel much like a diaphragm, does it?' she asked. 'That's because it isn't. It's a length of drainpipe with razor blades pushed through slits in the side.' Jenna clamped a hand on each of his buttocks, the muscles of her biceps standing proud as she locked him on to her. 'I was generous, Gordon, I used a nine-inch length, just in case, but I think you've got plenty of room in there.'

'Nnnh,' was the only sound that crackled from his throat.

'I think the word you might be looking for is ouch,' Jenna said. 'Come on, baby, ride me nice and hard. Fuck me out good and proper.'

Jenna used the movements of her body and her hands to force him up and down, in and out of her.

'Fuck!' he cried, finally organizing his shock and pain into a tangible word, giving it a voice.

'Yes. Yes. Yes,' Jenna called, laughing as she did. 'Oh baby, that feels so good.'

Jenna kept forcing him back and forth, ramming his body down on to hers as he writhed and attempted to free himself.

The brief focus of words was gone, his pain more desperate, needing quick release and bypassing the brake of language.

There was a liquid feeling inside her that started to seep and feel warm as it ran on to her legs. Jenna reached into the space between their bodies and let some of it smear her hand, raising it so Gordon could see the deep red blood.

'That can't be me, I'm not due on for another ten days,' she said. 'Keep going, I want you to rape me, Gordon.

Give it to me like the cunt I am, that's what you want, isn't it? Maybe we can do some oral in a minute.'

She gripped him and rolled their bodies over so she could ride him, wondering if there were anything left of him to be hard. There was movement within her, greater than just the contraction of her muscles, and the expression on Gordon's face took on a new tilt, as though a kind of complacency had been shattered, a belief that it could get no worse.

'They're swimming round my insides and now they're eating you,' she said, grabbing him round the neck and holding his face up so she could look into it, feeling a drain in the stiffness that kept him upright and alive. Jenna tried to ease up off of him, but she was held to him by something that was a part of neither of them. 'This is really going to fuck up your feng shui, I guess,' she said.

For several more minutes, the things inside her chewed on him, perched above his body as it was drained of life. He looked comatose as he slumped back, any colour that was once in his face now reduced to a dim mauve pallor, his lips already bluish.

When, independent of her own will, the grip was released, he almost fell away from her, a deep crater where his groin ought to have been, the area drier than she was expecting. Jenna put her head close to the site of the wound, fascinated by the criss-cross of tubing and fibre he had consisted of.

The clench inside her relinquished and the length of plastic grey tube fell out as though she had opened wider than she could have believed. Jenna picked it up, a piece of stray flesh dangling from the end. She ached, but she felt happy, pleased to have started the night so well.

Chapter 23

Jenna left her car a hundred yards down the lane, off the side of the road and leaning towards a ditch. Without the aid or need of streetlights, she found the familiar part of the hedge and pushed through it. Across the lawn, round the side to the conservatory, up on the rain barrel and then, the trickiest part, a few quick steps on the metal veins that held the glass of the conservatory in place, and she was on the window ledge near the thin pipe leading to the first flat roof. After that, there was a ladder and she was on top of the house and round to the attic window, which was the size of a small television screen with a single bar down its middle. Jenna pulled the bar sharply and it came away. From behind the drainpipe, she retrieved the thin plate of metal she needed to slide into the frame and lift the token catch on the inside. The only window in the house without an alarm was now open and she was pleased to still be thin enough to slide through.

The first time Jenna had used this route into her parents' house, she was twelve, and it had been her house too, she supposed. At that time, she was not breaking in, but returning from having broken out. The alarm system had been fitted to keep her in, not people out. Martin was away at boarding school while Jenna had been 'politely expelled' from two.

Carefully, her sonar-like knowledge of the stair creaks still intact, she made her way to the cupboard in the hall and disabled the alarm. She didn't want anyone hitting the panic button. There were no more live-in staff, just Bill and Ellen.

The house was not a place full of memories. It was just a continual unpleasant presence. She took the rucksack from her back, removed the red can and the carrier bag of essentials, and opened the bag out to its full size.

Jenna picked one of the pair of unused and over-polished candlesticks from the table under the mirror in the hall and put it in the backpack. Her blue reflection moved in time with her. In the dining-room, she opened the large drawer in the dresser and lifted two heavy silver forks from where they rested on crisp linen, laid out like surgical instruments. She also put the wooden letter opener shaped like a giraffe into the bag. A box with three of its twelve fat candles left. And a bottle of whisky.

She had to be quieter in the kitchen, its acoustics far more likely to reverberate her movements up to her sleeping parents. The hand blender and the concave attachment with the open blade, some dishwasher tablets, the bread knife with the grey handle, a potato peeler, a cheese grater, the meat tenderizer, some clear freezer bags. Salt. Tabasco. Lemons. One lime. Maple syrup.

Jenna detoured en route to the study, making a stop in the back part of the conservatory, retrieving a key from beneath a plant pot and also picking up a hammer and smiling when she found a blowtorch she remembered from when Bill had a go at stripping a cupboard. The electric screwdriver.

In the study, of course, the guns. Bill thought the key was safe under the pot. How much did he think she was ignorant of? The key opened a drawer on his desk and underneath that drawer, another key was taped, the one that opened the gun cabinet. It was as though her father thought the trail of keys would be too difficult for Jenna to follow. The dark green metal was pitted near the lock and when she opened the door, the smell of oil and gunpowder was on her instantly. Jenna removed a shotgun and the automatic .45 her father should not really have had. She filled the clip and loaded it into the butt. The rucksack was becoming heavy.

When she was at the top of the stairs, she took a moment to investigate the bathroom there, the only one that was not an en-suite. She closed the door and flicked on the light, adjusting to it in a matter of seconds. The inhibiting square space was hardly used. Jenna unbuttoned her jeans and pushed them down along with her knickers. She fell on to the seat and let the water release, enjoying its gush and now heedless of the noise it made in the bowl. There would still be blood in there from Gordon. When she had looked in the bowl at his house, she was sure there had been semen mixed in with the blood. At least he had had a good time, she thought. As she finished, she felt a tickle and turned round to look in the bowl. She was certain she had seen something, a long worm wriggling off down the toilet, its tail flashing as it disappeared. She looked in the cupboard with its dirty mirror door and there was not much. An old razor, some scissors and a deodorant spray. Sure. Extra Dry. She took them.

In the hall, she stopped and looked at the pictures of her mother. When Ellen Clare-Miller had been just Ellen Clare, she had been a model. A few shots from her portfolio had been mounted in picture frames; narrow waists, double-breasted pantsuits with oversized buttons widely spaced. In one, a red outfit with a black collar and matching gloves. On the opposite wall, a professional photograph of her mother and father shortly after they met. Her mother's face demure and feline, but slightly ill at ease next to the radiant confidence of her father. Her mother was nervous, as though she couldn't believe what she'd landed and was uncertain of her ability to contain it.

Jenna stood by the door of her old room. She opened it slowly but did not feel like entering. Jenna had occupied, left and reoccupied this room numerous times over the years, its décor evolving rather than undergoing major overhauls. Pieces of furniture that had been there since she was born still inhabited the room, as did others she had added. It would be nice to gut the whole room and start again. It would be nice to do that to myself, she thought. She could not cross the threshold into the room.

Instead, she moved silently down the corridor and gently shifted the handle of her parents' room. It amazed Jenna that they still slept together, but that was Bill, she was sure, insisting they inhabit the same bed whatever. And there they were, two feet apart, in deep and separate sleep. She doubted their bodies ever crossed paths in the course of the night, that when one of them turned, so did the other, fitting into the shape made for them. But then, she thought, I've never slept with anyone and felt like that either.

She had carried the can separately from the rucksack and unscrewed its black plastic lid with the big easy-grip bumps. Jenna walked to the bed and emptied all of the petrol over them as they slept, letting it douse the bedclothes fully before she allowed any to cover their faces and rouse them.

They both sputtered in confusion and flailed for a moment or two, her mother speaking her father's name, more of an enquiry than a cry for help. By the time they were both sitting up and her mother had managed to switch on the bedside lamp, Jenna had already lit the blowtorch and left it with a long yellow flame burning.

'If you try and get up, I'll throw this on to the bed. You haven't pissed yourself, although there is that sort of granny fanny flash-fire hazard smell in here. That's petrol you can smell, by the way.'

'Jenna?'

It was her mother, her voice slushy without her perfect teeth in. They were still in the same sad tumbler by the bedside.

Jenna wafted the blowtorch near her face, letting it catch her features in the dark.

'Jenna, what . . . ?' her father asked, coming fully awake and tapping at himself as though he had lost his keys. He sniffed the air.

'I told you it's petrol. Don't you believe me?' Jenna asked and walked a step nearer the bed, waving the flame about.

'What's going on, Bill?' her mother asked.

'Stay calm, Ellen,' he said.

'To tell the truth, I'd panic if I were you,' Jenna said, backing towards the door and switching on the main light in the room, an overblown frost of crystal that refracted the eight candle-shaped bulbs. She locked the door and put the key in her pocket. 'You said you wanted to travel, to see things. Well, we're going to take a fantastic fucking journey without even leaving this room. You'll be amazed the places I can take you.'

'What is the meaning of this?' her father asked, using a tone she had not heard since her mid-teens and shuffling as though about to get up.

'Don't get up on my account. I've come to talk to you both, because there are things I want to say to you and, to be frank, I find it quite hard to get your attention. I feel I have it now.' Jenna threw a small bundle on the bed. 'Those are cable ties, like the ones Father uses in his study. Mother, I want you to take his pyjamas off and then bind his hands and feet with them.'

No one spoke.

Jenna shook her head and massaged her temple with the thumb and little finger of her right hand.

'Now, please,' she said, quietly. 'Now!' she shouted, twisting the valve on the torch so that it hissed a violent blue flame. 'Do it fucking now!' she screamed and her mother cowered.

Jenna's mother was looking from one to the other and her father nodded at her, desperate as ever to be in control, even of being tied up.

'Pull them nice and tight,' Jenna instructed, enjoying the grating sound the plastic ties made when they were pulled shut around her father's wrists, her mother's hands shaking. 'Sit him up. Good,' Jenna said, eager to display her pleasure.

'Jenna,' her father said.

She ignored him. 'I don't really want to tie you up, Mother, but I'm worried you might try and run off on me. I was thinking about that on the way over. I thought I'd have a go at dislocating your hip. That should restrict your mobility somewhat,' she smiled.

'Jenna,' her father cut in, 'leave her out of this.'

'I'm going to get really bored with you saying that,' Jenna said, placing a foot on her mother and gripping her ankle.

There was a short cry and the sound of something inside her mother moving in a way that it should not have. Then the pain seemed to hit and she writhed, the agony making her movements throb. Her father was in a state of shock, a disbelieving expression on his face.

'That didn't go as well as I might have hoped. Let me just sort you out with some wire I have,' Jenna said to her mother, who continued crying. 'Could you shut the fuck up now or I might just have to set you alight.'

Her mother continued to sob as she was bound, sounding like a child. Jenna did not want to burn her yet and she tried to contain the anger she felt.

'You need to stop this now,' her father said.

'You might be right, but for all the wrong reasons as usual.'

'What is this about?' her father asked.

'You work it out,' she said.

'You are such an unhappy girl, Jenna Miller,' her father sighed, as though he might have been musing over it with a glass of brandy, ready for his after-dinner cigar and session of wind-breaking.

'Me? Me unhappy? When did I last see you smile? When did I ever see you smile, you miserable fucking bastard. Mother has a lovely smile, even in the glass. It's a pity you don't have a smile like that.' Jenna stopped, thought for a moment and then smiled. 'Of course, I can arrange for you to have Mother's smile, once we get your teeth out of the way.'

Jenna bent and rummaged in the sack, finding the hammer but then seeing something that presented even more possibilities of fun, for Jenna at least. She banged the blunt end of the long knife-sharpening steel against the frame of the bed, getting used to aiming the point at something as small as a tooth, then she went to work on her father, oblivious to his or her mother's screams.

'Open wide,' she said, forcing her mother's teeth into the bloody orifice his mouth had become, the odd stump of tooth still visible through his ancient gums. She was impressed that he had not passed out from the pain and shock. 'Don't bite me with Mother's teeth, or I'll get angry. Maybe you should nibble on one of her nipples with her teeth. Would you like that?' she asked her mother, who did not reply. 'Say something, Bill, let's hear how they sound. They must be well worn in by now, years of gnashing down and tongue-biting for Mother as she thinks what a boorish cunt you are.'

Her father said nothing.

Jenna took the potato peeler and made her mother cry out.

'I want to hear you speak and I'll carry on doing this until you do.'

This time her mother's moan was sorrowful enough even to get to Bill.

'Jenna, stop, please.' Except it came out sounding like he had food in his mouth that was spilling from it as he spoke.

'Give us a smile, Bill. Every time I hurt her, I want you to give me a nice big grin. When I think you look happy enough, I'll stop. If you don't, I'll take your lips off with the poultry scissors and make you watch her kiss them. Then you could both sit and watch them get a bit of her tongue.'

She held one of the silver forks high above her head.

'Try a bigger smile, Bill,' she said. 'That's a bit better, but not quite.' Her father flinched as he watched Jenna, but kept the teeth showing. 'Almost.'

With tears cascading down his cheeks, Bill Miller sat there grinning inanely with his wife's teeth.

'That's perfect,' Jenna said. 'You do have a nice smile when you want. I've got a treat for you, for being a good boy.'

With deft fingers, she unwrapped one of the dishwasher tablets and fed it to him like a sugar lump to a horse. He took it without complaining – he was learning.

'I read about this happening on an aeroplane years ago, I think,' Jenna said, as she unwound the coat hanger until it was a single length of wire, one end curved like the handle of an umbrella and the other a corkscrew with a sharp, slanting point.

Her mother became hysterical as she watched Jenna leaning over her father and she began to shake from side to side, throwing her head about, hair flying. A long spurt of his blood lifted in the air and streaked the bedclothes and her mother flinched from it.

'Fuck,' Jenna said, disappointed with her work. She grabbed the stapler and tried to meld two flapping edges of skin together with no success. 'Why are you so awkward, always?' she asked her father, but he was already dying and Jenna knew there was little point in arguing with him.

The hammer made a sound as though it were hitting wet mud, banging on the occasional stone. As he became less recognizable and her own enthusiasm grew, the task became easier for her, as though neither she or her father were themselves any longer.

'I think I've broken a couple of your teeth, Mum, sorry,' she said, giggling. 'Don't cry, please.'

The old woman did not respond. She was staring at her husband and trembling.

'I know,' Jenna said, agreeing with what she assumed her mother was thinking. 'They look strange when they're open, and they smell funny too. And slippery and goopey, like snot. Let me just get the wire cutters and I'll have you out of there.'

Jenna searched through the bag.

'Actually, I changed my mind,' Jenna said, spinning smartly and pointing the .45 at her mother, letting the whole clip off in a single salvo.

Chapter 24

The seaside town of Dray lies on the southeast coast of England in the throat of a natural bay. The bay is not especially large, but neither is Dray. The towns on either side of Dray do not touch it in any way, no scattering of houses along the coastal road so that the towns mingle and merge into one. As it has always done, Dray stands alone.

At what is known as the West End of town stand the remains of the grandest building in Dray. The Palace Hotel was owned by Clough Cameron and his wife Krista and it was their home between the wars and on until Clough Cameron moved himself, his wife and the two survivors of her triplets, Alexandra and Alexander, into a house in London, the first of many they were to live in.

By that time, the Cameron Trust owned many of the houses and most of the land that made up Dray – largely, it was rumoured, through the strength of the Camerons' link with the local council. In the Forties and Fifties, there were few families not connected in some way with the Camerons. The building of the hotel and the pier which extended from it brought much-needed work to the town as well as an air of glamour not seen before – or since.

Two incidents, separated by over forty years, served to rob Dray of the things that made it stand out from the weeds of other seaside towns in the vicinity.

In 1955, a fire broke out in the Palace Hotel and quickly took hold of the building's core, raging through the harsh granite structure as though it were a kiln. The stone withstood much of the heat, but the inside did not. One survivor, who broke her collarbone, both arms and a hip by jumping from the second floor into the gardens, said it was as though the fire moved through the building in an organized way, stalking through corridors and eviscerating anything in its path, looking for something. It was the first of many stories about the fire, its origins, its behaviour and its aftermath. But Dray was parochial enough that such talk did not have the power to move beyond its own confines, remaining as tales told by the old and endured by the young. When the fire happened the hotel, already past its glory, was practically empty in the cold off-season month of November. Still, three guests, eleven staff and two fire-men perished.

In 1997, once more in the silence of a cold winter night, the pier collapsed into the sea. The local paper had made something of the story, a bright local journalist able to make a connection and provide a small footnote remarking that there had been a fire the same night at a building in London which had once been the headquarters of the Cameron Trust. However, events far away, at the edge of the American continent where the ground had moved, occupied people far more than any kind of tragedy the loss of the pier might have generated. The structure had been listed and preserved but unused for eight years. The slow disintegration and eventual fall of the pier was never explained, more to do with lack of interest than any sense of mystery. Many in Dray had felt the pier was an eyesore, an unwelcome reminder of the past when the whole town had lived and breathed the Cameron family, as though the town had overextended itself. Now, there were enough generations between the past and present to blunt the memory of the family into myth.

Dray had begun and ended with the Cameron family. After the hotel was vacated post-war, their hold on the town began to loosen. Real power rested with the members of the Cameron family, and that meant it travelled with them. Once they had left, the hotel was run just as many felt it should always have been – as a hotel in a seaside town, not the plaything and home of a wealthy Scottish eccentric. The fire purged the last remnants of the family and it was rumoured that none of the Camerons even visited Dray to inspect the damage wrought by the blaze.

Instead, the building was closed up and left to stand that way. Along with the pier, it was the last monument and reminder of what Dray had been under the Cameron family.

Standing across the road from it to get a better view, Luke stared at the charred remains of the Palace Hotel, dirty waves of soot marking the walls like waves lapping from the nearby sea. He looked down at the postcard he had found in the box at home, shifting his gaze from one to the other. In the postcard image, the pier reached out from the hotel like an arm. Now, just a few stray posts pointed up from the sea, more like raised arms signalling for help. He put the postcard back in his bag, guilty at the sight of the Mars bar wrapper, the Doritos and the Toffee Crisp. A quick look round, then he'd take a shot, but he was too eager to see the hotel.

The building reminded Luke a bit of the Tower of London, or at least the memory he had of it from a school trip. It had the same squareness, the bricks small and almost like teeth. There was a turret at each end, a tower for a damsel. Whiter than the tower had been, the hotel looked solid and its windows expansive, even though Dray would have afforded very little in the way of a view. The rooms on the side facing the sea would have been nice, he imagined. Luke would have liked to curl up in a bed, snuggling down into the warmth and listening to the sea beating against the land. But the windows were shuttered with metal gates and the whole of the hotel was ringed by a uniform wooden fence, as effective as any moat would have been. A stark sign fended off curious people such as Luke.

It was the final building in the parade, separated from the few small hut-like shops on the seafront by the broad end of where the pier would have begun. Luke could tell from the picture that the wide entrance had snaked off into a much narrower pier, not as impressive as Southend. To the left of the hotel, nothing but seafront and a road that quickly wound round a hill, no hint of any life at the end of it.

Luke crossed the road.

The boards around the building were just too high to see over, about six and half feet tall. Plywood painted white, each panel was erected at such a stark right angle that it was sheer and unscalable. Luke walked all the way along the front of the building and round the left side of it, certain there would be an entrance of some sort, but there was nothing. The fence ran down as far as the seafront and then along the very back part of the hotel, sealing off whatever grounds it might have had behind it. Luke continued down the side, still expecting an entrance. When he had completed his circuit with no success, he found himself retracing his previous steps, closer to the fence this time, examining it as though a secret lock or handle might have been so well-concealed as to have escaped his first pass.

'What are you doing?'

The voice made Luke stand upright and draw in a breath of panic, his hands shaking.

Luke turned and saw an old man standing behind him. He looked to either side of him and off behind, trying to see where he might have come from. Up off the beach or from the sea itself?

'What are you doing?' the man asked again.

'Just looking,' he said. 'Who are you?' he asked, and it came out sounding cheekier than he had intended.

The man grabbed Luke by the arm, tight enough to cause him to make a face, and began to haul him along to the front of the building.

'Come and look at this then, son, if you want to look,' the man said.

Luke was having to trot to keep pace with the man. He was surprised at his strength and speed.

'What are you doing? Who are you?' Luke asked, agitation overtaking fear.

'There,' the man said, bringing him to a sharp halt at the front of the building. 'Up there.'

Luke looked up at the sign.

'What does it say? Read it,' the man said.

The voice, the demeanour, were familiar to Luke and he struggled to recall why. He stared up at the sign but ignored the words, gazing instead at the symbol. The same one he had seen outside the houses in Plymouth and Southend. The gangling knot, lines tumbling into each other like an orgy of snakes. The badge of the property company.

And he had seen it somewhere else, but where?

'What right do you have to be here?' Luke heard the man say. 'Are you listening to me, son? I'm security here. I look after this place.'

Luke reached dreamily into his pocket and pulled out the key with the name of the hotel and the room number. And the small knot pattern embossed on the corner of the brass tab. Several times, without really thinking about it, Luke had run his fingers over the pattern when the key had been in his pocket, taking comfort from the puzzling swirl.

'I have this,' Luke said, holding the key in his upturned palm for the man to see.

The man faltered for a moment and Luke studied his face, trying to dredge its familiarity up from memory and into his consciousness. There was something like consternation in the man's expression.

'Where did you get this?' he asked Luke.

'It's my mum's,' Luke said.

'Cross over the road with me,' the man said, seeming less like he was about to drag Luke this time.

They stood more or less where Luke had just been.

'One, two, three, four, five, six, seven, eight,' the man counted. 'Eight floors. Nine Twenty-Eight is the number on your key. Do you see nine floors?' the man demanded.

Luke counted them again.

'Do you?' the man asked. 'Why are you here, son?'

Luke listened to the man's words, then he looked hard at his face, forcing himself to remember. He looked down at the key, across at the building, the sign and the knot. He crouched and reached into the zip pocket inside his bag, handing the man the postcard and the two photographs.

The man stood and looked at the pictures. 'Where did you get these?' he said finally.

'They belong to my mum.'

'You're Bella's boy?' he asked, as though recognizing Luke now.

He nodded.

'Let's sit on that bench for a minute,' the man said, pointing at one on the front.

The wind lifted the flaps on the bottom of Luke's jacket and the sea air lighted on his face in a way that was familiar and welcoming.

'You know my mum?' Luke asked.

The man held up his hand. 'Just hear me out.'

As the man began to speak, he kept his head turned slightly to the left so he could look at the Palace Hotel, and his words were enveloped by the breeze and the splash of waves so much that Luke had to strain to listen.

'Dray seafront hasn't changed much since the hotel was first opened. The buildings get dressed up differently, but, underneath, they're all just the same. When Cameron wanted to buy the piece of land at the very end of the front, people thought he was mad. He stayed in a house over the hill and went away God knows where for weeks at a time. Every time, local gossip was they'd gone for good, but they always came back. He wanted that bit of land. Most of the front then was owned by the Wilding family. George Wilding didn't want to sell anymore than he wanted to build anything. They were a prosperous family, and probably had enough money for more than one life, but they still weren't rich like Cameron was. I don't think they liked the idea of him owning a piece of their Dray, although an agreement was reached in 1931 and work started not long after that.'

'So he bought the land?'

'Cameron acquired it. All that was said round here was that an agreement had been reached. Let me put it this way: George Wilding's lawyers weren't involved. The Wilding family practically ran the local council and soon news got out that Cameron was going to build a grand hotel and a pier. I always reckon it was the pier that swung the deal. Mr Wilding wanted himself a pier but couldn't afford to build one. We were going to be rivals to Southend. Two architects worked on the design. One came from India and the other was from Hungary. The local paper had a picture like the one you do of Mr Clough on the site when the foundations were being laid. Mr Clough Cameron and his adopted daughter Krista, they said.

'For the next year, all anyone talked about was the hotel. The Palace. Cameron sent a picture drawn by one of the architects to the paper and when it was printed, there were some letters complaining how ugly and out of place it would look, but the building of it provided plenty of local work in the Thirties. That wasn't all good news, mind. Nine people, including one of my uncles, were killed in the process of building this place. I remember being in a pub and someone saying it was like slaves building the ancient pyramids. I used to come and stand and watch when it was going up, and it did seem like it should be happening in Egypt, never in Dray. Everyone had something to say about it, that it was amazing or that it was awful. An eyesore, that it would attract unwelcome visitors. But as long as it went on creating work and the Wilding family didn't disapprove, no one could do much else but talk.

'When this place opened in 1932, he put an invitation up all around town requesting everyone to please attend a double celebration. The opening of the Palace and his marriage to Krista. Everyone thought he had adopted her. Nobody liked to think too much about it, but there were a few people stayed away from his wedding party because of it. They married in a private ceremony. I say private, secret was more like it. They held it over there, which couldn't have been a proper religious one, like in a church. That was in the Oak Room and that was also where they had the party afterwards. I think Cameron thought if he opened the doors to everyone, they'd flood in and take him to their hearts. He was simple like that in a lot of ways. The

Wilding mob was on parade along with the rest of the councillors, but mostly it was the sort of day where every-one spoke to each other in whispers.'

Luke stared at the building, trying to project the story he was hearing on to it, to imagine how words would have sounded spoken between the walls, footsteps along passages. The hotel gave nothing away. Along the beach, a tall woman in a long coat and a headscarf was letting herself be pulled along by a stalwart dog that seemed to push itself against the wind. Towards them, the lone figure of a girl ambled along, just avoiding the line of the tide as it left effervescent traces on the sand.

'Tony and me are not proper twins. We shared the same belly for nine months but we're not identical. Definitely not identical, thank Christ. I didn't know he was still in touch with Bella. Did he send you here to check up on me?'

The man's voice sounded like Tony Wood's.

'Brothers?' Luke said. 'So you do know my mum.'

'Not as well as Tony. My name's Terry.'

Luke felt a slight tingle and thought it was the cold.

'I'm Luke Smith,' he said, feeling strange introducing himself to someone as though he were a grown-up.

'And he sent you here to see me?' Terry asked.

'I've met him once, but I didn't even know about this place. He's doing a security thing at a swimming pool near where I live. I met him because I use the old car park as a short cut. He didn't tell me anything about you.'

'How is he?'

Luke wasn't sure what to say. He hadn't paid much attention. 'He looked alright.'

Terry snorted. 'And how's your mum? I haven't seen her in years.'

'How do you know her?' Luke asked.

'Tony knew her a lot better than me. She worked here for a little while, until the fire.'

'There are no rooms on the ninth floor of the hotel then?' Luke asked.

'There aren't even nine floors. Not really. There's an annexe on the top, towards the middle. Cameron used it as his office. They lived on the whole of the eighth floor. You could only get to the annexe from the eighth. No one called it the ninth floor. It's big, mind, but not big enough to be called a floor in its own right. Tell the truth, the eighth wasn't the only way to get there.'

'What do you mean?' Luke asked.

'Cameron had that building made so you could move around it without being seen. When I first started there, you could go through a door, along a corridor and end up somewhere you didn't think you should have. It's a fucking Chinese puzzle, that place.'

Luke looked at the building again. It had loomed over the whole conversation and it seemed to loom over the whole of the seafront. The Palace Hotel in Southend was nothing like it, much more ordinary and set back off the promenade. In Dray, the Palace could have risen up out of the waves, teetering almost on the edge of the land, ready to be reclaimed by the sea, like the pier, and like his brother.

As though gripped by a sudden weightlessness, Luke swayed on the bench and had to put a hand down quickly to stop himself from tumbling.

'You alright?'

'I have to take some medicine,' Luke said.

The man frowned, as though suspicious.

'I'm diabetic. I need to inject myself with insulin. Can we go inside? Please?' Luke asked.

'I'm not meant to have anyone inside the place.'

Luke pretended not to have heard him. Instead, he was imagining he was about to faint. There was something wicked about the pretence but any guilt he felt was nothing like the power of the need he had to get inside the hotel.

'Come on then,' the man said.

Chapter 25

The entrance to the hotel was at the front of the fence by the sign Terry Wood had shown Luke. It was obvious and easy to see once he was standing in front of it. Terry produced a key, slid it in and hushed him through a gap only just wide enough. Another two sets of locked doors and a flight of stone steps followed before Luke and Terry entered the now towering building and he found himself in the reception area, or what had once been the reception area.

Terry Wood, with his air of menacing deference, exhibited mannerisms close to those of his brother, although Luke had hardly spent enough time with either of them to judge properly.

'It might not look like much now, but it used to be.'

The reception area still had its front desk, but nothing else to indicate what the place had been. From the ceiling, stalks projected down where chandeliers would once have hung. A stairway clung to the far wall and curved round it, climbing to a mezzanine level that made for a gallery to view the reception from.

'How you feeling?' Terry asked, causing Luke to break his panoramic stare and look at the man instead.

Luke had forgotten he was meant to be feigning and had to recover his injured expression quickly.

'Is there somewhere I can go? To take my insulin,' Luke said, making a gesturing motion at his stomach with both hands.

Terry seemed to appreciate that this would require privacy. 'Use the office behind the counter. You need anything?' he asked.

'No, I can manage, thanks,' Luke said.

Five minutes later, after leaning against the wall in the

bare office, wondering if he should take a shot anyway, Luke emerged and smiled for the benefit of Terry, thinking he might be expecting him to look radiant now he had taken his magic potion. Terry was propped against the counter smoking a stubby cigar with an odour that quickly overpowered Luke.

'They stripped the place bare, took whatever the fire didn't,' Terry said.

The wallpaper was burned but in some places, like in the houses in Plymouth and Southend, there were patches where paintings had been removed. There was no carpet on the floor and no furniture, making the space seem hollow.

'The bar area was over there, through those doors. The big doors at the back there are for the Oak Room, and it has a veranda that looks out on to the sea. You got a nice view of the pier from the deck, specially when the lights were on it at Christmas. The main restaurant and kitchens were on this floor too and there was another bar and smaller restaurant up there.' Terry motioned to the gallery. 'There were also some offices and smaller function rooms up there. Down there,' he motioned at the floor, 'in the basement was the laundry, housekeeping and the boiler. At first, I thought that must have been where the fire started, but the bloke from the fire brigade didn't seem to think so.'

'Where did it start?' Luke asked.

'They never said. "Weren't able to determine the source or cause" was the phrase I seem to remember they used.'

'Can we look upstairs?' Luke asked.

'You were only meant to be in here because you weren't feeling too well, son.'

'I know,' Luke said, trying to be winsome without whining. 'Can I just have a look?'

'That key of yours won't fit nothing, you know. Maybe it was for the eighth floor and a bit got rubbed off the number. Show me.'

Luke and Terry both peered at the fob, but Luke already

knew it was not the case. He had studied the tab too closely for that.

'Maybe not then. This must just be a mistake,' Terry said.

Luke looked on and said nothing.

'Just a couple of floors, okay, then you should go,' Terry said.

Luke smiled. 'Thank you.'

Had his mother really worked here? he wondered as he followed Terry up the stairs, a little alarmed by the warning to keep near the wall as that was safer.

The floors that followed were a disappointment. Each was the same. Long corridors, countless doors, fire escapes. Any character that might have existed in the grandeur of the hotel's entrance was soon diminished by delving further. Everything was empty, completely bare.

'There're no handles on any of the doors,' Luke observed.

'They were taken off, probably melted down for scrap. There was enough metal on them.'

'There's really nothing here,' Luke said.

'Nothing to see. Just like I told you.'

They had made it as far as the fourth floor and were standing on its landing, the old man starting to wheeze slightly. He was going to suggest they turned back, Luke could feel it coming on.

'Can we take just a quick look up on the eighth floor, and in that office thing above it?' Luke asked.

'It's the same up there as it is down here. Empty rooms.'

'I've come such a long way to get here.' He fumbled with the key and let his words trail on into silence. Luke had neither the courage nor the guile simply to make a break for the eighth floor.

'I wish they hadn't taken those fucking lifts out of service,' Terry said as he started to climb.

'Thanks,' Luke said.

They rose all the way to the eighth without stopping to look at any of the other floors. Terry mumbled occasionally and Luke could tell he was unhappy with the situation. It seemed more like Terry was troubled at being soft than having to go all the way to the top of the hotel without the aid of a lift.

A set of heavy metal shutters blocked the way to the eighth floor, leaving them standing at the top of the stairs, little room to manoeuvre.

'Do you live here?' Luke asked as he watched Terry open the shutters with fluid movements.

'Most of the time I do. There's a room downstairs, right on the ground floor. Small but easy to keep warm,' he replied.

'But nobody ever tries to get in, do they?' Luke asked.

'They never have while I've been here.'

'I'd get scared here on my own,' Luke said.

'I do sometimes,' Terry said, as though unashamed to admit the power of the hotel was far greater than his own courage. 'Bad things have happened here, all those people through the doors, the lives lost building it, in the fire, the Camerons. There's bound to be a few ghosts rattling round the place.'

'It does feel a bit spooky. Why don't they just knock the place down?'

'Not allowed to. The Cameron family would never have heard of that in any case. This was still their most important place, even when they didn't live here any more. Old Cameron's children were born here, the boy and the girl.'

'What happened to them? Are they still alive?' Luke asked, thinking about what his mother had said about his dad.

'No. They're not. I don't want to go into that though, son, if you don't mind. You'll find the rooms on this floor a bit more interesting, in the way they're laid out,' he said, making an obvious change of subject.

It was dizzying, like being in a honeycomb. Rooms of differing sizes, spaces that did not seem to match each other, were connected by doors of wildly varying widths and heights.

'Most of these rooms were given over to the living area.

There was a nursery too and their own kitchen and a special chef. There was a little army of people looking after them.'

By the time they were done with the brief pointing tour, Luke had been in so many different interlacing rooms that the twists and turn had left him disoriented. He wanted to know where the sea was. They were standing in a windowless room, most likely towards the centre of the maze.

'Gets you that way. It took me a long time to get used to it,' Terry said. 'If there had been anyone up here when the building caught fire, they would have had a hard time getting out. Two firemen died up here. The blaze caught a second wind, I reckon, fanning through all these rooms. They must have opened a door and it just jumped them, like it was lying in wait.'

Luke stood in the quiet of the room, its air stale and a little damp. Claustrophobia was getting the better of him and he felt a twinge, as though his body were nudging him and reminding him that his blood/sugar level needed attending to.

On the large wall facing the door was a wooden carving of the symbol on the key tab and the board outside. Not as intricate, the carving was still complex and it boggled Luke's eyes as he strained to take it all in.

'This didn't get burned?' he asked, moving closer to it.

'It was the one thing in the whole building that was replaced. Cameron sent someone from London with an identical one to the one that got burned up and it was put up here.'

'What's so special about it?' Luke asked.

'Here you go,' Terry said.

He reached into the pattern and touched something on it. A panel in the wall, the size of a door, sprang open and Luke took a step back from it, feeling caution at the sudden piece of dark that had opened up before him.

'Where does it go?' Luke asked, not wanting to get too close in case it swallowed him.

'Either way. Up or down. Come on. You wanted to see.'

Terry reached into the dark and made it less so by flicking a switch. Luke went into the dimness and let his eyes become accustomed to it. A spiral staircase, the same black metal as the fire escapes he had seen on the other floors, went up towards a patch of what he realized was sky. He looked down.

'That one goes all the way to the bottom and then some,' Terry said.

Luke gave him a questioning look.

'It's a way in and out without being seen or heard,' Terry said. 'Only a few of us knew about this way to the annexe. You still want to go up?'

He nodded and stepped in front of Terry, not liking the idea of following and letting the darkness nip at his ankles.

Luke's eyes, which had only just become accustomed to the gloom of the stairwell, were now flooded by the light of the room into which he walked. The sky was visible through a window that was more like part of a wall. It was something like a greenhouse, the window running the length of one side of the long rectangular wall, starting halfway up it and curving up over his head and across at least a third of the broad ceiling. From the window, he could look out across the bay and beyond, into the steamy distance. The window enabled him to take in the sea but nothing of the drab Dray landscape that would have been behind him. There was a sense of relief and escape in the vista, able to wash feeling out of him for a while.

'This is fantastic,' Luke said, grinning although barely realizing it.

'It's a view alright, son. But nothing here. Empty as the rest of the place.'

The old man moved silently next to him and they stood close to the window. They stared together and it felt like a communal activity.

'What are they going to do with this place?' Luke asked.

'I don't think any one rightly knows who "they" are. Maybe they will pull it down one day, but it's been up long enough now. Reopen it, maybe, but who the fuck would come here? You must've been through the town on your way here.'

'You work for them, though.'

'They pay me, yes. The Camerons set up a trust for this place so it would be looked after. That's all we were told, Tony and me. All I do now is look after this place and that doesn't take much.'

'But Tony doesn't come here?' Luke asked.

'He does other things for them. We work for the same firm, though. He looks after properties, too.'

There was an awkwardness to Terry's words and Luke knew it indicated something not right between the twins. It seemed impolite to delve further.

'Did you work here when my mum did?' Luke asked.

'Tony and me have never, in all our lives, officially worked anywhere. We were around and we did things for old Cameron, but we didn't work here. That doesn't answer your question, does it? Sorry. Tony knew her a lot better than I did.'

Luke swallowed, and ventured a question that felt delicate. 'Was she his girlfriend?'

Terry chuckled and looked out to the sea. 'Tony's not the marrying sort.'

'Lots of people don't want to get married,' Luke replied and instantly realized what Terry meant. 'Oh,' was all he said.

'They were good friends. I wouldn't have minded knowing her better, but it didn't work out that way. If you want to know anything about what it was like when your mum worked here, Tony's the one to ask.'

'What was it like here on the night of the fire?' Luke asked.

Terry Wood looked out of the window but did not answer. Luke peered at him and saw a look on his face that was like guilt. For a moment, Luke thought the old man was about to cry.

'I wasn't here. I was in London. Tony was here, though. Ask him about the fire,' he said eventually.

'What do you mean?'

'Time to leave, son. I've got things to get on with and you need to be on your way. Say hello to your mum for me,' he said.

'And to your brother,' Luke added.

Terry did not answer.

Chapter 26

Luke felt dejected as he wandered away from the Palace Hotel, wondering if Terry Wood was observing him from one of the many windows he would have known so well. Luke had come to Dray and discovered nothing.

Almost as if he were being punished for lying his way into the hotel, he really was beginning to feel bad. He tried to separate the anger at the pointless journey from the sick feeling brought about by his blood sugar. He couldn't tell if he was high or low and he didn't care. Fuck it, he thought, I'll just pass out on the pavement, let someone else take care of me.

But he was too sensible for that, which made him angry as well. Across the road, pressed between an amusement arcade and an Indian restaurant, was a sweet shop. He went in and bought a bottle of Lucozade, feeling better even after a sip, the way he always did, whether or not it was making a real difference.

The arcade was open and pretty much deserted. It was so depressing the way some arcades in Southend would stay open almost all year, coaxing in nothing more than cold wind and rain and the odd schoolboy addicted to one of the machines. But this one was bright and noisy. Noisier than it should have been since it was almost empty. Glass was made hot by electric light, all the plastic surfaces greasy with the fingerprints of past customers. Most of the machines were electronic but there were a few games where real balls were thrown into hoops, darts into playing cards. Money fell into metal with captivating loudness somewhere off to Luke's right and then two voices cheered each other. The noise of the place gave him an instant headache.

Luke walked round a rink of unused kiddie dodgems, on

202

to the row of games machines lined against a back wall, the light they gave off the only illumination in the dark corner.

One machine in particular caught his eye. The Palace. Luke smiled at the irony of it and fished in his trousers for a coin as he made his way towards it. He set the Lucozade on top of the machine and dropped a coin into the slot.

The game was fairly basic fantasy, not the sort Luke liked. He preferred something with a space battle, some laser weaponry and lots of good explosions and blood. This looked like something out of one of those books he always avoided in shops, a boy on a horse, a woman in a chiffon dress, a castle floating on mist in the background.

Still, it was quite a fast-moving game, and soon his fingers tapped wildly on the buttons. He stuck his elbows out at the side as though trying to tilt the game like a pinball machine.

Luke was so caught up in the action, he wondered after noticing her with a quick glance over his shoulder how long the girl had been standing there watching him. She went and stood behind him, by his right shoulder. The brief glimpse had been enough for him to register that she was pretty. Maybe even very pretty. It made him feel self-conscious and he felt a light flush of heat in his cheeks.

Slowly, he sensed her ease herself nearer so he could see her reflection in the sloping glass of the machine. As she stood directly next to him, a computer-generated woman leaned out of the window of a high stone tower, boggle-eyed and arms waving, an evil ogre smiling in the background as it pawed her. A handsome blond prince was scaling the tower, dragons nipping at his feet.

A spike came from the wall of the tower, ran the prince through and left him wriggling like a worm for a few seconds before retracting and letting him fall to the open jaws of the dragons below. A few seconds of muted red butchery and dining followed.

The words GAME OVER flashed.

'Are you waiting to play this?' he asked, half turning to her, cringing at how confrontational it had sounded.

'No,' she said.

The girl seemed so taken with Luke it was as if she was looking at something even he was not aware of. He was sort of flattered, but it was also a bit creepy.

Luke knew there would be a point about fifteen minutes from now when he would be on his way back to the station and his head would be full of clear and precise things he could have said to her. Sentences that were so finely polished and honed she would throw back her head and laugh, perhaps reach out and touch his hand. Phrases that would pull her closer to him and then . . .

None of that would happen. He gave her a quick look, attempted something like a smile and began to walk away.

'You forgot your Lucozade,' she said, pulling up next to him.

He stopped and looked at her. 'Thanks,' he said, taking it and stepping forward once again. Say something to her, start her talking, a voice shouted in his head. She's nice. Very nice. A bit old, but, well, nice.

'My name's Lucy,' she blurted.

The knot tightened.

'I'm Luke. Luke Smith,' he said.

Chapter 27

For Wadlow, there wasn't really a place he could call home. No place like home, he thought, and smiled to himself. Click my heels three times and say it and where would I end up? What would be home? Gift? The town where he had lived until he was fourteen and then ran from after he had killed his brother Randall. Self-defence, Wad, you know you had no choice. Kill or be killed. Each gunshot was distinct in Wadlow's memory, as though every bullet possessed a personality of its own as it emerged from the barrel of Pa's gun. Sounds were what he remembered most from that night. The gunfire and hearing his brother Randall speak for the first and last time, begging Wadlow to end whatever silent turmoil Wad could see only in the frantic splash of ink on the pages of his brother's notebook. Gift was where he grew up, or so he believed, unless his other suspicion were true.

That his life had been made up by somebody else. I am not the person I think I am. I am the person someone else thinks I am.

When years later he had returned to Gift, a suffocating place in Tennessee, it was as though he or his family had never existed there. As if someone had planted memories in his head.

Gift had not been home.

Wadlow sauntered down the main street in Raynsford, the first time he had returned since closing the door of his bookshop almost four years earlier and setting off for California in search of an obscure English writer named Nancy Lloyd. That day he had left behind him the ashes of a lifetime's book-collecting, incinerating his collection in the bunker hidden beneath the shop.

He licked his lips which felt as dry as the rest of his

mouth. His mind was filled with 'what if' questions. If this pilgrimage was the same as his one to Gift, would he find familiarity but no proof he had ever existed? No one would recognize him now in any case, he reasoned. His new lean frame was an echo of the rotund figure that had earned him the reputation of local bogeyman and the nickname Waddler Grace, said behind his back but always loud enough for him to hear the cruel twist of his southern accent, impersonated to make it sound as though it really were his name.

It was an hour or so after lunch on a Wednesday afternoon and there were few people around – no one he recognized. The main street through Raynsford was wide, cars parked head-in on either side of a road that twisted off and up towards trees and the first hint of mountainous country beyond. Wadlow passed the drugstore and glanced in, wondering if Elanor Knowles was still there, playing out the drama of the town with flicks of her long grey hair and the knowing arch of her eyebrows. He saw no one and continued on, counting off the shops as he neared the end of the parade. Carlton Stanforth's craft-shop, an attempt to lure tourists with inappropriate and frankly awful postcards and lewd gifts, was boarded up. Ainsley Elton's barbershop was still there, the 'Closed' sign showing and the shop looking immaculate as it always did, chrome gleaming from the gloom as glints of sunlight caught it. Then there was the long gap between, before Wadlow reached the bookstore that had once belonged to him.

There was a gentle hum that Wadlow felt along his spine before the sound diminished to a low whirr and he realized a car had pulled alongside him. He stopped and turned and it was a ghost he saw.

The preacher's '55 Plymouth Belvedere stood beside him. It made Wadlow afraid and sad at the same time. Just as he remembered it, the first time he had seen it when he was fourteen, its chrome was polished so deeply it could have been silver, and even Ainsley Elton would have been jealous. Wadlow used to pull out his pocket comb and run it through his hair, using the side window as his mirror. The galleon hood ornament was almost blinding. The paint job was the kind of hopeful green you didn't see any more, a long white band along the side as delicious as cream next to a pie. All that was missing, thought Wadlow, was the sound of Elvis, bigger than any radio and bursting out the window. The sun on the windshield reflected his own image back at him and Wadlow was about to bend and look in when the door, the size of a decent gate, swung open and Alexander Cameron emerged.

'Hello, Wadlow. It's been some time. It is true, then. I almost didn't recognize you.'

Wadlow inhaled and felt an unexpected heave of fear. 'Since we've been face to face, yes, that has been more than some time, Mr Cameron. You knew I'd come here?'

The space between them on the sidewalk was uncomfortable. Neither of them seemed willing to cross it and make physical contact. Wadlow wondered if Cameron felt the same sense of unease he did himself, that it was coming from outside both of them.

Cameron nodded. 'I distracted you from your destination,' he said, looking over Wadlow's shoulder.

Wadlow realized he had not even looked at his old store. He took his eyes from Cameron and glanced at the car, wondering who was driving, before turning to look at his old home. Like Stanforth's, it was boarded up, except far more conclusively. The boards filled every window as though they were wooden panes of glass, made secure by the diamond pattern of the metal shutters that covered them. A sign, metal on closer inspection, and secured with wire so thick its twists would resist all but the strongest wire cutters, displayed a knot and the word Gordius.

'Did you really know I'd come out here?' Wadlow asked over his shoulder.

'Here, or back to Gift perhaps, but you did that a long time ago.'

Wadlow faced Cameron and held up Randall's notebook.

'It was this led me here, Mr Cameron. It's been my guide even though it's selfish with its secrets. Pulls me along but never shows any more than where I've been, everywhere I been. So many things I don't know,' he sighed.

Cameron was holding a key out in front of Wadlow's face. 'It would be a shame not to go in, don't you think?'

'You know, I came this far, but now it doesn't seem right to be going in. There's nothing in there for me. Made sure of that when I left the first time.'

'I think if you feel the need to see this place one more time, then you should, Wadlow. But I don't believe you came here for that or that you really know what you came here for.'

Cameron moved a step forward and laid a hand on Wadlow's shoulder, pressing the key into his palm.

'None of it was real, was it?' Wadlow asked.

'None of what?'

'Gift. Randall, my family.' Wadlow paused. 'Me.'

'We're here now, Wadlow. This is real.'

Wadlow looked at the main street and then the road that went into country, the hem of natural and man-made. Everything around him, under him, was made, nature fabricated into society, and yet none of it seemed authentic.

'You're not answering my question, Alexander.' Wadlow held Randall's notebook up as if it were a Bible he was about to swear on. 'This book isn't a record of what I've done, is it? I am the result of what's written in there. It's not about me. I'm about it.'

Cameron gave him a heavy stare, as though checking Wadlow was really there.

'There were things we did not know about, there still are. All we knew was that you would be there in Memphis, when the preacher went looking for you. We knew nothing of you before that, where you came from or what you had done. As far as we knew, still know, you grew up with your family in Tennessee.'

'But that might not be so.'

'If you remember it that way, Wadlow, then doesn't that

make it real, regardless?'

'The preacher knew where to find me,' Wadlow said quietly, the feeling of loss moving across the lower plane of his feelings.

'He was able to stay one jump ahead of the text. Some people have that ability. They can open a book like yours and see what is to be, not what has already passed. What we know of your past is based on what you told us.'

'But you let me believe Randall existed. We talked about him and my family. I've heard you talk about it to other people. Why?'

'I've told you why, Wadlow. There were things we didn't know.' Cameron's voice was firmer.

'You've always been more confident about what you didn't know than what you do, Alexander,' Wadlow said.

'There are few people for whom that does not hold.'

'The first time the preacher sat me down and told me about you, your family, Nathan Lucas, The Book, I lay awake for a long time wondering if you were the good man or the bad man.'

Cameron looked on, but said nothing.

'I realized,' Wadlow continued, 'that you were probably both and, more important, that it didn't really matter much either way.'

'Your life is not so different from anyone else's, Wadlow. You watch the ink in that notebook slowly become legible as you make your way through the story of your life. How much more does anyone else know?'

'I know there isn't very much ink left,' Wadlow said.

'There may not be for any of us, but we have no way of knowing that.'

'Tell me the truth, Alexander. Tell me the truth about me.'

'Wadlow, if there is truth, it comes through the telling of the story. You will come to it, trust me.'

'But first you want me to do something. That's usually the way. Build the collection of books, watch out for the signs, find Nancy Lloyd, take her to where she needs to be, look after Lucy Kavanagh, Mike Kavanagh. When does the story get to be about me, Alexander?'

The car's engine fired up, a sudden burst that gave Wadlow a start, but Cameron did not even blink.

'I have to be somewhere else,' Cameron said.

The door of the car swung open, silent and unaided.

'What do I do, Alexander?'

'I feel as if we've said goodbye a thousand times since we've known each other, Wadlow Grace.'

Wadlow was feeling panicked. Cameron was not paying attention. 'Where should I go? What do I do next?'

'How old were you when the preacher found you in Memphis?'

'Fourteen. You know I was.'

'What were you doing?' Cameron asked.

'What do you mean?'

'At the time you met the preacher.' Cameron was backing towards the open door of the car.

Wadlow stood on the sidewalk, trying to remember, surprised at the blind spot in his memory.

'I was trying to get something to drink. I was so thirsty. I hadn't had anything to drink all day. I'd been walking for so long.'

'You'll know the truth when you find it, Wadlow. Trust me. No, just trust yourself. Goodbye, Wadlow.'

Cameron disappeared into the open mouth of the car.

'Alexander. Wait.'

Wadlow stepped forward but the door closed. The car pulled along the main street and towards the mountains. He watched until it was out of sight and then looked down at the key, squeezing it and turning his attention back to the shop.

It was gone.

Chapter 28

'Cunt.'

It had been her idea to eat. They stood on the windy pavement, Luke not knowing what to say, when she suddenly marched towards a chip shop. Luke had agreed and was relieved to see the shop had a toilet. He mumbled and went straight to it, fumbling to inject himself properly, wondering about the Lucozade, what he should eat next and the right dosage, all of which meant he took longer than he wanted to.

'Cunt.'

He ordered just chips and two bread rolls, plain ones they told him they would have to cut specially. She didn't seem to know what she wanted to order, and he wondered if she'd ever been in a chip shop before. It was hard to tell how much older than him she was, but it felt too old, and Luke was less comfortable than he had been at the initial swaggering moment where her attentions had sent enough adrenaline through him to dilute anything like nerves.

'Cunt.'

'Is he going to stop saying that, do you think?' he asked, taking a quick look over his shoulder, but afraid to catch the man's eye in case it made him involved.

She smiled. 'He doesn't even look like a typical crazy,' she said. 'Whatever typical is.'

Luke picked up his glass, its once clear surface frosted from continual washing, and took his first sip. He winced.

'What's wrong?' she asked.

'This isn't Diet Coke. I asked them for Diet Coke,' Luke said, shaking his head disbelief they had got it wrong.

'I don't think she was listening when she took the order. We'd made her mad because we were taking so long.'

'I asked her for Diet Coke,' he said again, agitated and

anxious at the recollection the taste of the liquid had sent through him.

'She probably didn't mean . . .'

Luke ignored her and went to get it replaced. The lady was clucking and apologetic, but he was still finding it hard to relax. He shot a quick look back at Lucy. 'Can't keep your eyes off her? She's a looker,' the lady said to him as she handed him a new glass. Luke felt his face redden and the woman gave a little giggle, a saucy one.

'Sorry. I can't drink the other stuff,' he said, struggling to sit back in the chair that was fixed to the table, feeling awkward and ungainly.

'What was she saying to you?' Lucy asked.

'Nothing.' His face became hot again. 'She was just saying sorry.' Luke spun the glass slowly round on the blue Formica surface, some excess liquid on its base forming a seal.

'Cunt.'

'You don't live here then?' Lucy asked.

'I live in London, with my Mum,' Luke said, his mind racing along but coming across nothing further to say.

'I used to live in London,' Lucy said.

'You don't any more then?' he asked in response.

'I live in America now.'

'Really?' he replied, knowing he had made his eyes a lot wider than he had meant to, however interesting it was.

'I'm here visiting my dad.'

'Your dad lives down here?' he asked.

'Cunt.'

'No, I'm just here for the day. He still lives in London, but he's away at the moment.'

He tried to make himself look amused and said, 'I'm confused now.'

'Me too,' she said.

Luke was so grateful to see the food arrive, he almost fell into it. The plate of chips was big and easier to focus on than just the glass of Diet Coke. He grabbed the fork and ate a chip, then decided to use his fingers.

She was a looker, the lady was right. But she was also older than him, obviously so. But she came up to you. She was the one who said to come here. So now it's your turn to say something, he thought.

'You live with your mum?' she asked.

Luke grimaced internally. It made him feel like a boy, the question about his mum. 'Yeah, we used to live in Southend, but she sold our house there and we moved to East London.'

'When did she sell the house?'

'Just before Christmas,' he said. She's a nosy one, he thought. 'I preferred it in Southend. It's where I grew up.'

'I miss being in London,' Lucy said. 'That was where I was raised.'

He did not know what to say, so he filled his mouth with more chips.

'Do you mind me asking how old you are?' Lucy asked.

'Cunt.'

'Nearly sixteen,' he replied, giving his plate a downcast look, wishing he had lied.

Luke sneaked a glance at her. The girls at school, the new school, seemed curious about him mostly because he was new. When they learned about the diabetes, there were quite a few who were turned off, he could tell. That had happened in the old school as well. It was as if they could catch something from him or he was not clean. Others just saw him as an invalid when they found out, or a victim. He remembered one that had cried and then hardly spoken to him again.

She was looking at him, but did not seem to be concentrating, and her lips were moving gently, as though she were mumbling to herself.

'You're not eating anything,' he said. 'And you're talking to yourself. You're as bad as him,' he added, jogging his head back in the direction of the swearing man and attempting a charming smile.

'I'm not feeling very hungry,' she said.

'Cunt.'

Luke sighed.

'Cunt.'

The man had started to speed up.

'Cunt.'

'Shall we go?' she asked.

'Cunt.'

Luke nodded.

'Cunt.'

Chapter 29

Alone finally, except for the voices, Jenna stood under the flow of the shower in her bathroom and let the water jet over her naked body. For the first time, it was beginning to weigh on her, all that had happened. She felt it in her mind and her body. Weary, over-tired, excited, depressed. Contradictory states happily coexisted in her, getting in the way of the core self she believed to still be there. That was the thought that had started it all, in this same room. Is this all I am? she had asked herself, and it was as though the thought had opened a crack into which a demon had slipped.

Jenna's body was bruised, her stomach sore and swimming with whatever was resident inside her. There had hardly been a need for food or rest, as though all the exertion and its resulting tiredness had been stored in another place until now, when it had hit her like a dead weight.

No father. No mother. Nearly alone.

She turned up the hot water, twisting the tap until it would open no further. The stream of water she had been under for almost ten minutes became warmer. In turn, she revolved the cold tap in the opposite direction, the shower losing force but gaining temperature. When the cold tap was fully shut off, wound down hard, the water began to burn.

'Oh,' she said, the shock of the heat making her rear backwards.

At that back of her throat, something tickled as though it had come up her gullet and was about to expel itself. She opened her mouth, but nothing happened. Jenna put her face to the water and let it flow over her tongue and onto her tonsils. It burned the soft skin on the inside of her cheeks. The room was filling with steam which rapidly condensed as soon as it came into contact with the cool polished surfaces.

Jenna's insides, or what inhabited her insides, were swarming and she knew it was the heat. A pinprick sensation and then a throb in the corner of her eye. She snatched at it, trying to get a grip on the thread, but it slipped through her fingers. Pulling the showerhead from its holder, she soaked her skin in the scalding water, crying out in anguish as it seared the tender surface. Over her legs, between them, up her chest, over her breasts and then down her back, all the way to her behind, Jenna set her skin ablaze in the high temperature.

Her stomach rumbled as though she were hungry and then something heavy seemed to descend through her, flopping out from her vagina. Jenna felt it sort of pop and then droop against the inside of her left thigh. She dropped the shower attachment and grabbed at herself, taking hold of the viscera and gripping it as hard as she could. It was a meaty string perhaps nine inches in length – what she could see of it. With one hand on it, she held firmly and bent slightly to fit her other hand between her legs and take hold.

When she gave the first pull, the pain made the water seem like nothing. Jenna thought she was on the verge of uprooting some of her insides, the tendon pulling like elastic, until she realized it was working against her, snapping back in the opposite direction. Her skin felt as though it were separating into thin layers and that each would float away on the steam in the room, leaving her raw and wounded, able to see what was really going on beneath her surface.

Jenna tugged with greater force, heedless of what it might do to her. The thing she tried to hold and remove was stronger than her, more able to use her own body than she was herself. With a cry of frustrated anguish, she let it slither casually through her fingers and felt it work itself back up inside her.

How much longer did she have to hold it all in? When

would the release come?

She fell to her knees in the bath and cried with anger, gritting a single word through her teeth.

'Cunt.'

Chapter 30

'Cunt.'

He looked hungry, frail and tired to her, so Lucy had suggested eating. On the seafront, they stood in the breeze for a moment and then she saw the dark blue sign and the words FISH AND CHIPS and headed straight for it. She had stood at the counter and waited while he went to the toilet, worried that he had slipped out and away from her because he seemed to be taking so long.

'Cunt.'

When he did return, he looked even whiter than he had earlier. Lucy wondered if he'd been taking drugs in the toilet and then laughed at the thought, and then wondered again. He was too young, surely. Perhaps his confusion was from age and nerves. When she turned her attention to the uniform arrangement of greasy parcels and fish whose batter shone with oil, his wavering stopped and she almost followed him on the order of bread rolls and chips.

'Cunt.'

'Is he going to stop saying that, do you think?' he asked, glancing over his shoulder.

Lucy looked at the man sitting three tables down, on his own against a wall. In his late thirties and dressed in a grey suit that was either designer or from a charity shop, he was in all aspects neutral. Apart from the word cunt, which he spat at no one in particular every few minutes.

She tried to reassure Luke by smiling. 'He doesn't even look like a typical crazy,' she said. 'Whatever typical is.'

He picked up his glass, which had been filled to the brim when it was delivered to their table by an older woman with a faded red checked apron and flat shoes. Luke made a face as though it tasted bad.

'What's wrong?' she asked.

'This isn't Diet Coke. I asked them for Diet Coke.' He shook his head.

'I don't think she was listening when she took the order. We'd made her mad because we were taking so long.'

'I asked her for Diet Coke,' he repeated, as though he were personally affronted by what he had been given.

'She probably didn't mean . . .'

Her sentence was cut short as he stood and went back to the counter. He was out of earshot to Lucy, but she could see that he was having a hard time remaining calm and polite. He looked back at her once and Lucy was struck by how pretty he was, not yet masculine enough to be handsome. The woman said something to him and laughed. This was a coincidence, meeting him where I did in the way I did. She was here to appease her father, nothing more. Then what was so troubling? The same situation. An arcade. The same game. Even the same Lucozade bottle. The same boy?

'Sorry. I can't drink the other stuff,' he said, fitting his limbs back into the fixed plastic of the chair.

'What was she saying to you?' Lucy asked.

'Nothing. She was just saying sorry.' He played with the glass, turning it round on the surface of the table.

'Cunt.'

'You don't live here then?' she asked, assuming he did not as he had seemed uncertain where they might be able to eat.

'I live in London, with my mum.'

'I used to live in London,' she said.

'You don't any more then?'

'I live in America now.'

'Really?' he asked and seemed impressed.

'I'm here visiting my dad.'

'Your dad lives down here?' he asked.

'Cunt.'

'No, I'm just here for the day. He still lives in London, but he's away at the moment.'

He smiled and she watched his lips. 'I'm confused now.'

'Me too,' she said.

When the plate was placed in front of him, he dropped his head down and moved his shoulders closer to the table, almost like a dog. With long fingers, he picked up the heavy fork and pushed the chips around on his plate, selecting one, bringing it to the corner of his mouth and popping it in. Before he swallowed, he made a face, and then the food was gone. Setting the fork down, he used thumb and forefinger this time, licking his thumb afterwards and wiping half his face with the shiny harsh napkin. As he continued to eat, alternating between fingers and cutlery, his elbows stuck out and he looked gangling and boyish.

This isn't him. This is not Nathan Lucas. It is not possible, and if it were, this is not how he would be, Lucy was sure.

'You live with your mum?' she asked, confirming his earlier statement and feeling as though she were about to cross-examine him.

'Yeah, we used to live in Southend, but she sold our house there and we moved to East London.'

'When did she sell the house?'

'Just before Christmas,' he said, looking curious as to why she had asked him the question. 'I preferred it in Southend. It's where I grew up.'

'I miss being in London,' Lucy said. 'That was where I was raised.'

He did not answer. Lucy watched him eating, the skin of his jaws working. She remembered the hot afternoon in Leicester Square with Nathan.

'Do you mind me asking how old you are?' Lucy asked.
'Cunt.'
'Nearly sixteen,' he replied, not looking at her.

Or only fifteen, put another way, she thought. The age I was when I met Nathan. She had been starting to feel sorry she had become involved in this, letting her father convince her to come down to a small seaside town to look at a burned-out hotel he had dreamt about. It had been the one he was drawing, but why should she have to be handcuffed to her father's craziness? Had Dad known she would meet this boy? Feelings that had begun to calm themselves in the previous year and a half were rousing once again. Had she kept those anxieties so close to the surface that they could emerge like this, with only the smallest of coaxing? She did not want to think about it, to even be there.

'You're not eating anything,' he said. 'And you're talking to yourself. You're as bad as him,' he added, jogging his head back in the direction of the swearing man.

He gave a little smile, as though pleased at himself for making the connection and a small joke from it.

Lucy wanted to touch him and she was shocked and a bit embarrassed at herself, the lewd, intense thoughts she was allowing to traverse her mind.

'I'm not feeling very hungry,' she responded.

'Cunt.'

Luke sighed.

'Cunt.'

The man had started to speed up.

'Cunt.'

'Shall we go?' she asked.

'Cunt.'

Luke nodded.

'Cunt.'

Chapter 31

Kavanagh had only been in Los Angeles for three and a half hours, but he had already let memory get the upper hand.

This was a city he had so self-consciously avoided in the last four years, knowing instinctively what it would do to him the moment his foot touched the ground. A lot of his past was linked to this place.

He and Helen had travelled there, still students and in the early flush of their relationship. Making love on a floor in Westwood was something that Kavanagh had never forgotten. Helen and he were youthful and energetic enough that it certainly wasn't the most unusual place for them, or the best time, or the most fevered time. It stuck with Kavanagh because he knew that was the night they made Lucy.

Fifteen years later, Helen dead and Lucy a young woman, he found himself back there once again. In his hands, he held photographs he had taken of Lucy and Nancy Lloyd the afternoon they had gone to Disney. Lucy looked as though she were frying, all in black and the sun distorting her face, hiding whatever she might have been feeling, giant teacups spinning in the background.

Standing alone, holding one elbow while the other arm hung loosely, was Nancy Lloyd. The background was blurred around her as if speeding, sharpening the three-quarter profile. The white sleeveless top and straggling cut-off jeans should have made her look scruffy, but instead she appeared lean, healthy and inviting. Her blue-green eyes stared off and a breeze seemed to lift one side of her deep black hair, as though the world moved around her and she was there in its midst, beautiful and still. Kavanagh wanted to breach the photograph, step into it and take hold of her.

The picture had been taken the afternoon before they first slept together and looking at her brought back the expectation and desire he had felt. It was a delicate line between remembering the smooth skin of her legs, the taste of her mouth and her perfume and lapsing into something more desperate and pornographic. That or the other reaction he normally experienced.

Kavanagh sat on the edge of the bed, holding the picture and crying until he felt too sick to cry any more.

Chapter 32

They had been sitting on a bench looking out at the sea for ten minutes, Lucy feeling as though they were an old couple. He was fidgeting and it was both irritating and cute at the same time. Get up and get on the train out of here, she thought.

'I came here today because my mum's been lying to me,' Luke said.

He had spoken without prompting and she turned to get a better view of him.

'I thought she had always lived in Southend,' he continued. 'I went to stay with my Nanna down there, not my real Nanna, and she told me that Mum had lived in Plymouth before that. I didn't think it was true, but Nanna sent me there to the house where my mum lived. Nanna was right and Mum had been lying, but not just about that. I had a half-brother who died while Mum was pregnant with me. He drowned. She was too upset to stay in Plymouth, so she moved to Southend.'

'That must be really weird,' Lucy said.

'She used to live here as well, before she went to Plymouth, I suppose. I don't believe anything any more, nothing that she's told me. Everything was a lie. She made up things to cover up about Plymouth and she's doing the same about my dad, I know she is.'

He shivered and pulled his coat tighter.

'Why did you come here, to Dray?' Lucy asked.

Luke pointed at the hotel. 'She used to work there. I didn't even know it was shut down, but I wanted to come and see it.'

'Was it worth the trip?' Lucy asked.

'There was someone there who remembers my mum. Now there's someone else I have to talk to, back in London.'

'Your mum?' she asked.

'No. I'm not looking forward to seeing her. I'm frightened to go back,' he said, rubbing his palms together and biting his lips.

'You look cold,' she said. 'And earlier, you didn't look so well. Are you alright?'

'I'm alright. I'm not sick or anything.' He stopped for a moment. The sea chopped around, but the tide was too far out for it to be that noisy. 'I have insulin-dependent diabetes.'

'Where you have to have injections?' she asked.

'That's a part of it, but it's really keeping a balance between what I eat, what I do and what I take. Sometimes that's not easy and I have bad days.'

'You look so cold.' Lucy hated herself and the feeling, what it was about to make her say. 'Can I put my arm round you?' she asked.

He looked hesitant, but nodded.

Lucy held him against her chest and let her cheek rub the side of his head. As the blackened stump of the Palace hotel watched over them both, Lucy put her fingers in his hair making furrows before she caressed the smooth skin on the back of his neck.

The way she used to with Nathan Lucas.

Chapter 33

'You've seen Terry?' Tony Wood asked, looking at them through the small crack he had made in the doorway, his eyes widening with interest where previously they had been neutral. 'You'd better come on in.'

Luke and Lucy exchanged a quick glance, both equally apprehensive. Luke wanted to reach out and take her hand and feel some of its warmth. He stopped the thought and crossed the threshold.

'I suppose I should ask you how he is,' Tony Wood said over his shoulder, seeming as though he wanted to sound as uninterested as possible.

'He's alright,' Luke said.

All that came back was a snort and, Luke thought, possibly the whisper of the word cunt.

'Let's go into the changing rooms, there's more room in there,' Tony said.

The three of them sat on a table-like bench in the middle of what would once have been the ladies' changing rooms. It did not look much different from the boys' changing rooms at other pools Luke had been to. Lucy sat cross-legged on the low bench as though about to start meditating and Luke sat awkwardly beside her, wanting to stay as close to her as possible. Spread out on the bench were various belongings of Tony Wood's – a slim pack of cigars whose packaging looked like wood, a dainty lighter in rolled gold that seemed out of place, a sports bag half-opened and a toolbox. Tony pulled an ashtray across the surface of the bench and opened his pack of cigars.

'Is this your lady friend?' he asked.

Luke frowned in embarrassment but tried to smile.

'Pleased to meet you. I'm Tony Wood,' he said, reaching out his hand to shake Lucy's.

The bench was hard beneath him and Luke's posture was not comfortable. The only light in the room was afforded by two makeshift lamps on stands, obviously brought in for the purpose.

'I've got a bed in one of the old offices and a fan heater,' Tony said, obviously catching Luke's stare around the stark changing room with its tiles on the floor and walls, long empty lockers, some with doors closed, some open, some with no doors at all.

'You stay here? It must get cold,' Lucy said.

'I manage. What did Terry have to say for himself?' Tony asked.

'He showed me round the hotel.'

'You're privileged. He wouldn't even let me in last time I went down to see him, but that was eight years ago, nearly.'

Luke laid the postcard and the two photographs on the bench as though playing patience. He used a phrase of Terry Wood's, thinking it would have more of an effect on his brother.

'I'm Bella's boy,' he said.

'I know who you are, don't worry,' Tony said, completely unfazed.

Luke, by contrast, was slightly thrown. 'Why didn't you say so when I met you the first time?' he asked.

'Because it didn't matter.'

Luke did not understand the answer. 'Terry said that the both of you worked at the hotel, for the people who ran it, until it burned down,' he said.

'Dray's a long way to go just to hear that. Not much of a talker, our Terry. What's the old place like? I haven't been inside it for thirteen years.'

'Pretty dead. It's all boarded up,' Luke said.

'They left the building to stand, after the fire. It was more or less empty by then anyhow. Should have boarded up the whole fucking town,' Tony said.

'I thought my mum had lived in Southend all her life. I found out that wasn't true and that she had a house in

Plymouth too. There was another son, Luke Smith as well, that lived there. I was confused and then when I found those,' Luke said, pointing at the pictures, 'I knew there was more. That was how I ended up in Dray. Terry told me that you were good friends with my mum when she worked there.' Luke paused. 'I want you to tell me what's going on. How come there's a house locked up in Plymouth, that my mum worked at that hotel, that you're here so close to her now? I want to know if you know my dad.'

Tony drew breath. 'That's a bit of a list, son. Where should I start?' he asked, being jovial and opening the pack of cigars. 'We used to have all this old flannel about how we worked at the hotel, porters, odd job–men and all that? Handy with a screwdriver.' He laughed to himself.

Lucy shuffled on the bench.

'We didn't work for the hotel,' he went on. 'We worked for the Cameron family. That was different. Terry and me had a bit of a reputation around the town. You know what they used to call us? The Dray Twins.' He laughed. 'We knew who was who. If there was something or someone that needed sorting, we did it. Nothing heavy. We were just kids when we started out, only in our twenties me and Terry, but we fancied ourselves a bit. When we got wind that someone was looking to build a hotel on the end of the front, we knew he'd need a bit of help and we were ready to go to him and offer it. We didn't need to. He wasn't silly and he came to us. We were what he needed.'

'What do you mean?' Luke asked.

'People in Dray were backwards about things. They were frightened of change, didn't know what was going to happen if some old Scots loon came along and built a castle for himself in their little town. They probably thought he was going to make himself king. Some people needed per-suading.'

Luke thought about the way Tony Wood had been that first afternoon they'd met and how dangerous he'd seemed; the perfect comfort for certain situations in fact. He supposed it was just a case of practice. The more potentially violent situations you were in, the more you got used to it.

'Handy with a screwdriver.'

It was Lucy.

Both Luke and Tony looked at her.

'What do you mean by that?' Lucy asked quietly.

'It was a nothing really. There were all sorts of things we could have carried – razors or coshes – but we used to like a screwdriver. A driver has a bit more weight to it. You can do more damage that way.'

Luke heard the sound of Lucy swallowing.

'But you couldn't cut someone with one of those,' she said.

Luke looked at her, puzzled.

'That's not a problem. Get one with a diamond-shaped shaft so you've got an edge to sharpen. You can slice or dig that way,' Tony said.

'Do you still have yours?' Lucy asked.

With only a small move of his torso, he leaned down and flicked the catch on the blue metal toolbox, lifted the lid and laid a screwdriver on the surface of the bench. Lucy reached out for it and Luke thought she was going to cry.

'Be careful. It's still sharp,' Tony said.

Lucy was turning the screwdriver over in her hand by its handle. She seemed to be mumbling something.

'Does your brother still have his one?' Lucy asked.

'Terry lost his. That was about the time of the fire. I can still remember the last bloke I threatened with it. And the last one I put a stripe on with it. Now I keep it partly for old times' sake and partly because you never know when you might need it.' He sounded wistful.

'So why don't you and your brother talk to each other then?' Luke asked.

'After the fire, we had nowhere to go in Dray and nowhere we would go to together, but we were too important to the Cameron family. Old Cameron said to the both of us that we couldn't let our troubles stand in the way of our duties to the Trust. He was right. We owed them a lot. He'd not been in the hotel business since the war ended and he got more involved in the main business. The Palace was just a stopping-off point for them. They'd always bought plenty of property, but right after the fire they started to buy up even more. Me and Terry were starting to clean up our act. Old Cameron's operation was big enough that we could keep out of each other's way, Terry and me.'

It became apparent to Luke that Tony Wood was not going to enter into details about the rift with his brother.

'Terry said you knew my mum better than he did.'

'I took that photograph of her,' he said, nodding down at it and puffing his cigar. The smell was sweet, cloying but familiar. 'It was taken in the year of the fire. That car was only just imported from America and it was one of the first they'd made like it. Terry and me used to argue about who should get to drive it. We even had rows over who should clean the bastard thing. That day, I had it on the front giving it a polish-over and this woman comes up and asks me if I can take her picture with the car, hands me her camera before I've even got a chance to say yes or no. That was Bella and that was the first time I met her. 1955.'

Luke sat and felt thoughts assembling themselves without his conscious intervention. Something was wrong, he knew intuitively. 'That can't be right.' The numbers jumped about in his head. 'Mum would have been . . .' He calculated, feeling his forehead knit the figures together. '. . . only twelve when the hotel caught fire.'

Tony shook his head and took a short puff on the cigar. 'Son, as far as I knew she was nearly thirty. She might have lied about her age, but I think I'd have noticed if she was twelve, don't you?'

He gave a throaty laugh that had an implication Luke did not like.

'She was born in 1943. She'll be sixty in a couple of years. I should know, she goes on about it all the time,' Luke said.

'What about this then?' Tony asked leaning towards him and lowering his voice. 'Suppose she lied to you about her age? Thought of that?' There was no smugness in his tone.

'Why would she do that?' Luke asked.

Tony held his arms out expansively. 'You're asking me?' he said, shrugging.

'I thought you were good friends with her?' Luke asked.

'She was funny and I liked her. Bella needed work and I found her something casual at the Palace. We used to go out sometimes, but she never wanted to talk much about herself or about me. We just enjoyed ourselves.'

'But that means she would be seventy-four now. Sixty when I was born? What about this picture? Did you take that as well?' Luke asked

'No.'

'It's her other son, the one that died,' Luke said.

Tony nodded. 'Maybe she brought him down there for a day out, show him where she used to live.'

'The hotel's not burned in that picture.'

It was Lucy.

'What do you mean?' Tony asked.

'Luke said his brother would have been thirty now. If that was him, the hotel would have been burned by then. It looks fine.'

Tony Wood picked up the photograph and held it near his face, looking at it for a moment and then looking at Luke.

'Maybe it's your dad when he was a boy. There's a resemblance. Depends how old this picture is.'

Luke took the photograph from Tony and studied it, staring into the scowling face. The further he delved into his mother's past, the less sense it made.

'Where did she go after the fire?' Luke asked.

'Bella carried on living in a house in Dray until she moved to the house in Plymouth,' Tony said.

Luke rubbed his face and sighed. He felt Lucy's hand come to rest on his knee and he dropped one of his hands onto hers for a moment. He was about to speak when something made him pause. Under the aroma of the cigar was the scent of Tony Wood, the combination of him and his aftershave.

'You've been to our house, haven't you?' he said to Tony.

Tony nodded, tapping white ash from the cigar into the over-sized cut-glass ashtray, its once crystalline appearance now aged into an opaque yellow.

'I've been to all your mum's houses, son. I go visit them regular, the one in Plymouth and now in Southend.'

'Is that what the Cameron Trust pays you to do?' Lucy asked.

'Cameron Trust, Gordius, call it what you want. Right now, they've got me looking after this place as well. You think they'd tell me why? Course they don't. Terry keeps an eye on Dray, but that's all as far as I know.'

'Why?' was Luke's only question.

Tony Wood smiled.

'What?' Luke asked.

'When we first met Cameron and he told us about the work he needed doing, people that needed seeing to, we didn't have a problem with that. Once he had the hotel built, he said, there would be other things we could do for him. If we performed well, helping him by smoothing the way in Dray, there could be a lifetime of work in it. We were still in our late-twenties, but even then we were savvy enough to know we couldn't go on being hard lads all our lives. There was only one thing we would need to do in return for that, he told us.'

'What?' Luke asked.

'Never use the word why. He said we could give him advice, tell him what we thought, but when he asked us to do something for him, we were to do it. Come on, let me show you something.'

Tony Wood led them from the old changing room and through the empty troughs that would once have been foot baths. Their way was lit only by the faint glow of the emergency lights that were fixed at wide intervals along each

232

wall, modern and out of place against the cream and green of the tiles.

The area with the large swimming pool was much darker, hardly any lights in evidence, and it made Luke dizzy, fearful he could mistakenly wander over the edge and down a sheer ten-foot drop to the bottom of the deep end. The silence was troubling, but so was the click of their heels and the slightly laboured breathing of Tony Wood. No sound seemed to fit the hollow darkness. Luke felt Lucy take his hand and he breathed out, glad that she was there.

'Hold on there,' Tony said, so loudly Luke tightened his grip on Lucy's hand.

They stood at the shallow end of the pool, a gentle slope that eased away into unknown darkness.

'Are you alright?' she asked Luke.

'I think so. I'm scared, Lucy.'

'I know. So am I,' she replied, stroking the skin on the back of his neck and making him tingle.

The sudden light from the pool itself made Luke shut his eyes tightly. It was like switching on the bathroom light when he got up in the middle of the night.

After a few moments, his eyes became used to the glare from the lights that would have previously lit water. Now they flooded the empty pool, illuminating the shape at its far end, in the deep end. Luke gave Lucy a questioning stare.

It was the car from the photograph.

'That's what they've got me here looking after. They don't give a fuck about the building,' Tony said.

'How long has it been here?' Luke whispered.

'It got here not long before you did. It's been out once since I was here. They came and took it away, a whole group of them. The amount of time I've spent babysitting it and then when the Trust people arrive, I'm not allowed near it all of a sudden. Some things don't change. This is my last week here. It's due to be shipped to America at the end of the week. Can you believe that? Putting a car on a plane and flying it to another country, back to where it came from.'

'Why?' Luke asked.

Tony Wood rested his hand on Luke's shoulder. 'I don't use that word, remember. I think there's someone you need to go and talk to,' he said.

He was right.

'Go talk to your mum, Luke,' Tony said.

Chapter 34

Kavanagh had brought three of his old business suits with him, throwing them into his case without paying too much attention to them. Now he had laid them out in a line on the bed and was fascinated by them. It was as though the limp material were haunted by the ghost of his former life and he found himself remembering specific meetings he had attended in the double-breasted pinstripe, the dark blue suit he wore for formal presentations to new clients. Like echoes down a corridor, voices rattled in his head. All three outfits look tired and were patently out of fashion, although that might pass in America as loveable English eccentricity. It had been so long since he had donned a suit and he was uncomfortable at the prospect.

He wondered where Lucy was, if she was safe.

Kavanagh chose the double-breasted, the one that had always made him feel his most bullish, with its broad German tailoring. The trousers needed an extra pull together and a drawing in of breath to fasten, but they did not feel too bad. He put the brass tongues into the collars of his shirt and folded back the double cuffs, threading the thick gold bar of a pair of cufflinks through each. It took three goes for him to be happy with his tie, finding the balance of knot thickness and tie length.

'You look so old,' he said to the mirror.

His early evening appointment was half an hour away and he was feeling nervous. In that previous life, when he spent more time in a suit than out of one, meetings had been part of the everyday. He could pack his briefcase without thinking, filling it with everything he needed – his folder, pen, calculator, diary and his business cards. This was not going to be that sort of meeting and he needed only one thing, which was on the bedside.

The screwdriver.

Kavanagh was going to the heart of Gordius and he intended to stop it beating.

Reception called to tell him his car was waiting. He swallowed, left the room and rode the elevator in a sweat.

The discreet grey limousine was parked at the front of the hotel. Kavanagh stopped and stared halfway down the red carpet when he saw it. His instinct was to turn back, but as the door swung open, he felt himself drawn towards the gloom of the space, finding it oddly welcoming. Before he stepped in, he glanced back over his shoulder and looked up at the sky, as though charging himself up with the fading sunlight before disappearing into darkness.

A screen separated him from the driver, but Kavanagh was unsurprised by that. The seats were well-kept black leather, absorbing the sweat of his palms. The engine was silent and the ride smooth, bumps absorbed by the soft suspension. The tinted version of Los Angeles rolled past the window and Kavanagh studied his reflection in the glass screen in front of him. After a while, even the chill of the car could not alleviate the uncomfortable heat that prickled through him, the wool of his trousers scratching at the moist flesh of his legs, the collar of the shirt too tight and the cufflinks stopping the blood flowing in his arms. Kavanagh was ready to throw the door open and fling himself from the moving car when it came to a gentle halt.

Kavanagh gazed through the glass and then opened the door to step out.

It was hotter still and he squinted into the brightness. The car pulled away, revealing another parked in front of the building. Kavanagh walked around it. The word Plymouth was emblazoned along the rim of the bonnet and on its apex, a ship. It was the same car he had seen that night in Greenwich.

He did not know Los Angeles well, despite all that had happened there. He took a moment and then realized that he was on what had been Wilshire Boulevard, where the original offices of Jack Burns's company had stood. Many of its buildings had been lost in the quake and the new architecture that replaced it was less ambitious, as though the city were paying lip service to the power of its foundations. The landscape had changed far too much for him to know if he were in the exact spot of the Trellis headquarters, but Kavanagh guessed he would be. It seemed correct.

In front of him was a building of perhaps nine or ten stories, the stonework similar to that of the building he had drawn over and over, the Palace Hotel. There was no name on the building, nothing to indicate its purpose or function, other than a copper knot that loomed over the awning, the size of Big Ben's clock face. He felt into the breast pocket of his jacket, looking for the shaft of four-sided steel, needing some comfort.

The doors opened to reveal a lobby and then more doors before he was in the reception area. The airy grandeur of the old Trellis building was missing from this more modest entrance, which was more like a small mouth that would open out into something larger beyond. The walls were cool grey stone and the air-conditioning better than it had been in the car, for which Kavanagh was grateful. A man wearing a headset looked up at him from the reception desk, another knot sitting on the wall behind him.

'I'm Michael Kavanagh,' he said.

The man, who reminded Kavanagh of an airline steward in his white shirt and dark tie, looked down at the table and then pressed a button. Behind Kavanagh, a lift door opened.

'You can take that one,' the man said.

'Which floor?' Kavanagh asked, wondering if he were going to be issued with a badge.

'It only goes to one.'

The lift was similar to the one Kavanagh had rode each day when he was at Pendulum in London. How had he gone from there to here, taking such a large leap of the imagination in such a short space of time? he wondered, as he felt himself lifted. The doors parted and admitted him directly into a dim room, a single desk at its end concealed in shadow.

Kavanagh paced towards it evenly, trying to set a rhythm that would relax him. Almost four years ago he had made a similar journey across the boardroom of Trellis to meet with Arnold Long.

A light flicked on, illuminating the desk.

'Hello, Michael.'

Alexander Cameron was sitting behind the table.

'Hello,' Kavanagh replied.

'Have a seat, do,' the old man said, his eyes scanning Kavanagh. 'You were expecting me, it seems. I am not sensing much in the way of surprise. I'm almost disappointed.'

'If anyone were to be at the heart of all this, I would have expected it to be you, Alexander. And the car, I remembered it from our last encounter.'

'The car?' Cameron asked.

'The Plymouth you were in last time we met in Greenwich.'

'It's here?' Cameron wore a look of mild consternation that subsided into resignation. 'So you think I am at the heart of it all? I saw Wadlow Grace recently and he told me he could never understand if I was a good or a bad man,' Cameron said.

'What did you tell him?' Kavanagh asked.

'Nothing. I never got the chance to answer before Mr Grace told me. He thinks it likely that I am both. You think that also. And so do I.'

Cameron was wearing the same type of clothes Kavanagh had seen him in each time they had met – washed out browns and greys, as though he were fading away. The first time had been in a similar context, a room and a table, truths and myths passing across it from the old man to Kavanagh.

Kavanagh fished with difficulty into his tight shirt collar, and pulled the chain out and lifted it over his head. He unthreaded the knots and laid them both out on the surface of the desk.

'Sometimes it's hard to comprehend that it is all about these,' he said. 'My wife died because of them, Nancy is gone. Your family.'

'I know, Michael,' Cameron said, touching his hand.

'Lucy has the third knot, doesn't she?' Kavanagh asked. 'It's inside her head the same way it was with Nancy. There must be a way of reaching it, not like with Nancy.'

'I hope so.'

'But you don't know,' Kavanagh said.

'No, Michael, I don't.'

'Are you behind this? Gordius – the Movement and the Corporation?'

'When control of the Trust began to slip away from my father and me, I believed there were only two options. I could give it up or I could try and fight it. Then a third way, a new beginning, presented itself, a way to maintain as much control as I could. I came to think of that as a kind of passive resistance through active compliance.' He smiled. 'Even though the merger of Pendulum and Trellis, the fuse that would have led to the Trust becoming Gordius, was not going to happen, Nathan Lucas knew it would spark the Gordian Movement along with the change in the Trust. These were plans he had laid since before you or I even existed, Michael. I thought about this for a long time until the third way became clearer in my mind.'

'What did you decide to do?' Kavanagh asked.

'To stay at its heart and in its mind, beating and thinking away, unseen. I used the time I had as well as I could, making sure that I had enough control and contact. The Trust was, as you know, far bigger than any single person, too big even for Nathan Lucas. The networks that traverse it are almost infinite in the way they feed back and forth into each other,' Cameron said, glancing briefly into the lamp's bulb.

'As intricate as the knot itself,' Kavanagh murmured, looking at them on the table.

'Yes. I have intimated myself into that network, the almost invisible lines that join Gordius and the Gordian Movement, made myself an important part of it. There are people in the Gordius Corporation who are working on my behalf without even knowing it. Whatever it may have turned into, Gordius still came from the Cameron Trust, and that came from the Camerons, which, now, is just me. I have given it a heart and a brain.'

'You're the heart of Gordius?' Kavanagh asked.

Cameron smiled and shook his head. 'I am the thought process, the brain. We knew we needed a heart for it, one we could place right in the centre of the organization, knowing it would be willing to stop when the time was right. That was when my father and I began casting around for the right person.'

'That long ago?'

'We came to the States in the late Fifties because we felt someone had presented themselves. That was Jack Burns Junior. He was still in the middle of a seemingly permanent education, but we made contact and then we waited almost forty years. Then, as you know, he was heading up Trellis and he would have done the same with Gordius, whatever you were being told at the time.'

'How many people knew?' Kavanagh asked.

'At that time, only Jack Burns, my father and I.'

'And now?'

'And now, only you, Jack Burns and I. Jack Burns is the man in control of Gordius and the Gordian Movement He is its heart and he belongs to us. In the Movement and in the Corporation, he is listened to. The Gordian Movement has lost an important symbol. Its blind figure-head is no more. But Jack is the one giving direction, controlling the finances. By the end of tomorrow, he will be gone and the slide will begin, the commencement of financial problems that will lead to one of the most spectacular collapses seen. The Movement and the Corporation will finally be publicly united, in downfall.'

'And what about these?' Kavanagh asked, sliding the knots about on the surface of the desk.

'That is where you come into this, Michael. You and Lucy. None of this happens by accident. Even if it appears to, that is just accident by design. You have done well for us so far and I trust you to do the same again.'

'Done well for you so far?' Kavanagh asked, disbelief in his voice. 'Sixteen thousand people died here in that earthquake, people who had nothing to do with me – gone. And the people I knew directly, the lives lost there. I don't think that is doing anyone well.'

'You carry two thirds of eternity round your neck. That is a heavy weight and I don't believe it was meant for you, not forever. You have to take the weight of all three knots, feel it, and then unburden yourself, let them go. Then there will be a new beginning.'

'How will it end, Alexander?'

'I'm afraid I can't see beyond this point, where we are now,' Cameron replied.

'You've had foresight through all of this, why not now?' Kavanagh demanded.

Cameron reached out and Kavanagh thought he was going to touch him. Instead, he reached into Kavanagh's jacket and retrieved the screwdriver, laying it out on the surface of the table.

'Because this is the point where it ends for me,' Cameron said.

Kavanagh looked down at the long blade of the screwdriver, one side sharpened and ready.

Cameron picked up the two knots and cradled them. 'Nathan Lucas made one child for each knot, myself and my two sisters, Camille and Alexandra. Reunite the family, Mr Kavanagh. Put all three of them back on The Book, where they belong, and ensure it gets into the right hands.' He paused. 'A new beginning.' He handed the knots back to Kavanagh. 'Put those on the chain and back round your neck, where they belong for now.'

When he had done so, Cameron stood and handed Kavanagh the screwdriver. He removed his jacket and pulled open the buttons of his shirt, revealing a wrinkled torso with long wisps of grey hair.

'Begin the end, Mr Kavanagh,' he said, coming round the table to offer himself.

Chapter 35

They looked once more, going through every room in the house.

'Your mum's room seems sort of old-fashioned,' Lucy said.

'Does it?' Luke hadn't seen enough women's bedrooms to know.

'Of course it is. Look at these,' she said, going to the clothes rail and flicking quickly through the dresses on it. She stopped suddenly.

'What is it?' he asked.

Lucy had pulled out the dress his mother always wore whenever there was a celebration of his birthday. The sight of it made him feel nervous.

'Hmm,' Lucy mumbled, hardly opening her mouth.

'What?' he asked, not hearing.

She suddenly mumbled several sentences, none of which he could hear properly.

'Lucy?'

'Do you believe in ghosts?' she asked him.

'I suppose so,' he replied.

'Mum and me used to think our house was haunted. That there was the ghost of a lady that used to live there. Mum used to see her and I started to as well, when I was little. After Mum died, I still used to see her. She wore a dress like this.'

'So you believe in ghosts?' he asked her.

'I believe I saw things, but I don't know if I believe in ghosts. After my mum died, things got worse, for a long time.'

Luke looked at the dress where Lucy had hung it at the front of the rack. Off to one side, in the full-length mirror, Luke's reflection listened in on them.

'Shall we go downstairs?' Luke asked, feeling spooked in his own house.

'How did your mum die? Is it alright to ask?' Luke said.

They were in the kitchen and the kettle was hissing comfortingly in the background.

Lucy reached over and touched his hand. Luke assumed it meant it was okay to ask. He liked the feel of it and was disappointed when she moved it away again.

'My mum was murdered in our house, almost seven years ago. It happened in the afternoon and I found her body when I got back from school. She had a workshop in the attic where she made jewellery and that was where I found her. Her body had been cut up, badly. They thought it might have been a ritual killing, the way she had been slit open.'

'And you found her,' Luke repeated to himself, trying to imagine it. 'Did they catch the killer?'

She shook her head quickly.

'That just must be so horrible,' Luke said.

The kettle clicked and it made him jump.

'It was, but then it got even worse. Just before the third anniversary of Mum dying, my dad was given the chance to do a deal that would have made him so much money he could have retired. I never really understood what he did. All that finance stuff was just boring to me. Dad took Mum's death a lot harder than he would let on. I was seeing a counsellor, being looked after, but he needed some help too, except he was too stubborn to ask for it. When this deal came along, it really was too good to be true. I should have seen that at the time. We all should have.'

Luke was going to offer to make tea, but he wanted to listen to her, drawn in by the gentleness of her tone and troubled by the hurt she had suffered. He wanted to do something, as though he could help in some way, even though that seemed stupid.

'What happened?' Luke asked.

'There was a man that worked for my dad and he went mad, became unhinged, call it whatever. He killed his father, and his mother, and two other people that worked for Dad's company and then I think he set the fire that burned the building down. Dad was going backwards and forwards to America while this was going on. He'd met another woman while he was in America doing the deal. It was funny because I'd met this boy called Nathan, so we were both starting to put things into place. I even thought I might get better. It didn't work out like that.'

'Why?'

'After he was done over here, this man who was killing people went out to America after my dad. Dad went missing and I went spare. I ended up in America with my boyfriend, worried about where Dad was. We were going to stay with Nancy, the woman Dad had met.'

Lucy paused and gave a look as though she were trying to focus on something in the distance.

'Do you remember the earthquake in Los Angeles in 1997?'

Luke nodded.

'Nathan and Nancy were killed in that. Well, like a lot of people that night, they just disappeared.'

'What about your dad?'

'I remember the earthquake, how it felt under my feet and even in my bones, but I don't remember where it happened. Nancy had gone out and the last thing I remember was Nathan leaving, to go to the shops,' Lucy said, laughing as though it were ironic, 'and then a knock at the door. Dad was okay. Our friend, he's our friend now, sort of rescued him.'

'God,' was the best Luke could manage.

'You're supposed to offer me a cup of tea about now,' Lucy said. 'Where do you think your mum is?'

'I don't care,' Luke said, shaking his head bitterly.

'You don't mean that,' she said, touching his arm again.

They sat in silence, her touch turning to a slight caress. Luke tried not to shiver, but it was hard to control his nerves. He looked down at her hand, wondering what was going through her mind, if it was the same as he was thinking. To test it would involve crossing a boundary and if he were wrong, the situation would get awkward. He was still thinking about what to do when her hand moved to his hair and smoothed through it.

Once they were upstairs, perched on the edge of the narrow bed in his room, the earlier confidence and excitement Luke felt had dissipated and now he felt awkward.

'Don't worry,' she said, as though she could read his thoughts.

Gently and slowly she leaned forwards and brought her mouth into contact with his. She tasted a bit like metal, but there was sweet undertow to it. He felt the tension in his face muscles begin to slacken and he went with the direction of the kiss.

When she knelt on the bed and he craned up to look at her, the light in his eyes, he saw how absorbed she was, completely caught in something, possibly not even what they were doing. As she unbuttoned his shirt, he wanted to say something, make sure everything was alright, but he was too afraid to break her concentration.

This was new to him, whatever had happened before. The motions and the actions were similar, but they were fused with something else – a mutuality. Luke tried to focus on what he was feeling, not wanting to think too much about it.

She stroked his bare chest and kissed it, letting her tongue make wet trails on it. When her hand rubbed over his stomach, he shivered with the familiarity of it, lighting so close to the concentrated area of his desire. He watched her hands as they opened his trousers and then removed them, working them off his feet and taking his socks with them.

'Can I?' he asked quietly, touching the buttons on her blouse.

'Of course you can. After I get you out of these,' she said, hooking her thumbs into his boxers and rendering him naked in one smooth tug.

He tried not to be shy as he removed her blouse and

246

fumbled with the clip on her bra. His eyes stung and he wondered what was wrong with him. As he cautiously removed her underwear, he realised tears were running over his cheeks. Silent tears, the sob that might have helped muffled by anger and confusion.

'Sorry,' he said.

'What's wrong?' she asked, pulling him to her chest and soothing his hair with a light hand.

'Nothing. I'll be alright.'

For a few minutes he let his body rock with only the minimum of tears, afraid that if he really did start crying there might not be a way to stop. Luke could feel her heart and her breathing. As he enclosed himself in the warmth of her body, he began to feel safe, desire seeming to fade. He lifted his head from her chest and looked at her. She wiped one corner of his eye with a thumb and smiled.

'Luke, this is my fault . . .'

'Shush. It's okay. It's okay.'

'We don't have to. We can sleep, rest,' she said.

'No. I don't want to.'

Luke ran his hand along the side of her body and let it sweep across her groin, coming casually to rest in her lap. He raised himself up and planted a bold kiss on her mouth.

When he mounted her, he felt inept and embarrassed to be in such close quarters to her, as though it would give away who he really was, a gauche fifteen-year-old, out of his depth entirely.

Lucy stroked his hair again and caressed his back, making it tingle. With care, she slipped her hand between their bodies and let it roam into the area where Luke was longing for them to be joined. With adroit fingers, he felt her guiding him. He gave a gasp that was a mix of surprise, satisfaction and pure lust as he felt the sudden soft and wet warmth of her. His eyes were bulging wide, he could tell, but it no longer worried him. We don't have to, she had said. And, because of that, he had wanted to.

'That feels so nice,' she whispered, so close to his ear the heat of her breath made him shudder.

Luke felt enveloped by the warm sensation in his groin and the physical proximity to her. Slowly and cautiously, he started to move himself back and forth, his hardness a painful strain but one that promised a release.

At the end, it was hard to be gentle and he gave himself up to the frantic jerking of his body, burying his face into her shoulder and nuzzling it hard with his forehead. It built in him like a shudder that was about to rip his whole body open and he knew she could sense it too, encouraging him with her own body, gripping his behind with her hands and pushing him into her. His breathing was far beyond his control and as he gritted his teeth and made ready, she gave the tiniest of whimpers, the noise enough to send him over the edge he had brought himself to and had teetered on painfully for the previous few minutes.

The feeling shocked him, stronger than anything he had experienced on his own – or when he had been made to. Luke wanted to shout, laugh, cry, be gentle, be violent, a whole mixture of feelings and desires.

He lay on top of her for what felt like a long time, trying to get his breath back and listening to the soothing words she said, the feel of her hands over him, intimate but changed by what they had done.

'We shouldn't have. I shouldn't have,' he said, raising his eyes and looking into hers.

'We can't both go on apologizing to each other,' she said.

He squinted and shook his head.

'Are you alright?' she asked him.

'I need to have an injection and to eat.' He stopped, obviously looking embarrassed. 'It says that it can make you go a bit hypo. Doing it,' he said.

She smiled at him. 'You're going to run off and hide now, like you've done every time.'

'I don't do that.'

'You do,' she said.

'You can do it for me if you want. Mum usually does.'

She did not answer.

'You're frightened now, aren't you?' he asked her,

mocking her gently with his tone.

'No. You should be the one who's scared. I wouldn't let you near me if it was the other way round.'

Luke talked her through it, explaining about air, about the different types of insulin, about his blood glucose levels. He was surprised at how much he knew. He had not really had to explain it to anyone before.

They were both still naked as he lay back on the bed with his legs apart to make a space for her to lean over and gingerly point the needle at his stomach. Eventually he pinched a lump of belly between his fingers and put his other hand on hers, driving it down against the resistance she put up.

With both their hands on the hypodermic, his thumb on top of hers on the plunger, Luke pressed down and closed his eyes.

The Final Knot

And after the earthquake a fire;
But the Lord was not in the fire;
And after the fire a still small voice.
I Kings 19:12

Chapter 36

Ryan Summer sat by his grandfather's bed and waited for the old man to die.

All the air in the room had been cooked, the curtains blocking out any fresh light and making the one shaft of sunlight struggling through seem as old and yellow as everything else in the room. Father's bed – Ryan always referred to his grandfather by the name Father – was an old metal-frame, one with aching, extended springs that had long ago given up any resistance. Hanging on the side of the bedstead was a rosary, white feathers stuck through each decade.

Behind him, other members of Ryan's family shuffled and whispered and he was conscious of their eyes on him as he sat on the stiff high-backed chair that had been placed there by his mother almost four weeks ago, when Father had taken to his bed and made ready for the cancer to wash him away. That was when Ryan and his mother knew they had to move into the old man's house – not so much a house as two rooms formed by uneven clapboards. They wanted to wait for the end and ease him into another beginning. Father had refused to move to Ryan's and his mother's home.

There had been so much waiting over the previous month as a stillness gradually crept over the house, the place dying along with him. The bedroom and the kitchenette were separated by a small door, although both sides of the threshold were equally gloomy. Ryan could remember all the furniture from when he first started visiting, about the same time as he first began having memories. Out back, in the unkempt yard, Father had shown him how to catch a ball efficiently enough to stop him being laughed at in school. Sitting on the back step, Ryan pressed in tight to Father who had a big arm round him, they would make knots with a length of rope, the weave gradually getting warmer in their hands. He also showed Ryan how to baste a bluefish in maple syrup and then broil it until the whole kitchen filled with the sweet, peppery fragrance. Father let Ryan try beer and taste whisky, and puff on one of the tightly rolled cigarettes he kept in the breast pocket of his checked shirt.

Father had been a big man, his chest like a pigeon's, shoulders you could stand on and even as he got older, only a bit of a belly. Now the old man was on his back and the great, huge chest was hardly moving. Ryan wondered if such a chest would take more air to inflate than a normal one, more breath than even Father had. Ryan had always been able to make Father's whole body shake with laughter, goofing around, making up silly words or just acting up in general. My little clown, my heyoka, Father called him.

Ryan's aunt Janice and his mother were exchanging hushed words. Two of his older cousins had been standing near the door for over ten minutes, afraid to get too near the bed, yet Ryan could feel their jealousy, that he was the one chosen for the vigil. His aunt said something, the precise words unclear but their tone perfectly evident. They did not feel wanted here. The cousins left. Ryan's mother came to his side and stroked the back of his head, smoothing the hair all the way down to the collar of his shirt. He was afraid even to glance away from Father in case that was the moment he chose to move on. His mother rested a hand on Ryan's shoulder for a few moments and then withdrew.

Father's face was intense, the very top of his nose, right at the join of his eyes, a mass of stress wrinkles that spread out in a circle across his face, like the flat surface of a pond disturbed by a stone. He was the only full Native American in the family, his own wife only a quarter so. The line had diluted itself in Ryan to the point where he was sometimes asked where he was from. Ryan's skin was not as dark as

Father's, his lips not as pursed and his nose not as proud. They shared cheekbones and a roundness of face, as though Father had been a blueprint, a mould from which successive castings had resulted in Ryan. Where Father could appear stern or stolid, Ryan was slightly cheeky and more pretty. It seemed so long since Ryan had seen Father's eyes open that he was beginning to forget their serene darkness, cool and deep in the surface of his face.

The breathing had been winding down for most of the last two days. Just when Ryan would think it could get no slower, that the end was almost there, then the rhythm changed. The worst had been the awful wheezing, the rattle, like a car begging to start. Don't let it be like this, Ryan had prayed. Now, the pattern was unnervingly slow, as though it had nowhere else to go.

Aunt Janice and his mother were arguing, and for the first time in hours, Ryan turned and shot the two women a glance, surprised at how stiff his body felt and how angry they had made him. Both women looked guilty but glared at each other just the same. A couple more sentences passed between them and, their business obviously unfinished, they left the room.

'Sorry about that,' Ryan whispered.

On the nightstand was a squat white beaker made of plastic. It had two handles on either side and a spout to drink from. When offered it, Father had sucked on it like a baby, his lips dry and wrinkled.

There was a gurgle, phlegm breaking loose in the back of Father's throat, and Ryan sat up, leaning forward to survey the old man. The breath came stronger, as though trying to dislodge whatever was blocking it. With growing power, as though he were inflating himself, Father's breath speeded up. The familiar rattle came back. Ryan stood, ready to call Mother, until he thought he saw a flicker in the leathery eyelids. He waited in case it happened again, but it did not. He turned, in a slight panic, ready to leave the room and find someone.

'Rrr . . .'

It came like the growl of an animal.

'Ryan.' Father's voice was crackling, like a radio station incorrectly tuned.

Ryan turned back and Father's eyes were wide open but he stared at the ceiling as if blind, peering into nothing.

'Father?'

He heaved a great breath and the cover rose. Ryan moved his hand over the front of Father's face, signalling to him, but his eyes did not register the movement. Perhaps he was blind. Was that part of the sickness? But Father did not seem blind. Instead, he was concentrating on something, his face registering all the expressions of seeing.

'Father, what is it? What do you see?'

'He comes from water, walking backwards. He brings time, ready for the long journey.'

Father's words were clear, carried on a strong breath. Ryan moved closer and watched as the old man minced his mouth before speaking, as though shaping the words with his lips.

'He comes from water, walking backwards. He brings time, ready for the long journey.'

They were not Father's words. Ryan could feel their power, recognize them in some way. It was as though they had hung in the air for all time, waiting to attach themselves to someone who could become their vessel. Ryan knew this because Father had told him of these things, of words that were there all the time, an endless conversation going on under the silent surface of everything, occasionally tapped into by those who were on its plane.

Full of their old flame, Father's eyes were recharged. All that remained of his life might have been embodied in them, as though he were about to take a final look at the world, committing it all to memory before moving on. Ryan leaned over and stroked the veins on the top of Father's right hand, as big as it had ever been and yet rendered powerless as all his cells turned in on themselves and he imploded.

It would not be long.

Father's hand turned over, shot out and grabbed Ryan's wrist so suddenly and with such unexpected strength that it made Ryan recoil, a bolt of something that was akin to fear running through his body. Then Ryan realized that there was fear, but it was in Father and he was gripping him to feel safer.

'It goes on forever, but you can see it.'

Ryan looked hard into his grandfather's eyes, the shattered glass of the veins firing off from the sides of his pupils. Deeper in and closer to the centre, the tiny arteries were more like forked lightning. Ryan moved his head nearer, realizing he was doing so because Father was pulling him by the wrist. Ryan was standing with only one foot on the floor and a knee on the bed. His eyes aligned themselves with Father's and they were all he could see, black circles filling his vision. Father's face became nothing more than a blur as surely as his eyes grew sharper.

Far, far inside them, the veins were dancing, swirling around as though floating through a thin liquid. The slim tubes moved around like worms, touching each other, bonding into a line and then separating once more. The longer he watched, the more Ryan saw there was a pattern forming and a rhythm underlying the motion.

'It goes on forever, but you can see it.'

As the veins became purest gold in the darkest black, Ryan let himself synchronize with them.

The long gold trails in each eye began to join up. They formed an endless loop, one long arc that spun around on itself forever, no beginning or end. The complexity of the design swallowed Ryan's brain and he felt the shape engraving itself into his consciousness.

'It goes on forever, but you can see it.'

The words made perfect sense as he stared into the universe of the old man's eyes, and yet Ryan could not say why.

He wanted to surrender, to let himself fall into the welcoming golden net that now surrounded him, but Ryan knew to do so would be the end of him. In his throat he felt a slight pulse of vomit, as though something beneath the skin of the movement was not as it should be.

'He comes from water, walking backwards. He brings time, ready for the long journey.'

The voice and the words belonged neither to Father nor to Ryan.

Somewhere underneath all that was before him, so real and yet so utterly unreal, Ryan could sense that Father had already left his body behind and the knowledge saddened him. The hand no longer gripped his wrist.

The knots spun faster and faster, dizzying him and his thoughts, confusing them so they could be rearranged into a new configuration without him even realizing it.

'It goes on forever, but you can see it.'

A blinding flash and then grey normality once more, death in its midst.

Ryan fell on to the old man's empty chest. The door to the room opened and he heard the voices of his mother and Aunt Janice, a strange concert suddenly between them.

He comes from water, walking backwards. He brings time, ready for the long journey.

Ready for the long journey.

Chapter 37

Lucy sat up in bed and watched Luke as he slept. Did she know Nathan Lucas well enough to convince herself that she could recognize him whatever the circumstances? Their time together had been almost nothing, but she believed it had been enough, that she would know him however much he might have changed. Seeing her father for the first time in nearly two years, she had noticed him ageing, as though he were wearing away like an old piece of clothing, shiny in places, ready to tear in others. Nathan would be different and it would require Lucy to use her imagination in reverse, to take years off Nathan and see if it added up to, or, more correctly, reduced to Luke Smith.

Luke was more beautiful, but she told herself that was what she wanted to see. The self-assurance and the cockiness of Nathan were gone, worn away perhaps by the fragile part of being a teenager, a part she remembered well. I was the same age as Luke is now when I met Nathan, she thought. Did she seem so much older to him? Wiser? What had she done? she thought, staring at the boy in bed next to her.

With Nathan, the first time, her first time, it had been sudden and then it tipped into something more volatile, Lucy not certain she could control what she had helped unleash. After that, the next time, the tenderness was something that could still trigger tears when recollected.

This isn't him.

Lucy felt as though she had forced this boy, taken him somewhere he should not yet have gone, but there was more to it.

She leaned over on the bed and kissed one of the bony points that stuck through his shoulderblade. The skin had a sheen of gold, dappled with freckles occasionally bursting

259

into moles that looked like splats of paint. Lucy put her face closer and studied one of the small imperfections in his skin and the delicate derma it rested on. Lucy was on all fours now, her hands placed carefully either side of him, no part of her touching Luke. She made gentle contact with a blotch on his skin by using the tip of her tongue as lightly as she could. Sitting back and inching down the bed, she pulled the sheet with her, uncovering more of him with each movement. Lucy lifted the rough white cotton clear of his back, uncovering his rear and then his legs. Finally she pulled the bundle of material off his feet and stood at the end of the bed.

His feet were callused along the edges, his little toe clawing inwards and the nail barely visible. The soles of his feet were smooth in the centre and riffled along the outside. Was this the way she remembered Nathan? Luke's calves were hairless, as were the backs of his legs and his behind. Nathan had had a fine weave of hair, a typical blond boy, but what would he be like younger?

Recall was all she had and Lucy stood, letting her mind wander, searching for a feeling that would connect with the present and help her be sure.

Possessed by memory, no longer in control of her actions, Lucy's hand traced the outline of the tattoo on her arm, following its pattern as though it were a roadmap. When her arm was tingling sufficiently that it no longer needed the stimulation of her fingertip, her hand wandered to her breasts, over her stomach and on to the border of hair at the top of her legs.

Abruptly, she shifted her position, softening one of her knees into a crouch, giving herself easier access. Afraid to wake him, she worked herself in a way that was so urgent it made her feel ugly and desperate. Trying to contain the noise brought her to the verge of tears, of pain, of frustration and passion. The loudest noise in the room was where her hand made contact with herself.

On tiptoe, Lucy shivered and closed her eyes, letting her breath whistle lightly through a small gap in the corner of her mouth. The knot burned on her arm, more painful than when it had been put there. Pressure eased from her body through the flex and release of muscle. For a few obliterated seconds she was connected to past and present and it was underpinned by a certainty about the future – who she would become and what would happen to her.

And what was lying on the bed.

Chapter 38

Jenna breathed out and felt herself become part of the world once again.

The machines around Martin's bed hummed, bulbs twinkling in soothing, safe green. She remained still, trying to minimize her presence in the room and let herself gauge whether or not Martin was conscious. It was harder to tell with Martin as his waking state involved such a low level of consciousness. Sending a thought out like radar, she picked up on the waves, tuning in her hearing until she picked up the weary thud of his heart. Electricity from his brain crackled with static, the pattern making no sense. The current was not strong enough to lock on to. He was sending out incomplete signals.

Jenna remembered the first time she had seen Martin sleeping after he had come out of the comatose state. A spasm of panic had gone through her, the fear that he had willingly lapsed into a place she would not be able to reach. Jenna had prodded his leg, the nearest piece of him to her at the time, and then she shook it. Only then did she realize that he would not wake because he could not feel what she was doing. But her hand stroking and then agitating the skin on his face did rouse him.

Can his body really be that dead? she wondered. If she were to anaesthetize the remainder of his brain, would she be able to remove his legs without him knowing? A bit more of his torso, his stomach perhaps? Jenna giggled as she imagined peeling him away until all that remained were a few vital organs squirming and pulsing on the bed, connected to his head by indecipherable entrails. Bring him round from the stupor and then whip away the sheet like a magician, letting him see what he was made of. Then she could prod at his heart with the point of a pencil, or squeeze down hard on his kidney, hard enough for even his lame brain to feel it. She smothered the laugh by inhaling.

She was not going to let him be absent, asleep. There were things she wanted him to hear.

Jenna found his electricity in the air once again and let it mingle with a bolt of her own, pressing it back at him. She felt him feel it and knew he was awake, possibly thinking he had been dreaming, if he really dreamt. Of what? Walking? Talking? Thinking?

Martin's breathing changed, its pattern more alert.

'It's me. Your sister,' Jenna said, hidden in a shadow.

The sheet around his neck rustled as he moved his head to see her.

'All in good time. I want to talk to you first and I don't think I can look at your face while I do that. At least you won't answer back. I've been to see Mum and Dad, to sort a few things out. They thought it was my fault you ended up like this, which is right, of course. I was going to tell them what really happened, how I pushed you off that balcony, but I didn't want to overload them. I wanted them to have an appreciation of why I am me and I think they do now. Well, they did. They won't understand much of anything any more.'

His breathing grew louder and more urgent, as though he were arguing without words. His brain activity had climbed to the point where it was an interference, white noise in her own head.

'You weren't meant to answer back, Martin. This is about me. Me, me, me. How I am, who and what I am,' she said, rolling the words like Dr Seuss. 'Part of it was Father's fault and I realize that now. All that time and I just kept it hidden, put away behind something in my head until it started to come back through, the reason I was the way I was and why I am the way I am now. Nothing lets it out and you have the sort of feeling that you are choking, that crying would be like taking a drink you're really thirsty for, but there's nothing there, no drink that will shift the thirst, no way to release it.'

Jenna paused, her chest wavering. She waited to see if the tremor would spread to her face and if she would burst into tears, but there were none. Quietly, she took a step through the shadows. She pressed the button on the back of the Anglepoise lamp, illuminating it like a dull flower. Martin flinched, as though even the low level of light were uncomfortable for him.

'I've brought a special game for us. Some new things to learn. A whole new language. Well, some different words for our vocabulary.'

Jenna held the plastic board high in the air before placing it in the middle of their respective eye-lines.

'Not too many pictures – even you can follow this one. That's me, obviously, when I was younger. There you are, a bit older than me.'

Jenna watched his eyes move through the dim cast of the lamp, following her words. They stopped, sharpened and then looked at Jenna through the plastic.

'Yes. That's us too,' she said, nodding at him.

He moved his head from side to side, the effort uncomfortable even to look at.

'Of course it is. Don't pretend, Martin. You have to believe your eyes. Look at that next one. You seem to be enjoying yourself. I was probably a bit thinner than that and I don't think my tits were that big at that age, maybe not even now, but drawing isn't my best subject. You get the picture, though.'

A state something like panic seemed to power Martin and Jenna thought he might be about to move, but all he managed was a shaking of his head from side to side, in a way that was almost sorrowful.

'You were so strong, so much bigger than I was. All that power. I might as well have been . . .' Jenna trailed off and went in the direction of a new word. 'I might as well have been paralysed.'

She put the board to the side of the bed and shifted the direction of the light, its joints creaking like an elbow.

'What am I doing?' she asked, as though she could read

his thoughts.

Jenna could not read his mind with any precision, but she could sense his consternation, the fear he would be feeling as she drew the sheet back and exposed his chest and lower body to the glare of the light. 'This is like an operating table,' she said. 'Except I don't have to use any anaesthetic.' Jenna slapped his thigh where it was exposed, the flesh dead to the touch. 'I bet you wish you could move your head upright, so you could see what I'm doing.'

She pulled a pillow from behind him, his head flopping back, and laid it on his chest, blocking what little view he might have had.

'Now you won't know what I'm up to. I could be stroking your cock, licking it a bit, once I've taken the catheter out.'

For a moment, she was silent, using all her strength as she went about her work. His flesh gave off noises as she worked on it and it amazed her that he felt no pain. When she was done she looked up and over the pillow to speak to him. 'You'd give anything to feel again, wouldn't you Martin? And to speak. Do you want me to let you? I can make it happen, really.'

Jenna leant on to the pillow on his chest and looked into his face, moving close enough that he flinched an eye at her breath.

'I could make you talk and I could make you feel, move as well.'

He stared at her and she could see all the familiar stubbornness, the arrogance of their father seeping through him as though he were possessed.

For just a few seconds, she let the fibres connect, no idea how she was making it happen. Jenna looked at her brother and made him connect to himself, switching on the pain cells.

A hot wave of agony sent him into motion, his back arching, the force throwing Jenna up off his chest and backwards, the pillow falling to the floor. It was as if he had just received a high-voltage charge, unused muscles and tendons suddenly overloaded with energy. Martin's eyes widened in surprise and his mouth opened, letting out a soundless scream.

And then she switched him off again.

'Not all feelings are good, Martin,' she said, putting her hand behind his head and lifting it so he could look down at his legs. 'That's the big knife, the one from Mum's drawer. I blunted it a bit on her which is why it took so long to work it in and find a tendon, but I managed. Sore? Are you glad the pain's gone away now? Does it make you feel any better about the way you ended up?'

A noise gurgled in his throat, one that had more force than the usual wheezes and sighs where his body made space for the invasive equipment that helped sustain it. Martin wanted to form a word. Somewhere between the physical damage to his spinal cord and the lobe in his brain, in the midst of the harmonics of madness that she knew overlay his psyche, he was trying to speak to her.

Jenna pressed the button that raised the back of the bed so he could get a full view of the knife that was buried into his inner thigh. Jenna propped him up with some pillows. 'You can have your say in a moment. I think you need a bit more of an incentive to speak, a nice wake-up call,' she said.

When she was satisfied with his view, she took the knife by the handle and worked it down his leg, turning the clean puncture into a long and fleshy gash, his skin tearing with a sound like fabric ripping. It was very meaty, a nest of muscle, bone and tendon, compacted together.

'I'm going to have a go at cutting through the inner leg muscle,' she said. 'A bread knife might have been better for that, I suppose,' she continued as she began to make a sawing motion across the muscle. There was a scraping sound. 'That was your femur. Sorry.' She sawed faster. 'I thought that would have made a twang when it went. You're bleeding a lot more than I expected, but there are one or two arteries floating about there. Let's give you a little feel.'

Martin howled, nothing that sounded even animal, let

alone what Martin himself used to sound like. Jenna let the pain course through him for a full minute, turning his voice off so it was sealed within him.

When she let him return to the numb paralysis, she watched as he struggled to breathe, fascinated by the sheer exertion pain required.

'Go on then,' she said. 'Say it.'

He drew a breath and Jenna waited for him to expel it as words, wondering if his voice would sound the same or if she could really remember how his voice sounded, sure it was nothing like the nasal reproduction heard on family-gathering videos.

'Nuh.'

'You can do better than that, you arrogant bastard,' she said, sweetly.

'No.'

'See,' she said.

Martin was hyperventilating

'I.' He exhaled, the word ventilated with laboured breath.

'I am sorry. That's what you're trying to say, Martin.'

'I.'

Jenna sighed. 'I'm with the I part, Martin. I know you want to say something about yourself.'

'I.'

She looked at him, exasperated, but also afraid. He was so intense, so much energy forcing itself into such a simple act made him seem possessed, and even though he was paralysed it seemed as if he might just leap from the bed and grab her.

'I. Didn't. Do. Any. Thing,' he said, each word a sentence.

'Liar,' she said, like a coquette.

'Get the other board,' he said, startling her with a full, well-oiled sentence.

Jenna looked at him and then reached behind the bed, finding their usual picture board. 'What do you want with this?' she asked, holding it between them.

A boy. The sea. The arrow that pointed to the left. The clock. The aeroplane. The arrow that pointed to the right.

'You did that last time and it didn't make any sense then,' she said.

Martin followed the six images the same way he had previously.

'I never did anything, Jenn. It's been put there for you, but it isn't real.'

'No,' she said.

'Yes,' he replied, scanning the images on the plastic.

'Why do you keep looking at those?'

'I was in a motorbike accident, on one of Father's four hundred fours. You remember the old Triumphs, we used to sit on them and pretend to race when we were little. I rounded a corner so fast I ended up on the opposite side of the road, then off it, right into an old trailer parked halfway down a ditch.'

'No. You know what you were trying to do to me and you got what was coming. That was why I pushed you off that balcony.'

'Jenn, it never happened. You're being used. The memories are false. Trust me.' His eyes scanned the plastic once again.

'Why do you keep doing that?' she asked, angry.

A boy. The sea. The arrow that pointed to the left. The clock. The aeroplane. The arrow that pointed to the right.

'Since that day nearly four years ago, since the accident, that is all I have been able to think. The same words go through my head again and again, endlessly. It's like there's a loop of tape that will never stop playing. I'm tuned into something, a bigger voice. I hear it in my head, but it isn't me, Jenna, I'm not the one saying it.'

'Saying what?'

A boy. The sea. The arrow that pointed to the left. The clock. The aeroplane. The arrow that pointed to the right.

'He comes from water, walking backwards. He brings time, ready for the long journey.'

'What does it mean?'

'I don't know,' Martin replied, almost crying. 'You hear the voice too, don't you, Jenn?'

'Stop it, Martin. Don't talk your way out of this. I'm the one that's letting you speak.'

'He comes from water, walking backwards. He brings time, ready for the long journey,' Martin said, the rhythm the same as the other repetitions. 'Do you know what it's like, just those words as my life? I'm trapped by them. Stop them for me, Jenna, and then make them stop in your own head. Find your own voice in there and listen to it.'

Martin stopped and Jenna realized that he was not going to speak again – ever.

It only took her a few minutes to see to it that he would no longer hear the voice. She pulled his limp body up by the shoulders so she could say goodbye.

'You're dead now, Martin. All you're watching is a memory of life that I'm pumping through your brain. You don't have to be afraid to die because you already have. What you need to be afraid of now is me switching you off, letting the memory run out of power. I wanted you to know what it was like to be dead before I let you slip into it forever, that's why I dropped you in there and pulled you back out. I thought it would be nice for you to see me one more time, when there was no pain and no voice. Goodbye.'

Jenna blinked and he was gone.

Chapter 39

Kavanagh walked away from the jet which had touched down softly on the private airfield adjoining the impressive and spare building he approached. After a silent plane ride with a pilot who was as discreet as the earlier driver of his car, Kavanagh had eyed the ground from his window, trying to get everything into perspective. The house stood alone, nothing visible in any direction, and Kavanagh wondered how secluded it was. It was easy to see why someone would come here to hide, he thought. Lit only by night and the short throw of the landing-strip lights, its shape was irregular and hard to comprehend, as though it were concealing corners from him. A single light eyed him from one side of the facade, on the ground floor.

The noise of the jet engine was comforting in the desert, placid even.

Kavanagh jumped, as though he had seen a figure move in the shadow at the side of the house, instead of just catching sight of the inanimate object that stood sheltered by an arm of dark.

The car.

Cameron had told him he would be expected by Jack Burns, and the front door was open, admitting him into a dark hall, the light he had seen from outside now only a dim shaft off to his right. Without fear and driven on by questions, Kavanagh entered. He moved through the dark, heading for the glow, drawn to it and paying little attention to what was around him, barely conscious of the tiled floor beneath his feet.

The door to the lit room was ajar and he pushed it back, the sudden illumination a strain for his eyes as he tried to assimilate the burst of light and translate it into images. He blinked, squinted, and before him, in the middle of a perfectly square room with a high ceiling, sat Jack Burns. Directly above, a long wire dangled, suspending a single bulb close to Burns's head. The room was spartan and windowless. Burns was hunched uncomfortably into a director's chair, as though afraid it would give under his weight. The walls were stone, the colour of biscuits, and the floor grey slate. The room was like a burial chamber, ready to be sealed and contain its occupants for eternity, the air tasting clean enough to preserve a corpse.

Behind Burns, like a frame, was a large mirror. Kavanagh looked at himself in it and then studied the back of the old man's bald head, the skin of his neck in rolls.

'Mr Kavanagh, I've been expecting you.'

Burns stood, seeming glad to do so. The chair creaked with equal relief as he left it. He placed his hands behind his back and squared his shoulders, eyeing Kavanagh as if on parade and awaiting inspection. He was wearing a thin robe of white cotton which exposed the greying hair of his chest where the material fell away.

'Alexander Cameron said you would come.'

'When did you speak to him?' Kavanagh asked quickly, almost afraid he was going to say ten minutes ago or that he was in another room of the house.

'Well, the first time he told me you would come here tonight was the first time I met him. That, as you know, was forty-five years ago.'

'The party at the end of the Fifties. What really happened there?' Kavanagh asked.

'Alexander and his father were travelling. I'd been led to believe they were trying to find partners, ways of bringing money into the Cameron Trust. Business didn't interest me at that point in my life. I remember getting very drunk, being an arsehole, which I did a lot at the time. I'd been in and out of a bunch of universities and I was already far too old to still be studying. I was on my way to becoming just a burned-out burden with a rich father.'

Burns paused, looking over his shoulder and into the mirror for a moment.

Kavanagh listened to the gentle purr of silence in the room. The stillness held everything in place and he simply stared at the short, bald man trying to piece things together in his mind.

From outside, the engine of the jet roared and then became quieter with each second. At first Kavanagh was alarmed, but then he knew the jet would not be the way out of here. He stroked the chain through his shirt, feeling the bumps of metal at its end.

'They were there to talk to me, not my father. And I realized it wasn't money they wanted – they had plenty of that. They were there because they wanted me and all they had to offer in return were words.'

'What did they tell you?' Kavanagh asked.

'They told me that my life was just one small story knotted together with millions of others,' Burns said, looking at Kavanagh. 'All these strands were massed together into a single story and within that I had a simple purpose, even if it would take most of my life to fulfil it. In fact, it would *take* my life. There was more to it than that, of course. They told me things, shared words with me. Up to that day, I had believed simple led to complex. I saw it was the opposite. Using the unbelievably complex to engineer the very simple.'

'And they told you we would be here, now?' Kavanagh asked.

'They knew a lot. Gordius was already the word being used. Nathan Lucas, as he was calling himself then, had grafted it into his story, wanting it to serve his purposes, to undermine the logic of the one story he had no control over – his own. How frustrating that must have been, to have the power to write every story in the world except your own. He will die as surely as you and I, but with even more precision. He will get to zero. We don't know where our own personal number comes. Most of us,' he added after a short pause.

'Why all the artifice? Why didn't you just go ahead and let the Trust swallow up Trellis? Why spend all that time building your own business, then the proposed merger?'

'Because I had to behave precisely in character. I was meant to be at the head of Gordius. That was the way Nathan Lucas had intended it to be and the Camerons had gleaned that also. They sought me out, revealed the true purpose that would lie behind actions I would have considered to be voluntary. Don't you find that ironic, that we were able to dupe Nathan Lucas in that way?' Burns smiled. 'I have gone through my life in the motions that Nathan Lucas intended and yet my own intentions, inside my head, are the opposite of that.'

'How did the Camerons find out about you?'

'There was someone they had with them who could read into the text of the story in a way others could not. There was a chain of events. He found them, told them things they already knew, things no one else should have known. Then he revealed facts they did not know. He was with them briefly when they were travelling, but he had his own loose end of the story to take care of. They called him the preacher,' Burns said.

Kavanagh nodded and thought of Wadlow Grace and where he might be.

'Cameron said he was the brain of Gordius but that you were its heart.'

'The earthquake gave birth to the Gordian Movement as Nathan Lucas had scripted it to. When the fusion of the corporations went ahead in any case and it was renamed, I began to make sure there was no link between the two in the eyes of the world. Of course, that served to make the link itself even more powerful.'

'And Nathan Lucas was behind that?' Kavanagh asked.

'I've never met him. As far as he is concerned, I am nothing more than an innocent character acting out something that serves his purpose, a purpose I know nothing of. And so was the blind man.'

'And now the blind man is dead,' Kavanagh said.

'Yes. And once I am gone, it will bring Nathan Lucas back into the text, out from the substructure he has slumbered in for so long. The movement caused by my erasure will be so profound it will reach the foundations of the text, shaking it like an earthquake.'

'And then?'

'He will retrieve the third knot and try to reunite it with the two you have. He will look for a new beginning. You, Michael, have much to gain and lose in that. The Camerons and the preacher knew of the role you would be called on to play. And your daughter. That has been part of the story.'

Kavanagh drew in a sharp breath. 'Going through the motions,' he muttered to himself.

'That was necessary, Michael. At our first meeting, if I had sat down and told you what you now know, what would your reaction have been?'

'I don't know what my reaction is now,' he said.

'To be where you are now and who you are now, Michael, you needed to have made the journey that placed you there. That is the process, the way the story unfolds. For Nathan Lucas, his story folds in on him.'

'No choice. No chance. Nothing random,' Kavanagh said. 'Why am I here?'

'You know why. To close off my involvement in this, to cause the rupture and open the wound in the text that will allow him to slip back through.'

Kavanagh's right hand flexed and he made an instinctive grabbing motion, his fist closing around something.

'It is so very strange to have lived forty years knowing when it will end, what you last words ever will be,' Burns said, sounding as though the energy in his body was winding down into a relaxed state.

Silence. A moment of preparation. Kavanagh watched, almost in respect, as the man prepared to utter his last word.

Jack Burns stared hard into Kavanagh and said a final word.

'Please.'

Kavanagh looked down at his right hand and saw the

screwdriver, its solid handle and long four-sided shaft. He twisted it so the sharpened edge of the barrel pointed upwards. When he looked back up, Burns stood with his robe open, waiting.

With a lunge propelled by all his body weight, Kavanagh sank the screwdriver into Burns's stomach just under the navel. It brought their bodies close, almost like an embrace that could lead to a kiss. Kavanagh looked at Burns and watched the shocked expression on his face turn to one of relief.

Kavanagh wrenched the blade upwards and as he did, a figure appeared in the mirror.

Chapter 40

Feverishly, Jenna untwisted the plaits of green wire, the harsh edges sticking into her fingers as she went at it like a child opening a gift. The closure of the fence was fresh and tight and Jenna could still sense trace-heat from the last fingers that had touched it, feel the slight grease of finger-sweat on the green plastic that covered the harsh core. Once the knot of the binding was open, she was able to rip the fence open as easily as tearing paper and the sound it made, coupled with the pleasingly wide stretch of her arms, gave Jenna a moment of satisfaction as she paused and readied herself for the next barrier.

Doors were not going to stop her, she knew that. Keeping virtually the same pace with which she had approached it, she raised her right foot as she was almost upon the padlocked door and lunged the sole of her boot into its middle. Force came back at her and jolted her hip, the bone quivering in its socket, but she was the stronger and the door gave way with a splitting noise.

'I can see in the dark,' she said aloud and to no one in particular, marching down a badly lit hallway.

Jenna stopped. Above the rustle of a rat and the scratching sound of a spider moving under the crack in a brick near the floor, she heard a muffled cry. Blocking out all of the peripheral sound, she focused, trying to imagine she really did have a radar in her head. The rustle of fabric, quite a porous, busy sort of material. A woman's dress. A creak of wood, the sighing sound of an old chair protesting under the weight of its occupant. Jenna moved in the direction of the sounds' source.

'This is going to be even better than I was expecting,' Jenna said, giggling as she stood at the lip of the shallow end of the empty swimming pool.

Submerged in nothing but depressing half-light was an old woman on a chair, tape across her mouth and hands behind her back.

Next to the car, she looked small, cowering and partly hidden by the cast of its long shadow. Were the pool to fill with water, the car looked as though it would simply lift and glide off through it like a submarine. Like most American cars, it reminded Jenna of something with a face, the opal of the headlights and the angular jawline of the bonnet. A sneering, satisfied sort of personality.

On the other side of the woman, off to her left just behind her, out of her view Jenna guessed, was the strewn and lifeless body of an old man. She peered at the prostrate form and made it larger. The man's tie was balled up and had been forced into his throat until his airway had been blocked. Jenna traced the feeling backwards, picking up the final flinching moments as his body ran away to nothing. Fear, panic, it was all there. And something else, almost like danger, a warning of some kind.

'I thought I would have to do some of this work myself. How thoughtful to have you here, trussed and ready for me. Who should I thank?' Jenna asked into nowhere.

She jumped down the two feet from the edge of the pool and into the shallow end. She took a couple of steps forward, resisting the urge to run down the slope and build up speed as she approached the woman. This was not a time to rush.

'I've spent the last five minutes opening things up,' Jenna said, brandishing the largest Sabatier knife she had been able to find in her parents' house. There was a chip in the middle of the blade, an odd sort of V-shape, but Jenna quite enjoyed it because it was like a notch. Maybe she would put another one in after she had finished with the old woman.

'You'll be the easiest of all to open, so I'll take plenty of time. I wouldn't want you to miss anything.'

Jenna was a third of the way down, the sides of the pool beginning to lower around her. The old woman was flinching, squirming around on the chair as though taking comfort from the illusion that she might be able to break free.

'Even if you could untie yourself, you wouldn't be able to outrun me. Be patient. Think about what I'm going to do.' Jenna held the knife in the air and let it catch the light. She tried unsuccessfully to reflect it into the woman's eyes.

'This is the one chance you'll get to see what's going on inside you. How many people get to see that, to really see themselves for what they are? I'm getting quite good at it now. I know just what to do to keep your attention for long enough.'

Halfway there and the woman was still struggling, the smell of sweat evident. Urine was not far behind it. Jenna could hear it swirling inside the woman and imagined the other struggle that was going on inside her to keep control of her bladder.

'Let it go, I won't mind. I'd prefer you to be a bit cleaner on the inside in any case. We're going to see that piss whatever happens. Both of us. Okay, hang on to it then.'

There was energy and panic and struggle. Adrenaline whipped up into her nostrils. Something was missing, though, and it troubled Jenna.

'I've got this sort of narration now, where I can explain exactly where I'll be cutting and what the things are you'll see. We'll go through it a couple of times before I strip you. Then I'll draw a line, like you see television doctors do, for the incision.'

The old bitch was not afraid. That was missing. Fear.

'Skin is a bit like glue, holding all those bits in. There must be so much pressure inside, like a balloon waiting to pop. I'm going to take the pressure away for you, make it better.'

Still no fear.

Jenna made long whistling cuts into the air with the knife, disappointed that it did not make the kind of slicing sound she would have liked. She varied the angle of the blade until she found the best noise, but it was not enough. A demonstration would be necessary.

'Perhaps you don't feel any pressure? There's no point in me doing this favour for you if you're not interested. You have to really want it. I can make you want it. I'll make you beg for it. It doesn't have to be quick.'

She was talking loudly into the echo now, enjoying the sound of her voice as it came back to her.

'I wonder if there are more areas on the body that can feel more pain than pleasure. They are the same thing, you know, just measured along a scale of sensitivity. I'll pick the most sensitive areas and I'll make them feel good and then I'll make them feel bad. Will you be able to tell when it's meant to stop being nice? Then we can find somewhere else and start with the bad, letting it get a bit better.'

Finally the gentle energy of the woman's fear reached Jenna and it was nourishing. She tightened her grip on the handle and spent a few seconds imagining what she would do.

'I can whip most things out now to give you a chance to look at them before you go to sleep forever. I'm going to go for my record tonight.'

She took another look at the man and the car, both lifeless and uninteresting to her. In front of her on the chair, that was what she needed – something pulsing, reverberating with life.

'I've come for you,' Jenna said.

And then, without warning, it all stopped. As though a switch had been thrown somewhere – not a switch inside her, but one controlled by an unseen hand – everything came to an abrupt halt and Jenna stood in the cold and dark silence.

The old woman rose to her feet and Jenna saw there had been nothing restraining her, no rope round her swollen ankles or skeletal wrists. The old woman drew back a shoulder and then threw her arm forward into Jenna's face.

Bella Smith ripped the tape from her mouth. 'You silly girl,' she said. 'Did you really think you were in control? That this is how it was going to happen?'

The headlights of the car flicked on.

Chapter 41

Luke slid from the warmth of the bed, one foot first followed by the rest of his body, ending up in an ungainly but nonetheless quiet posture on the carpet. He sat still until he was familiar enough with the rhythm of Lucy's slumber to know he had not disturbed her.

Naked, he crept along the landing, pausing to listen for his mother, but the house was empty, he was certain.

In the spare room, he approached the mirror and stood a good five feet from it, shuffling until the streetlight that tipped in through the high windows picked him out and made his pale skin silver. His reflection gazed back in a perfect impression of him. Luke wondered how hard it was for it to do that, anticipating every move he made and moving in the opposite direction to it. Luke held his arms outstretched, palms up, as though offering himself to it. The reflection did the same, not giving the Luke the satisfaction of a contrary motion.

Sometimes, when he went into Mum's room and played about with the triptych of mirrors on her dressing table, he could rearrange two of them so it was possible to see the back of his head reflected in a cascading infinity. He found it hard to imagine the reflections went on forever, collapsing into an eternity of decreasing size, but in that mirror, he was safer, as if the cross-flows of light and image frightened his reflection.

Luke did not look at himself often without clothes on.

As though it had picked the thought out of Luke's head and refracted it through the mirror, the reflection stroked its hands over its chest. Through its hair, round its neck, along its sides, sweeping down its chest and stomach, lighting across its groin and then over the front of its legs. Smiling directly into Luke's face, so mocking it touched his heart, the reflection manipulated itself.

Annoyance made Luke feel bolder and he moved quickly to less than two feet from the glass. The image went back to just being Luke. He and his reflection faced each other, neither of them twitching.

From inside the mirror, less than an inch from its surface, a man stepped into view, reached out and pulled Luke through.

Kavanagh had let the dead body of Jack Burns fall heavily to the ground as soon as he had seen what was in the mirror. Nathan Lucas, naked and splashed with the fresh blood of Kavanagh's wife, stood in the glass, brazen and smiling. Kavanagh reached into the glass and it felt like water over his hands. He grabbed Nathan and pulled him through and threw his naked body against the table.

He growled, following the direction of Nathan's body and getting close to him, not wanting to give him any time to recover.

Kavanagh grabbed his bony shoulder, spun him round by it and landed a punch in the boy's stomach. He crumpled to the floor, as lifelessly as Burns had, and Kavanagh kicked into the foetal form, aiming the toe of his shoe into the soft fleshy area of the stomach. The body closed together in a reflex of pain and Kavanagh disengaged his foot, bringing it back farther this time and back in harder still, the contact making the boy cry out. Kavanagh dropped to one knee and rolled the body half towards the floor, exposing another soft area of flesh and punching into the kidney three times.

Nathan was crying and he continued to sob when Kavanagh rolled him over and sat on his chest, leaning over him and into his face. Kavanagh slapped the boy hard on the right cheek and he howled.

This was not Nathan Lucas. Kavanagh froze, confusion paralysing him.

The boy who had been so passive, such easy prey, seemed to sense his chance and his hand shot up and landed a clenched fist into Kavanagh's balls. His grip loosened on the boy's throat as the pain robbed him of any strength. He felt the body wriggling underneath him, getting away. The boy was lithe and more agile than Kavanagh, and while he still reeled in agony, the boy had twisted and slipped away.

Kavanagh stood, hyperventilating, worried the boy would bolt for the door. He looked through watery eyes.

There was no longer a door. The bare bricks that had previously made the walls and left a gap for the doorway were now the only thing, top to bottom.

Apart from the mirror.

Kavanagh looked up just in time to see the boy hurtling towards it. There was no complementary reflection and it looked as though he were charging a window that led to somewhere else. The glass swallowed him as though it were a liquid.

'No!' Kavanagh screamed into the dry acoustics of the room. 'Wait!' he called after nothing.

Then he ran towards the mirror, his own reflection approaching him at the same speed.

Lucy was woken by a sound she was certain had been the tinkle of breaking glass. She shivered from fear rather than cold, a tingle down one side of her body at the thought of someone breaching the house by smashing a window. Tentatively, she felt into the small section of the bed Luke had occupied, her hand finding nothing but the cover turned back and the undersheet chilly. The room was unnerving without him in it. She debated whether or not to venture out and down into the house to look for him, wondering if his mother had come back. Lucy did not want to run into her, but nor did she want to stay in the bedroom. The mattress on the bed was thin, the wallpaper looked damp and the furniture as though something mouldy was hidden at its core. Unless you're just feeling guilty, she told herself, looking round at the boyish accoutrements that littered the room. Just a boy.

How could they live like this, he and his mother?

Lucy slipped from the bed and dressed, readying herself to make a quick exit.

The landing and the stairs that led down were in complete darkness. Lucy stood and kept as quiet as she could, seeing if she could hear anyone, voices or activity. The sounds of the resting house came back at her, nothing else.

'Luke?' she whispered into the black, and then wondered why she was whispering. 'Luke?' she said in a normal voice and then more loudly, the sound of her own raised voice frightening her, as though it might rouse something best left slumbering. A panicky heat flushed through her and she needed to get moving instead of standing in the tickling dark of the landing, imagining shapes were forming.

'Luke?' she tried, standing in the doorway of his mother's room. The Lady's dress seemed to radiate light and she turned and ran when she saw it glinting in the dark.

'Luke!' Her voice more desperate now, drowning in the blackness and gagging on his name as she opened the door into the empty spare room they had looked in earlier. When a figure moved towards her in the darkness, Lucy's heart jumped so hard she left the ground. She froze for a second and then spun to face them head-on. It was her reflection in a large mirror the size of a door. She gazed at herself, moving closer.

A shadow moved behind her and again she made a tiny shriek, turning to catch whoever was behind her, her arm prickling with a sweaty heat. There was nothing there.

As she turned back, she caught the movement again, but this time it seemed more like it had happened inside the mirror, rather than it being a reflection of what went on in the room. It felt more like the room was a reflection of the mirror.

Afraid to stare any longer, she fled the room, pulling the door to behind her and bounding down the stairs, not caring who she bumped into, wanting only to be away from the upstairs of the house.

Finding the light switch at the foot of the stairs, she flooded the space with light, letting it wash away the animate shadows and grateful for the pain in her eyes. She went through each room downstairs, no longer expecting to find him, but checking in case, wondering if something had happened to do with his diabetes.

Where might he have gone? Lucy did not know very much about Luke Smith. When she added what little facts she had together, she realized there was only one place she could think of where Luke might have gone – and she was not sure she could remember how to get there.

Ten minutes and two wrong turns later, Lucy was at the swimming pool, scanning the outside of the opaque building and hoping to see a square of light, any hint of life. A memory of being with Nathan, going to the Pendulum building late at night, fired off in her mind. She was disoriented and needed to make almost two complete circuits of the building before coming across the door with the bell they had pressed to summon Tony Wood earlier that evening. Lucy pressed it, but somehow it did not feel like it was ringing anywhere.

Thinking how much easier it would be to turn back, go to Dad's house, or to Wadlow's, Lucy pushed the door, but it did not move. As she looked further down its surface, she saw the knot, fat and round, that served as a handle, almost concealed in the shadow because it was so close to the jamb. She rotated it, feeling the pattern on her palm, and opened the door.

The security lights were still on. She took some comfort from them, despite the morbidity of their weak glow. She was in a utility corridor, a bare vein running beneath the skin of the building. Exposed pipes marked the way along to the changing room they had been in before, but it was empty, no evidence of Tony Wood on the bench.

Lucy heard something, muffled and distant, its force dissipated by the reverb. Had there been a hundred such noises, it would have been more instantly identifiable as a human voice echoing around a swimming pool. Lucy tripped on the step as she went through the dormant showers and stood at the shallow end of the pool.

The car was still there and next to it, in the shadow it cast, was someone sitting on a chair.

Lucy jumped into the pool, trying to make sense of the shapes and shadows.

'Hello?' she asked, not using Luke's name because it did not seem like him, even from this distance.

The muffled sound again, a woman's vioce, and coming from the chair. Lucy approached, keeping her eyes on the chair as the sides of the pool grew higher around her.

The headlights of the car switched on without a sound and Lucy involuntarily brought her hand to her eyes. She continued walking and was less than five feet from the chair before her sight had adjusted.

'Oh,' Lucy said when she saw how the woman was bound to the chair, her face stricken. 'I'm going to help you, okay?'

The woman nodded, biting into the gag as though it were choking her.

Bent over the woman to release her from the bindings, Lucy did not see the punch as it whistled round the periphery of her vision and hit her solidly on the left side of her face. As it knocked her upright and backwards, all she could think was that the blow would not have hurt so much if it had been on her stronger right side. The blow that then came from behind was heavy enough to make her feel sick even as she passed out.

Chapter 42

With less than a page of indecipherable ink left for him in Randall's notebook, Wadlow sat on the deck of the coffee shop, looking out on to the water. He could not see the road that ran along the lip of the coast, but every once in a while the sound of a slow-moving car reminded him of its presence. The ocean was fascinating. Vast, it seemed to behave like a creature, something with a sort of consciousness.

Following Cameron's departure in Raynsford, Wadlow had stood gazing at where his shop had once been, had been only moments earlier. Then, perhaps for the last time, the notebook had granted him some sense, given him the chance to read ahead. The result had been like a map with a set of directions. Wadlow knew where he had to go, was there right now, and knew what would happen to him shortly, if the notebook and Alexander Cameron were right. If he were able to decipher that dwindling block of code, get to the end of his own story, would that give him the truth? Perhaps it was selfish of him to expect a revelation. After all, how many people got that?

Today, as the notebook had cut him some slack, so Wadlow had given himself a break. Into the sixteen-ounce foam cup of Java, he had trickled Half and Half in place of his usual fat-free milk and, in the same halting voice a teenager might have asked for prophylactics, he had mumbled, 'I'll take a piece of toffee-crunch pie also.' Wadlow dabbed moist chocolate from his lip with the edge of a paper napkin and fidgeted on the white iron-framed garden chair. Not so long ago, he would have spilled unflatteringly over each side of the chair as it failed to accommodate his haunches and in his mind he was already imagining the pie inflating him like a balloon. Coffee and sugar soared through him and Wadlow felt light-headed, like after the first few swallows of beer. His trousers felt tight, he was sure.

Wadlow took the last mouthful of pie, scraping the plate with the side of the fork, and drained the rest of his coffee from the cup. From below, somewhere nearby, he could hear the sound of banging. Wadlow checked his watch and stood.

It was time to move through what he knew would happen and arrive at ignorance once more.

Descending the stairs, still high on sugar and nervous, Wadlow felt the power of The Book as it scripted him. There was no escaping it. It was every story, good or bad. Only as good or as bad as the person it read. And his brother's notebook, a small offshoot of The Book, was the same. The mangled spillage of his dead brother's brain painted on to the page.

The source of the noise was two shops along. As calmly as he could, Wadlow approached.

'Fuck,' the boy said, slapping at the machine and then clenching his fist and hammering against the reinforced glass as though it were a door, the solid rectangle as heavy as a safe and not moving an inch. There was a matte black plinth around the base of the machine and he launched a kick at it, the metal reverberating noisily but the machine still silent, unyielding and mocking.

Wadlow stood watching, uncomfortable he had yet to be noticed, making him feel like a trespasser. Tears filled his eyes and he had to blink. When the preacher had found Wadlow in Memphis, he had been kicking a soda machine for a good five minutes, trying to get a bottle to drop, thirst scratching his throat to shards. This machine was supposed to dispense cans, not bottles, of soda and stood on the porch of a shop which could as easily have been a house. Wadlow stood at the bottom of the three steps which led up to where the boy continued to vent his anger.

Randall's notebook had been wrong, or at least silent, on one aspect. Wadlow was unprepared for how striking the boy was. His nose turned up a fraction, pointing towards the soft honey colour of his eyes, set off against skin that was ever so slightly olive. Black hair that shone like well-aged leather was swept back away from his face and flowed in a neat and even wave all the way to his shoulders. Wadlow gulped and realized he was studying the boy's frame, solid-shouldered and firm. The Book was taunting him.

By the time the boy turned to leave, a disgusted sigh his parting gesture, Wadlow's smile was broad enough to border on a laugh. The boy looked at him and anger remained for a moment before it faded into embarrassment. He paused on the middle of the three steps.

'Summer's so far gone now,' Wadlow said, looking up.

The sky had the tone of autumn, white cloud leaded grey, the photograph switching from colour to black and white. People on the beach kept moving, hunching into the wind with collars turned up and buttons fastened. Shops along the boardwalk had stopped hanging things outside – beach balls, Frisbees and towels imprisoned behind glass. Narrow doors which would have opened out like welcoming arms were now snapped closed.

'It's getting colder,' the boy replied.

He stood with both hands fitted into the pockets of green combat trousers that looked as though they belonged to someone else. The fabric shone from the press of an over-hot iron that had left creases behind it. Over a black T-shirt that was greying from continual washing, he wore a military sort of jacket. The boy's heavy work boots seemed to be an anchor, his body shifting with nervous energy atop them. Wadlow wondered if he was anxious to get away from him.

The boy walked down the steps so he was on the same level as Wadlow, almost the same height. He reminded Wadlow, just a little, of himself, although Wad knew in truth he had not been that fine as a teenager.

'You're a lot more handsome than I was expecting. Thinner too,' the boy said.

'How long have you been walking? You look tired.'

'Almost three whole days, sun up to sun down. I hitched as far as the bottom of the Cape, but then I just wanted to walk.'

'Wadlow Grace.'

'Ryan Summer.'

Wadlow realized they had spoken each other's name, not introduced themselves.

Ryan held out his hand and Wadlow met it halfway, ready to shake. Instead, he found himself cradling the delicate hand, not wanting to let go. Ryan stroked the top of Wadlow's hand with his free one and neither of them spoke.

Chapter 43

'I've had a life like you wouldn't believe, where things have happened and been done to me that shouldn't have and I've spent years trying to get over it, but the memories stay there, hiding in shadows and around little corners where you can't see them, and they can jump out on you and surprise you, sometimes a lot if you don't recognize what it is you're remembering because then it's just as bad as when it happened the first time, however old you were then and are now, no matter how many tablets you take or people you talk to about it and even if you go after the people who were bad to you in the first place and you're bad to them, it doesn't make you feel any better since even though they're not there any more, hiding in the dark or around the next blind corner, the dark and the corners are still there and you start to realize that they're the problem, all those fucking corners and that fucking dark stuff.' She turned her head. 'I'm Jenna Miller, by the way.'

Lucy was not certain at which point the drone had become words in her wakening mind, but the words weren't addressed to her in any case. The woman on the seat next to her was simply issuing them into the world as though she wanted to expunge them from her head. Lucy's own head hurt, the left side aflame with the ache, but her whole consciousness was woozy from the blows, her thoughts adrift and bumping into each other.

They were in the back seat of the car Lucy had seen in the swimming pool. She looked out of the window and her only landscape was the small rectangular tiles of the swimming pool wall. Lucy moved forward but got no more than an inch from the seat back when she felt the restraint.

'That's just the seatbelt, but it's been fastened tightly so you keep nice and still,' the woman said.

'Who are you?' Lucy asked.

'I'm Jenna Miller, I told you that. The real question is, who is Jenna Miller,' she said, shrugging her shoulders.

Lucy's hands were free but the woman was out of reach and even so, there would not have been much Lucy could do, strapped tightly into the well-preserved leather of the seat.

'The old woman,' Lucy said, remembering.

'She is a cheeky one, but I was pleased to see she had you as fooled as I was.'

'What do you mean?' Lucy asked.

'We're going on such a lovely trip.'

The woman's face was bruised on the left side, apparently from a blow. Her eyes were focused on something that might have been only inches from her face, wherever she was looking. She made clenched and unclenched fists with her hands more or less in time with her breathing. Being in such close and restricted proximity with someone in this state made Lucy sweat and her heart pulse more quickly, so she could feel it expanding against the weave of the seatbelt.

'Where's the old lady?' Lucy asked, trying to sound firm.

'I have no idea.'

'Where are we going?' Lucy asked

'You ask so many questions. Just like me. Are you squeamish?'

'What do you mean?' Lucy demanded, pushing back into the seat harder, wondering if she could muster a kick.

'I don't know. Supposing I was to take your hand and use my teeth to chew off the end of one of your fingers. Would you be squeamish about that?'

'It would hurt, I suppose,' Lucy said.

'A finger is a bit bony, though, and probably not that sensitive. One of your nipples would hurt, I expect. Both might give the pain too much of a balance, but that's about pain, not about being squeamish or feeling discomfort. Pain is overrated and it's far too direct and physical. Just a simple chemical reaction. What about something more intimate and cerebral than that?' the woman asked, her eyes suddenly tuning in on her.

Lucy said nothing and just stared back at the woman, determined she would not blink.

'Do you think I could make you have an orgasm, even against your will?' she asked Lucy.

Again she did not reply.

'See?' the woman went on. 'Isn't that even better than pain? You're sitting there now wondering if I would reach across and fit my hand in between your legs. What if I did and said all you had to do, to walk away from this, would be to let me make you come, no faking of course, would you? Would you rather I chewed something off?'

'I think I'd rather you chewed your own finger off in that case,' Lucy said, the veins in her neck throbbing.

The woman laughed. 'That's very funny, Lucy, even at a time like this.'

'You know my name?'

'We had a mutual friend and I was able to learn a lot about you. Then I opened my mind and I was able to learn everything about you, things you don't even know yourself.'

'Who?' Lucy asked.

'You still think you're going mad, don't you, Lucy? There's part of you that thinks this could be another part of the dream, the next stage. You'd so like to believe that you're just dreaming about what happened to your dad, the way the madman held him in the swimming pool and that the car is in the dream because you saw it in the swimming pool with Luke earlier on.'

'Who are you?' Lucy asked.

'We've been over that. I have no fucking idea who I am. I'm just a name. Do you want me to tell you the moment I knew that it wasn't madness, for me?'

Lucy stared at the back of the seat in front of her, trying to gauge the weight of the moment, to discern if this were indeed a vivid dream and she was still lying sleeping next to Luke Smith.

'When it happened in front of others. Things I had thought were secret to me, happening in my sick mind. This isn't just in your mind, Lucy. Even if you don't believe me now, when we get to the end of the journey, you will.'

'Where does the journey end?'

'At the beginning, of course,' Jenna said, laughing as though it were funny and obvious at the same time. 'A new beginning. But we have to get there first.'

There was a swishing noise and Lucy jerked her head to the side. Water was rising just above the window level of the car, green and thick. Had it been rising the whole time or did it just appear there out of her imagination? Lucy struggled against the belt, not knowing what she would do even if she were to get free. She replayed events in her mind, trying to find possible boundaries where she may have lapsed into a dream without realizing it. Or been taken prisoner by her own hallucinations.

'We'll drown,' Lucy said, watching the steady progress of the water, now over halfway up the window on her side, the bonnet covered and water lapping like waves over the windshield.

'Maybe we will. Better take a deep breath and see if you can hold it forever, although that would be just the same as being dead of course.'

The air pressure in the car felt greater and Lucy's ears popped, a bit like being on an aeroplane. The glass of the windscreen was warping, more like it was melting than giving under pressure.

There was a sound like an explosion and then a burst of light that went far beyond her visual range, blinding her. Under her, she felt a jog and realized the car had started to move through the light, gently and easily. Why was there no water? she wondered. The liquid had transformed itself into light. Lucy could not see or hear the woman next to her. In fact, there was only silence and smooth motion.

The car stopped moving but the light did not. It passed through her and at that moment Lucy knew for certain that what had happened in the swimming pool was real. This conviction was based on the fact that Lucy knew she was about to pass into something completely unreal and fabricated.

Chapter 44

In the room of the guesthouse, Wadlow repeated a ritual.

He fetched a bowl of hot water, gently unlaced Ryan's boots, removed his socks and cleansed the boy's feet. Dabbing the sore flesh with a towel, he nourished the wounds with antiseptic cream, applied good-sized plasters and finished by putting a pair of his own fresh socks on the boy's feet.

'Do your boots have to go right back on?' Wadlow asked.

Ryan nodded. 'We need to be going soon.'

'Should I check out of here?' Wadlow asked.

Again, the nod.

As the day faded and Wadlow Grace watched his last sunset, he silently followed the boy along the sidewalk and then, when there was no more sidewalk, the side of the road, until the town was behind them and they were approaching the Interstate.

'Where are we going?' Wadlow asked, shrugging his shoulders so his backpack lifted to a more comfortable position.

'Not very far. I couldn't walk much farther. Just to the dunes.'

'For what?' Wadlow asked.

'To spend the night,' the boy said over his shoulder, sounding irritated by the question.

Wadlow continued to follow in silence.

Abruptly, Ryan turned off the side of the road, heading through some trees that opened into a thin piece of forest before the first signs of sand appeared, streaked like salt across the dark peat of the earth.

'We should gather wood for a fire,' Ryan said.

They collected some dry twigs and bigger branches they came across in the short walk through the forest.

The day was almost over when they began to trek across the dunes that led to the ocean, out there somewhere in the grey. The terrain sloped up and down and the soft sand made it tiring, twigs prodding at Wadlow through his shirt.

'Are your feet holding up?' Wadlow asked.

'Yes,' Ryan almost spat back. 'Thanks,' he added, softening.

'Are we looking for somewhere particular?'

'I've been here before. So has Father. And his father.'

'Your pa?' Wadlow asked.

'Grandfather. It skips through generations, the gift.'

'Will you tell me about the gift?'

'In good time, yes. That's partly why we're here. Look, just over there.' Ryan was pointing to a flat section of sand at the bottom of a short but steep slope. 'It gives good shelter from the wind.'

Ryan made the fire while Wadlow sat on the soft sand and watched. The boy coaxed the fire into life, nudging the wood so the flame took hold. The boy sat the other side of it, watching Wadlow through the fire.

The sound of the fire mixed with the air and the water and it was a perfect balance, calming and soothing. It would be a shame to break the ambience with words, but Wadlow knew that that was their reason for being there. It was not his place to begin and he looked at the boy expectantly. Their eyes held each other across the glow and Ryan began to speak.

'The culture has many stories, stories that belong to the one who tells them. They are a part of him, of his breath and his being. The stories are kept alive because they pass from the mouth of one into the mouth of the other. Imagine the words, the sentences of the story, are a great long chain and the people are the links of the chain. The circle of the chain will go round forever, unless there is one link that is crucial, both its first and its last. My father, his father and his father. The chain that passes the story. I am that link. I am where the chain ends and begins again. I am the father to my father and the father to his father. I am me and I am Father. We are all one and the same. That is why I have been here before, Wadlow Grace, and why I will be here again.'

'Why am I here?'

'You are a part of the story. You make no sense outside of that. Listen and then your place and purpose will become clear.'

Like a boy scout, under the cover of chill dark and accompanied by the crackle of a campfire, Wadlow listened.

'We have been on this piece of land for a long time, eating what comes from it, catching what runs across it and fishing what comes from the water around it. That might have gone on forever, until he came. From water. Walking backwards. By the time he came, Father and his people were used to visits from the other side of the water and when the strangers came they would abandon their homes, taking to the cover of their surroundings until they knew they were in no danger. Countless stories have been written about this, but no page can contain this story because it has never been written down.

'On this day, when the chain began, it was Father who saw it first. I call him Father, because he was Father, but he was also only fifteen years old when this happened to him. There had been recent burials, many lost to plagues that later they would learn were brought by the strangers. He had no special reason for looking where he did, when he did. They had been fishing in the bay and were readying themselves to go back, already had their backs to the ocean. Father turned and there it was. A small spot, so distant it could have been a full stop on a page. But this was where things would begin, really begin. They went back to the village and warned people that it was time to become invisible again.

'It troubled Father that he had turned when he had and seen what he had. It had been no accident. He walked alone through the deserted village and found a place on the shore where he would not be seen. The ship had dropped its anchor and Father looked for the smaller boat that would carry the strangers to the shore. He waited but nothing happened, as though the ship were empty. It drifted on its mooring but it did not move.

'Father was like a fish, and from the side of the shore he carefully made his way to the water and into it, wanting to get closer to the ship. He swam as though he were a part of the water itself, barely above the surface even when he came for air, which was not often. Father took a longer course so that he could come from the rear and not be seen. When he made it and broke the surface, he saw something he did not recognise. Drawings on the wood. Many of them, but none of them able to tell him a story.

'M A Y F L O W E R.'

Wadlow stopped breathing for a moment.

'There was a movement, from the water, from the land, from everywhere. A wave that went through Father, the sea rushing towards the land as though it were afraid, wanting to get away from what it now contained. Something was moving through the water towards the land and Father knew he had to be there before it, to fend off the danger it brought. He swam for the shore, the waves pushing him in, aiding him.'

Ryan stopped.

'This happened when the *Mayflower* set down?' Wadlow asked, his throat dry.

'Yes, look in the books, Wadlow. It stopped in Provincetown before ending up in Plymouth. The tales of the Nauset talk of it and so do the books. What is the first thing those books tell you the men did when they put their feet on our land? They wrote. They began to embody the land and the people in their own words. But so much more than just that occurred on the beach.'

'What was the danger?' Wadlow asked.

'The danger was that we could become locked into a pattern of words that was not of our making. On the shore once again, Father fought the water from his lungs and tried to fill himself with air. The waves subsided, the wind stopped, the sun gave off no heat. There was perfect and awful silence. The water was like a sheet of paper.

'His head broke the surface of the water, the back of his head. He was emerging from the sea and he was walking backwards. His progress was unhurried, his posture calm. As he drew closer, his back still to Father, the book he carried was visible. Father did not know what to do – to run, to confront, to hide?

'The man turned and faced him, holding the book out in front so Father could see its cover, the metal that shimmered on it, the veins that connected them. It was hard to look away, the shape leading him into the cover and through it, into the pages which could trap him forever. This was the thing that later would be referred to as Nathan Lucas. This man was older than all time, was from before all time and had the power to stretch beyond all time. Father tried to pull his stare away from the lines that rolled over each other like snakes, like long worms, but he was pulled closer and closer.'

The fire crackled.

'The world itself took on the shape and movement of what Father watched, as though reality were remaking itself in a new pattern. Things were shifting beneath the surface, somewhere on the outside of everything, a place where there should be no outside. This man, this thing, that could do so much and looked so old, was in truth very young. Time was falling away from him. He needed to stop that happening.

'Words flooded Father and he felt himself melding with the pages of the thing in front of him and the thing itself was getting under his skin. In the sickening spin of all that was around him, he knew that the man and the book in front of him were almost one and the same. All the stories of the world flowed through Father in a single moment, a moment that should have killed him with its power. All of his brain, every single cell, was screaming with every voice that had ever lived, would ever live. Every tale and poem, story, truth and lie, became a part of him for one single deafening moment.

'In the silence that followed, the single arc of the story was left. The truth that flowed through the middle of every story. The Book. In every story.'

Ryan moved himself round to Wadlow's side of the fire, casting a shadow across him. Ryan sat, still cross-legged, but leaning forwards into Wadlow's face, a foot or so from it. The words touched him harder across the shorter distance.

'That day, as they faced each other across The Book, things came into the world that had no rightful place within it. Father and the man were able to conjure things purely through their speech. They were able to breathe life. The rest was locked away in words and patterns that no one could decipher, constellations of the mind that were so intricate and personal they were available to no one else. Those secrets, the stories that were in The Book, of where it would begin and end, were sent into the world, made flesh by the words of those who whispered the story.'

Ryan stretched to be even nearer, so close Wadlow could almost have touched the boy's lips with his own.

'And other things were made that day. A being fabricated from nothing more than the combined sound and breath of a great line of men. A being that would serve the purpose of the story, something that would be its only purpose. The Man of Words. Since that time, they have been passing you down from mouth to mouth. Through time, you have served the point of the story, touching it, being a part of it. The story, this story, is almost at a close.'

Wadlow blinked slowly.

'For this story to end and a new one to begin, there must be no trace. The Man of Words is a character of the old story. He can have no place in the new beginning. Do you understand that, Wadlow Grace?'

Wadlow held Randall's notebook up. 'My whole life is in here and it was written for me.'

'It was spoken for you,' Ryan said.

'And now it ends,' Wadlow said.

'A new beginning,' Ryan said, reaching out, and Wadlow thought the boy was about to take his hand.

Tossing it like a Frisbee, Ryan threw Randall's notebook over his shoulder into the fire. Wadlow jumped as he saw it go in, expecting to feel the burn on his own skin as his life was consumed by flames. There was no feeling at all. From his bag he brought Nancy Lloyd's old notebook and his own, heaving them onto the pyre with Randall's. The fire took hold of all three with a speed that was surprising, as though the pages had been tinder-dry, ready. Wadlow wondered if this is how all the books in his great underground bunker had looked when he set it alight four years earlier, turning it into a crematorium.

Ryan had stopped speaking the best part of ten minutes earlier and all that could be heard was the sound of the fire crackling in the wind, small flakes of smouldering wood and paper popping as they took flight. The wind made the flame liquid, pushing it in several directions.

Wadlow stared into the heart of the flames until his vision became blurry. The same way as at their first meeting, Wadlow felt the weight of Ryan's hand on his own and the gentle caress of his other.

He looked at Ryan, his eyes taking a moment to adjust. Wadlow touched Ryan's cheek, working his fingers in the hairline, feeling the fine strands and the roots. Ryan stroked the inside of Wadlow's wrist, running a fingertip over the pulsing vein. They made equal distance to meet halfway and kiss, Ryan's mouth as delicate as Wadlow had secretly imagined it would be. Working his mouth off Ryan's, Wadlow let it wander over the boy's chin and down his neck, licking at the Adam's apple before placing his mouth over it and sucking lightly, hearing the gasp.

They undressed each other in an unhurried, almost ceremonious way, the gentle curvature of Ryan's chest making a shadow across the top of his belly. Wadlow felt self-conscious as the boy helped him off with jeans and underwear, but once they were both naked in the short glow of the fire, he realized it was the clothes themselves that were embarrassing and now he felt natural and unencumbered.

This would be the one and only time and it put a brake on them both.

When Ryan crouched over Wadlow as he lay on the sand, their eyes met as their bodies became joined, the boy tensing his features and whole body as he entered into union with Wadlow. Finally, he was sitting astride his prostrate body, and he leaned forwards to feather his hands over Wadlow's torso. Wadlow had to sit up and kiss, stretching his neck and upper back to do so. They shuffled about until Wadlow was also in a sitting position and Ryan held him by locking his fingers behind his neck.

Ryan's gauze-clad heels dug into the sand as he moved himself back and forth and Wadlow dug his own feet and hands in, trying to anchor himself and find a complementary friction. The noise they made now was climbing higher than the elements around them, the wind carrying their wordless cries out to the sea and into the core of the flame.

There could, Wadlow realized as the orgasm swallowed him, have been no words for the moment in any case. All he could describe to himself was its effects; even as it was happening, he could tell the way it would feel beyond the escape.

Under a soft fur blanket, they lay as the fire dwindled into dark, bodies pressed close, wordless and together.

Chapter 45

Wadlow clung to Ryan as tightly as he dared without waking the boy. He had slept intermittently, his mind in a thousand places and his body in only one. The chill of the night was giving way to the warmth of the sun as it rose above the crest of a dune, the windbreak sheltering them from draught, the animal pelt trapping the warmth generated by their own skin.

He had been expecting morning to bring a new hunger, a need to make love with Ryan one more time, but it did not. All he wanted to do was hold on and breathe in time with Ryan as he slept in serenity.

Ryan turned and looked at Wadlow with a sleepy smile. 'Morning,' he said.

'Morning,' Wadlow repeated, lifting his arm to let Ryan move into its hollow. They lay listening to the ocean wash the sand, Wadlow smoothing the skin of Ryan's back with a gentle hand.

'We should get moving,' Ryan said, breaking away gradually and sitting up.

Wadlow followed the long arc of Ryan's back with his eyes.

He stood and Wadlow watched him scratch his head and rub his stomach as though hungry. Unselfconscious about his nudity, he gathered his clothing up piece by piece, putting it all in a pile before turning his attention back to Wadlow.

'You too,' he said.

'I know. I just want to lie here for a while longer,' Wadlow said. 'Watching you,' he added. Now, desire did have a hold and Wadlow adjusted the skin blanket around himself.

'Sure,' Ryan said, bending to lift his shorts from the top of the pile.

When he was dressed, Ryan made a similar mound for Wadlow, handing him his underwear.

'Where are we going?' Wadlow asked, hopping from leg to leg into his shorts and then standing one-legged to put his socks on.

Ryan was staring at him and Wadlow chided himself, knowing that their paths were about to diverge as suddenly as they had merged.

'Okay,' Wadlow said, fastening his pants. 'Where am I going?'

'Home,' Ryan said.

Wadlow stood still, his shirt only half pulled up his arm. 'Where are you going?' he asked.

'Home,' Ryan repeated, picking up the blanket and giving it a shake.

Without words, they trooped across the dunes, the noise of boots in sand almost covered by the breeze and the sound of the water. They walked down into the bottom of a sandy basin and then climbed again. At the peak, Wadlow turned and looked at the ocean.

'Walking backwards, he brings time,' Ryan said, the words drifting into Wadlow's ear.

'Ready for the long journey,' Wadlow finished.

The natural spill of the sea and the whine of the early air was fractured by the sound of a truck's horn, an engine shifting gear as it altered speed. Wadlow turned from the ocean and followed Ryan, who was already heading in the direction of the highway. The soft carpet of sand hardened and became dirtier until they were trekking through a small gorse thicket, finding themselves on the side of the highway.

'Where's home?' Wadlow asked, eyeing the long tongue of road that pointed to the north of the Cape.

Ryan touched his own chest and then his head. 'I won't ever let you die, Wadlow Grace. You live on in here,' he said, touching his chest again, 'and in here,' he finished, touching his head once more.

'Mama Grace was a singer, a big lady, and Pa Grace was

a carpenter. He made things. My brother Randall, they said he was backwards, on account of him not speaking. I was my Mama's angel,' Wadlow recited, clinging to the words, knowing they were his life. 'I was the preacher's angel too. All those books, all those years. They used to call me Waddler. Ma. Pa Randall. The Preacher.' He paused. 'Nancy Lloyd.'

'You will see them all again, Wadlow, I promise you that. I won't let your story die. Each time I breathe it, it is you that breathes through it. And your family. Everyone that had been special to you. Everyone,' Ryan said.

'I know, but I'm scared. This is the end of the story for me.'

'Kiss me,' Ryan said.

Wadlow touched his mouth onto Ryan's, as cautiously as he had the night before. The boy's breath seeped into his mouth and his lips were slightly wet. Wadlow tried to imagine not feeling anything, to be dead in a place beyond words. He took Ryan's head in firm hands and positioned it so he could open his mouth wider and explore, until he felt the yawning and excruciating strain in his jaw, his tongue writhing with the boy's. He pressed so hard he could feel the pain far down in his bones, the fluidity of the kiss pouring him into Ryan. It became harder to breathe and they moved their faces about, hands pulling hair and small snorts escaping nostrils.

Wadlow broke away from the kiss and looked over Ryan's shoulder as a sooty smudge on the horizon of the road moved closer, its speed so even it might have been floating.

The preacher's '55 Plymouth cruised to a stop and the door opened.

Ryan was looking at him, on the threshold of heaving tears, and Wadlow wanted to tell him it was alright, that he wasn't afraid any more, but there were no words left. The text had no further use for him. The ink had run away into nothing and he had reached a final full stop. He stepped into the car, feeling the familiarity of the seat beneath him.

The car jogged into motion and then Wadlow felt nothing, words beginning to fail him.

Preacher. Memphis. Seven days. An angel. Plymouth. Randall Grace. Ryan Summer. Nancy Lloyd. Forest Lawn Memorial. Fine things. This is the real secret of God's Gift. Something very special and very nice. Wadlow Grace. Talking to be done. Don't be starting me, child. Emetic. Singer. Carpenter. House. Ghost. The Book. Nathan Lucas. He comes from water, walking backwards. He brings time, ready for the long journey. A small spot of light on a distant page. Is that your life. Man of Words. Wadlow Grace. Wadlow. Grace. Wad. Wadlow . . .

Chapter 46

It was still early when Ryan arrived at the sea. The world had fused into the sound of the wind, washed out by the breaking of the waves. The Man of Words was gone, but Ryan did not feel alone. He was the page, the doorway, the filter, the context in which the story would play itself out.

He sat cross-legged, just short of where the sea's power diminished. He stared out across its horizon, letting his eyes glide across the flat plane that appeared to go on forever.

'He comes from water, walking backwards. He brings time, ready for the long journey.'

There were people out there in the world, at that moment, who needed to get to a place it was possible only for Ryan Summer to create. He was the fabricant and it was his mind that would build the world in which they might come to the end of the story.

The doorways were already there pressed onto his mind and he could sense presence at their thresholds, people travelling towards them, but it was down to Ryan to create a place for them to go. He was the clean page that would provide the context.

The water calmed before him and a tension whose existence he had not been aware of, released. Ryan felt as though he had been clenched all of his life, prepared for something that had been kept a secret from him.

As though it were nothing more than the clean white page of a book ready for ink, Ryan opened his mind.

Chapter 47

The mirror spat Luke out as though he tasted bad. He flew forward too fast for his legs and fell on his face, tasting sand.

Luke stood and brushed at himself, looking down and realizing he was back in clothes, his school uniform. He stared out across the flat, bare desert, straining his eyes to find the seam of the horizon. Agoraphobia and claustrophobia vied in his head. A low wind lifted the lightest grains of sand and while it was hot, it was certainly not what he would have expected for a desert.

He turned 180 degrees and stopped, halted by the two things he saw.

The Palace Hotel, grim granite, the same small windows and the turrets, stood at the top of a small mound, free from the fence that had imprisoned it on the seafront. Instead, it was planted here on the eternal beach, all sand and no sea to relieve it. It was like something out of Egypt, he remembered Terry Wood saying to him. The old man had been right at the time, but here it was even more pronounced. This is what it would be like to see a pyramid, Luke thought.

Next to the hotel was the car Luke had seen in the swimming pool with Tony Wood and Lucy. The car his mother had been photographed with.

Luke regarded the building and could tell he was also being watched, perhaps by the building itself. Something about the edifice troubled him, not just the fact that it was robbed of the context he had seen it in previously. He was more familiar with the building than he had thought. Luke fingered the key in his pocket, letting it roam to the brass tag and its raised bumps.

One, two, three, four, five, six, seven, eight.

Nine.

There were nine floors, not eight.

Ignoring the car, he approached the Palace, or whatever the building really was.

The two front doors, highly polished brass, the same sort as the key and its label, swung back in oiled silence.

Luke walked through, wondering if he would see the hotel in its fire-damaged state or as it would have been before, in its heyday even.

Neither.

Luke panicked, jerking from side to side, feeling the pain in his neck as he tried to avoid the endlessly replicated images of himself.

Everything was a mirror – floor, ceiling and walls. Each surface was highly polished glass, reflective and dazzling. No matter where he looked, Luke was taunted by himself. The space was similar in size to the reception he had stood in with Terry Wood in Dray, but that was all.

He turned to run back through the doors and was confronted only by his own reflection, the opening no longer there. He did the only thing he could, forcing his eyes closed against the blinding sight, knowing it would still be there once he opened his eyes again.

The key in his pocket gave a jangle. Would the stairs be there? His way up to the ninth floor. Bracing himself, he opened his eyes and quickly scanned across the infinity of repetition, desperate for a way up and out. It was there, but it was the same as everything else, a stairway of mirrors ascending into unknown light.

Luke was afraid to make the dash across the floor, as though the crossfire of reflection would trap him like a laser beam. In the periphery of his vision, the army of his reflections had begun to disobey the movements of his own body. They had broken free from Luke, no longer taking him as a reference point. He turned to the nearest wall and the reflection there, about twenty feet from him, stopped in a mocking posture, mimicking Luke's own. He could see the expression on its face and knew it did not correspond to his own. For the larger part of a minute he stood and faced the glass, trying to stare himself out.

A shudder erupted behind his ears and quickly ran the length of his vertebrae. Something inside him unclenched and he could not get a fix on what was happening until he returned his concentration to the mirror.

The image was trying to get free of the glass. It no longer needed Luke, that much was clear, but now it was trying to cross over from the thin layer of its existence and into the world. It moved forward, anxious and annoyed at its weakness.

'Oh God,' Luke said aloud. The acoustics of the space were completely dead and they smothered the words, almost gagging him. 'No,' he shouted, wondering why his words would not ricochet around all the glass.

He broke his concentration and ran for the stairs. His feet were making no sound and he looked down at them as they began to make the climb. Moving fast enough to stop himself focusing on any single point, Luke kept count of the floors, not even sure if the landings he passed really led anywhere. All the time he listened into the soundless void he had left behind him, ready for the metallic tinkle of glass and the sound of footsteps closing in on him. When he got to seven, he looked ahead, knowing he would need to see where he was going. Eight, the walls and the steps still flooding his likeness back into his senses.

Past the landing of the eighth and he looked directly ahead.

Welcoming darkness. He would never have expected to be so glad to see an absence of light, a place where he could be without seeing himself. The rectangular patch was the size of a door, growing as he approached it. Luke wanted to look back, in case something was following him or he ended up needing to retreat from the dark. In truth, Luke did not know if there was any way forward or back. All he had placed his trust in was the key in his pocket, and that led only forward.

Darkness. Silence. But – real silence. He could hear the sound of his own body in the world once more, the labour of his breathing and the troubled rhythm of his heart.

This was just the landing, the same as the ones he had seen in Dray, except there were no corridors leading off. Only one ordinary brown oak hotel door and the number nine twenty-eight. He turned the key in the lock, opened the door and entered.

'Hello, Lucas.'

It was his mother.

They were in the spare room in the house in . . . where? Southend? London? Plymouth?

She sat on a chair, in familiar repose, as though she were on the border of sleep or about to faint. Her face was not made up. Without their carefully painted borders and filled-in pout, her lips were thin and frail and her eyes small and barely noticeable, as if lost on her face.

Nervously, Luke glanced to his right, moving only his eyes to see if the mirror was there. It was.

'Don't be afraid of that,' his mother said.

'Where is this? Where are we?' he asked.

She looked around.

'Home,' she said. 'Don't you recognize it?'

'I don't know where we are,' he said.

'And that makes you afraid? Are you afraid of me, Lucas? I was never scared of you. You felt very powerful the last time I saw you, didn't you? I remember how ferocious you were with me.'

Luke chewed his bottom lip and looked to his right once more.

'Don't be scared of that, babe. Sit down. Things are going to be alright, I promise you.'

'Where are we?' he asked again, thinking of the long dash he had made up the stairs, knowing there was no way he could do that again. 'How do we get out?'

'All in good time. Sit,' she said.

Luke sat on the floor in front of her, cross-legged.

'When we did this the last time, you were angry with

me, asking about your father, where you came from, what I'd been doing in Plymouth and why I had lied to you. That was all for your sake, babe.'

'You're lying to me again,' he said.

The room felt so much like the one in London and Southend, it was hard to believe they were not in one or the other.

'You've asked where we are,' his mother said. 'Where do you think we are?'

'I saw a hotel like this one, from the outside, when I went to Dray. Except it was burned down, in 1955.'

His mother nodded, as though indicating he had said something correct, or expected.

'And what made you go to Dray?'

'These,' he said, laying out the postcard, the two photographs and the key.

'Which you found among my things when you went looking,' she said, touching below her throat where the key for the box used to be. 'One key led you to another key and you hope that will lead you through a door and into answers for all those questions.'

'Both pictures were taken in Dray, where this – where the hotel – is.'

'Look at me, Lucas. I'm old, older than you realize. I was almost thirty when I first laid my hand on the car in that picture, the year of the fire at the hotel.'

'That was . . .'

'Forty-five years ago,' she finished. 'I will be seventy-five years old soon.'

Luke swallowed. Tony Wood had said as much at the swimming pool.

'Is Tony Wood my dad? Did you meet him here, in Plymouth, or Southend?'

'Tony is a good man. Terry as well. They saw me alright, babe. Tony's not your dad. They worked here for the man who owned it.'

'Cameron. I know,' he said. He paused. 'Not Cameron? Cameron's not my dad. You said he had money. Is it him?

It's not.' Luke halted the babble of questions and accusations.

She pointed at the picture on the floor.

'That's Luke, isn't it, the other one?' he asked, pointing at the picture of him sitting on the wall.

She shook her head.

'No, no it isn't. That's your father. And it's Luke's father.'

Luke looked up from the picture and at his mother. 'You said we were half-brothers, that we had different dads.'

'That's Luke's father,' she said, with such matter-of-fact conviction Luke was drawn to the truth of the words, as though it were the first time she had ever told him anything that was not some sort of lie. 'That's Luke's father. And it's Luke. And it's your father.'

She looked him in the eyes.

'And it's you as well.'

'I don't understand you, Mum.'

'There're things I should tell you that you don't know about me or even about yourself, and you should. You have to. There's no choice in that. It took me fifteen years until I believed that.'

'Mum, who is this in the picture?'

'I told you. It's Luke's father. And it's Luke. And it's your father. And it's you. Can't you see it?'

'But that doesn't make any sense.'

'If you were there, then, surrounded by someone with real charm, it blinded you, you drowned in it. I was so charmed by him, even though he was older. He was much older than me, almost twice my age, in his sixties.'

Luke sat looking at her, this woman who was his mother but had been so much else before he existed. She seemed like that other person to him, someone from a past he knew nothing about.

'When I touched that car for the first time, that was what led me to meet him, the nearest you had to a father. You think I've been unkind to you, don't you, Lucas?'

'All I want is for you to explain things to me, properly.

No lies. Tell me about the other Luke and his dad, and then tell me about my dad.'

'In Dray, in 1955, I touched the door of this car as the man who had been cleaning it took my picture, the one you have there. The car, I found out, belonged to a man called Nathan Lucas. He was a friend of Clough Cameron, the man who owned the hotel, the one you just mentioned. I spent one weekend with him, that was all.'

'He's Luke's dad? What about me?'

She was ignoring him. 'We talked for almost two whole days, when we weren't laughing or . . .' his mother gasped.

Luke looked up at her and flinched when he saw what she was doing to herself, the posture of her legs and the urgent movement of her hand.

'Stop it!' Luke shouted. 'Stop and talk to me, Mum, please.'

'He gave me that photograph,' his mother said, pointing to the other Luke. 'And he told me that would be my first son. And that it would also be the father of my first son. I was going to carry part of him and then, when the time came, I would carry that part over again. And again.'

'I don't understand,' he said, afraid that he might and of where it would lead.

'Neither did I, babe, at first,' she smiled. Wind gusted around the outside of the room, making tunes with the edges of the hotel. 'He brought me to this room, on a floor of the hotel I never knew about, and he showed me that mirror, and what was living in it.' She motioned to the photograph. 'He tried to explain it to me, how he had a part of himself that was separate as well as being a part of him.' She stopped.

Luke looked at her.

'It's funny,' she continued. 'I feel shy now with you, even though you are still that same part of him, reformed through me. You would think I could tell you this without embarrassment, considering the things I did with him. And the things we have done.'

'I want you to tell me,' Luke said.

'Nathan showed me the mirror. I stood in front of it and looked at what was in there. I wanted it. I wanted to be able to walk through that glass as though it wasn't there and take what was on the other side. Nathan knew that. He could see it on my face and feel it in my mind.' Bella looked at him. 'He was so, so sweet. So beautiful, just the way you are, and he was standing in the glass gazing back at me, wanting me.'

The sound of the wind was more intense now, and it felt like they were in an oven.

'I held my hands out to him and he came to me. I had made it happen. I used to wonder if I could have just turned and walked out of this room and gone away. But I didn't, because I didn't want to. I wanted him, in the way I wanted what came from him, and what came from that. And you.'

An angry roar came from the wind and it made the room feel smaller.

'Nathan watched, gave instructions, encouraged his own flesh to become a part of mine.' Her own hand soothed herself once more, less passionate and more delicate. 'It was rougher than I wanted it to be, but I understood what was going on. I could feel him everywhere, insinuating himself into me. When the moment came, where this boy was going to finally lose control of himself, Nathan covered my eyes with his hands, pinning my head to the table. The pain of childbirth is something, but this was more than that. You boys were more strain going in than forcing out. There was a sense of pain that I couldn't give you words for. I could hear Nathan making encouraging noises and then the part of the boy that was forced into me seemed to dissolve and I was filled with something different. I could feel them touching me everywhere, finding their way inside me and looking for a safe place. Long tendrils that stroked and elongated me. Nathan gave me something to bite on and I clenched my teeth around it. I could feel it being conceived in me, not in that usual warm way. I could actually sense it knitting together with me, the way he was becoming a part of me. Nathan had given me a part of himself and let himself be made into something else.'

Luke was trying to piece it together, uncomfortable with the explicitness.

'Where was the boy from the mirror?' he asked.

She laid her hands around her stomach. 'In here, waiting. The fire had razed the hotel to the ground and I was moved to a house that had been in waiting, without my realizing. A week later, in 1955, I gave birth to a baby boy and he was called Luke. I raised him in Dray near the sea and by the time he was twelve, he knew that what was in the mirror was not really himself, so I began to make preparations. When he was fifteen, in 1970, it was time. A house had been made ready for me in Plymouth, so we moved there, again the water. You've seen that house, of course. The story is very similar. I watch and I wait, until you begin to get a sense of who you are not, and of who you might be. That came a little earlier when we were in Plymouth, as though you had grown ahead. You had only turned ten when you thought the man in the mirror was following you. I contacted Tony and I was told Southend would be there when I needed it.'

'He knew?' Luke cut in.

'No. He knew I needed it, that was all. The awareness troubled you for longer in Plymouth, because you had still turned fifteen when the time came, and I knew there must have been a reason for that. In 1985, you were born in Southend-on-Sea , a painful birth. You're the most beautiful of them, Luke. I loved you so much when you were born and a little boy. When the diabetes was diagnosed, I was afraid that something was happening I didn't know about. I know there are reasons for all of this that I will never know.'

'There were no other dads, ever?' Luke asked, thinking of all the various times throughout each year she had told him it was his birthday.

Bella shook her head. 'Just you. And him. I've had this talk with you three times now,' she smiled.

'But this isn't the same, not like the other times,' he said.

'You're right. It isn't. It's time for you to go home.'

'No,' he said.

'Listen to the fire. Can you hear it, Lucas? It knows you, it remembers you.'

She was right. It hadn't been wind he heard whipping the building from outside, it had been fire taking hold of the building's insides and incinerating them.

The fire crackled and popped from behind the closed door. Luke could see the red seep under it, more than just a reflection. It was trying to get in.

'What are you doing?' he shouted at his mother as she walked calmly to the door.

She touched the handle and there was a hissing sound. Luke looked at the knob and saw steam rising from his mother's hand as the white heat of the brass turned skin to vapour. She was smiling and her chest rose and fell in deep strokes.

'Don't!' he screamed as she threw the door back.

Luke expected the fire to send a hot blast in that would render his mother to ashes, but instead the orange wall just bayed at the door. Perhaps it was going to shoot a snake-like tongue at her, wrap around her waist and take her deep into its hot mouth.

She turned and spoke to him.

'This is where you came from, how you were born the first time. My sweet boy. This is you.'

Two arms of flame reached from the mass and encircled her. She did not seem to burn.

'Lucas. Nathan. I love you.'

A circle of flame lifted around her ankles and Luke saw it redden her skin. It was burning even if she did not feel it. He moved forward, ready to grab her.

And she was gone.

The fire did not burn her. She had literally been consumed by the flames. The circle had lifted around her like a cowl, covering her and then incorporating her into itself. The mass of heat seemed more alive than ever, its sound

317

like breath. Several long arcs of flame spurted and whistled past his face, not touching him, but he felt the caress of the air. He stared into the fire and it was bottomless. He imagined it heating through the mirrored floors he had run up, reflecting into itself, feeding on itself.

This was not the way out. It was not meant to be.

Luke turned and looked in the mirror.

He had never felt more separate from what looked back at him. Now he was able to give it a name, and it was not his own. This was not him. I am not you. You are not me, he thought.

Nathan Lucas smiled at him.

Luke could see behind himself in the mirror. The fire had burned away most of the wall and doorway and was spreading out, up, down and across. Soon there would be nothing but a sea of it, and the mirror.

Nathan stared out of the mirror, no longer smiling. He waved Luke in, encouraging him to make the journey away from the flames and into the mirror, into himself.

Sweat trickled down one side of Luke's face. He looked down and saw the floor smouldering. Behind the mirror, a fire about three feet high was advancing quickly up the wall.

Nathan held his arms open, as though ready to welcome Luke.

Fuck you, Luke thought to himself, and ran headlong at the glass, as fast as he could.

By the time Nathan's faked look of surprise had turned to a satisfied smile, it was too late to turn back and Luke felt an explosion, a fireball that swept him towards, through and into the mirror.

There was heat greater than he had ever known and the smashing sound was lost in the roar as the elements around him were pulverized and the mirror reverted back to its natural state.

Sand fell around him and he realized he had passed through the mirror and was on a beach.

Chapter 48

Three strips, land, sea and sky, filled Luke's vision. All the places of the world in a single glance, earth, water and air. Luke had never stood on this beach, he was certain. As certain as he was that he also knew where it was, and that he had been there before. He knew what it felt like to have a vivid dream or experience a déjà vu, and this felt like neither of those. If he had to design a beach, was asked to write one in a story, this was how it would look. Am I making this up? he asked himself. After the painful contortions of the Palace and its mirrors, Luke could sense that his surroundings were real, at a level so deep, it was beyond the reach of words or even thought.

Thoughts followed him like an energy trace, coming through the mirror just after him and planting themselves back in his head. What had he and his mother talked about? He remembered and the dread plummeted through him.

'.yenrouj gnol eht rof ydaer, emit sgnirb eH. sdrawkcab gniklaw, retaw morf semoc eH'

Luke turned to the source of the sound.

A boy about his own age stood in front of him, like a ghost. At first, Luke was afraid it was the reflection of himself, the thing that had tried to break free of the mirror in the Palace. Then he saw it was not the distorted reflection of himself. The boy was darker-skinned and had shining black hair the colour of oil and almost touching his shoulders.

'.yenrouj gnol eht rof ydaer, emit sgnirb eH .sdrawkcab gniklaw, retaw morf semoc eH'

Luke made a face, almost as though he were in pain, as he tried to understand the twisted words that came from the boy. He was talking backwards.

'He comes from water, walking backwards. He brings time, ready for the long journey.'

The words had changed their direction and made sense, at least individually. The sentence meant nothing to Luke.

'Where are we?' he asked.

'In a place beyond the text. Where the story ends. This is a place of confusion, a bad place, where things began, a long time ago. You can understand me, can't you?

'Yes,' Luke replied.

'My name is Ryan Summer. Many things cross on this beach, have touched each other in the past and the present. We are caught in those lines and there is only one key that will bring sense and a kind of harmony to this.'

'What?' Luke asked.

'He comes from water, walking backwards. He brings time, ready for the long journey.'

Luke stared at Ryan.

Ryan said it again. He repeated it several more times, always with the insistent and troubling rhythm, making it sound like a spell.

'He has travelled across all time, against time, ready for this moment. He was on this beach almost four hundred years ago, bringing The Book with him,' Ryan said. 'It was there, like my ancestor, only to serve this one moment. He has come backwards from outside of everything and he is waiting to meet with you.'

This was worse than not being able to understand. Now the words had meaning, they just made no sense.

'I don't understand,' Luke said.

'He comes from water, walking backwards. He brings time, ready for the long journey. There is one word missing. An obvious word. Forward. He is ready to start his journey in a new direction, a new beginning. He will no longer travel backwards against time. Instead, he will use you to go forwards. You are his vessel, his method to go in the opposite direction.'

'Tell me where we are,' Luke said.

'We are somewhere that is real and yet beyond the text.

This is a place of Notext. You have to make the choice, Luke Smith. The road is forwards, but there is more than one path. You must choose the road. I am just the con-text, the fabricant, the one who makes this possible. You must choose the way into the new beginning.'

The boy looked at something over Luke's shoulder, and Luke turned to look also.

Across the calm surface of the ocean, a ripple. Luke eyed it and saw something moving beneath the surface of the water.

'You must choose,' the boy said, resting his hands on Luke's shoulder.

'What is it?' Luke asked turning.

The boy had gone, and yet it felt like he was everywhere at once, his eyes – no, his mind and thoughts – a part of the place.

The car broke the surface of the water about twenty feet out and Luke recognized it immediately. Like a submarine, it came from the depths, headlights dim in the water. It made steady progress up the slight slope and towards Luke, dripping water. The small ship crest on the bonnet surfaced and for a few moments looked like a tiny galleon floating unaided. The word Plymouth became visible. The car stopped in front of him and one of the doors opened.

'Luke.'

It was Lucy. He let air escape from his lungs and realized he had been holding his breath in expectation and fear.

Lucy was staring at him and he saw that she was crying, almost without movement or sound, as though sadness were seeping from her.

Luke went closer and released Lucy from the seatbelt and they embraced with force.

'I'm frightened, Lucy. I don't want to be here.'

Her hands stroked the length of his back, squeezing him and making him feel better.

'Don't leave me, please,' he whispered into her ear, wanting to cry but feeling as though he should stay as calm as he could. 'What's happening?' he asked, pulling back to look into her face.

'I don't know, but I won't leave you, Luke. I promise.'

He kissed her and it was as though the place they were in had dissolved and she was the only place he needed to be. If they could have stayed that way forever, Luke would have accepted it.

Hands gripped the back of his shirt, tugging him back, the sound of tearing.

It was the man he had seen in the room, the one who had attacked him. He was on top of Luke once more, trying to do the same thing again, blows raining in on him.

The man's fist flattened against Luke's chin, opening the ripe skin of his lips and sending the taste of blood into his mouth. Lucy was behind the man she had called her father and was pulling at his shirt, slapping his head and shouting at him to leave Luke alone. As the man turned to shout at Lucy, Luke surprised himself with an uppercut that caught the man directly under the jaw, closing his mouth with a force that was too great for several of his teeth, which broke audibly.

Luke heaved the weight off him and stood.

'This is for last time,' he spat and swung a long kick into the man's stomach.

'Stop!' Lucy screamed.

'!potS'

Luke's leg flew out of the man's stomach and he was back on the floor, the man on top of him. His fist pulled away from the man's jaw and then the man was looking at Lucy. The man's punch reversed out of Luke's mouth and the blood filled his lips, the skin sealed once more.

They were standing once again, but Luke was no longer embracing Lucy.

'Dad, Dad, it's not him. Stop it.'

Nausea drifted over him, his head fuzzy. Luke had heard exactly what she said and yet he could not get the words to make any sense. He no longer understood what she was saying. The rhythm of her sentence, the pattern made by the arrangement of words were all unintelligible. Down to each single word, nothing meant anything. Each letter making up each word was a dead and soulless body.

'Luke,' she said.

Luke gave her an empty stare, the sounds she made bouncing straight off him, nothing absorbed. 'Oh God,' he said.

'What's wrong?'

'Luke?'

'Help me, please. Don't hurt me,' Luke said. He could feel the memory of Lucy fading, erased from the space inside himself. Soon, he knew, she would be a stranger to him. 'Please, Lucy. I can't understand what you're talking about. Can you understand me?' he said, wondering what she was saying to him. Her words were like a foreign language. He continued to retreat from the noise, still followed by her.

'What did he say?'

'He's talking backwards, Luce.'

'Be careful, Lucy!' Luke shouted. He tried to point at the woman who had emerged from round the side of the car and was approaching Lucy, but as he raised his arm, it flew off behind him.

Luke wanted to warn her, to help her so much, that he forced himself to make sense, to do what was needed, surprised at the throb of power he felt through himself as he tried to reverse himself, or them. Either way, he needed to be synchronized.

'!ycuL'

'Lucy!'

It was too late.

Luke's arm pointed just as the smiling and confident woman stood directly behind Lucy and lifted the short length of wire above her and then down round Lucy's neck, moving her hands together as though tying a knot.

Lucy sputtered and lost her balance as the woman dragged her back so she rested against the car.

Both Luke and Lucy's father moved forward.

'Uh-uh. Don't do that. One more step and I'll cut right through. This is a sharp wire and I'm strong enough at the moment to take her fucking head off.'

A sore-looking red line had already appeared on the skin of Lucy's neck.

The ground gave a tremor that made Luke's legs buckle. He looked at the ground and then out to sea.

In the ocean, beneath its surface, a wave began and reverberated out, pushing water aside as its sheer force cut a path towards the shore. As Luke looked at the sea, it appeared bigger and more alive than it had before, filled with the energy of the current running through it. There was a feeling of the depth and power of what was before him, its ability to smother him. A second wave pulsed and Luke felt it in the ground beneath him, the sand momentarily becoming concave.

From the midst of the waves, fifty feet from the shore, a head popped up, as though a swimmer had surfaced up for air. Gently, the shape emerged from the sea, almost lost against the background of water.

He was walking backwards.

Luke wanted to turn and see if Lucy was alright, but he was not able to take his eyes off what was coming up the beach. They all stood and watched as a boy emerged from the depths, his shoulders visible, then all of his upper body and finally his legs.

Luke fixed his eyes on the back of the boy walking in his direction as though guided by an unseen force. He was holding something out in front of him. When he was five feet away from Luke, he turned and held out The Book to him. Involuntarily, Luke's arms lifted as though he too were holding it. It was Nathan Lucas, the other half of his perverted reflection made flesh.

'Hello.' When Nathan spoke, Luke's jaw moved in time with it and the same words came from his mouth. 'This is confusing for you, I appreciate that. You are a son, a brother and a father to me. You are me. I am you. It is time for us to be together.'

Nathan's eyes flitted round the other figures on the beach.

'Hello again, Mr Kavanagh, it's been some years. Lucy,' Nathan said. He turned his attention back to Luke. 'We are outside. We are beyond the text, hiding in the small spaces between words and the worlds created by them.'

Still Luke's jaw was mirroring that of Nathan's, his mouth uttering the same words.

'Who are you?' Luke asked.

Nathan spoke the same words at the same time, identical in shape and sound.

'I am you. You are me.'

Luke was not sure which one of them had said it. He put his hands on his head and pressed hard, angry and almost trying to force the thoughts from his head. Nathan copied him.

'Stop.'

The unison was so precise it made Luke want to scream.

'Are you thinking exactly the same thoughts as me?'

Luke fought to find the core of himself, the sense of certainty about who he was and what separated him from everyone else, even this boy who looked almost the same as him and was reflecting everything he said, did and, perhaps, thought.

'It's time for us to be together. We will begin the long journey forwards. Thanks to Mr Kavanagh, Alexander Cameron is finally gone, Burns too. Even the blind man. Gordius is waiting for us now. The time is right for us to emerge, to lead. We have all time at our disposal. A new beginning.'

They spoke with one voice.

Nathan took two steps forward and Luke mirrored the movement, his hands coming to rest on The Book.

'Don't,' Luke heard Lucy gurgle and then she gasped, the wire pulled tighter.

Luke and Nathan stood either side of The Book as though it were a pivot. Luke's hands began to tingle.

'Even now, it has power. Can you feel it? We can write

any story we wish with this. All we need is the knotwork that flows through the stories like their arteries.'

Luke had stopped speaking in time with Nathan. His hands were beginning to hurt, but he did not feel as though he could let go of the dark green volume, ancient and damp.

'I think you know what I'm going to ask you for now, don't you, Mr Kavanagh? And you know what I'm going to offer you in return, don't you?' Nathan said, glancing over at Lucy and the woman.

'Luke.' It was Lucy, and as she spoke, he felt the grip of The Book loosen, a flash of her in his mind, their embrace, the kiss. Nathan had felt it too, Luke knew, because he blinked, trying to hide his surprise.

'I know you have no trust for me, Mr Kavanagh, and I have never given you cause for any. That is why it seems simpler to give you no choice. Our friend there will happily garrotte your daughter's head off. I actually think she would like to do that in any case and I may not be able to stop her. Let me have the chain round your neck, please,' Nathan said.

'And then you'll let her do it anyway?'

'Dad, don't give them up,' Lucy said.

'Shut your fucking mouth,' the woman said.

'What do you think, Luke? Will I let her do it anyway?' Nathan said.

'I won't let it happen, Lucy. I promise. I promise you that,' Luke said, calling over his shoulder to her. 'But if your dad doesn't give me the chain, I'll come over there and do it to you myself.'

Nathan smiled and the hold of The Book released. Lucy and her father fell silent at Luke's words.

'Please don't try and stop me doing this,' Luke said, lifting the chain over Lucy's father's head, unable to make eye contact with him.

'You're killing her, me and yourself by doing this, you know that, don't you?' her father said quietly.

Luke said nothing. Instead, he looked at Lucy, who

shook her head slightly. He pulled the chain through the thread and held the two knots in his palm. Luke went to The Book, Nathan still holding it out, and inserted them on the cover.

Light flickered in the arcs of the knots, running from one piece of metal through the veins on the cover of The Book and then into the other. There was short circuit, a crater where the energy could not flow.

'We are missing a sibling,' Nathan said.

'No,' Lucy's father said.

Luke went to Lucy. She looked at him, but was not going to speak.

'This is where I was meant to be,' Luke said.

Luke took the woman's hands and made them unfold the wire from around Lucy's neck. He faced both of them, Lucy breathing heavily. He gave her a long look and then raised his hand, making Lucy flinch and her father move towards him. Luke took the woman's hand and walked away from Lucy.

'Luke,' she called after him in a painful voice.

The woman stared through Luke, her eyes burned out by all they had seen, her body worn from the things she had done. Her short blonde hair was falling out in tufts, exposing bald patches of skull, as though she were having chemotherapy.

She pulled his body towards hers and he wondered what she was about to do.

'I can hear it,' she said to Luke, quietly so only he would hear.

'What?' he asked her.

'My own voice. Who I am. Finish this. Please.'

The beach was silent except for the piping of the wind as it searched for harsh edges on which to make a tune, and, in the unformed wash of sound, Luke and the woman danced.

Luke could almost hear their feet dragging in the sand as they gathered speed and waltzed silently. The way Luke and his mother used to.

She made eye contact with Luke, but it seemed empty to him, nothing inside her head. Nathan gave him the familiar smile, the expression he had learned well from such long study in the mirror. He could see himself in there even more now, as though Nathan, and Luke himself, were melding into each other.

They both moved as if hearing the same music, lost in their own dimension. Luke kissed her and felt the tendons of his neck tensing and standing proud. Their mouths pressed together for an aching length of time and Luke could hardly breathe. She seemed to be growing weak at the knees, drowsy.

'Do you understand why I have to do this?' Luke whispered to her, soothing.

She did not speak, but he felt the movement of her head as it nodded against his shoulder.

'Tell me your name. Tell me who you are,' he whispered and pulled her hand to his mouth, planting a kiss on its back.

'Jenna.'

She dropped to her knees in front of him and he stroked her hair, patting her head as though she were a dog. He ran the tips of his middle two fingers down her forehead, along the slide of her nose and over the bow of her lips, tracing further until his hands were on her throat. Luke gave her neck a squeeze. She was floating in a haze, peering through barely open eyes. It would be so easy to squeeze, block the flow of life until there was nothing left. Luke did not tighten his hands. Instead he resumed the journey with his fingertips, retracing his previous route, Jenna shivering under the feather of his touch.

Her eyes opened wide when he forced his hand into her mouth.

Luke pressed the tips of all four fingers and his thumb together so they made a single blunt point and got four fingers into the cavity beyond her lips with almost no effort. Her teeth scratched at him but he ignored it and worked the four fingers in until they were up to the middle knuckle; then he crouched a little, softening the joints of his knees to improve his leverage. Luke felt sick just from watching himself do it. When he made it as far as the final solid ridge of his knuckles, she really did gag and Luke tried not to think about it, the alien feel of his fingers in her mouth, fingernails scratching at the back of her throat, touching the pharynx. She coughed, trying to force air around the blockage Luke had created.

Before he made the final push, Luke wormed his thumb in as well, slipping it between her stretched bottom lip and the underside of his fingers. He wiggled his whole hand, readying it.

Luke could not take his eyes from her face, alternating his gaze from her eyes to her mouth. Her eyelids pulled high across her irises and she swallowed, like someone taking a final gulp of air before submerging, as if she knew what was coming next.

His hand disappeared into her mouth. It tore the skin at the corners, her mouth pouting around Luke's wrist, feeding on his arm as if she were a baby. His shoulder jerked, working hard to keep his hand moving. Her eyes had gone from an alert stare to a nothingness. Blood trickled along his inner arm. Luke realized his hand was being guided, because as he looked at Nathan, he saw him making clenching movements in mid-air. Nathan was using him to rummage around inside the woman's head. Luke thought about the story of the monkey's paw as he looked down at his wrist. The bone and flesh of her head was so supple it seemed to dissolve with his touch, something else, fine and ticklish, lighting on his fingers. He was making scooping motions when his arm tensed unexpectedly and his fingers closed around something hard and sharp.

Luke wrenched his hand out of the woman's mouth and she fell dead to the sand.

He held the mass of ragged flesh and writhing tendrils above his head. As the meat fell away from it, Luke looked up and saw something glinting.

He was holding a shining metal knot.

'Luke. Luke.' Lucy was calling and he blocked it from his mind, certain about what he needed to do.

For a few moments, he stood in front of Nathan Lucas, The Book between them at their feet. He held the knot up like a communion host.

Luke bent as though to place the knot in the final crater, the tome seeming excited to see it. When he was in the position he wanted, he stood abruptly and swung the knot as though backhanding a racquet, slashing Nathan across the soft skin of his throat. The slit flapped open immediately.

'Don't be foolish. You'll die without me,' Nathan shouted, as though oblivious to the gaping wound.

Luke sliced again, on a different part of Nathan's throat this time. He wanted to get him down on the ground, so he threw his weight into him, using the knot as a blade on his face, running its edge into Nathan's cheek as he made contact with him and they fell to the floor.

He carved messily at Nathan's face, cutting his hands when he held them up as a shield. Ignoring the bloody cuts, Nathan grabbed Luke's wrist, his strength maniacal, and the knot was poised in mid-air. Nathan squeezed Luke's wrist until the feeling began to ebb from it and his hold on the knot weakened. With his other hand, Nathan took the knot from Luke, who was afraid he was about to be cut with it.

Instead, Nathan reached a quivering arm towards The Book, his ruined hand trying to find the place for the knot. Luke panicked and tried to reach Nathan's hand, but it was extended too far. The muscles under Luke's arm strained, as did his back, and the weight of his own body began to make him fall. The edges of the knot touched the cover and sparks flew, small forks of lightning. As they did, Luke felt himself become one with Nathan for a brief second, a glimpse of all time. He struggled harder. Nathan's fingers turned the piece of metal and it found the first edge, Luke's brain screaming with the pain he felt from the touch.

'No.' Lucy's foot stamped down on Nathan's wrist and she bent and picked up The Book, moving away with it, the knot falling into the sand.

Nathan's arm went limp. 'Don't do this, Luke,' he said. 'You can write any story you want for her in the new beginning. Come with me. If you do this to me, I will take the final knot with me and you will be lost here with no way back. The final knot belongs to me. If I go, it goes. Don't do this.'

Luke took the knot from the sand. It was warm in his hands and he could feel the throb of Nathan Lucas in it.

The mirror. The house in Southend. London. Plymouth. His mother. Lucy. All of it travelled through his mind. Nathan Lucas. The Book. The knot. The reflection.

'There will be no way back. Kill me and you kill the final knot. Any story we want, Luke. Together. You and I as one.'

Luke held the knot high and buried it into his father's chest. He fell into Nathan's torso and split the ribs as though they did not exist. The anger and the energy that held him in their grip obliterated his sense of time and Luke could not tell how long it took to reduce the form under him to nothing more than a mass of fleshy strips. Back and forth he worked the blade of the knot, conscious of the cries of Lucy behind him. Eventually, he was slopping his hands through something almost liquid.

He knelt in the remains, covered in the blood of Nathan Lucas, a thing he had been a part of as certainly as it had been a part of him. The remnants of Nathan Lucas seeped into the sand and the tide began to lick at them. Back and forth, it carried the mess off and left only clean beach in its place. Luke held the dead knot tight in his hand and cried into the salt water.

Lucy was still holding The Book. Luke placed the dull piece of metal in the last crater on its cover.

Nothing. The final knot was as dead as Nathan Lucas.

'He's gone,' Luke said.

'But we're still here,' Lucy said.

'I wouldn't have let anything happen to you. You believe me, don't you?'

She was about to nod when she cried out. Lucy dropped

The Book and grabbed at the left side of her head. She fell almost straight into Luke's arms. He took the brunt of her weight, lessening the fall and lowering her to the ground. Her body went into a hunched spasm and she gripped at the side of her head with both hands.

'No,' her father said in a way that sounded forbidding rather than desperate, as though this was not meant to happen. He would not allow it.

'What's wrong?' Luke asked, falling to one knee next to Lucy and gripping her shoulder. Her body was in the hold of the jerking movement, as if she were having a fit. 'Lucy. Lucy.'

Her father was kneeling on the other side of her, his face stricken as he grabbed at his daughter and tried to stop her body convulsing. She kicked out with her right leg and it caught her father in the arm, hard enough to make him recoil.

Luke thought you were supposed to put something between a person's teeth if they were having a fit, although he couldn't really remember why.

'Uh. Uh.' Lucy was snorting a sound of pain down her nose, her jaw clenched, face twisted and hands still on her head.

'It can't be. It can't be in her,' her father said.

Lucy's hands released their grip on her head and she started to flail, digging into the sand and whipping it around, some of it making Luke flinch as it scratched his cheek. She arched her back, her spine curved with tension, and seemed as though she were reaching out to the sky with her hands.

'Look,' Luke said, pointing at her jeans.

A dark patch, too dark to be urine, had appeared on the inner thigh. Dark enough to be blood. Luke hesitated for a second, embarrassment able to overtake the situation. He pulled the front of Lucy's jeans apart and recoiled when he saw the heavy red on her white underwear. The wild movements of her legs were restricted by the jeans acting as a restraint halfway down her thighs. On the front of her knickers, the stain was spreading. Her father had missed a beat, Luke could tell, so he quickly pulled her free of her jeans and underwear.

A long gush of almost brown blood-like fluid streaked her inner thigh, leaving her body with more force than muscles alone might have provided. Lucy's face shone with sweat that trickled around her contorted features. Her eyes were wrinkled from the tightness with which her lids were pressed together. Luke wished she would open them, as though a brief moment of eye contact might tell him what to do instead of floundering in the way he was currently.

Down between her legs, she was beginning to dilate and Luke thought he saw something move, a shape that was not part of her and yet was inside her. Lucy screamed almost in time with the movement and writhed on the sand. Another movement and this time Luke was not mistaken. A small nub of something brown had poked through for a second, as though peering into the outside world

A groan escaped her that sounded like it could not have belonged to anyone human and then she seemed to just open up as whatever was inside her disengaged itself and came into the world.

On the sand, in the space between her open legs, was a pulsing lump of brown meat, raw and sinewy, grains of sand flecking it from where it moved, inflating slightly as though it were respiring. With each breath, it grew in size, now far too big to ever have been in Lucy.

Luke's first instinct was to back away from it, but then he wanted to approach it, stop it. He moved closer to it and raised his foot high, ready to stamp down into the soft mass, not certain what it would feel like.

'No!'

It was Lucy.

'Don't,' she said.

Her legs were covered with blood and what looked like mucus. She sat upright and scooted back a foot or so from the growing mass. Luke was transfixed by the expression on her face, rather than what was in front of her. The shifting landscape of her features was relaying emotion directly into Luke.

The brown faded from the thing on the beach and it became paler, the colour of bone. There were deep reds embedded in there too. It sprouted, small offshoots worming from the central mass. Luke realized it was not just growing in the way a plant might. It was forming itself as though alive and being born. The mass was taking a form, a human form that writhed in agony, encased in a membrane nothing like flesh, a solid white skin.

Lucy was staring at the thing in front of her as it heaved itself into life, the arms still painfully and comically short, but thrashing into the sand as it tried to pull itself along.

The skin broke and Lucy screamed. So did what had burst from it.

A naked woman lay face down on the sand, fighting for breath and obviously alive. Like a newborn, she began to cry, but it had more vigour and purpose than the unfocused and primal need of a child. She had a flowing shock of curled black hair.

Lucy's father was on his knees next to the woman.

'Oh my God,' he said, putting his hands on the side of his head and tears beginning to flow from his own eyes. 'Nancy.'

'Nancy?' Lucy said, and was quickly up on all fours.

Luke stood as the three of them huddled together in the sand, hugging, crying, kissing.

He watched for a moment longer, then took the dead knot and went to the seam of land and sea, facing the ocean. Luke threw the knot through the air and it skimmed the surface of the water three times before it plopped and sank.

Luke waited.

'What are we going to do?'

It was Lucy's father, standing behind him with his arm around the woman, Lucy at their side.

'There,' Luke said, pointing.

At a point close to where the knot had sunk, the back of a head emerged. Long black hair floated until the dark-skinned shoulders were visible. The boy walked backwards from the sea, confident and steady. He faced them and spoke to Luke.

'You have chosen well.'

It was the boy Luke had spoken to when he had first arrived on the beach.

'Now it is time for the story to come to an end,' Ryan said.

'We don't have the final knot,' Lucy's father said. 'There's no way out of here.'

'There is one way,' the boy said.

'How?' Lucy asked.

'Change the knot,' Ryan said. 'A new beginning.'

Luke handed The Book to Ryan, who nodded and gave a small smile of acknowledgement.

'How?' It was Nancy Lloyd this time.

The boy looked at Lucy and walked towards her.

Luke saw her father bristle as he approached.

'It's okay,' Luke said, holding up a hand.

The boy touched the side of Lucy's head and smiled. Lucy smiled back, nodding as though reading a silent thought.

'It's okay, Dad,' she said.

Lucy pulled at the sleeve of her shirt and revealed the tattoo of the knot, holding her arm up for the boy.

'Goodbye,' the boy said to all of them.

'What will be on the other side of the page?' Luke asked.

'Nothing. Just a blank page,' Ryan said. 'Then, a new beginning.'

They all stood and watched silently as the boy placed The Book on Lucy's arm.

Luke stared at her, knowing he would know her on the other side of the page, but that they would know nothing of this. Any of them. They would be on a different knot and in the new beginning.

Lucy smiled at him.

There was a blinding flash of light that became dark.

And became nothing.

The Book turned the page.

After-Text

A New Beginning . . .

The boy washed up onto the shore in the first year of the new century. A couple taking an early morning walk on the beach in Provincetown saw it happen. They watched as the ocean rose in a tongue-like wave that carried the boy in and threw him onto the sand as though the sea were spitting him back.

He was alive, just.

At the hospital, emergency measures were taken to raise his body temperature, hypothermia the only ill-effect he appeared to have suffered. Subsequent tests showed him to be diabetic and his blood/sugar level was monitored closely, until, four days after the diagnosis, his diabetes was gone.

A specialist was called to make a thorough examination of the vocal cords and the boy was pronounced free of any apparent physical bar to his speaking. The CAT and NMR scans showed nothing. Some inconclusive EEG readings revealed an unusual Alpha wave pattern and several days of observing his REM sleep patterns suggested the boy did not have any dreams.

His age was somewhere between 15 and 19, and he was dark-skinned, of Native American appearance. After five weeks, no one had come forward to claim the boy and for three days he was the subject of dispute between doctors and social workers, neither a medical nor a social case.

Two nights later, he disappeared from his bed and has not been seen since.

Acknowledgements

I would like to thank the following people, who may or may not know how helpful they were with various parts of *Gordius*:

Andrew Wille. The two Marys. Elizabeth Pattison. Saul Schneider. Julian Spencer. Jeremy Mattson. Simon Blair. Daniel McKernan. Dan Beach. Darrin Parker. Nico Garcia. Helen Pisano. Mic Cheetham. Ollie Cheetham. The Marsh Agency. Jo Tapsell, Andy McKillop, Kate Farquhar-Thomson, Michael Mascaro and everyone at Random House.

GOD'S GIFT

John Evans

The Book want to read you. Step closer . . .

Let it unravel the knots of your mind and make new patterns. For centuries, for millennia, The Book has been every story. Now, in Garth Richards it has found a new vessel. Through him, Mike Kavanagh, a disenchanted financial wizard in London, and Nancy Lloyd, a British writer in Los Angeles, will be drawn together by The Book's plan . . .

As the story and the knots which bind it come together, Mike and Nancy slowly understand they are caught in an ancient tale. And of the inconceivable evils that stalk them, Garth is the very least.

John Evans has written a fantastical thriller which takes in two continents. Like Clive Barker and Dean Koontz he creates terrors both awesome and utterly believeable. He coolly draws the reader into this tale, daring them to guess the profoundly shattering end.

OTHER TITLES AVAILABLE

❑ God's Gift	John Evans	£5.99
❑ Memnoch the Devil	Anne Rice	£5.99
❑ Servant of the Bones	Anne Rice	£5.99
❑ Taltos	Anne Rice	£5.99
❑ The Feast of All Saints	Anne Rice	£5.99
❑ Red Dragon	Thomas Harris	£5.99
❑ The Silence of the Lambs	Thomas Harris	£5.99
❑ Green River Rising	Tim Willocks	£5.99
❑ Bloodstained Kings	Tim Willocks	£5.99
❑ The Chosen Child	Graham Masterton	£5.99
❑ Flesh and Blood	Graham Masterton	£5.99

ALL ARROW BOOKS ARE AVAILABLE THROUGH MAIL ORDER OR FROM YOUR LOCAL BOOKSHOP AND NEWSAGENT.

PLEASE SEND CHEQUE/EUROCHEQUE/POSTAL ORDER (STERLING ONLY) ACCESS, VISA, MASTERCARD, DINERS CARD, SWITCH OR AMEX.

EXPIRY DATE .... SIGNATURE ....

PLEASE ALLOW 75 PENCE PER BOOK FOR POST AND PACKING U.K.

OVERSEAS CUSTOMERS PLEASE ALLOW £1.00 PER COPY FOR POST AND PACKING.

ALL ORDERS TO:
ARROW BOOKS, BOOKS BY POST, TBS LIMITED, THE BOOK SERVICE, COLCHESTER ROAD, FRATING GREEN, COLCHESTER, ESSEX CO7 7DW.

NAME ....

ADDRESS ....

....

Please allow 28 days for delivery. Please tick box if you do not wish to receive any additional information ❑

Prices and availability subject to change without notice.